The DYBBUK and the Yiddish Imagination

Judaic Traditions in Literature, Music, and Art
Ken Frieden and Harold Bloom, *Series Editors*

The

DYBBUK

and the Yiddish Imagination

A HAUNTED READER

Edited and Translated from the Yiddish by

Joachim Neugroschel

Includes a New Translation of
S. Ansky's *The Dybbuk*

Syracuse University Press

First Edition 2000

00 01 02 03 04 05 06   7 6 5 4 3 2 1

Regarding performance: Professionals and amateurs are hereby warned that this material, being fully protected under the Copyright Law of the United States of America and all other countries of the Berne and Universal Copyright Conventions, is subject to a royalty. All rights including, but not limited to, professional, amateur, recording, motion picture, recitation, lecturing, public reading, radio and television broadcasting, and the rights of translations into foreign languages are expressly reserved. Particular emphasis is placed on the question of readings and all uses of this book by educational institutions—permission for which must be secured from the author's representative: Georges Borchardt, Inc., 136 East 57th Street, New York, New York 10022.

The paper used in this publication meets the minimum requirements of American National Standard for Information Sciences—Permanence of Paper for Printed Library Material, ANSI Z39.48-1984. ♾

Library of Congress Cataloging-in-Publication Data

The dybbuk and the Yiddish imagination : a haunted reader / edited and translated from the Yiddish by Joachim Neugroschel.— 1st ed.
   p. cm. — (Judaic traditions in literature, music, and art)
"Includes a new translation of S. Ansky's The dybbuk."
   ISBN 0-8156-2871-4 (cloth : alk. paper) — ISBN 0-8156-2872-2 (pbk. : alk. paper)
   1. Jews—Folklore.   2. Spirits—Folklore.   3. Legends, Jewish.   4. Tales.
   5. Yiddish literature — Translations into English.   I. Neugroschel, Joachim.
   II. An-Ski, S., 1863–1920. Dibek. English.   III. Series
GR98.D93 2000
398.2'089'924—dc21   00-037016

Manufactured in the United States of America

Contents

Joachim Neugroschel has translated 180 books from French, German, Italian, Russian, and Yiddish, including works by Thomas Mann, Franz Kafka, Sholem Aleichem, and Elias Canetti. A winner of three PEN Translation Awards, he has also received the French-American Foundation Translation Prize. In 1996 he was appointed a chevalier in the Order of Arts and Letters of the French Republic.

Acknowledgments

Like a movie, this book required many hands to make my work light. Many people helped me enormously with directions, explanations, suggestions, recommendations. In alphabetical order: Dina Abramovicz, Zachary Baker, Dan Ben-Amos, Marc Caplan, Itzik Gottesman, Kim Guise, Mikhl Herzog, J. Hoberman, Eli Katz, Tony Kushner, Mark Lamos, Aaron Lansky and his National Yiddish Book Center, Sid Leiman, Matti Megged, Max Mermelstein, Edna Nahshon, Simon Neuberg, Dovid Roskies, Mordkhe Schaechter, Jeff Sharlet, Michael Steinlauf, Dov Taylor, Erika Timm, Iosif Vaisman, Bina Weinreich, Seth Wolitz, Neil Zagorin, Sara Zfatman, Harry Zohn—and countless employees of countless libraries.

I am also very grateful to the Lucius Littauer Foundation for a tremendously generous and helpful grant.

My translation of "The Possession" by Jacob ben Abraham of Mezritch, copyright 1976 by Joachim Neugroschel, was originally published in *Great Tales of Jewish Fantasy and the Occult* by Joachim Neugroschel (1986, 1987), and is reprinted with the permission of the Overlook Press. Some of the Yiddish works that I have translated in *A Haunted Reader* may still be in copyright, but since those Yiddish publishing houses no longer exist, it was impossible for me to track down any estates.

Introduction

Ansky's *The Dybbuk* and the Yiddish Imagination

On Translating *The Dybbuk*

My interest in S. Ansky's drama *The Dybbuk* (1914–1919) was re-
kindled when the American playwright Tony Kushner approached me
about my doing a new translation, which he would then adapt. In preparing my version I came up not only against countless problems (to be
expected in any translation) but also against many questions that might
go unanswered.

Right off I was struck by a conundrum. Unlike the wealth of fanta-
sies in Yiddish fiction and poetry, there are few supernatural theater
works in the Yiddish repertoire. Yet the two best-known Yiddish plays,
composed around the same time, deal with the metaphysical: S. Ansky's
The Dybbuk and H. Leivick's *The Golem* (1921). Despite their mystical
substance, however, both were inspired, at least partly, by the same historical events: the Russian pogroms, especially during and (in Leivick's
case) after World War I.

In Ansky's drama, the Khmielnítsky massacres (1648–1649) have a
strong background presence in the joint grave of a bride and groom who
were murdered by the pogromists before their nuptials were completed.
Contrary to normal practice, the grave lies not in the cemetery but in the
town square—a daily reminder of past and present horrors. These passive victims contrast with the living characters, who both actively and
passively take part in the sacrificial rite: Khónen and Leah must pay for
the sin committed by her father, who broke the promise he made to his

A note on the transcriptions of Yiddish and Hebrew words: As usual, I have generally
followed the YIVO transcription system except for words, names, and titles that have
entered the English language or that might be mispronounced.

xi

friend, Khónen's father. Through the lovers' atonement in death, the collective is made whole again. Metaphysically Leah is passive, but psychologically, by admitting or imagining the dybbuk, she is active.

The reference to Khmielnítsky's hordes is the sole mention of Christian existence in the world of this play; the characters are all Jewish—a figment prevalent in much of Yiddish literature and even documentation. Thus, in his own autobiography, Sholem Aleichem's brother Volf Rabinovitsh (*My Brother Sholem-Aleichem* [Kiev, 1939]) pointed out that their home town had far more Gentiles than are mentioned in the humorist's memoirs (*Fúnem Yaríd—Home from the Fair*). The fabrication of an all-Jewish world allows an exclusive focus on the Jewish collective; it counteracts the move of the Jewish individual from the thick of Jewish life to a marginal twilight zone between Jewish and Gentile culture. In traditional Jewish life, the individual serves the collective by serving God—and serves God by serving the collective. Assimilationists and secularists give up their participation in Jewish centrality—a process that Ansky (1863–1920) went through in his odyssey of assimilation and return. By coming back to Jewish life with Yiddish as its national language, he created the illusion of a completely Jewish life—even though he apparently never felt totally at home in it. As I have written in an Introduction to my forthcoming Ansky translation:

> Ansky's almost fanatical devotion to Jewish life [after living as a Russian for a long time] conceals an ambivalence that lurks in his writings. The actual title of *The Dybbuk* is: *Between Two Worlds.* Indeed! And in his satirical miniepic *Ashmedai,* Lilith, queen of the demon world, eventually returns to the Jewish fold—but is punished for her iniquities: She is never fully accepted by Jews or by demons. Then again, in his humoresque *Letters from the Beyond,* Ansky pokes fun at Russian Jews who try to live as both secular Russians and observant Jews.

By translating Ansky into English, a non-Jewish language, we assimilate the author into a Gentile world. Translation tends to be more curatorial, adaptation more transformative. Both are imperialistic in that they wrench a text from another culture, a foreign context, and shove it into its new home. We take from the "other," giving little in return.

Transferring a text from a Jewish to a non-Jewish language presents an unusual problem. In European cultures, language and ethnicity belong to the fundament of identity while religion is part of the superstructure. But for Jews, religion has usually been the overall basis, and any other cultural expression, including language, has been built on religion—what Max Weinreich calls *Dérekh-ha-Shás* (the Talmudic Way).

With Zionism and the creation of a Jewish state, Hebrew shifted from its religious position in the religious foundation to its ethnic position in the ethnic foundation (with religious and political rationales). Other Jewish languages, while lodged in a given superstructure, are nevertheless rooted in religion, no matter how secular a literary work may be.

The very script in which they are written suggests the religious bedrock of these languages. Alphabet follows religion: The Latin alphabet is used by Catholic and formerly Catholic languages; the Cyrillic alphabet by Orthodox languages; and the Arabic alphabet by Muslim languages (including Persian, an Indo-European tongue). The Hebrew (originally Aramaic) alphabet, retained by nearly all two dozen Jewish languages, is a visual reminder that Jewish religious life, including the alphabet, existed long before these tongues ever developed (just as the Jewish Bible was set down long before the existence of most of the languages into which it has been translated—usually by Christians). Each letter of the Jewish alphabet is a stylized ideogram: *gimel* (camel) still hints at the camel's hump; *bet* (house) suggests a foursquare abode more permanent than a desert tent.

Building a Play

Ansky's *The Dybbuk,* about a girl's possession by the spirit of her undead beloved, deals with popular and traditional religious beliefs. An ethnographer and historian as well as a playwright, Ansky shaped his drama as an omnigatherum of the old shtetl life that was collapsing in Eastern Europe. The author splices Hasidic tales and parables into the action almost as if they were arias; these narratives are cases of hearsay rather than straight depiction. Like the words of the messenger in a Greek play, they describe what has happened offstage, mediating instead of showing, keeping us at arm's length from vital (spiritual) action. Ansky's Messenger, suggested by Konstantin Stanislavsky, but resembling the Ashkenazi version of the ever-helpful Prophet Elijah, provides what Bertolt Brecht was to call an "alienation effect." Or consider Manuel Puig's *The Kiss of the Spider Woman.* This novel progresses entirely in dialogue between two cellmates without even a desirable "he said." Narration, as in the secret police report, is the tool of the tyrannical Latin American regime. Ansky's Messenger, however, is nonmalignant (don't forget that in Hebrew *malakh* [angel] means "messenger"); he virtually interprets the events for us, though without full explanations.

Ansky further popularizes by rendering sacred texts into Yiddish—

say, the chant opening the play or the passage from the Song of Songs. The latter, perhaps the most sexual portion of the Bible, is doubly shocking: for being in Yiddish and for being erotic. The Hebrew text begins *Doddee lee v'anilo* (My beloved is mine, I am his). But *doddee* also means "uncle," and children in Hebrew school were protected against moral turpitude by being taught that the opening verse means "My uncle is mine, I am his" (see Joseph Opatoshu's novella *Hibru* [Hebrew School] (Vilna: Kletskin, 1927) for a description of this puritanism). Sholem Aleichem satirizes this censorship in his vaguely incestuous novella, "The Song of Songs," in which a little boy falls in love with his older brother's daughter: He is both "uncle" and "beloved."

The Biblical Song of Songs has a more sexual function in the Yiddish movie version of *The Dybbuk* (1937), whose supposedly gay director, Michal Waszynski, added a foreplay linking the two fathers in a profound and transcendent bond that is both spiritual and erotic. Yet despite its own erotic mood, Ansky's stage play is antisexual. There are only two couples: the dead bride and groom, and finally Leah and Khónen, who likewise die before consummating their marriage. The most unabashed sexuality in the play occurs when Leah kisses the Torah and, later on, when her beloved's ghost enters her body; however, the young lovers achieve spiritual but not physical fusion (see my commentary to *Béria and Zímra*, pages 81 to 94).

Style, Structure, and Language

The parables and wonder stories are not the only factors that make *The Dybbuk* seem like a postmodern collage. We are faced with a different genre in each act. Act I is a romance with an unhappy ending; Act II is virtually a musical with dance numbers and a macabre twist; Act III is a ghost story; Act IV is a trial and an exorcism with a bizarre and ambiguous outcome.

As for the style of Ansky's drama, linguistic politics play a crucial role. The original Yiddish or Russian manuscript was lost, and the author had to turn it *back* into Yiddish from Khaim Bialek's neo-Hebrew version. Thus the extant Yiddish text is actually a second-degree translation. But there is nothing unusual about that in a culture with three internal tongues (Yiddish, Hebrew, and Aramaic) and several external Christian tongues (German, Russian, Polish, Ukrainian, etc.). Children in elementary schools spent their days orally rendering Biblical and Talmudic passages into a literal Yiddish. Beyond that, most medieval and some modern Yiddish literature consists of translations and adaptations that have joined the core of the Yiddish literary imagination.

The language of Ansky's play is a mixture of everyday vernacular, sometimes journalese (with numerous words from modern German), heavily charged rhetoric, conventional poetic diction, and a large number of traditional borrowings from Hebrew and Aramaic (the latter being the language of the Talmud, which plays a far greater role in the daily life of devout Jews than the Hebrew Bible does). These loan words in the play may be influenced by the fact that the final Yiddish text was retranslated from Hebrew. But more likely they are due to the religious subject matter and the Hasidic component, since these areas of Yiddish rely strongly on Biblical and Talmudic vocabulary. In the conventions of Yiddish melodrama, the overwrought dialogue of *The Dybbuk* is often grandiloquent, reaching an intensity that was perfectly acceptable to, indeed demanded by, its audience, but which might sound comically overcharged in English.

Given all these peculiar problems, I have steered my version toward a blend of colloquial and slightly elevated English while taking over the funny bits as deliberate comic relief. In addition, though Ansky incorporates no other poetic passages (aside from a rhymed rap chant in Fradde's monologue with Leah), I often employ a fusion of free verse and blank verse for the more mystical characters. This is especially true of the amorous passages, which, in a culture that was very buttoned-down about displaying love, sex, or even affection, had a profoundly erotic impact that would otherwise be blunted in translation. Camouflaged by the uneven Yiddish, the inherent poetry of the play ought to be expressed in a lyrical English. Indeed I was influenced by German stage adaptors, who, when translating fairy-tale plays like Jean Giraudoux's *Ondine,* cast the foreign prose in German blank verse. To a German audience, fantasy means poetry.

My efforts may look like adaptation—and they are. But they focus on arousing the same emotions, the same reactions, that the original drama, in its fashion, touches off in readers and spectators. For instance: The French phrase, *Ce n'est pas catholique* (verbatim: "It is not Catholic"), is best rendered in English as "It is not kosher": the less literal, the more accurate (in solid geometry a curve can be the shortest distance between two points). The director is then charged with the next phase of a play translation—the transfiguration on the stage.

The Origins of Dybbuks

The Yiddish word *dybbuk* (pronounced *díbbik*) stems from a Hebrew root meaning "adhere." But according to Gershom Scholem (*On the Mystical Shape of the Godhead* [New York: Schocken, 1991], 223 n. 60), *dybbuk* was actually coined in Yiddish, first occurring about 1680 in a text from Volhynia. It was then absorbed into Ashkenazi Hebrew and eventually into a number of other European tongues. Earlier and later Yiddish and Hebrew writers used other terms for the undead entity that takes over a human being. For instance, the author of *The Tale of the Evil Spirit in Korets* (Prague, 1665; see page 61), employs *rúekh*, from Ashkenazi Hebrew *rúakh*. While this noun more or less refers to "spirit" in both languages, it has various meanings in different contexts.

Take 1 Sam. 18:10, which tells us that "the evil spirit [*rúakh*] from God came upon Saul." This word may refer simply to a wretched mood since Saul was fiercely angry at David's increasing popularity; or it may describe a possession that was exorcised when David played his harp—it all depends on the exegete. But whatever the (mis-) interpretation, *rúakh*, the noun applied in these Biblical verses, may have influenced the terminology of subsequent Yiddish and/or Hebrew portrayals of possessions.

A two-pronged usage can be found in A.-M. Dik's *The Gílgul* (published in 1867). Throughout the Hebrew phrases initiating many of the paragraphs, *rúakh* generally indicates the wandering soul; while in the Yiddish text, the term is *neshómme* (spirit, soul, from Ashkenazi Hebrew *neshómmah*, with the same meaning)—though Dik occasionally resorts to the Yiddish *rúekh*.

These disparate usages would indicate that the Hebrew and Yiddish words are virtually interchangeable among these authors. In fact, a later writer, Der Nister, who presents a lyrical and spiritual universe of demons (see pages 258 through 274), uses *rúekh* as one of several terms for his often benign supernatural beings. Another of these words is *shed* (from Hebrew); earlier and later Yiddish writers use feminine forms such as *shédekhe* for the evil she-demon that "adheres" to a man against his will, or because he is sexually drawn to her, or because he has committed a sin that allows her to take possession of him.

What is usually missing from the diverse timbres and nuances of these terms is the Midrashic structure of five levels of potential consciousness:

Nefesh (appetitive awareness)
Rúakh (emotional awareness)
Neshómmah (intellect)
Khayah (divine life force)
Yekhidah (uniqueness . . . wherein all the soul's faculties are unified
   with G-d). (*Midrash rabbah*, Gen. 14:11; quoted after Gershon
   Winkler, *Dybbuk* [New York: Judaica Press, 1997])

Rabbi Nakhman of Braslev evokes some of these distinctions in "The Tale of the Seven Beggars" (Joachim Neugroschel, *Great Tales of Jewish Fantasy and the Occult* [New York: Overlook Press 1987]). And given the religious training that most Ashkenazi boys underwent, Yiddish writers must have known about this hierarchy yet chose to ignore it. All five terms are common in Yiddish, but with less definite meanings than in the Midrash quoted above. Few Yiddish writers follow these specific Midrashic categories, which are vastly outweighed by the more colloquial and less mystical usages.

The various exorcisms described in these texts seem to have become more "Jewish" through the centuries. In "The Tale of the Evil Spirit in Korets [Korzc] During the Turmoil of War" (Prague: 1665), the procedures may hark back to earlier non-Jewish practices. Indeed, this story describes one conjuration that, involving a barrel and incense, seems quite ancient and most likely pagan in origin. See *Midrash Tanchuma, Chukas,* no. 8, and *Midrash Rabba,* Num. 19:4.

> "Were you ever possessed by an evil spirit?" the rabbi asked.
> "No," said [the Roman].
> The rabbi then asked: "Have you ever seen a person possessed by an evil spirit?"
> "Yes," said [the Roman].
> "What do you do for him?"
> [The Roman] replied: "We bring special herbs and burn them underneath him and spray it with water, and so the spirit is driven away." (Adapted from the quotation in Gershon Winkler, *Dybbuk* [New York: Judaica Press, 1997], 5.)

Later exorcisms, however, including those in Ansky's play, appear to rely almost entirely on Jewish religious customs—fasts, prayers, promises of celestial (Jewish) redemption, divine forgiveness, etc. The earlier trappings have been replaced by the overwhelming powers of a well-nigh preternatural or supernatural rabbi.

The Origins of Gílguls

A dybbuk enters a body that it shares with the original tenant. By contrast, a *gílgul,* Hebrew and Yiddish for "transmigration," "reincarnation," and ultimately for the transmigrating soul itself, is reborn as the sole tenant of a new body. The goal of rebirth is to give the imperfect soul a chance to perfect itself. The doctrine of reincarnation, unknown in the Torah and the Talmud, was condemned by Jewish theologians. Yet, according to Gershom Scholem, it was taken for granted by the very start of the Cabala (*Sefer ha-Bahir*, ca. 1180); and the later Cabala also maintained that human souls could return in the bodies of animals.

In this connection, it might be interesting to look at a Midrash that depicts the seven ages of a human being in terms of higher and lower creatures (*Midrash Tanchuma, Pikudei*, 3; *Midrash Rabba, Koheles* [Eccles. 1:3]). In his mystical rumination *A Human Life* (1910), Ansky very freely adapts this metaphysical belief—even replacing the pig of the original text:

> When it is time for a person to be born, the angel named Laila forces him out of his mother's innards.
>
> And from that day on, a human being goes through seven worlds.
>
> In the first world, he is like a newly crowned emperor, who is welcomed by all, greeted with joy and with gifts.
>
> In the second world, he is like a billy goat, who feeds on muck, capers about cheerful and carefree, and devours grass that he hasn't sown.
>
> In the third world, he is like a young colt, who knows no hindrances, and is intoxicated with freedom and passion.
>
> In the fourth world, he is like a swift horse, who runs merrily in its harness and doesn't feel the weight of the wagon and the light passengers.
>
> In the fifth world, he is like a donkey, who is burdened with a load and struggles under the driver's lashes.
>
> In the sixth world, he is like a dog, who shamelessly drags everything it can and barks at anyone who comes close.
>
> In the seventh world, he is like a monkey, who looks like a human being and yet is not the same as a human, and it acts crazy, so that everyone laughs at it and no one heeds it. (For the complete Yiddish text see Ansky's *Collected Works*, vol. 1 [Warsaw: 1928]; 9–20; for a full English translation, see A. Ansky, Tony Kushner, and Joachim Neugroschel, *A Dybbuk* [New York: TCG, 1998].)

Text and Context

In putting together this reader, I have experimented with recreating an historical and cultural environment that provides a more thorough grasp of the countless themes making up Ansky's drama. The possession and the exorcism are certainly key elements, but there are so many other aspects. We find: quests; amorous union beyond death; a trial (stage trials are actually plays within plays); a parental vow that binds children;

the belief in true love between soulmates; the fear of demons and other supernatural entities; the concept of transmigration—a dybbuk who, by possessing, is himself possessed and obsessed—and on and on. To clarify these various facets, I have included some two dozen Yiddish stories and one play.

When we read something produced by our own culture, we experience that work within our familiar milieu. But when we read a translation, the direct opposite occurs: We have to infer the cultural context from the given work. So while each piece in this anthology illuminates one or more factors in Ansky's *The Dybbuk*, the totality forges a context that can assist us in perceiving Ansky's drama as manipulating codes in an intricate historical and cultural system. Some of these works directly influenced Ansky, some may or may not have done so, while others simply help to paint an overall background. I have deliberately ignored the chronological order since we normally experience cultural entities in a nonchronological fashion, as pieces in a huge and iridescent mosaic.

I would like you to read Ansky's play first, then the rest of the material. I hope you will find my comments beneficial. When you have finished reading this anthology, try rereading *The Dybbuk*—and see if you understand it in a different way.

Joachim Neugroschel

The DYBBUK and the Yiddish Imagination

S. ANSKY (1863–1920)

From A Letter to Khaim Zhitlovsky

The Yiddish text of this letter can be found in Leksikon fun Yidishn Teater *New York: TCG, 1931), 73. It was originally published in* Literarishe Bleter *11 (1924).*

My play, needless to say, is a realistic drama about mystics. Its only nonrealistic element is the Messenger, not Leah's dialogue or visions. I've deliberately limned the Messenger with mystical features. Actually, he was not in my original version. It was [Konstantin] Stanislavsky who advised or rather told me to add him, and I thereby automatically broadened my overall conception, adding a higher level beyond the theme of the "lovely and pleasant."

Throughout the play there is a battle between the individual and the collective—more precisely, between the individual's striving for happiness and the survival of the nation. Khónen and Leah struggle for their personal happiness, while the tsaddik's only worry is that "a living branch will wither on the eternal tree of the people of Israel." Which side is right?

Upon first confronting Leah/Khónen, the tsaddik wants to satisfy himself that the striving of their souls (for personal happiness) has deep roots and is not licentious or obstinate. It turns out that in the celestial palaces it is assumed that Khónen has been drawn by a higher power. And when the tsaddik expels Khónen by blasting the shofar, he feels that "some powerful entity must be helping him!" However, the tsaddik cannot deviate from his path. Ultimately Khónen and Leah are the victors. But is the tsaddik wrong?

The Messenger comes from a higher world, a world in which "Its fire melts the highest mountain tops,/dissolving them into the deepest valleys." For the Messenger, both sides are right—right and even more

1

righteous in their battle. The Messenger holds with the tsaddik—that is, he holds him back; and at the height of the battle, when the tsaddik shouts out his anathema, and Khónen loses his last spark of strength, the Messenger says: "The final spark has blended with the flame"

S. ANSKY (1863–1920)

The Dybbuk (1914–1919)
or Between Two Worlds
A Dramatic Legend in Four Acts

Characters

SENDER OF BRÍNNITZ
LÉAH, his daughter (*in Hebrew the name means "despondent"*)
FRÁDDE, her old nurse
GÍTL, Leah's friend
BÉSSYE, Leah's friend
MENÁSHE, Leah's fiancé
NÁKHMAN, Menáshe's father
MENDL, Menáshe's rebbe (*Hasidic rabbi*)
THE MESSENGER
RABBI AZRÍEL OF MÍROPOLYE, a Hasidic rebbe (*the Hebrew derivation of his name means "God's help"*)
MIKHL, his *gabbe* (*overall manager and administrator*)
RABBI SHIMSHIN (*Sampson*), rabbi in Míropolye
FIRST JUDGE
SECOND JUDGE
MÉYER, *shammes* (*beadle*) at the synagogue in Brínnitz

Translator's note: Names of historical figures are transcribed according to their normal English spellings. All the names of the characters, including those deriving from the Bible, are transcribed according to their standard Yiddish pronunciations. For instance: King David (Biblical), but Rabbi Dúvid. For a performance, any of the characters' names can be changed if they are too difficult to pronounce, unless the director wishes to retain the etymological overtones. However, some names, as clarified in the text, are discussed in terms of their numerological Cabalistic values. So obviously, those names would have to be kept.

3

KHÓNEN (*the name derives from the Hebrew root for "merciful"*), yeshiva student

HÉNEKH, yeshiva student

ÓSHER, yeshiva student

FIRST IDLER

SECOND IDLER

THIRD IDLER

(*The* IDLERS *are usually paid by the Jewish community to stay around in order to take part in a minyan, a quorum of ten men, if need be.*)

FIRST HASID

SECOND HASID

THIRD HASID

AN OLD WOMAN

A WEDDING GUEST

A POOR HUNCHBACK

A POOR CRIPPLE

A LAME OLD WOMAN

AN OLD WOMAN WITH ONE ARM

AN OLD BLIND WOMAN

A TALL PALE YOUNG WOMAN

A YOUNG MOTHER HOLDING A BABY

HASIDS, YESHIVA STUDENTS, HOUSEHOLDERS, SHOPKEEPERS, WEDDING GUESTS, PAUPERS, CHILDREN

Scene and Time

The first and second acts take place in the town of Brínnitz, the third and fourth in the town of Míropolye. Three months go by between the first and the second acts, two days between the second and the third acts, twelve hours between the third and the fourth.

Act I

Before the curtain goes up to reveal utter darkness, we hear something like a soft, mystical chanting in the distance.

Why, oh why,

Did the soul descend

From the highest height

To the deepest end?

The greatest fall

Contains the upward flight.

The curtain slowly rises.

A small, very ancient wooden synagogue with black walls. The roof is held up by two posts. At the center of the ceiling, an old brass lamp hangs above the sloping bimah (the platform from which the Torah—Pentateuch—is read to the congregation). The bimah is covered with a dark tablecloth. On the rear wall, several small windows indicate the women's gallery. A long bench, and in front of it a long, wooden table with sacred tomes scattered across it; among them, lower than the books, a few clay candle holders with two burning tallow candles. To the left of the bench and the table, a small door leading to the rabbi's private room. In the corner, a bookcase containing sacred tomes. At the center of the right-hand wall, the Holy Ark (the repository of the Torah scrolls); to its left, the cantor's reading stand, on which a thick wax memorial candle is burning. There is a window on either side of the Holy Ark. Benches with several bookstands along the full length of the wall. On the left-hand wall, a huge tile stove; next to it a bench with a long table also with scattered holy books. A ritual washstand with a towel hanging from a ring. A wide door leading to the street. Near the door, a chest; above the chest, a niche with an eternal light (ner-tomid).

At a pulpit near the cantor's stand, HENEKH *sits, absorbed in a holy book. At the table by the front wall, five or six yeshiva students, sprawling wearily, are studying while dreamily humming a Talmudic melody. At the bimah,* MEYER *stands, leaning, and laying out pouches containing prayer shawls and phylacteries. The three* IDLERS, *starry-eyed, thoroughly lost in thought, are sitting around the table. On a bench by the tile stove, the* MESSENGER *lies, with his head on a sack.* KHONEN, *lost in thought, stands with his hand resting on the top of the bookcase.*

It is evening. A mystical atmosphere pervades the synagogue and its shadowy corners.

THREE IDLERS. (*Finish chanting*).
Why, oh why,
Did the soul descend
From the highest height
To the deepest end?
The greatest fall
Contains the upward flight.
A long pause. All three sit motionless, lost in thought.
FIRST IDLER. (*As if telling a fairy tale.*)
Rabbi Dúvid of Talne—may his good deeds deliver us from evil—had a golden chair, and seven words were engraved in the gold: "David, King of Israel, He Lives Eternal." (*Pause*)

SECOND IDLER. (*In the same tone.*) Rabbi Yisróel of Ruzin—blessed be his memory—lived like a real monarch. His meals were always accompanied by a twenty-four-piece orchestra, and he always traveled in a coach drawn by six horses in tandem.

THIRD IDLER. (*Rapturous.*) And people say that Rabbi Shmúel of Kamink would go around in golden slippers (*ecstatic*)—in golden slippers!

MESSENGER. (*Sits up on the bench, speaks in a soft, quiet voice as if from far away.*)
The holy Rabbi Zúsye of Anipólye
was a pauper all his life. He lived on alms
and he wore a peasant smock with a rope around his waist.
Yet his achievements were as great as those
of Rabbi Yisróel or Rabbi Dúvid.

FIRST IDLER. (*Annoyed.*) If you don't mind my saying so, you have no idea what we're talking about, yet you butt in all the same. When we praise the greatness of these rabbis, do you think we mean their material wealth? Are there so few fabulously wealthy men in the world? Don't you see that the golden chair and the orchestra and the golden slippers contained deep secrets, hidden meanings?

THIRD IDLER. It's so obvious. How can anyone misunderstand!

SECOND IDLER. Anyone who had open eyes could see. People say that the first time the Rabbi of Apt encountered Rabbi Yisróel of Ruzin, he fell to the ground and kissed the wheels of his coach. And when the Rabbi of Apt was asked what his action meant, he shouted: "You fools! Can't you see that this is the Divine Chariot, the one that Ezekiel saw in his vision, the one that took Elijah to Heaven?!"

THIRD IDLER. (*Ecstatic.*) Oh, oh, oh!

FIRST IDLER. The point is that the golden chair was not a chair, the orchestra was not an orchestra, and the horses were not horses. Those things were nothing but fancies, reflections; they were just clothes, just envelopes for their greatness.

MESSENGER. True greatness doesn't need a lovely wardrobe.

FIRST IDLER. You're wrong! True grandeur should wear the finest garments!

SECOND IDLER. (*Shrugs.*) Their grandeur! Their power! They were beyond measure.

FIRST IDLER. Their power was remarkable! Did you ever hear the story of Rabbi Shmelke of Nikelshberg and his whip? It's worth hearing. Rabbi Shmelke once had to judge a dispute between a poor man and a rich man. The rich man had influence at the royal court, and everyone was terrified of him. Rabbi Shmelke listened to both sides and then he ruled in favor of the poor man. The rich man was very annoyed and he refused to abide by the rabbi's judgment. So the rabbi quietly said: "You will go along with my decision. When a rabbi issues an order, you have to obey." The rich man grew angry and began yelling: "The hell with you and your rabbinical judgments!" Now, Rabbi Shmelke stood up to his full stature and shouted: "You are to obey my order this very instant. Otherwise—I'll use my whip!" The rich man hit the ceiling! He started cursing and swearing at the rabbi! So Rabbi Shmelke opened the drawer in his desk—and out jumped the Original Serpent, the one from the Garden of Eden, and it coiled itself around the rich man's neck. Well, you can imagine the commotion. The rich man screamed and wept: "Help me, Rebbe, forgive me! I'll do anything you say, but please take away the Serpent!" Rabbi Shmelke replied: "You will tell your children and your children's children to obey the rabbi and to fear his whip!" And he removed the Serpent from the rich man's neck.

THIRD IDLER. Ha ha ha! A fine whip! (*Pause.*)

SECOND IDLER. (*To the* FIRST. I think you've made a mistake. The story couldn't have involved the Serpent from the Garden of Eden. . . .

THIRD IDLER. Huh? What do you mean?

SECOND IDLER. It's quite simple. Rabbi Shmelke couldn't have used the Serpent. The Original Serpent in the Garden of Eden was the Devil, the other side . . . Lucifer—God help us! (*Spits.*)

THIRD IDLER. C'mon! Rabbi Shmelke knew what he was doing!

FIRST IDLER. (*Offended.*) I don't know what you're talking about! I described an event that took place in public—dozens of people saw it with their own eyes. And now you claim it couldn't have happened. You think it's all mumbo jumbo?

SECOND IDLER. God forbid! But I figure there are no incantations or conjurations for summoning the Devil! (*Spits.*)

MESSENGER.
There's only one way to conjure up the Devil:
You have to utter the Holy Name twice:
Its fire melts the highest mountaintops,
dissolving them into the deepest valleys.
(KHONEN *looks up and listens carefully.*)

THIRD IDLER. (*Nervous.*) Isn't it dangerous to use the Great Name?

MESSENGER. (*Thoughtful.*)
Dangerous? . . . No. . . . The vessel can burst
only under the impact of great lust—
the lusting of the spark for the flame. . . .

FIRST IDLER. In my shtetl there's a rebbe who can perform the most incredible miracles. He can start a fire just by pronouncing the Holy Name and he can put it out in the same way. He can see what's happening for hundreds of miles around. He can tap wine from the wall with his fingers. . . . He once told me that he knows spells for doing all sorts of things: creating a golem, resurrecting the dead, becoming invisible, summoning demons . . . and even conjuring up the Devil. (*He spits.*) I heard it from his very own lips.

KHONEN. (*Has been standing motionless, listening carefully, now walks over to the table, looks at the* MESSENGER, *then at the* FIRST IDLER, *and speaks in a dreamy, faraway voice.*) Where is he? (*The* MESSENGER *gazes at* KHÓNEN, *never once removing his eyes.*)

FIRST IDLER. (*Surprised.*) Who?

KHONEN. Your miracle worker.

FIRST IDLER. Where else? Back in my shtetl—if he's still alive.

KHONEN. Is it far from here?

FIRST IDLER. My shtetl? It's very far away! Deep in Polisia.

KHONEN. How far?

FIRST IDLER. How far? It would take you at least a month to walk there. . . . (*Pause.*) Why are you asking? Would you like to visit him? (*KHONEN remains silent.*) The name of my shtetl is Krasne. The miracle worker's name is Rabbi Elkhonen.

KHONEN. (*Surprised, speaks to himself.*) Elkhonen? El-Khonen? The God of Khonen?

FIRST IDLER. (*To the other* IDLERS.) I tell you—he can perform the most incredible miracles! Once, in broad daylight, he used a spell to—

SECOND IDLER. (*Interrupting.*) That's enough! We shouldn't talk about these things at night! Especially in a house of prayer. You might accidentally blurt out a spell, a formula—God forbid!—and something awful could happen. Such mishaps have occurred—Heaven preserve us! (*KHONEN slowly exits. The others peer after him. Pause.*)

MESSENGER. Who is that boy?

FIRST IDLER. A yeshiva student. (*MEYER closes the doors of the bimah and walks over to the table.*)

SECOND IDLER. A prodigy, a genius!

THIRD IDLER. That boy has a mind like a steel trap! He's already memorized five hundred pages of the Talmud, they're at his fingertips!

MESSENGER. Where is he from?

MEYER. Somewhere in Lithuania! He studied at our yeshiva, he was the first in his class, and he was ordained as a rabbi. Then all at once, he vanished, no one knew where, and he didn't turn up again for a whole year. People said he was doing penance, wandering in exile. He returned a short time ago, but he was no longer the same boy. He's always lost in thought, he fasts from one Sabbath to the next, he constantly goes through ritual cleansings. . . . (*Lowering his voice.*) They say he's dabbling in the Cabala. . . .

SECOND IDLER. (*Quietly.*) The townspeople are also talking about it. . . . Some are even asking him for amulets. But he won't give them any. . . .

THIRD IDLER. Who knows who or what he is? Perhaps he's one of the great scholars? Who can say? And it would be dangerous to pry. . . . (*Pause.*)

SECOND IDLER. (*Yawns.*) It's late. . . . Time to go to bed. . . . (*To the* FIRST IDLER *with a smile.*) Too bad your miracle worker isn't here. He could tap some wine from the wall. I wouldn't mind a shot of something. You know, I haven't had a bite all day!

FIRST IDLER. I've practically been fasting myself. After praying, all I had was a buckwheat cookie.

MEYER. (*Half-secretively, content.*) Just wait, I think we'll have more than enough to drink soon. Sender has gone to see a bridegroom for his daughter. If he signs an engagement contract, God willing, then he'll treat us all to a fine round of drinks!

SECOND IDLER. Ah! I don't believe he'll ever sign a contract. He's already gone to see three bridegrooms, and he's always come back empty-handed. Once he didn't like the boy, the second time the family wasn't good enough, another time the dowry wasn't big enough. He shouldn't be so persnickety!

MEYER. Sender can afford to be picky. He's rich, he comes from a good family, he's got a fine and beautiful daughter—may Heaven preserve her.

THIRD IDLER. (*Ecstatic.*) I like Sender! He's a true Hasid, he's a follower of the Rebbe of Míropolye, and his faith is very ardent! . . .

FIRST IDLER. (*Coldly.*) He *is* a good Hasid, there's no denying it. But if he wants to find a husband for his daughter, he ought to think about his standards.

THIRD IDLER. Huh? What do you mean?

FIRST IDLER. In the old days, whenever a rich man with a fine background had to find a husband for his daughter, he didn't look for money, he didn't look for a good family tree. All he cared about was the boy's character. He would travel to the Great Yeshiva with a lovely present for the director, and the director would then select a student, the finest in the school, the crème de la crème. Sender could try the same approach.

MESSENGER. He might also find the right husband in this yeshiva.

FIRST IDLER. (*Surprised.*) How do you know?

MESSENGER. Just speculating.

THIRD IDLER. (*Hurriedly.*) Well, well, well. Let's not gossip, especially about good friends. A marriage comes about if the bride and groom are meant for each other. (*The door flies open and an* OLD WOMAN *hurries in, leading two children by the hand.*)

OLD WOMAN. (*Hurries with the children to the Holy Ark, shouting and weeping.*) Oh, oh, God, oh God! Help me, Lord! (*Runs to the Holy Ark.*) Children! We're going to open the Holy Ark, we're going to kneel before the Torah scrolls, we're going to weep and wail, and we're not leaving until we obtain a complete cure for your mother! (*She opens the Holy Ark, kneels down, thrusts her head inside, and launches into a tearful recitative.*) God of Abraham, God of Isaac and Jacob, look at this disaster, look at the sorrow of these little children. Their mother is so young—please don't take her away from this world. Holy Torahs, please intercede for a poor, unhappy widow! Holy Patriarchs, dear Matriarchs, go to God, run to the Lord of the Universe, scream, beg! Don't let the tender sapling be torn out by its roots, don't let the baby dove be hurled out of its nest, don't let the gentle lamb be wrenched from its herd! . . . (*Hysterically.*) I'll destroy the world, I'll split the heavens! I won't leave here until God restores the apple of my eye! . . .

MEYER. (*Goes over, touches her quietly, speaks calmly.*) Khanna-Esther, should we gather a minyan and recite psalms?

OLD WOMAN. (*Pulls her head out of the Holy Ark. Looks blankly at* MEYER. *All at once, she blurts out.*) Oh! Get a minyan together, have them recite psalms. Now! Hurry, hurry! Every minute is precious! She's been flat on her back for two days now, unable to talk, struggling with death!

MEYER. I'll get ten men together immediately! (*In a beseeching tone.*) But we have to give them something for their trouble. . . . They're very poor.

OLD WOMAN. (*Rummaging in her pocket.*) Here's a ruble! Just make sure they recite!

MEYER. A ruble!? . . . That comes to just a few kopeks per man! . . . It's not exactly generous. . . .

OLD WOMAN. (*Paying no attention.*) C'mon, children! We have to hurry to the other synagogues! (*Hurries out.*)

MESSENGER. (*To the* THIRD IDLER.) This morning, an old woman came to the Holy Ark to pray for her daughter, who's been in labor for two days already and the baby still won't come out. And now an old woman has come to pray for a daughter who's been struggling with death for two days.

THIRD IDLER. Well? What's your point?

MESSENGER. (*Musing.*) When the soul of a person who hasn't yet died has to enter a body that isn't yet born, there is a struggle. If the sick woman dies, then the other woman will bear the child. If the sick woman recovers, then the baby will be stillborn.

THIRD IDLER. (*Surprised.*) Oh my! How blind people are! They never see what's happening under their very noses!

MEYER. (*Goes over to the table.*) Well, the Good Lord has sent us something for a drink. We'll recite some psalms, we'll drink to our health. So God will take pity on the woman, and she'll recover completely.

FIRST IDLER. (*To the* YESHIVA STUDENTS *sitting drowsily at the large table.*) Boys! Who wants to recite psalms? Each of you will get a buckwheat cookie. (*The* STUDENTS *get up from the table.*) We're going into the private room. (*The* THREE IDLERS, MEYER, *and all the* YESHIVA STUDENTS *but* HENEKH *go off into the private room. They soon launch into a mournful recitation of the First Psalm: "Blessed be the man who walks not in the counsel of the ungodly. . . ." [This recitation may be in Hebrew.] Meanwhile the* MESSENGER *has remained immobile at the smaller table, his eyes glued to the Holy Ark. A long pause.* KHONEN *enters.*)

KHONEN. (*Very tired, lost in thought, walks aimlessly toward the Holy Ark. Noticing that the Ark is open, he halts in surprise.*)

The Holy Ark is open? Who opened it?

Whom did it open for at midnight? (*Peers inside the Ark.*)

Torah scrolls. . . . Huddling together, calm, silent. . . .

And they conceal all the mystical meanings,

All the allegorical meanings,

all the combinations of letters and numbers—

from the Six Days of Creation to the end of time.

And it's so hard to grasp a single secret,

a single allusion, it's so difficult. (*Counts the Torah scrolls.*)

One, two, three, four, five, six, seven, eight, nine.

A magical number, the numerical sum

of the letters in the word *EMES* (truth)

—and each of the nine scrolls has four wooden handles,

four "Trees of Life" . . . which adds up to thirty-six. . . .

I keep running into that number all the time—

and I still don't know what it means.

But I feel it contains the essence of the truth. . . .

How about the letters in the name *Leah?*
Lamed is thirty, aleph is one, hey is five. . . .
That adds up to thirty-six.
Three times thirty-six makes 108,
the numerical value of the name *Khonen.*
But *Leah* also breaks down into
"lo" (not) and the letter "hey"
—the symbol of God. No God! . . . Not through God. . . . (*He trembles.*)
What a horrible thought . . . and how tempting. . . .

HENEKH. (*Looks up, scrutinizes* KHONEN.) Khonen! You keep wandering around in a dream. . . .

KHONEN. *Moves away from the Holy Ark; lost in thought, he slowly walks over to* HENEKH.)
Endless secrets, endless allusions,
and I can't see the straight and narrow path. . . .
(*Brief pause.*) The shtetl's name is Krasne. The rebbe's name is El-khónen. . . .

HENEKH. What did you say?

KHONEN. (*As if awakening.*) Who me? Nothing. . . . Just thinking out loud. . . .

HENEKH. (*Shaking his head.*) You've gotten lost in the Cabala, Khonen. You haven't touched a holy book since your return.

KHONEN. (*Not comprehending.*)
A holy book? What sort of holy book?

HENEKH. How can you ask? The Talmud. . . . The Commentators. . . .

KHONEN (*Still not quite conscious.*)
The Talmud? . . . The Commentators?. . . I haven't touched?
The Talmud is all cold and dry. . . .
The Commentators are all cold and dry. . . .
(*Comes to all of a sudden, grows lively.*)
Beneath the earth there is another world
just like our surface world.
It has fields and forests, oceans and deserts, towns and villages.
And powerful hurricanes blast across fields and deserts,
and huge ships sail across the oceans there,
and the dense forests are haunted by eternal terror,
and thunder keeps on thundering and thundering. . . .
Yet one thing is missing from that netherworld:
It doesn't have a lofty sky

with fiery lightning and a dazzling sun. . . .
And that's what the Talmud is like.
The Talmud is profound, it's grand and splendid.
But it shackles us to the earth,
it doesn't let us soar to the heavens.
(*Ecstatically.*) The Cabala, however! . . . The Cabala! . . .
It tears the soul away from the earth!
It carries us to God's highest palaces,
it opens all the heavens to our eyes.
It takes us straight to Paradise,
it draws us all the way to endlessness!
It lifts a corner of the infinite curtain. . . .
I'm worn out. . . . I feel faint. . . .

HENEKH. (*Very earnest.*) That's all true. But you're forgetting something: Soaring in ecstasy is the greatest danger. You can easily drop and fall into the abyss. . . . The Talmud raises the soul aloft, very slowly, and it protects us like a loyal sentry who never sleeps or dozes. It surrounds us like an iron armor and it never lets us leave the path of righteousness, it never lets us go right or left. Unlike the Cabala. . . .

You remember that story in the Talmud. . . . (*He switches into a Talmudic melody.*)

Four rabbis entered Paradise:
Rabbi Ben Azzai, Rabbi Ben Zoma,
Rabbi Aher, and Rabbi Akiba.
Rabbi Ben Azzai looked around and died.
Rabbi Ben Zoma looked and lost his mind.
Rabbi Aher "laid waste the plants"—that is,
he abandoned Judaism and seduced the young.
Rabbi Akiba was the only one
who entered Paradise unscathed
and came out unscathed. . . .

KHONEN.
Don't try to terrify me with those rabbis.
We don't know how they went or why.
Perhaps those men were yielding to temptation,
perhaps they stumbled because they went to look
and not to purify their souls. . . .
We know that others entered after them—
the saintly Ari, the holy Baal-Shem-Tov—
and none of them were sinners.

HENEKH. Are you comparing yourself to them?

KHONEN.
I'm not making any comparisons.
I'm just following my own path. . . .
HENEKH. Which path is that?
KHONEN. You wouldn't understand.
HENEKH. I want to understand. My soul also yearns for the highest
spheres.
KHONEN. (*Thinking for a while.*)
Our saints all have the task of cleansing human souls,
they root out the evil spirit of sin
and restore our souls to radiant perfection.
It's a hard task because "sin lurks by the door."
When one soul has been purged and purified,
another takes its place immediately,
a soul that's tainted with far greater sins.
When one generation has repented,
another takes its place immediately,
a generation with a stiffer neck.
And people keep growing weaker and weaker,
and sins keep growing stronger and stronger,
and saints keep growing scarcer and scarcer.
HENEKH. Then what do you think we should do?
KHONEN. (*Quiet but very confident.*)
We must never wage war against sin,
we should simply try to ameliorate it.
It's like a goldsmith tempering gold in an intense fire,
or like a farmer separating chaff from wheat.
That's how we have to purify sin:
Remove all impurity and leave
nothing but holiness. . . .
HENEKH. (*Surprised.*) Holiness in sin? How is that possible?
KHONEN.
Everything that God has created
contains a spark of holiness.
HENEKH. It wasn't God who created sin, it was the *sitra-akhra,* the
other side—the Devil!
KHONEN.
And who created the other side? God!
The *sitra-akhra* is the other side of God.
And since the Devil is a side of God,
he must contain a spark of holiness.

HENEKH. (*Shocked.*) Holiness in the Devil? I don't understand! I can't! Let me think. (*He buries his head in his hands on the lectern. Pause.*)

KHONEN. (*Goes to him, bends over him. In a trembling voice.*)
Which sin is the worst?
Which sin is the hardest to conquer?
The sin of lust. Isn't that so?

HENEKH. (*Without lifting his head.*) Yes. . . .

KHONEN.
And if you purify that sin in powerful fire,
the vilest sinfulness becomes
the most exalted holiness
—it becomes the Song of Songs. (*Breathless.*)
The Song of Songs.
(*Standing up straight, he begins to croon softly and ecstatically.*)
You are beautiful, my beloved, you are beautiful.
Your eyes are like doves,
peering out from under your brows.
Your hair is like a flock of goats
scampering down from Mount Gilead.
Your teeth are like a herd of sheep
that have just bathed,
and they are all twins,
and there are no barren sheep among them. . . .

(*MEYER emerges from the private room. We hear a quiet tap on the door; it grates softly and opens hesitantly. LEAH enters, holding FRADDE's hand. Next comes GITL. They halt by the door.*)

MEYER. (*Surprised to see them; in a flattering and ecstatic voice.*) What? Sender's daughter? Leah? . . .

LEAH (*Timidly.*) Don't you remember? You promised to show me the old embroidered curtains on the Holy Ark. (*The instant he hears her voice, KHONEN stops crooning and stares at her wide-eyed. From now on, he stands there, either gaping at her or closing his eyes ecstatically.*)

FRADDE. Meyer, please show her the oldest and most beautiful curtains. Leah promised she would embroider a curtain for the anniversary of her mother's death. She'll use gold thread and she'll embroider lions and eagles into the finest velvet, the way women did in the old days. And when they hang the curtain on the Holy Ark, her mother's pure soul will be so happy in Paradise.

(*LEAH looks around shyly, she notices KHONEN, her eyes drop, and she makes an effort to keep them down.*)

MEYER. Of course, of course! I'd be absolutely delighted! I'll bring the curtains out right away, the oldest and most beautiful. (*Goes over to the chest by the entrance door and takes out some curtains.*)

GITL. (*Grabs* LEAH's *hand.*) Leah, aren't you scared to be here at night?

LEAH. I've never been inside a synagogue at night before. . . . Except for Simkhes-Torah, the rejoicing in the Torah. That night, the synagogue was radiant and cheerful, but now. . . . How sad it is, how sad.

FRADDE. Girls, a synagogue has to be sad. At midnight, the dead come to pray and they leave their sorrows here.

GITL. Fradde! Don't talk about ghosts, I'm scared!

FRADDE. (*Ignoring her*).
And every morning, when the Almighty weeps
for the destruction of the Holy Temple,
his holy tears flow into all the synagogues.
That's why their walls are always damp—with tears.
And the walls must never be whitewashed.
If ever they were, they would get angry and hurl stones.

LEAH.
The synagogue is old, so very old.
I couldn't really tell from the outside.

FRADDE. It's old, it's very old, my darling. They say it was discovered under the ground, intact. There's been so much destruction here, the whole town's been wiped out by so many fires—and yet the synagogue has always survived unscathed. One time only, the roof caught fire, but doves came flying, masses of doves. They beat and beat their wings until they blasted out the flames.

LEAH. (*Not hearing her, talking to herself.*)
How sad the synagogue is and how sweet!
I don't feel like leaving, I'd like to kneel
at the tear-stained walls and embrace them lovingly
and ask them why they look so sad and dreamy,
so silent and gloomy. I'd really like to—
I don't know what. But it's heart-wrenching, I feel
so much pity for them, so much tenderness. . . .

MEYER. (*Brings curtains to the bimah and spreads one out.*) This is the oldest curtain, it's over two hundred years old. We only hang it up on Passover.

GITL. (*Delighted.*) Look, Leah, isn't it glorious! It's made of brown velvet and there are two lions embroidered in thick gold thread. They're holding a Mogen Dovid, a Shield of David, and they're flanked by two trees with doves! You could never get such heavy velvet today or such rich gold thread.

LEAH. The curtain, too, is sweet and sad.

(*She smoothes it out and kisses it.*)

GITL. (*Clutches* LEAH'*s hand, speaks quietly.*) Look, Leah. There's a boy standing over there and he's staring at you! He's staring at you so strangely!

LEAH. (*Dropping her eyes even more intensely.*) He's a yeshiva student . . . Khonen. He sometimes had meals in our home.

GITL. He's staring at you as if he were trying to call you with his eyes. He wants to come closer, but he's afraid.

LEAH. I wonder why he looks so pale and sad. He must have been sick. . . .

GITL. He's not the least bit sad. His eyes are sparkling.

LEAH. His eyes are always sparkling . . . and they're so incredible. And whenever he talks to me, he becomes breathless. And so do I. . . . After all, it won't do for a girl to speak with a strange boy. . . .

FRADDE. (*To* MEYER.) Meyer, you have to let us kiss the Torah scrolls. How can we pay God a visit without kissing his Holy Torah!?

MEYER. All right, all right! C'mon! (*He goes ahead,* GITL *leads* FRADDE, *then comes* LEAH. MEYER *takes out a Torah scroll and hands it to* FRADDE, *who kisses it.*)

LEAH. (*Right across from* KHONEN, LEAH *pauses for a moment, speaks softly.*) Good evening, Khónen. So you've come back?

KHONEN. (*Breathless.*) Yes. . . .

FRADDE. Leah, come and kiss the scroll! (LEAH *goes over to the Holy Ark.* MEYER *holds out the Torah. She embraces it and kneels down, kissing it passionately.*) Fine, my child, that's enough! You shouldn't kiss a scroll too long. After all, a Torah is written with black fire on white fire! (FRADDE *is suddenly startled.*) Goodness, look how late it's getting! C'mon, you two, we have to get home as fast as possible. (*They hurry out.* MEYER *shuts the Holy Ark and goes out behind them.*)

KHONEN. (*Stands a while with closed eyes, then continues to croon the Song of Songs from where he broke off.*)

Your lips are like a scarlet thread and they
are beautiful; and your temples are like
pomegranates under your bridal veil.

HENEKH. (*Raises his head, looks at* KHONEN.) Khonen! What are you singing?! (KHONEN *breaks off. Opens his eyes, looks at* HENEKH.) Your earlocks are wet—you've been to the ritual bath again.

KHONEN. Yes.

HENEKH. When you cleanse your body, do you recite incantations? Do you use spells and rituals from the Book of Raziel?

KHONEN. Yes.

HENEKH. And you're not afraid?

KHONEN. No.

HENEKH. And you really fast from one Sabbath to the next? It's not hard for you?

KHONEN. It's harder for me to eat on the Sabbath than to fast all week. I've lost all desire for food. (*Pause.*)

HENEKH. (*Intimately.*) Why do you do all those things? What are you hoping to achieve?

KHONEN. (*Almost to himself.*)
I want. . . .
I want to find a clear and sparkling diamond.
I want to melt it into tears and soak
the tears into my soul. . . . I want to find
the rays of the Third Heavenly Temple,
the Third Divine Emanation . . .
the Sphere of Tiferet—Beauty.
I want . . . (*He suddenly becomes very agitated.*) Yes! I still have to get two small barrels of gold coins. . . . For the man who can only count money. . . .

HENEKH. (*Astonished.*) What are you saying? Listen, Khonen, you're walking on a slippery path. . . . You won't get all those things with holy forces. . . .

KHONEN. (*Eyes him boldly.*) And if I don't use holy forces? If I don't use holy forces?

HENEKH. (*Terrified.*) I'm scared of talking to you. I'm scared of standing next to you! (*Hurries out.* KHONEN *remains motionless, with a bold expression.* MEYER *enters from the street. The* FIRST IDLER *emerges from the rebbe's private room.*)

FIRST IDLER. I've recited eighteen psalms—that's enough. After all, eighteen is the symbol of life. I'm not going to recite all one hundred fifty psalms for just a few lousy kopeks. But there's no way of talking to the others, they're absorbed in their psalms, and once they get going— forget it! (OSHER *comes dashing in, very excited.*)

OSHER. I just ran into Borekh, the tailor. He's back from Klimóvke—Sender went there to meet with the bridegroom's parents. Borekh says they failed to reach an agreement. Sender wanted them to put the couple up for ten years, but the boy's parents wouldn't go beyond five. So they just went their separate ways.

MEYER. That's the fourth bridegroom he's rejected!

THIRD IDLER. It's heartbreaking!

MESSENGER. (*To the* THIRD IDLER, *smiling.*) You yourself said that a marriage comes about if the bride and groom are meant for each other.

KHONEN. (*Stands up straight; highly enthusiastic.*) I've won again! (*Collapses on the bench and sits with a blissful expression on his face.*)

MESSENGER. (*Picks up his sack, removes a lantern.*) It's time I got going.

MEYER. What's your hurry?

MESSENGER. Look, I'm a messenger. My wealthy clients hire me to deliver important messages and precious objects to one another. So I have to hurry. My time is not my own.

MEYER. Why don't you wait till dawn?

MESSENGER. The dawn is far away, and I have far to go. So I'll be leaving around midnight.

MEYER. It's pitch-black outside.

MESSENGER. I've got a lantern, I won't get lost. (*The other two* IDLERS *and the yeshiva students emerge from the private room.*)

SECOND IDLER. Mazel tov! May God grant the sick woman a complete recovery.

ALL. Amen! Amen!

FIRST IDLER. We ought to spend our ruble on some liquor and cookies.

MEYER. It's all been taken care of. (*He takes out a bottle and some cookies.*) Let's go to the anteroom. We'll have our drinks there. (*The door opens wide and* SENDER *walks in. His coat is unbuttoned, his hat pushed back; he is in high spirits. He is followed by three or four men.*)

MEYER AND IDLERS. (*Together.*) Ah, Sender. Welcome, welcome!

SENDER. I was driving past the synagogue, so I thought I'd drop in and see how my friends are doing. (*Notices* MEYER'*s bottle.*) I figured you'd be studying a holy book or talking about some Talmudic dilemma. But I see you're about to have a drink! Ha ha! True Hasids!

THIRD IDLER. You'll have a sip, too, won't you, Sender?

SENDER. C'mon now! I'm going to be treating you to a drink, and a fine drink. Congratulate me! I've signed the engagement contract for my daughter—thank goodness!

(KHONEN *jumps up, he is shaken.*)

ALL. Mazel tov! Mazel tov!

MEYER. Hey, we were just told you couldn't work things out with the boy's father, so the engagement was off.

THIRD IDLER. We were devastated!

SENDER. It did look hopeless, but at the last moment the boy's father came around, and so my daughter's engaged.

KHONEN. Engaged? . . . Engaged? . . . What do you mean? How can that be? . . . (*In great despair.*)
Were all my efforts useless—all my fasts,
my ritual ablutions and my spells,
and all the mortifications of my flesh?
Was everything for nothing? . . . And what now? . . .
Where should I go? Where can I get the strength?
(*Grabs at his chest, straightens up, with an ecstatic face.*)
Aah! . . . Aah! I see the revelation now.
The huge, the twofold utterance of the Name.
I . . . see it now! I. . . . I. . . . I've won! I've won!
(*Collapses on the floor.*)

MESSENGER. (*Opens the lantern.*) The candle has burned down. I have to light a new one. (*Terrifying pause.*)

SENDER. Meyer! Why is it so dark here? Can't you light some candles. (MEYER *lights a candle.*)

MESSENGER. (*Quietly walks over to* SENDER.) So you've come to terms with the boy's father?

SENDER. (*Looks at him in surprise, slightly amazed.*) Yes. . . .

MESSENGER. Sometimes parents accept a condition, but then they don't keep their word. Sometimes people have to go to a rabbinical court. You've got to be very careful. . . .

SENDER. (*Frightened, to* MEYER.) Who's that man? I don't know him.

MEYER. He's not from here, he's a messenger. . . .

SENDER. What does he want from me?

MEYER. I don't know.

SENDER. (*Calming down.*) Osher! Zip over to my house and tell them to set out drinks, preserves, and other treats! Hurry! Get a move on! (OSHER *dashes out.*) In the meantime, let's sit for a while and talk. . . . Maybe somebody can tell us some news about our rebbe—a story, a miraculous feat. Every gesture of his is more precious than pearls.

FIRST IDLER. (*To* MEYER.) Put away your bottle. It'll come in handy tomorrow. (MEYER *puts it away.*)

MESSENGER.
I'll tell you a story about him:
The rebbe had a visitor, a Hasid,
A very rich but very stingy man.
The rebbe took him by the hand and led
him to the window, saying, "Have a look!"

The rich man then peered out into the street.
The rebbe asked him: "Well, what do you see?"
And the rich Hasid answered: "I see people."
And then the rebbe took him by the hand
again and led him over to the mirror,
and said: "Now have a look. What do you see?"
The wealthy man replied: "I see myself."
The rebbe went on: "Do you understand?
"The window is made of glass
"and the mirror is made of glass.
"But the glass in the mirror has a thin silver coat.
"And because of that silver,
"you can't see other people,
"you see only yourself."

THIRD IDLER. Ohhhh! Our rebbe's words are sweeter than honey.

FIRST IDLER. Sacred words! . . .

SENDER. (*To the* MESSENGER.) Hey! Was that a dig?

MESSENGER. God forbid.

SECOND IDLER. We ought to sing something. (*To the* THIRD IDLER.) Hum the rebbe's special melody. (*The* THIRD IDLER *launches into a soft, mystical, Hasidic melody. The others join in.*)

SENDER. (*Gets up.*) And now a dance, a *rikudl*! C'mon! My daughter's getting married and no one's dancing?! What kind of Hasids are we? (SENDER, *the* THREE IDLERS, *and* MEYER *each puts his hand on the next man's shoulder and they form a round. Starry-eyed, they chant a repetitious mystical tune while slowly moving in a circle.* SENDER *merrily dashes out of the circle.*) And now, a merry dance. All of you—get over here!

THIRD IDLER. Boys! Boys! All of you get over here. (*Several* BOYS *go over.*) Henekh! Khónen! Where are you? We're dancing our socks off!

SENDER. (*A bit confused.*) Aha, Khónen! Our Khónen ought to join us. Where is he? Where is he? Bring him here immediately!

MEYER. (*Sees* KHONEN *on the floor.*) He's sleeping on the floor.

SENDER. Wake him up, wake him up!

MEYER. (*Tries to waken him; terrified.*) He won't wake up! (*The others join him; they bend over the boy and try to waken him.*)

FIRST IDLER. (*Cries out in terror.*) He's dead!

THIRD IDLER. The book's fallen out of his hand, it's The Book of the Angel Raziel! (*All of them are shaken.*)

MESSENGER. He's been destroyed by the demons!

CURTAIN

Act II

*Three months later. A square in Brínnitz. To the left, the old wooden syna-
gogue, ancient in its architecture. In front of the synagogue, slightly off to
the side, a mound of earth with an old gravestone bearing the inscription:
"Here lie a pure and holy bride and groom who were martyred in the year
5408 [1648]. Blessed be their souls." Next to the synagogue, a narrow lane
with some tiny houses merging into the backdrop. To the right,* SENDER's
*home, a large wooden house with a porch; next to the house, a wide gate
leading into a courtyard; then a tiny alley with a row of shops, which also
merge into the backdrop. On the backdrop, to the right near the shops, a
tavern and an aristocratic mansion with a large garden. A wide road
runs down to the river. On the high bank on the other side of the river, a
Jewish cemetery with headstones. To the left, a bridge across the river and a
windmill; nearby, a bathhouse and a poorhouse; in the background, a dense
forest.*

The gates to SENDER's *courtyard are wide open. In the courtyard, long
tables stick all the way out into the square. The tables are set, and beggars
and cripples, old and young, are sitting around them, eating ravenously.
Waiters emerge from the house with huge platters of food and baskets of
bread, which they place on the tables.*

*In front of the shops and houses, women sit, darning stockings, their
eyes glued to* SENDER's *home. Householders and students with prayer shawls
and phylacteries emerge from the synagogue; some go into shops or houses,
others form small groups. Music, dancing, and noisy conversation are
heard from* SENDER's *courtyard.*

*It is evening. In the middle of the street, in front of the synagogue, we
see the* WEDDING GUEST, *an elderly man wearing a long satin frock, with
his hands tucked into the back of his belt. Next to him, the* SECOND IDLER.

GUEST. (*Looks around the synagogue.*) This is a grand synagogue
you've got here. . . . It's huge, it's beautiful. The shekhina, God's spirit,
is resting on it. It looks very old.

SECOND IDLER. It's ancient. Our old people say that even their
grandparents couldn't remember when it was built.

GUEST. (*Spots the gravestone.*) And what's this? (*Walks over and reads
the inscription.*) "Here lie a pure and holy bride and groom martyred in
the year 5408. Blessed be their souls." A bride and groom were martyred here?

SECOND IDLER. Yes, they were killed by Khmielnítsky—may he rot in
hell. He and his Cossacks butchered most of our people in this area.

When they attacked Brínnitz, they slaughtered half the Jews—including a bride and groom, just as they were being led to the wedding canopy. Afterwards, the two of them were buried in one grave and in the very spot where they'd been murdered. Ever since, it's been known as the Holy Grave. (*He murmurs softly, mysteriously.*) Now, whenever the rabbi marries a couple, he hears sighs coming from the grave. . . . And so we have an old custom here: After a wedding ceremony, we dance around the grave and entertain the buried couple.

THE GUEST. A fine custom! (MEYER *emerges from* SENDER*'s courtyard and comes over.*)

MEYER. (*Raving.*) What an incredible banquet for the poor! I've never seen anything like this in all my life.

THE GUEST. It's not surprising. Sender is marrying off his only daughter.

MEYER. (*Ecstatically.*) Everyone is getting a piece of fish, a slice of roast, and then carrot stew! And before the meal, they were served cake and brandy. It must be costing millions—it's beyond belief!

SECOND IDLER. Sender knows what he's doing. If you don't treat an invited guest properly, it's no big deal, he'll just pout and get huffy. But if you don't go out of your way for the poor, then you're skating on thin ice. . . . You never know who may be dressed in beggar's clothing. Perhaps a pauper or perhaps someone else. A hidden saint, or even a *lámmed-vóvnik*—one of the thirty-six righteous men. . . .

MEYER. And why not the Prophet Elijah—Elly-ha-nóvi? He always comes disguised as a beggar.

THE GUEST. You should treat everyone decently, not just the poor. You can never tell who a person is, or who he was in an earlier life, or why he was reborn. (*The* MESSENGER, *with a sack slung over his shoulder, enters from the street on the left.* MEYER *spots* MESSENGER, *goes to him.*)

MEYER. Shólom aléikhem—peace be with you! So you're back in our town?

MESSENGER. I've been sent here again.

MEYER. You've come at the right time. We're having a sumptuous wedding.

MESSENGER. People are talking about it all over the district.

MEYER. Did you happen to run into the bridegroom's family on your way here? They're late.

MESSENGER. The groom will arrive on time. (*Goes over to the synagogue. The* GUEST, *the* SECOND IDLER, *and* MEYER *go into the courtyard.* LEAH, *in her wedding gown, emerges from behind the tables, dances with each of the poor old women in turn; other paupers come over to her. The ones who have finished dancing go out into the square, where they form small groups.*)

WOMAN WITH A CHILD. (*Contented.*) I danced with the bride.

LAME WOMAN. So did I. I took her in my arms and we danced. Hee hee!

HUNCHBACKED MAN. Why is the bride only dancing with women? I'd like to take her in my arms and whirl her around. He he he!

SEVERAL PAUPERS. He he he! (FRADDE, GITL, *and* BESSYE *come out of the house and stand on the porch.*)

FRADDE. (*Nervously.*) Oh my! Leah is still dancing with the paupers. She's going to be too dizzy. Girls, please go and get her. (*She sits down on a chair.* GITL *and* BESSYE *go over to* LEAH.)

GITL. That's enough dancing, Leah. Come on.

BESSYE. You're going to get very dizzy. (*She and* GITL *take* LEAH *by the hands and try to lead her away.*)

THE POOR WOMEN. (*Clustering around* LEAH, *with pleading and tearful shrieks.*)

She hasn't danced with me yet! Am I any worse than the others?

I've been waiting for hours to dance with her!

Let me. I'm supposed to dance with her after Elke.

She's spun around ten times with that cripple Yakhne, and not even once with me! I never have any luck!

MEYER. (*Comes from the courtyard and sits down on a chair. Chants loudly like a wedding jester.*)

The father, the rich man, he asked one and all
To come to his home for the big wedding ball!
He said he'd distribute his alms to the poor—
Ten kopeks for everyone who came to his door!

THE POOR. (*Dashing, shoving, jostling their way into the courtyard, shouting excitedly.*) Ten kopeks! Ten kopeks! (*The square empties out. The only people remaining are* LEAH, GITL, BESSYE, *and the* BLIND OLD WOMAN.)

BLIND OLD WOMAN. (*Grabs* LEAH.) I don't need your charity. Just dance with me. Just spin around with me once. I haven't danced in forty years! Oh, how I danced when I was a girl, how I danced! (LEAH *and the* BLIND OLD WOMAN *dance, the* OLD WOMAN *refuses to let go, she pleads.*) More, more! (*They keep dancing, the* OLD WOMAN *becomes breathless, hysterical.*) More, more! (GITL *yanks away the* OLD WOMAN, *leads her to the courtyard, and returns; then she and* BESSYE *take* LEAH *to the porch and they all sit down. The* WAITERS *and* SERVANTS *take in the tables and lock the gates.*)

FRADDE. You're pale as a ghost, Leah. You must be exhausted!

LEAH. (*Her eyes closed, her head bowed, she speaks almost dreamily.*)
They grabbed me, they crowded around me, they crushed against me,
they touched me with their cold, dry fingers. . . . My head whirled, I felt
faint. . . . Then someone lifted me up and carried me far, far away. . . .

BESSYE. (*Frightened.*) Leah! Look at your wedding gown, it's
smeared and crumpled! What are you going to do now?

LEAH. (*In the same tone.*) If the bride is left alone before the ceremony, evil spirits come and carry her off. . . .

FRADDE. (*Frightened.*) Leah! What are you saying! You mustn't use
their real names. They lurk and hide in every nook and cranny, in every
hole and crack. They see everything, they hear everything, and they're
just waiting for someone to use their real names, their unclean names—
then they leap out and attack. (*She spits three times to ward off evil.*)

LEAH. (*Opens her eyes.*) They're not evil. . . .

FRADDE. And never trust a demon. If you do, he goes berserk and
starts playing his pranks. . . .

LEAH. (*Very self-confident.*) Fradde!
The spirits that surround us aren't evil.
These are the people who died before their time.
And now their souls watch everything we do
and listen now to everything we say. . . .

FRADDE. God help you, darling! What are you saying! Souls? What
souls? Pure souls fly to Heaven and rest in the brightness of Paradise. . . .

LEAH. No, they're here, with us!
(*Her tone of voice changes.*)
When a person is born,
he can look forward to a long, long life.
But if he passes on before his time,
what happens to the life he hasn't lived?
What happens to his joys and sorrows?
The thoughts he had no time to think?
The deeds he had no time to do?
What happens to the children
he had no time to conceive?
Where does everything go? Where? (*Musing.*)
Oh. . . . Once upon a time there was a boy.
His soul was lofty, and his mind was deep.
A long, long life stretched out ahead of him. . . .
Then all at once, in a split second,
his life was cut short.

And strangers buried him in a strange soil. (*Mournfully.*)
What happened to the life he never lived?
The words he never spoke, the prayers he never prayed? . . .
Fradde, when a candle goes out, we light it again,
and it keeps burning down until it's gone.
So if a life has not burned down,
how can it be possibly be snuffed forever?
How can that be?

FRADDE. (*Shaking her head.*) Darling, you shouldn't think about such things! The Good Lord knows what He's doing, but we are blind, we know nothing. (*The* MESSENGER *comes over unnoticed and stations himself somewhat behind the others.*)

LEAH. (*Ignoring* FRADDE, *self-assured.*)
No, Fradde,
no human life is ever lost forever.
If anybody dies before his time,
his soul comes back into the world and lives
the lifetime that he should have lived on earth.
it does the deeds he never got to do,
it feels the joys and pains he never felt. (*Pause.*)
Fradde! You told me that the dead
come to the synagogue to pray at midnight.
You see, they come to finish up the prayers
that they had no time to recite. (*Pause.*)
My mother died when she was very young.
She had no time to do and feel and know
the things that she was destined for on earth.
So now I'm going to the cemetery,
I'd like to ask her to attend my wedding
and lead me to the canopy with my father.
And she will come and she will dance with me. . . .
And that's what always happens to the souls
that leave the world before their time is up:
They lurk among us, but we never see them,
we never feel their presence. . . .
(*Softly.*)
But Fradde, if we wish very hard, we can see them and we can hear their voices and even understand their thoughts. . . . I know. . . .
(*Pause. She points to the gravestone.*)
I've known the Holy Grave since childhood,
I know the bride and groom who are buried there.

I've seen them so often,
in my dreams and in the flesh,
and they're as close to me
as my own family and my friends. (*Musing.*)
When they walked to the wedding canopy,
they were young and beautiful.
A long life lay ahead of them, a lovely life.
But all at once,
evil men attacked them with hatchets—
and the bride and groom lay dead on the ground.
The two of them were buried in one grave
so they could be together for all eternity.
And at every wedding, when people dance around their grave,
their ghosts emerge and they participate
in the joy of the newlyweds.

(LEAH *stands up and goes over to the grave.* FRADDE, GITL, *and* BESSYE *follow her.* LEAH *spreads out her hands and holds them high.*)

Holy bride and groom! I invite you to my wedding!
Please come and stand at my side under the canopy.

(*Suddenly we hear a lively klezmer march.* LEAH *cries out in terror and nearly collapses.*)

GITL. (*Holding her.*) Don't be scared. It's probably the bridegroom coming. They must be welcoming him with music.

BESSYE. (*Excited.*) I'm gonna sneak over and have a look at him.

GITL. Me too. Then we'll come and tell you what he's like. Do you mind?

LEAH. (*Shaking her head.*) No. . . .

BESSYE. She's embarrassed! Don't be embarrassed, silly. We won't tell anyone. (*They hurry off.* LEAH *and* FRADDE *return to the porch.*)

FRADDE. A bride always asks her friends to go and look at the groom. Then they tell her what he's like, and whether his hair is blond or black or brown.

MESSENGER. (*Comes closer.*) Bride!

LEAH. (*Trembles, turns around.*) What do you want? (*Peers intently at him.*)

MESSENGER.
The souls of the dead do return to the world,
but not as spirits without bodies. There are souls
that transmigrate through several bodies,
trying to purify themselves.

(LEAH *listens more and more attentively.*)

The sinful souls come back as animals,
as birds, as fish, or even plants—but they're unable
to purify themselves and so they wait
until a holy man, a tsaddik,
can liberate them and bring them salvation.
And there are souls that enter a newborn baby
and purify themselves through their own deeds.

LEAH. (*Trembling.*) Go on! Please tell me more!

MESSENGER.
And there are homeless souls that find no rest,
and so they enter living bodies
to purify themselves.
Such a soul is called a dybbuk. . . .

(*He vanishes.* LEAH *remains astonished.* SENDER *emerges from the house.*)

SENDER. Why are you sitting there, my darling?

FRADDE. She was entertaining the poor people at their banquet. She danced with them, and now she's exhausted, so she's resting.

SENDER. Ah! Entertaining the poor. That's a very good deed, a great *mitzvah!* (*Looks at the sky.*) It's getting late. The bridegroom and his parents have arrived. Are you both ready?

FRADDE. She still has to go to the cemetery. . . .

SENDER. Go on, dear, go and visit your mother's grave. (*Sighs.*) Cry your eyes out and invite your mother to the wedding. Tell her I'd like her to join me so the two of us can lead our only daughter to the canopy. . . . Tell her I've done everything she asked me to do when she was dying. I've devoted my entire life to you, I've brought you up, I've raised you as a virtuous Jewish daughter. And now I've found you a studious and God-fearing husband from an excellent family. (*Wipes his tears and goes back inside, his head lowered. Pause.*)

LEAH. Fradde, when I go to the graveyard, can I invite other people to my wedding?

FRADDE. Only next of kin. You can invite your grandfather, Fraim, and your Aunt Mírrele.

LEAH. I'd like to invite someone . . . who's not a relative.

FRADDE. That's not allowed, darling. If you invite an outsider, the other dead people will be jealous, and they might do something awful. . . .

LEAH. No, he's not really an outsider. . . . He was like a member of the family. . . .

FRADDE. (*Quiet, frightened.*) Oh. . . . Darling, I'm scared! . . . They say he died a horrible death. . . . (*LEAH weeps softly.*) Oh, c'mon, please don't cry, don't cry. Invite him. I'll take the responsibility. (*Tries to remember.*) But I don't know where his grave is located, and it won't do to inquire.

LEAH. I know where it is.

FRADDE. (*Surprised.*) How do you know?

LEAH. I dreamt about his grave. (*Closes her eyes, muses.*)
I dreamt about him too.
He told me what was happening with him. . . .
He asked me to invite him to my wedding.

(GITL *and* BESSYE *come hurrying back.*)

GITL, BESSYE. (*In unison, excited.*) We saw him! We saw him!

LEAH. (*Shaken.*) Who? Who did you see?

GITL. The bridegroom! He's got dark hair, dark hair!

BESSYE. No, he's got blond hair, blond hair!

GITL. C'mon, let's have another look! (*They hurry off.*)

LEAH. (*Stands up.*) Fradde! Let's go to the cemetery.

FRADDE. (*Sad.*) I'm coming, darling. Oh, me. . . . (LEAH *pulls a black shawl over her shoulders, and she and* FRADDE *exit into the right-hand lane. For a while, the stage remains empty. Music is heard. From the street on the left,* NAKHMAN *comes with* RABBI MENDL *and* MENASHE, *a short, skinny, terrified boy with huge, gaping eyes; next come the bridegroom's parents and relatives in their holiday best.* SENDER *goes out to meet them.*)

SENDER. (*Shaking* NAKHMAN*'s hand.*) Shólom aléikhem, Nakhman, welcome! (*They kiss.* SENDER *greets* MENASHE *and kisses him, and then greets the others.*) How was your trip, Nakhman?

NAKHMAN. We've had a very arduous and confusing trip! Somehow we left the road and wandered through the countryside for a long time. Then we wound up in a swamp and we almost sank in, we barely managed to crawl out. I began to think that the demons—God spare us!— were trying to keep us from traveling. . . . But in the end, we managed to arrive in time, thank goodness!

SENDER. You must be exhausted. Would you like to rest a little?

NAKHMAN. There's no time to rest. We still have to discuss our obligations—the dowry, the gifts, the fees for the rabbi, the cantor, the beadle, the musicians.

SENDER. By all means! (*He puts his arm around* NAKHMAN*'s shoulder, and the two fathers start walking up and down the square, talking quietly.*)

RABBI MENDL. (*To* MENASHE.) Now remember! During the meal, you have to sit quietly at the table and not leave, and always keep your eyes down. . . . Right after the wedding dinner, the clown will announce:

"The groom will now deliver his Talmudic discourse." At that point, you have to get to your feet immediately, stand up on your chair, and begin. You have to chant in a loud, clear melody—the louder, the better. And don't get stage fright! Do you hear me?

MENASHE. (*Mechanically.*) I hear you. (*Softly.*) Rebbe, I'm scared. . . .

RABBI MENDL. (*Startled.*) Why are you scared? Have you forgotten your speech?

MENASHE. No, I remember it. . . .

RABBI MENDL. Then why are you scared? . . .

MENASHE. (*In deep sorrow.*) I don't know. . . . The instant we left home, I started feeling terrified: The places we drove through were alien to me, I've never seen so many strangers in my life. . . . I was frightened whenever they looked at me. . . . I was scared of their eyes. . . . (*Trembles.*) Rebbe! There's nothing I'm so scared of as the eyes of strangers!

RABBI MENDL. You've been harmed by an evil eye. I'll have to exorcise it.

MENASHE. Rebbe! I'd like to be alone and hide out in some nook. I'm surrounded here on all sides by strange people, and I have to talk to them, answer their questions. . . . As if I were being led to the gallows! (*In mystical fear.*) Rebbe! Most of all, I'm terrified of her . . . the girl! . . .

RABBI MENDL. Get a hold of yourself! Conquer your fear! Otherwise you'll forget your speech, God forbid! C'mon, let's go to the inn. You can rehearse your speech one more time. (*They start walking.*)

MENASHE. (*Spots the Holy Grave, trembles, grabs* RABBI MENDL*'s hand.*) Rebbe! What's this? A grave in the middle of the street? (*They stop, silently read the inscription, then, with lowered heads, walk off into the left-hand lane.* SENDER, NAKHMAN, *and the* IN-LAWS *enter the house. One after another, the beggars, with sacks slung over their shoulders and sticks in their hands, come out of* SENDER*'s courtyard. Sad and silent, they plod across the square and disappear into the left-hand lane, some of them pausing for an instant.*)

TALL PALE WOMAN. Now the banquet for the poor is over, as if it had never been. . . .

LAME OLD WOMAN. We were told that each of us would be getting a bowl of broth, but we got nothing.

HUNCHBACKED WOMAN. We got tiny bits of chalah. . . .

MAN ON CRUTCHES. With all his money he couldn't afford to serve each guest a whole roll?

TALL PALE WOMAN. He could have served us pieces of chicken, you know. For the rich guests, they prepared hens and geese and stuffed turkeys. . . .

BLIND OLD WOMAN. What's the difference? . . . When we're dead, there'll be nothing but worms. Oh my, oh my! (*They slowly go away. The stage is empty for a while. The* MESSENGER *slowly walks across the stage and enters the synagogue. Dusk. The shopkeepers close their shops, leave. Candles are lit in the synagogue and in* SENDER's *house.* SENDER, GITL, *and* BESSYE *come out on the porch, look around.*)

SENDER. (*Nervous.*) Where's Leah? Where's her nanny? Why are they spending all this time in the cemetery? I hope nothing's happened, God forbid.

GITL, BESSYE. Let's go and meet them. (LEAH *and* FRADDE *enter hurriedly from the right-hand street.*)

FRADDE. Hurry, hurry, Leah, we're horribly late! (*Women emerge from the house.*) Why did I ever listen to you! Now I'm scared something awful might happen, God help us!

SENDER. Well! Here they are! What's been keeping you? (WOMEN *come out of the house.*)

WOMEN. Take the bride indoors, she has to bless the Sabbath candles. (*They take* LEAH *indoors.*)

FRADDE. (*Softly to* GITL *and* BESSYE.) She fainted. I barely managed to bring her around. I'm still shaking. . . .

BESSYE. She's fasting, that's why she fainted.

GITL. Did she cry a lot at her mother's grave?

FRADDE. (*Waving her hand.*) Better not ask what happened there! I'm terrified! (*A chair is placed next to the door,* LEAH *is brought out and she sits down on the chair. Music is heard. From the left-hand lane come* NAKHMAN, MENASHE, RABBI MENDL, *and the groom's* PARENTS. MENASHE *is carrying a bridal veil in both hands, he goes over to* LEAH *and places it on her head and her face. The* MESSENGER *comes out of the synagogue.*)

LEAH. (*Tears off the bridal veil, jumps up, pushes* MENASHE *away, and shouts.*) You are not my bridegroom! (*Commotion all about. The others surround* LEAH.)

SENDER. (*Shaken.*) Leah! My darling daughter! What's wrong?!

LEAH. (*Tears herself away, runs over to the gravestone, spreads out her arms.*) Holy bride and groom, protect me, save me! (*She collapses. The others run over to her, lift her up, she looks around wild-eyed and screams in a strange voice, a male voice.*) Aaah! Aaah! You buried me! But I've returned to my beloved, and I'll never leave her! (NAKHMAN *goes over to* LEAH. *She screams into his face.*) Murderer!

NAKHMAN. (*Terrified.*) She's lost her mind.

MESSENGER. A dead soul has entered the body of the bride: a dybbuk. (*Great commotion.*)

CURTAIN

Act III

Miropolye, two days later. RABBI AZRIEL*'s house. A huge room. To the right, a door leading to the other rooms. In the middle of the front wall, the front door, with benches on either side. Windows in the wall. To the left, for almost the entire length of the wall, a broad table covered with a white tablecloth. On the table, piles of sliced chalah for the blessing of the meal. At the head of the table, an armchair. At the right-hand wall, next to the inner door, a small Holy Ark and a reading stand. Opposite the Ark, a small table, a sofa, several chairs.*

Saturday night, a short time after evening prayer (Maariv). There are HASIDS *present.* MIKHL, *the beadle, stands at the table, dividing the piles of chalah. The* MESSENGER, *sitting next to the Holy Ark, is surrounded by a group of* HASIDS. *Other* HASIDS *are sitting apart, perusing holy books.* FIRST HASID *and* SECOND HASID *are standing by the small table in the middle of the room. From the interior rooms, a soft singing emerges: "Got fun Avrom, fun Yitzik un fun Yankev. . . ."* (God of Abraham, of Isaac, and of Jacob).

FIRST HASID. The guest is telling such amazing stories. . . . They're terrifying. I'm afraid to listen. . . .

SECOND HASID. What kind of stories?

FIRST HASID. The symbols are too deep, they don't make sense. They're probably inspired by the teachings

of Rabbi Nakhman of Braslev. . . . Who knows? . . .

SECOND HASID. The older Hasids are listening, so there's probably nothing to worry about. (*They join the group around the* MESSENGER.)

THIRD HASID. Tell us another story.

MESSENGER. It's getting late. There's not much time left.

FOURTH HASID. It doesn't matter, the rebbe won't be going out so soon.

MESSENGER. At one end of the world, there is a high mountain, and on that mountain, there is a huge rock, and from that huge rock a pure spring comes gushing out. And at the other end of the world, there is the heart of the world, for everything in the world has a heart, and the world itself has a big heart. And the heart of the world gazes and gazes at the pure spring and it can never see enough of it, and it longs and yearns and thirsts for the pure spring, yet it cannot take even the smallest step toward it. For the moment the heart so much as stirs from its place, it loses sight of the mountain peak and the pure spring, and if the heart of the world ever loses sight of the pure spring for even an instant, it loses its life. And at the very same time, the world starts dying. Now the pure spring has no time of its own and so it lives on the time it receives from the heart of the world. And the heart of the world gives it only one day at a time. . . . And when that day has faded, the pure spring begins to sing to the heart of the world. And the heart of the world sings to the pure spring. And their singing spreads all over the world, and radiant threads emerge from the singing and they reach the hearts of all things in the world and they reach from one heart to the next. . . . And there is a righteous and gracious man who wanders about the world and gathers the radiant threads of the hearts and weaves them into time. And as soon as he finishes weaving an entire day, he passes it on to the heart of the world, and the heart of the world passes it on to the pure spring. And so the pure spring lives for another day. . . .

THIRD HASID. The rebbe is coming! (*They all lapse into silence and stand up. Through the right-hand door comes* RABBI AZRIEL, *a very old man in a white caftan and a shtreyml—the fur-edged hat worn by rabbis and Hasidic Jews on the Sabbath and holidays.*)

RABBI AZRIEL. (*Lost in thought, he trudges slowly and wearily, settles arduously into his easy chair.* MIKHL *stations himself at the rabbi's right, the* HASIDS *sit down around the table. The older ones sit down on the benches, the younger ones stand behind them.* MIKHL *distributes chalah to the* HASIDS. RABBI AZRIEL *raises his head and slowly begins chanting in a quivering voice.*) Do hi soodássa d'dovid malka m'shiekha. This is the banquet of King David the Messiah. (*The others respond, recite the blessing on the bread, then they start chanting a sad, mystical melody without words. Pause.* RABBI AZRIEL *sighs deeply, rests his head on both hands, and sits there for a while, absorbed in his own thoughts. A fearful silence.* RABBI AZRIEL *raises his head and speaks in a soft, trembling voice.*) There is a story they tell about the holy Baal-Shem-Tov—may his merits deliver us from evil. (*Brief pause.*) Once some German acrobats came to his town and they performed stunts in the streets. They stretched a rope all the way across the river, and one of them walked across the rope. People came running from all over town to watch this amazing feat. And the holy Baal-Shem-Tov also came to the river and stood there with everyone else, watching the tightrope walker. His students were astonished to see him there and they asked him what it meant: Why had the holy Baal-Shem-Tov come to watch the stunts? And the holy Baal-Shem-Tov replied: "I wanted to see a man walking over a deep abyss. And as I watched him, I thought to myself: If that man could work as hard on his soul as he worked on his body, then just imagine what deep abysses his soul could cross on the very slender string of his life!" (*A deep sigh. Pause. The* HASIDS *exchange rapturous glances.*)

FIRST HASID. As high as the world!
SECOND HASID. Marvels and wonders!
THIRD HASID. The finest of the finest.
RABBI AZRIEL. (*Softly to* MIKHL, *who is leaning over to him.*) There's a stranger here. . . .
MIKHL. (*Looking around.*) He's a messenger. . . . He seems to be a follower of the Cabala. . . .
RABBI AZRIEL. What sort of message has he brought?
MIKHL. I don't know. Should I ask him to leave?
RABBI AZRIEL. God forbid! Absolutely not! We have to show respect to an outsider. Offer him a chair. (MIKHL, *slightly surprised, offers the* MESSENGER *a chair. No one notices.* RABBI AZRIEL *glances at one* HASID, *who is chanting a mystical melody without words. Pause.* RABBI AZRIEL *as before.*)

God's world is huge and holy. The holiest land in the world is the Holy Land. In the Holy Land, the holiest city is Jerusalem. In Jerusalem, the holiest site was the Temple; and in the Temple, the holiest place of all was the Holy of Holies. (*Brief pause.*)

Now there are seventy nations in the world. The holiest nation is the people of Israel; and of the twelve tribes of Israel, the holiest of all is the Tribe of Levi; and in the Tribe of Levi the holiest men are the priests. Of all the priests, the holiest was the high priest. (*Brief pause.*) Now there are 354 days in the year, and some of them are Holy Days. The holiest of these days are the Sabbaths, and the holiest Sabbath of all is Yom Kippur, the Day of Atonement—the Sabbath of Sabbaths. (*Short pause.*)

Now there are seventy languages in the world. And the holiest of them all is the Holy Tongue, Hebrew. And the holiest Hebrew of all is the Hebrew of the Holy Torah, and the holiest part of the Torah is the Ten Commandments, and in the Ten Commandments the holiest word of all is the *Shem-ha-Váwyaw*, the name of God. (*Brief pause.*) And once a year, at a specific moment, the four holiest holies in the world used to join together: That was on Yom Kippur when the high priest entered the Holy of Holies and uttered the *Shem-ha-Mfóyrosh*, the complete and ineffable name of God, the Tetragrammaton, the Four Letters: Yud, Hey, Vov, Hey. And because that moment was immeasurably holy and fearful, it was the most dangerous—both for the high priest and for the entire Jewish people. For if at that moment—God forbid—a sinful thought had come to the high priest, an impure thought, a *makhshóvve zórre*, then the world would have been destroyed. (*Pause.*)

Any place where a man raises his eyes to heaven is the Holiest of Holies; every man whom God has created *b'tsálmoy ukhd'músoy*, in His

Own Image and after His Own Likeness, is a high priest. Every day of a man's life is Yom Kippur, the Day of Atonement, and every word that a man speaks artlessly is the *Shem-ha-Váwyaw*, the name of God. Hence, every sin and every injustice that a man commits will destroy the world. (*In a trembling voice.*)

Human souls. . . . They pass through great sorrows and sufferings, through many transmigrations and incarnations, drawn to their origin like a baby to its mother's breast, drawn aloft, to the *Kísse-ha-Kóved*, the Throne of God. But sometimes, when a soul reaches the highest levels, then suddenly—God preserve us—the evil spirit wins out, and the soul stumbles and falls. And the higher the soul has soared, the deeper it plunges. And when such a soul falls, then the world is destroyed and all the celestial temples are overcome by darkness and all the Ten Spheres of Heaven, the Ten Emanations of God, weep and wail. (*Pause. As if awakening from a trance.*)

My children! Today the Sabbath dinner, the *melaveh-malke*, will be shorter than usual as we usher out the Sabbath. (*Everyone but* MIKHL *leaves quietly, under the spell of the rebbe's words. A brief pause.*)

MIKHL. (*Walks over to the table, unsure of himself.*) Rebbe! (RABBI AZRIEL *gazes at him, sad and weary.*) Rebbe, Sender of Brínnitz has come to see you. . . .

RABBI AZRIEL. (*As if echoing him.*) Sender of Brínnitz. . . . I know. . . .

MIKHL. Something horrible has happened to him. His daughter is possessed by a dybbuk—God help us.

RABBI AZRIEL. A dybbuk. . . . I know.

MIKHL. Sender has brought his daughter to you. . . .

RABBI AZRIEL. (*As if to himself.*) To me? . . . To me? . . . How could he have come to me since my "me," my "I," does not exist? . . .

MIKHL. Rebbe, the whole world comes to you.

RABBI AZRIEL. The whole world. . . . A blind world. . . . Blind sheep following a blind shepherd. . . . If they weren't blind, they wouldn't come to me, they would go to the only one who can say "I," the only "I" in the world.

MIKHL. Rebbe, you are His emissary. . . .

RABBI AZRIEL. That's what the world says, but I don't know. . . . I've been sitting in a rebbe's chair for forty years now, and I'm still not sure that I am the emissary of God—Blessed Be He. . . . There are times when I feel so close to Him, and I'm not assailed by any doubts, I feel confident, and I have power over the higher worlds. But there are also times when I lose my confidence, and then I'm as tiny and feeble as a baby. And then I'm the one who needs help. . . .

MIKHL. Rebbe, I remember something. . . . You once came to me at midnight and asked me to recite psalms with you. And all through the night, we recited psalms and we wept. . . .

RABBI AZRIEL. That was long ago. Now I feel a lot worse. (*In a trembling voice.*) What do they want from me? I'm old and weak. My body needs rest, my soul craves solitude. Yet I attract the sorrows and sufferings of the world. Every request that someone aims at me pricks my flesh like a needle. I have no strength. . . . I can't! . . .

MIKHL. (*Frightened.*) Rebbe! Rebbe!

RABBI AZRIEL. (*Moans.*) I can't anymore! I can't! (*Weeps.*)

MIKHL. Rebbe! You mustn't forget that entire generations of saints and holy men stand behind you—may they all rest in peace: your father and your grandfather, the great man, who was a disciple of the Baal-Shem-Tov. . . .

RABBI AZRIEL. (*Comes to, raises his head.*) My ancestors: my holy father, who saw the Prophet Elijah three times; my uncle, Rabbi Meyer Ber, who ascended to heaven whenever he recited the Sh'ma Isroel. . . . My grandfather, the great Rabbi Vélvele, who could bring the dead back to life. (*Turns to* MIKHL; *lively.*) Mikhl, my grandfather was able to drive out a dybbuk without resorting to spells or incantations! All he had to do was yell at the dybbuk, just yell! Whenever I face a difficult moment, I turn to him, and he helps me out. And he's not going to desert me now. . . . Call in Sender. (MIKHL *exits and then returns with* SENDER.)

SENDER. (*Stretching out his hands with a tearful plea.*) Rebbe! Take pity! Help me! Save my daughter!

RABBI AZRIEL. How did the disaster come about?

SENDER. Well, the groom was placing the veil on her head—

RABBI AZRIEL. (*Interrupting.*) That's not what I'm asking. Why did this disaster come about in the first place? A worm can make its way into a fruit only after the fruit starts rotting.

SENDER. Rebbe! My daughter is a God-fearing Jewish girl. She's modest and humble, and she obeys me in everything.

RABBI AZRIEL. Children can be punished for the sins of their parents.

SENDER. If I knew of any sin that I've committed, I would do penance. . . .

RABBI AZRIEL. Did anyone ask the dybbuk who he is and why he's possessing your daughter?

SENDER. He won't answer. But we recognized his voice: He was a student at our yeshiva. Several months ago, he died very suddenly in our synagogue. He used to dabble in the Cabala, and that damaged his soul.

RABBI AZRIEL. What forces damaged him?

SENDER. Supposedly, the evil spirits. . . . Several hours before he died, he told a friend that we shouldn't wage war against sin. He also said that there is a spark of holiness in the Devil—God help us! And he tried to create two barrels of gold by using magic. . . .

RABBI AZRIEL. Did you know him personally?

SENDER. Yes. . . . He sometimes had meals in my home—like other yeshiva students.

RABBI AZRIEL. (*Looks sharply at* SENDER.) Did you offend him in any way, did you disgrace him? Think hard.

SENDER. I don't know. . . . I don't remember! (*Despairing.*) Rebbe, I'm only human. (*Pause.*)

RABBI AZRIEL. Bring in the girl. (SENDER *exits and returns immediately with* FRADDE, *who leads* LEAH *by her hands.* LEAH *halts at the threshold, refuses to enter.*)

SENDER. (*Tearful.*) My darling daughter, have pity. Don't shame me in front of the rebbe. Please come in.

FRADDE. Come in, Leah darling. Come in, dear.

LEAH. I want to go in but I can't.

RABBI AZRIEL. Leah! I order you to come in. (LEAH *crosses the threshold and goes to the table.*) Sit down.

LEAH. (*Sits down obediently. Suddenly, she leaps up and shouts in an alien voice.*) Leave me alone! I don't want to! (*She tries to run away, but* SENDER *and* FRADDE *hold her fast.*)

RABBI AZRIEL. Dybbuk, I order you to tell me who you are.

DYBBUK.

Rebbe of Míropolye!

You know very well who I am,

and I won't reveal my name to anyone else.

RABBI AZRIEL. I didn't ask you for your name. I ask: Who are you?

DYBBUK. (*Silent.*) I am one of those who looked for new paths. . . .

RABBI AZRIEL.

A person looks for new paths only if

he wanders from the path of righteousness.

DYBBUK. The path of righteousness is far too narrow. . . .

RABBI AZRIEL.

Those are the words of a wanderer

who couldn't find his way back. (*Pause.*)

Why have you entered this girl's body?

DYBBUK. I am her destined bridegroom.

RABBI AZRIEL.

According to our Holy Torah, the dead

may not linger among the living.

DYBBUK. I have not died.

RABBI AZRIEL.

You've left our world, and you have no right to come back
until the Great Shofar, the ram's horn,
is blown on Judgment Day.
Therefore I order you to leave the girl's body.
Otherwise a living branch will wither
on the eternal tree of the people of Israel.

DYBBUK. (*Shouting.*)

Rebbe of Míropolye!
I know how strong you are, how omnipotent!
I know you can command angels and seraphim.
But you can do nothing to me!
I have nowhere to go!
All paths are blocked for me, all roads are barricaded,
and evil spirits lurk on all sides, waiting to grab me.

(*In a trembling voice.*)

There is Heaven, there is earth,
and there are worlds beyond number throughout the cosmos,
but there is no place for me anywhere in the universe.
And now that my bitter and banished soul
has found a haven,
you want to drive me away!
Have pity on me, don't expel me.
Don't exorcise me.

RABBI AZRIEL.

Homeless soul!
I pity you from the bottom of my heart,
and I will try to save you from the demons.
But you must leave the body of this girl.

DYBBUK. (*In a decisive voice.*) I'll never leave!

RABBI AZRIEL. Mikhl, go to the synagogue and round up a quorum
of ten men. (*Mikhl exits and soon returns, followed by ten men, who station themselves on the side.*) Holy minyan! Do you give me the authority,
in your names and with your power, to expel, from the body of a daughter of the Jewish people, a spirit that refuses to leave of its own accord?

ALL TEN JEWS. Rebbe! We give you the authority, in our names and
with our power, to expel, from the body of a daughter of the Jewish
people, a spirit that refuses to leave of its own accord.

RABBI AZRIEL. (*Stands up.*)

Dybbuk! Soul of a man who left our world:

In the name and with the power of a holy minyan of Jews,
I, Azriel the son of Hadas,
order you to leave the body of this girl,
Leah, the daughter of Khanna.
And I order you not to injure her
or any other living creature as you leave.
If you refuse to obey,
then I will curse you, I will conjure you,
hurl maledictions and anathemas at you,
with all the power of my outstretched arm.
But if you obey,
then I will focus all my power on your salvation,
and drive out all the demons and the devils that surround you. . . .

DYBBUK. (*Shouting.*)
I'm not scared of your conjuring and cursing,
I have no faith in your assurances!
No power in the universe can help me!
Nothing is so lofty and sublime
as my resting place here,
and no abyss is so dark
as the one that awaits me!
I refuse to leave!

RABBI AZRIEL.
In the name of Almighty God,
I beseech you one last time.
I order you to leave the girl's body.
Otherwise, I will excommunicate you
and then hand you over to the demons. (*A terrifying pause.*)

DYBBUK.
In the name of Almighty God,
I am joined forever with my destined bride,
and I will not leave her in all eternity.

RABBI AZRIEL. Mikhl, bring in a white robe for every person in this room and also seven rams' horns and seven black candles. Then get seven Torah scrolls from the Holy Ark. . . . (*A terrifying pause, during which* MIKHL *exits, then returns with rams' horns and black candles. He is followed by the* MESSENGER *with white robes.*)

MESSENGER. (*Counts the robes.*) There's an extra robe here. (*Looks around.*) Is someone missing?

RABBI AZRIEL. (*Nervous, recollecting.*) In order to excommunicate a Jewish soul, one has to obtain authorization from the town rabbi. . . .

Mikhl, hold on to the rams' horns, the candles, and the robes. Take my staff, go over to Rabbi Shimshin, and ask him on my behalf to come here immediately! (MIKHL *takes the rams' horns and the candles and exits together with the* MESSENGER, *who is carrying the robes.* RABBI AZRIEL *speaks to the* TEN MEN.) You can go out in the meantime. (*They exit. Pause.* RABBI AZRIEL *raises his head.*) Sender! Where are the bridegroom and his parents?

SENDER. They're spending the Sabbath at my home in Brínnitz.

RABBI AZRIEL. Send a horseman to them on my behalf. He should tell them to wait there until I summon them.

SENDER. I'll send one right away.

RABBI AZRIEL. Meanwhile take the girl to the next room.

LEAH. (*Wakes up, speaks in her own voice.*) Fradde! I'm scared. . . . What are they going to do to him? And to me?

FRADDE. Don't be afraid, child! The rebbe knows what he's doing. He won't do anything bad. The rebbe would never do anything bad. (FRADDE *and* SENDER *lead* LEAH *into the next room.*)

RABBI AZRIEL. (*Sits absorbed in his thoughts. Then, as if awakening.*) And if the higher spheres decree otherwise, I will reverse the divine judgment. (RABBI SHIMSHIN *enters.*)

RABBI SHIMSHIN. Good day, Rebbe!

RABBI AZRIEL. (*Stands up to greet him.*) Good day to you, Rabbi. Please have a seat! (RABBI SHIMSHIN *sits down.*) I have taken the liberty of asking you to come here because of a dreadful problem. A Jewish girl has been possessed by a dybbuk—God preserve us—and he refuses to leave her body. We have no choice, we're forced to use our last resort: We are going to drive him out with curses and excommunicate him. So I would like to ask your consent. That way, the *mitzvah* of saving a life will stand you in good stead.

RABBI SHIMSHIN. (*Sighs.*) Anathema is a harsh punishment for a living Jew and even more so for a dead Jew. . . . But if there's no other way, and if a godly man like you considers it necessary, then I grant my permission. . . . But first, Rebbe, I have to reveal a secret that pertains to this matter.

RABBI AZRIEL. Really?

RABBI SHIMSHIN. Rebbe, think back twenty years. Do you remember a young man who used to come here from Brínnitz? He was a Hasid and also a practitioner of the Cabala: Nissin, the son of Rivka.

RABBI AZRIEL. Why yes, eventually he moved far away, and he died at a very young age.

RABBI SHIMSHIN. Exactly. Well, last night, that very same man, Nissin, the son of Rivka, appeared to me in three dreams and asked me to summon Sender of Brínnitz before a rabbinical court.

RABBI AZRIEL. What is his grievance against Sender?

RABBI SHIMSHIN. He wouldn't tell me. All he said was that Sender had spilled his blood.

RABBI AZRIEL. When a Jew asks another Jew before a rabbinical court, then naturally a rabbi cannot refuse—especially if it's a dead man, for he can demand a hearing before God's own tribunal. . . . But what does all this have to do with the dybbuk?

RABBI SHIMSHIN. There's a connection. . . . I've been told that the dead boy who entered the girl's body as a dybbuk was Nissin's son. . . . I've also heard that Sender had a certain obligation toward Nissin and that he failed to honor it. . . .

RABBI AZRIEL. (*Thinks for a while.*) In that case, I'll put off the exorcism until noon tomorrow. We'll interpret your dream after morning prayers, God willing, and then you'll summon the dead man for the rabbinical trial. After that, with your authorization, I'll drive out the dybbuk by means of an anathema. . . .

RABBI SHIMSHIN. Rebbe, a rabbinical trial between a living man and a dead man is very unusual and extremely difficult. So I would like to ask you to officiate as the presiding judge.

RABBI AZRIEL. I accept. Mikhl! (MIKHL *enters.*) Bring in the girl. (SENDER *and* FRADDE *bring in* LEAH, *who sits down with closed eyes.*) Dybbuk! I will give you exactly twelve hours, until noon tomorrow. You must leave of your own free will by the stroke of twelve. If not, then, with the permission of the town rabbi, I will drive you out by means of a very harsh anathema. (*Pause.*) You can take out the girl now. (SENDER *and* FRADDE *are about to take* LEAH *out.*) Sender, please stay a bit longer. (FRADDE *takes* LEAH *out.*) Sender! Do you remember your old friend Nissin, the son of Rivka?

SENDER. (*Startled.*) Nissin? . . . Why, he's dead. . . .

RABBI AZRIEL. I have to tell you that last night the town rabbi dreamt about him three times. (*Points to* RABBI SHIMSHIN.) He demanded the right to bring charges against you before a rabbinical court.

SENDER. (*Shaken.*) A rabbinical court? . . . Oh my God! . . . What does he want from me? . . . What should I do, Rebbe?

RABBI AZRIEL. I don't know what he's accusing you of, but you must agree to the trial.

SENDER. I'll do as you say.

RABBI AZRIEL. (*In a different tone of voice.*) Send the fastest horses to Brínnitz without further delay and bring the bridegroom and his parents.

They are to get here tomorrow morning before noon. The instant the dybbuk is driven out, we will perform the marriage.

SENDER. Rebbe! They may not want to be related to me now. Suppose they refuse to come? (*The* MESSENGER *appears in the doorway.*)

RABBI AZRIEL. (*Firmly.*) Tell them that I order them to come. Just make sure the bridegroom arrives in time.

MESSENGER. The bridegroom will arrive in time.

(*The clock strikes midnight.*)

CURTAIN

Act IV

Twelve hours later. The same room as in Act III. At the left, the long table has been replaced by a small table closer to stage front. An armchair flanked by two other chairs has been placed behind the table. RABBI AZRIEL, *in his prayer shawl and phylacteries, is sitting at the table, flanked by the two rabbinical judges.* RABBI SHIMSHIN *is standing at the table. Further off:* MIKHL. *They have just finished interpreting* RABBI SHIMSHIN'*s dream.*

RABBI SHIMSHIN. *Khélmo tóvo khózze*, I have dreamt a good dream. *Khélmo tóvo khózze*, I have dreamt a good dream.

RABBI AZRIEL AND BOTH JUDGES. *Khélmo tóvo khazéyso*, you have dreamt a good dream. *Khélmo tóvo khazéyso*, you have dreamt a good dream. *Khélmo tóvo khazéyso*, you have dreamt a good dream.

RABBI AZRIEL. Rabbi, we've interpreted your dream, and it's going to work out for the best. So please join us as a judge. (RABBI SHIMSHIN *sits down next to* RABBI AZRIEL *at the table.*) We will now summon the dead man to the rabbinical court. But first I want to draw a circle. He is to remain within its circumference and he will not be allowed to leave. Mikhl, hand me my cane! (MIKHL *hands him the cane.* RABBI AZRIEL *goes over to the left-hand corner of the room and draws a circle with his cane from left to right. He sits down again at the table.*) Mikhl! Take my cane and go to the cemetery. When you get there, close your eyes and grope your way with my cane. Halt at the very first grave that my cane touches, tap the grave three times and say the following words:

"*Mes tóhor*, righteous dead man: Azriel, the son of the great and saintly Rabbi Itshele of Míropolye, asks your forgiveness for disturbing your rest, and he enjoins you, by ways you are familiar with, to tell the righteous dead man, Nissin, the son of Rivka, that the rabbinical court of Míropolye requires his immediate appearance and orders him to wear the clothes in which he was buried."

You are to repeat those words three times, then turn and come back. Pay no heed whatsoever to the shouts, shrieks, and cries that you may hear behind you, and do not let go of my cane for even an instant. Otherwise you will be in mortal danger. Go, and God will protect you, for someone who is performing a good deed, a *mitzvah,* cannot be harmed. . . . Before you leave, send in two men to put up a partition for the dead man. (MIKHL *leaves. Then, two men bring in a sheet, which they hang up, so that the edge reaches the floor, thereby covering the entire left-hand corner. They leave.*) Call in Sender. (SENDER *comes in.*) Sender, have you done what I told you? Have you dispatched horses to summon the bridegroom and his parents?

SENDER. I sent out the fastest horses, Rebbe, but the bridegroom and his parents haven't arrived yet.

RABBI AZRIEL. Send out another horseman, he is to tell them to drive faster.

SENDER. Yes, Rebbe. (*Pause.*)

RABBI AZRIEL. Sender! We are notifying the righteous dead man, Nissin, the son of Rivka, that he is being summoned to the rabbinical court to settle a dispute with you. Will you accept our judgment?

SENDER. I will accept it.

RABBI AZRIEL. Will you do anything we tell you to do?

SENDER. I will do anything you tell me to do.

RABBI AZRIEL. Then go and stand on the right.

SENDER. Rebbe! Now I remember. . . . Nissin, the son of Rivka, probably wants to take me to court because of an agreement we once made. . . . I failed to keep my pledge, but it wasn't my fault. . . .

RABBI AZRIEL. You can explain later, when the plaintiff presents his grievance. (*Pause.*) Soon a man from the True World, the realm of the dead, will appear before us, so that we can settle his dispute with a man from our Illusionary World, the realm of the living. (*Pause.*) A trial like this proves that the laws of the Holy Torah rule all the worlds and all the creatures, and these laws apply to both the living and the dead. (*Pause.*) Such a proceeding is very difficult and frightening. It will be watched from all the heavenly palaces. And if the rabbinical court should deviate from the law by even a hair's breadth—God forbid!—then there will be loud protests from the celestial court. We therefore have to conduct our trial with fear and trembling. . . . Fear. . . . And trembling. (*He nervously looks around, focuses on the sheet and lapses into silence. A fearful silence.*)

FIRST JUDGE. (*To the* SECOND JUDGE, *softly, timidly.*) I can feel he's here.

SECOND JUDGE. (*In the same tone.*) He *is* here, I can feel it. . . .

RABBI SHIMSHIN. He is here. . . .

RABBI AZRIEL. Righteous dead man, Nissin, the son of Rivka, the rabbinical court decrees that you shall not step beyond the circle and the partition that have been prepared for you. (*Pause.*) Righteous dead man, Nissin, the son of Rivka, the rabbinical court orders you to state your complaint and grievance against Sender, the son of Henya. (*A terrifying pause. All listen, petrified.*)

FIRST JUDGE. (*As before.*) I think he's answering. . . .

SECOND JUDGE. I think he's answering. . . .

FIRST JUDGE. I hear a voice, but I hear no words.

SECOND JUDGE. I hear words, but I hear no voice.

RABBI SHIMSHIN. (*To* SENDER.) Sender, son of Henya! The righteous dead man, Nissin, the son of Rivka, claims that when you were young the two of you were fellow students in the yeshiva, and your souls were joined in true friendship. You both married in the same week. Later, when you met at the rebbe's home for the Days of Awe, the two of you made a pledge: When your wives got pregnant, and one bore a girl and one a boy, the two children would someday be united as man and wife.

SENDER. (*In a trembling voice.*) Yes, that was our agreement.

RABBI SHIMSHIN. The righteous dead man, Nissin, son of Rivka, further claims that he soon left your town and moved to a remote place, where his wife gave birth to a son at the very same moment that your wife gave birth to a daughter. A short time later, he passed away. (*Brief pause.*) Then, in the True World, the realm of the dead, he learned that his son was blessed with an exalted soul and that he was rising to loftier and loftier heights. And Nissin's heart swelled with fatherly pride. And he also saw that when his son grew older, he went out and wandered across the world, roaming from village to village, from town to town, from country to country, for his soul was seeking his beloved. Now one day, he came to your town and he frequented your home and he sat at your table. And his soul was drawn to your daughter's soul. But you are rich, and Nissin's son was poor. And so you completely ignored him and went looking for a son-in-law with a noble family and a large settlement. (*Brief pause.*)

And Nissin watched his son suffering in profound despair, and the boy began roaming the world again, searching for new paths. And the father's soul was filled with grief and anxiety. And the powers of darkness, upon seeing the boy's despair, spread their nets before him and caught him and snatched him from the world before his time. And his soul wandered about until it entered his beloved's body as a dybbuk. (*Short pause.*)

Nissin, the son of Rivka, states that with the boy's death, he, the father, has been cut off from both worlds. He is unremembered—without a name, without an heir, without a son to say Kaddish for him. His candle was snuffed for all eternity, and his pride and joy plunged into an abyss. And so he asks the rabbinical court to judge Sender, according to the laws of our Holy Torah, for spilling the blood of Nissin's son and his son's children and his children's children until the end of time. (*Terrifying hush.* SENDER *sobs.*)

RABBI AZRIEL. Sender, son of Henya, have you heard the grievance of the righteous dead man, Nissin, son of Rivka? What is your response?

SENDER. I can barely speak, I have no words to justify what I did. But I beg my old friend to forgive me for my sin, because it was not ill will on my part. A short time after we swore our oath, Nissin moved away, and I never knew that his wife had given birth, I never learned about their son. Eventually, I heard that Nissin had died. I received no further news about his family, and little by little I forgot all about him.

RABBI AZRIEL. Why didn't you make inquiries? Why didn't you try to investigate?

SENDER. Normally it's the groom's family that takes the first step. I figured that if Nissin had had a son, he would have notified me. (*Pause.*)

RABBI SHIMSHIN. Nissin, son of Rivka, asks why it was that when his son visited your home and sat at your table, you never once asked him who he was or where he came from?

SENDER. I don't know. . . . I can't remember. . . . But I swear that I constantly felt a longing to make the boy my son-in-law. That was why whenever someone proposed a husband for my daughter, I made such exorbitant demands that the parents always refused. And so three possible engagements didn't work out. However, this time the mother and the relatives insisted. . . . (*Pause.*)

RABBI SHIMSHIN. Nissin, son of Rivka, says that in your heart of hearts you recognized his son, and that was why you were afraid to ask him who he was. You wanted a rich and cozy life for your daughter, and so you hurled his son into the abyss. (SENDER *weeps quietly, covering his face. An intense pause.* MIKHL *arrives and hands the cane to* RABBI AZRIEL.)

RABBI AZRIEL. (*Speaks softly with* RABBI SHIMSHIN *and* THE JUDGES. *Stands up, takes hold of the cane.*) The rabbinical court, having heard both sides, has now come to the following decision:

Whereas it is not known whether their wives were already pregnant when Nissin, the son of Rivka, and Sender, the son of Henya, made their agreement; and whereas according to our Holy Torah, an agreement has no validity if it refers to something that has not yet been created, we cannot determine that Sender was obligated to keep his promise. On the other hand: Since the heavenly palaces accepted the agreement, and since they planted in the heart of Nissin's son the thought that Sender's daughter was his destined bride; and since Sender's subsequent behavior caused great calamities for Nissin and his son, it is the judgment of this rabbinical court that Sender must donate half his wealth to the poor; furthermore, for the rest of his life, he is to burn memorial candles and recite Kaddish on the anniversaries of Nissin's death and his son's death, as if they were his own kinsmen. (*Pause.*) The rabbinical court asks the righteous dead man, Nissin, the son of Rivka, to grant full and complete forgiveness to Sender and also to exert his paternal authority by ordering his son to leave the body of the girl, Leah, the daughter of Khanna; otherwise a living branch will wither on the fruitful tree of the people of Israel. And the Almighty will then show his vast grace to Nissin, the son of Rivka, and to his homeless son.

EVERYONE. Amen! (*Pause.*)

RABBI AZRIEL. Righteous dead man, Nissin, the son of Rivka, have you heard our judgment? Do you accept it? (*A fearful pause.*) Sender, son of Henya, have you heard our judgment? Do you accept it?

SENDER. Yes, I accept it.

RABBI AZRIEL. Righteous dead man, Nissin, son of Rivka, the litigation between you and Sender, son of Henya, is terminated. Now you have to go back to your rest. We enjoin you not to hurt any human being or any other living creature on your way. (*Pause.*) Mikhl! Remove the partition and bring us some water. (MIKHL *summons two men, who take down the curtain. With his cane* RABBI AZRIEL *draws a circle in the same place as before, but this time from right to left. The servants bring in a bowl and a pitcher. They all wash their hands.*) Sender? Has the bridegroom's family arrived?

SENDER. We haven't heard them yet.

RABBI AZRIEL. Send another horseman out to meet them. They should drive their horses as hard as they can. Set up the wedding canopy and alert the musicians. Have the bride put on her wedding gown. That way, the instant the dybbuk leaves her body, the ceremony can take place. Make sure that everything is ready. (*Takes off his prayer shawl and phylacteries and folds them up.*)

RABBI SHIMSHIN. (*Softly to the* JUDGES.) Did you notice that the dead man did not forgive Sender?

FIRST AND SECOND JUDGES. (*Softly, terrified.*) We noticed.

RABBI SHIMSHIN. Did you notice that the dead man did not accept the judgment?

FIRST AND SECOND JUDGES. We noticed.

RABBI SHIMSHIN. Did you notice that he did not say "amen" to Rabbi Azriel's words?

FIRST AND SECOND JUDGES. We noticed.

RABBI SHIMSHIN. A very bad omen!

FIRST AND SECOND JUDGES. A very bad omen!

RABBI SHIMSHIN. Look how agitated Rabbi Azriel is! His hands are trembling. (*Pause.*) We've done what had to be done, now we can go. . . . (*The* JUDGES *steal out unnoticed.* RABBI SHIMSHIN *is about to leave, too.*)

RABBI AZRIEL. Rabbi, stay here until the dybbuk leaves. And then you can perform the ceremony. (RABBI SHIMSHIN *sighs and, lowering his head, he sits down off to the side. An oppressive silence.*) Lord of the Universe! Obscure and wondrous are your ways. But the path that I take is illuminated by the blazing flame of your sacred will. And I will not deviate from this path either to the left or to the right. . . . (*Raises his head.*) Mikhl, is everything ready?

MIKHL. Yes, Rebbe.

RABBI AZRIEL. Call in the girl. (SENDER *and* FRADDE *bring in* LEAH. *She is wearing a white wedding dress with a black cape on her shoulders. They seat her on the sofa.* RABBI SHIMSHIN *sits down next to* RABBI AZRIEL.) Dybbuk! On behalf of the town rabbi, who is sitting here, on behalf of a holy minyan of Jews, on behalf of the Great Sanhedrin of Jerusalem, I, Azriel, the son of Hadas, issue this order one last time: You are to leave the body of the girl, Leah, daughter of Khanna!

DYBBUK. (*Resolutely.*) I will not leave!

RABBI AZRIEL. Mikhl, bring in the men and the white robes and the rams' horns and the black candles. (MIKHL *goes out and then comes back with fourteen men, plus the* MESSENGER. *They bring in smocks, rams' horns, and black candles.*) Get the Holy Torahs! (MIKHL *takes out seven Torahs, distributes them to seven men. Hands out seven rams' horns.*) Obstinate spirit! Since you refuse to submit to our decree, I am placing you under the authority of the higher spirits, and they will pull you out with all their violence. Blow the horns! Blow *tekiah.* (*They blow the horns.*)

LEAH (*DYBBUK*). (*Jumps away, thrashes, screams.*) Stop it! Stop pulling me! I don't want to! I can't leave!

RABBI AZRIEL. Since the higher spirits cannot control you, I am placing you under the authority of the middle spirits, those that are neither good nor evil. And they will pull you out with all their cruelty. Blow the horns! Blow *shvórim!* (*They blow the horns.*)

DYBBUK. (*With waning strength.*) Oh God! All the powers in the universe have risen up against me! I'm being pulled by the most horrible demons, the most ruthless devils. Great souls and righteous souls are confronting me, and my father is among them, and they are ordering me to leave. But so long as there's even a spark of strength left in me, I'll keep fighting and I won't leave.

RABBI AZRIEL. (*To himself.*) Some powerful entity must be helping him! (*Pause.*) Mikhl! Put the Torahs back in the Holy Ark. (*They are put back.*) Now shroud the Holy Ark in a black curtain. (*MIKHL does so.*) Now light the black candles. (*They are lit.*) Now put on the white robes—all of you! (*Everyone, including* RABBI AZRIEL *and* RABBI SHIM-SHIN, *dons a white robe.* RABBI AZRIEL *stations himself and raises his arm high and fearfully.*) Rise up, oh Lord! May your enemies flee and disperse. Let them scatter the way smoke scatters. . . . Sinful and obstinate spirit! With the strength of Almighty God and with the power of the Holy Torah, I, Azriel, the son of Hadas, rip apart all threads that tie you to the world of the living and to the body and soul of Leah, the daughter of Khanna. . . .

DYBBUK. (*Shrieks.*) Oh God!

RABBI AZRIEL. And I anathematize you and expel you from the community of Israel!! *Terúah!*

MESSENGER. The final spark has blended with the flame.

DYBBUK. (*Powerless.*) I can't fight anymore. . . . (*They blast terúah on the rams' horns.*)

RABBI AZRIEL. (*Stops the blasting. To the* DYBBUK.) Do you surrender?

DYBBUK. (*In a dying voice.*) I surrender. . . .

RABBI AZRIEL. Do you swear in good faith to leave the body of Leah, the daughter of Khanna, and never return?

DYBBUK. (*As before.*) I swear.

RABBI AZRIEL. By the same power and authority with which I anathematized you, I hereby revoke your anathema. (*To* MIKHL) Snuff the candles and remove the black curtain. (*MIKHL obeys.*) Put away the rams' horns. (*MIKHL gathers them.*) All of you, take off your robes. You may leave. (*The fourteen men take off the robes and leave together with the* MESSENGER *and* MIKHL. RABBI AZRIEL *raises his arms high.*) Lord of the Universe! God of mercy and goodness! Behold the great suffering of the homeless and afflicted soul who stumbled because of someone else's sins and errors. Avert Your eyes from this soul's transgressions, take into account his earlier good deeds, his great torments, and the merits of his ancestors. Lord of the Universe, clear away all the demons from his path and grant him eternal rest in Your heavenly palaces. Amen!

ALL. Amen!

DYBBUK. (*Leah shudders violently.*) Say Kaddish for me. My time is running out.

RABBI AZRIEL. Sender! Recite the first Kaddish!

SENDER. *Yisgadál ve-yiskadásh shmey rabó b'olmá di b'rà khiruséy.* . . . Magnified and sanctified be His Great Name throughout the world that He has created according to His will. May He establish His kingdom in your lifetime and in your days, and in the lifetime of all the House of Israel, soon and speedily; and say amen— (*The clock strikes twelve.*)

LEAH (*DYBBUK*). (*Leaps up, terrified.*) Ohhhh! (LEAH *falls on the sofa, unconscious.*)

RABBI AZRIEL. Take the bride to the canopy! (MIKHL *comes running in.*)

MIKHL. (*Very agitated.*) The last horseman has just returned. He says a wheel broke on the groom's carriage, and the family is continuing on foot. They're almost here. Look! They're on the hilltop, we can see them now!

RABBI AZRIEL. (*Greatly surprised.*) Whatever must be must be! (*To* MIKHL.) Leave the old woman here with the bride. The rest of us will go out to welcome the groom. (*With his cane, the rebbe draws a circle around* LEAH *from left to right. He takes off his robe, hangs it up by the door, and exits, gripping his cane. He is followed by* SENDER *and* MIKHL. *Long pause.*)

LEAH. (*Wakes up; her voice is very weak.*) Who's here with me? . . . Oh, it's you, Fradde? Dearest Fradde? I feel so heavy. Help me. . . . Cradle me. . . .

FRADDE. (*Caressing her.*)
You shouldn't feel heavy, my darling.
Let the rat feel heavy, let the black cat feel heavy.
Your heart should be as light as a bit of down,
a puff of breath, a white snowflake.
Let holy angels fan you with their wings.

(*We hear a klezmer band playing a wedding tune.*)

LEAH. (*Shuddering, clutches* FRADDE*'s hand.*)
Do you hear that? They're dancing at the Holy Grave,
they're entertaining the dead bride and groom!

FRADDE.
Don't shiver, my darling, don't be afraid.
You're surrounded by a ring of powerful guards.
Sixty sturdy men with drawn swords
will protect you against any misfortune.
Our holy Patriarchs and Matriarchs
will protect you against the evil eye.

(*She gradually passes into a rhythmic chant.*)
Soon you will walk to the canopy
In a good moment, in a happy moment. . . .
Your saintly mother will come from Heaven,
Will come from Heaven,
All decked out in silver and gold.
And two angels will welcome her,
Will welcome her with all their might.
They will take her hands,
One left, one right:
"Khanna mine, Khanna fine,
"Why are you in gold and silver,
"Why do you shine?"
Khanna answers without a whine:
"Why shouldn't I wear silver and gold?
"Today is a great holiday!
"My only daughter is being given away,
"My darling girl is marrying today!"
"Khanna mine, Khanna fine?
"Why is your face full of sadness and pain?"
Khanna answers without a whine:
"Why shouldn't I grieve? Why should I smile?
"Strangers are walking my daughter to the canopy,
"And I have to stand on the side and pine. . . .
"The bride will be taken to the canopy,
"Old and young will come to see.
"The Prophet Elijah will join the spree.
"He will take the goblet in his hand. . . .
"And he will bless the entire land.
"Amen! Amen!" (*She falls asleep. Long pause.*)
LEAH. (*Closes her eyes, sighs deeply, opens her eyes.*)
Who sighed so deeply?
KHONEN'S VOICE. I did.
LEAH. I hear your voice, but I can't see you.
KHONEN'S VOICE. We're separated, you're in a magic circle.
LEAH.
Your voice is as sweet as a violin
weeping in a hushed night. . . .
Tell me—who are you?
KHONEN'S VOICE.
I've forgotten. . . .
I can remember only if you remember me. . . .

LEAH.

I do remember. . . .

My heart was drawn to a radiant star. . . .

In hushed nights, I shed sweet tears

and I kept dreaming about someone. . . . Was that you?

KHONEN'S VOICE. Yes. . . .

LEAH. I remember. . . . Your hair was soft and delicate, and your eyes were mild and sad.

Your fingers were long and slender. . . .

You haunted me day and night. . . . (*Pause. Sadly.*)

But then you left me, and my light went out

and my soul shriveled,

I felt like a sorrowing widow

when a stranger approached me. . . .

All at once, you came back, and in my heart

death brought life and sorrow brought joy. . . .

Why did you desert me again?

KHONEN'S VOICE.

I smashed all barriers, I conquered death,

I flouted all the laws of time and space.

I wrestled with the powerful, the ruthless.

And when my final spark of strength was snuffed,

I left your body so I could return to your soul.

LEAH (*Tenderly.*)

Come back to me, my bridegroom, my husband. . . .

I'll carry you in my heart as a dead man,

and in dreams at night we'll cradle our unborn babies.

(*She weeps.*)

We'll sew shirts for them,

we'll sing lullabies to them.

(*Sings tearfully.*)

Weep, oh weep, my babies sweet,

No cradle for you and no sheet.

Babies dead and never born,

Babies lost in time, forlorn. . . .

(*A wedding march is heard from outside, coming closer.* LEAH *trembles.*)

They're going to marry me off to a stranger!

Come to me, my bridegroom.

KHONEN'S VOICE. I've left your body, I'm coming to your soul.

(*Wearing white for his wedding, he appears at the wall.*)

LEAH. (*Joyous.*) The circle is broken! I can see you, my bridegroom!

Come to me!

KHONEN. (*Echoing.*) Come to me!

LEAH. (*Stands up joyously.*) I'm coming to you.

KHONEN. (*Echoing.*) I'm coming to you.

VOICES. (*offstage.*) Take the bride to the canopy!

(*A wedding march.* LEAH *leaves the black cloak on the sofa and, all in white, she approaches her bridegroom to the rhythm of the wedding march. She reaches him and fuses with him.* RABBI AZRIEL *comes in, holding the cane. He is followed by the* MESSENGER. *They halt by the door.* SENDER, FRADDE, *and the* OTHERS *appear in the doorway.*)

LEAH. (*In a distant voice.*)

A giant light is pouring all around us. . . .

I'm joined to you forever, my beloved. . . .

We'll float together, higher, higher, higher. . . .

(*The stage grows darker and darker.*)

RABBI AZRIEL. (*Lowering his head.*) Too late. . . .

MESSENGER. *Bórukh dáyan ho-émes.* Blessed be the true judge. May they rest in peace.

(*The stage becomes pitch-black. In the distance, we hear.*)

Why, oh why,

Did the soul descend

From the highest height

To the deepest end?

The lowest fall

Contains the upward flight. . . .

CURTAIN

S. ANSKY (1863–1920)

From The Ethnographic Expedition

Questionnaire

In 1913 S. Ansky headed an ethnographic expedition to Eastern Europe's Jewish communities, collecting Jewish folk material—songs, stories, pictures, superstitions, and the like. Using a very long questionnaire, the gatherers interviewed scores of informants; and while the answers have not come down to us, part one of the questionnaire, covering human beings from conception to resurrection, was published as a separate book. The questions are aggressive when judged by modern rules of scholarship, but they do add up to an outline of what Ansky thought Jews thought. The various motifs recur not only in The Dybbuk *but throughout many of his folk tale–like narratives—both serious and humorous. See Joachim Neugroschel,* Great Tales of Jewish Fantasy and the Occult *(New York:Overlook Press, 1987).*

Selected Questions

5. The Angel of Death, the Dumah [Guardian Angel of the Dead], the Soul after Death, Gilgul, Dybbuk

1967. How do people picture the Angel of Death? His appearance, his characteristics?

1968. What weapons or instruments does the Angel of Death employ: a sword or poison or both together?

1969. Do people think that a sick person can possibly survive once the Angel of Death is in that person's home?

1970. Is there a notion that the Angel of Death gets into a debate with the soul?

1971. What is an easy death and what is a difficult death?

1972. Is the Angel of Death glad to take a human soul or does he do so only because he's been given an order?

1973. Is the Angel of Death accompanied by his servants, and who are they?

1974. Is it possible to fool the Angel of Death? What stories do you know about such cases? Do people think that you can fool the Angel of Death by changing your name?

1975. Do people think that the Angel of Death appears to a sick person a while before his death?

1976. Do people think that the Angel of Death has no power over a person who is studying the Torah?

1977. Does a sick person always see the Angel of Death?

1978. Do people believe that a dying person yells when breathing his last and that his yell resounds from one end of the earth to the other, but is heard only by the roosters?

1979. Do people believe that the Angel of Death can harm the surrounding persons?

1980. Does the Angel of Death ever kill the same person several times?——[text illegible]

1981. Does a tsaddik [righteous man] have the power to drive the Angel of Death away from a sick person's bed?

1982. How long before a sick person's death does the Angel of Death come to his bedside?

1983. Where does he stand: at the head of the bed or at the foot? And what does his position signify?

1984. Where does the Angel of Death enter a sick person's home and where does he leave?

1985. Does the Angel of Death pull the soul from the body or does the soul come out by itself?

1986. Can the Angel of Death visit many sick people in different places at the same time?

1987. How do people picture the soul?

1988. Do people think that the soul refuses to leave the body?

1989. Does the soul weep when it leaves the body?

1990. Do you know any stories about a debate between a soul and the Angel of Death?

1991. Through what part of the body does the soul leave?

1992. Where is the soul once it leaves the body?

1993. After a person breathes his last, do any senses remain in the body? For instance, the ability to feel grief, to hear the weeping of the surrounding people, and so on?

1994. Does the soul remain next to the body until after the burial?

1995. When does the soul fly up to Heaven?

1996. Does the soul know and feel everything that happens to the body in its grave?

1997. Do people believe that angels accompany the funeral of a tsaddik [righteous man] while demons throw a wicked man to his grave?

1998. What stories do you know about that?

1999. Do people believe that the dead parents and relatives come to welcome the dead man during a funeral?

2000. Do people believe that the Dumah comes to a dead man the instant he is put in his grave?

2001. What do people believe about the appearance and the characteristics of the Dumah?

2002. What is the reason for his coming?

2003. What does the Dumah do with a dead person who has forgotten his name?

2004. Does the Dumah beat him or chop him up with a sword or a chain?

2005. What happens to the dead person after the Dumah leaves him?

2006. What does the *Khibit-ha-keyver* [beating after death] consist of? Which Angels of Destruction [*Malakhe-Khabole*] punish the dead man? How long does the beating last?

2007. Do people believe that if a Jewish woman has fornicated with a non-Jew, he comes to her grave after her death?

2008. Do people believe that a tsaddik's corpse doesn't decay and that worms have no power over him?

2009. What stories do you know about graveyard worms?

2010. Do people believe that the corpses lying in their graves can socialize with one another?

2011. Do the corpses leave their graves at night, and what do they do?

2012. Do people believe that a corpse can take over another corpse's grave?

2013. Do people believe that, if a corpse doesn't return to his grave by cockcrow, he is grabbed by demons?

2014. Do people believe that corpses, like living people, hear everything that visitors tell them when they visit their graves?

2015. Do people believe that all corpses or only some go to pray in a synagogue at night?

2016. Do you know any stories about two dead people involved in a litigation presided over by a rabbi?

2017. Can a dead man come before the Celestial Council of Justice or go to the Patriarchs and Matriarchs to intercede for living people if he wants to or only if he is summoned to the Celestial Council of Justice?

2018. Whom does the Celestial Council of Justice consist of?

2019. When is a dead person judged? Right after his death or only after his beating in the grave?

2020. How does the judgment at the Celestial Council proceed? Who weighs the sins and good deeds, and so on?

2021. What kind of punishment is doled out for each kind of sin?

2022. Does the body also appear during the trial, or only the soul?

2023. Is there a belief that because of certain sins a [deceased] person must return to the world in the form of a human being, an animal, or a bird in order to expiate his sin?

2024. As what creatures is such a sinner reincarnated?

2025. Is there a belief that a sinner can be reincarnated as a tree or another kind of plant?

2026. Is there a belief that he can be reincarnated as a rock?

2027. Is there a notion that a person can be reincarnated several times, and in what shape does he return the first time?

2028. How can each kind of gílgul [wandering soul] find redemption?

2029. Do you know any stories about a cow or a beast that suddenly began talking because it contained a gílgul?

2030. Do you know any stories about a log that was burning in a stove and that suddenly began to scream because it contained a gílgul?

2031. Is there a belief that if someone makes a blessing over a thing that contains a gílgul, the soul will be redeemed?

2032. What should you do if you recognize a gílgul?

2033. Do you know any stories about any kinds of reincarnations?

2034. Do you know any stories about a dead person's soul that finds no rest and that turns into a dybbuk and enters a living person?

2035. What does a dybbuk normally say and shout?

2036. Because of what sins does a dybbuk enter a person?

2037. Does a male dybbuk ever enter a female and vice versa?

2038. Do most dybbuks enter a male or a female, a young person or an old person?

2039. What antidotes or remedies can be effective in such a case?

2040. Does a dybbuk ever harm other people [outside the person it enters]?

2041. Which tsaddiks were famous for exorcising dybbuks?

*6. Gehenna, Kafakál [Limbo, Purgatory; also the Infernal
Punishment in Which Evil Spirits Hurl the Soul Back and Forth];
The World of Chaos*

2042. How do people picture the place where Gehenna is located?

2043. How big is Gehenna?

2044. How do people picture the Seven Halls of Gehenna?

2045. What punishments are applied in each hall? For what sins?

2046. What demons and Angels of Destruction exist in Gehenna?
What do they look like?

2047. Is the body in Gehenna the same as the one in the grave?

2048. Does the grave remain empty the whole time that the body is
in Gehenna?

2049. Is the soul also in Gehenna? Is it attached to the body there?

2050. Are the punishments in Gehenna only physical or also mental?

2051. Is there a custom of pushing back Maariv [evening prayer] on
the evening of the Sabbath because the wicked return to Gehenna at
night only after Maariv?

2052. Do all the wicked in Gehenna rest on the Sabbath?

2053. Do people believe that even the greatest sinner cannot be
sentenced to more than twelve months in Gehenna?

2054. Do people believe that even a tsaddik [or other righteous
man] has to go through Gehenna?

2055. Do you know any stories about tsaddiks who had a chance to
see Gehenna while still alive?

2056. When is the sinner sentenced to Kafakál? Before Gehenna or
after?

2057. Are there any sins that are given eternal punishment in
Kafakál?

2058. Where is Kafakál located? How do people picture it?

2059. What punishments are meted out in Kafakál?

2060. Is the wicked person hurled there from place to place by the
Angels of Destruction?

2061. Are these the same Angels of Destruction as in those in
Gehenna?

2062. How do people picture the World of Chaos?

2063. Is that where sinners wander if the earth does not wish to take
them?

2064. What stories do you know about people who wander about in
the World of Chaos?

7. Paradise, Resurrection of the Dead

2065. How do people imagine the place where Paradise is located?

2066. Where is the Earthly Paradise? Where is the Supreme Paradise?

2067. How many halls are there in Paradise?

2068. What kind of reward do the tsaddiks get there for their deeds?

2069. Who comes to welcome a tsaddik?

2070. Is he welcomed by the Patriarchs and Matriarchs with dancing and singing?

2071. Does the Lord of the Universe ever visit Paradise?

2072. Does he study [the holy texts] with the tsaddiks?

2073. Are holidays observed in Paradise?

2074. What do the tsaddiks in Paradise do when Jews [on earth] are victimized by persecutions and evil decrees?

2075. What are the degrees of greater and lesser tsaddiks in Paradise?

2076. Is there a special Paradise for women, and how does it differ from the one for men?

2077. Do people eat and drink in Paradise?

2078. Do people believe that every tsaddik in Paradise receives the pleasures he did not receive on earth?

2079. If two tsaddiks have quarreled in this world, do they make peace in the afterlife?

2080. Do you know any stories about a tsaddik coming from the next world and revealing the mysteries of the Torah?

2081. How do people picture the Resurrection of the Dead?

2082. Will all corpses roll to the Holy Land through the earth?

2083. If a dead person has been reincarnated several times, in which body will he come alive at the Resurrection?

2084. Which sinners will not be resurrected?

2085. Will the virtuous non-Jews also be resurrected?

2086. What will happen to Gehenna and Paradise after the Resurrection?

2087. What will life be like after the Resurrection?

JACOB BEN ABRAHAM OF MEZRITCH

The Possession

This story is number 157 in The Mayse Book *(Basel; 1602) by Jacob ben Abraham of Mezritch.*

Long though the Jewish tradition of exorcisms may be, this is, so far as I know, the first Yiddish story about a possession. While more women than men (roughly a two-to-one ratio) may have been taken over by evil spirits, this narrative about a possessed male contains numerous elements of both actual and literary possessions in subsequent centuries, especially: the evil spirit as a male (nearly all cases), the intense eroticism, the development from evil spirit to gilgul, transmigration as punishment (especially reincarnation as animals), moralizing of many stories, and so on.

Once, an evil spirit entered a young man. The wise men tried to get the spirit to tell them his name or his wife's name. And whenever they reminded him of his wife, he began shrieking and said that she was an agunah, a woman whose husband had vanished. This meant that she couldn't remarry even though he had drowned at sea. And the wise men could not allow her to take another husband.

The spirit wanted the wise men to allow the woman to marry again. And he gave them many signs to prove he had drowned at sea. But they didn't know where he had been at home, so they said: "We cannot permit it."

And now he shrieked because she had become a whore, since they didn't allow her to take another husband.

The wise men asked him why he had had no rest and what sins he had committed.

He said he had committed adultery. The wise men asked who the woman had been.

But he wouldn't tell them because she had been dead for a long time. "It wouldn't help you if I did tell you." And he added: "I am the kind of man who our sages said ought to be punished with all four

59

capital punishments— stoning, burning, killing by the word, and strangling—for committing adultery. But I was not punished."

And as they were talking, the young man got to his feet. The wise
men asked him: "Why are you standing now?"

And the young man said: "Because a scholar is about to come in."

They looked around. And just then a scholar came in, exactly as the
young man had foretold. And he was followed by a group of young
men. They also wanted to hear what was going on. Whereupon the evil
spirit said: "Why have you come here? To see me? There are some
among you who have done what I did, and you shall be as I am now."

The young men were terror-stricken. Then the evil spirit said: "Why
are you so surprised? That's the one, standing there in white clothes. He
lay with a man. That's as bad as lying with a married woman."

The young men were terror-stricken and peered at one another.
Meanwhile the young man in white clothes began shouting: "It's true,
by God! I did it, and so did he!"

And they owned up to their bad deeds.

One of the wise men now asked: "How did you know what they had
done?"

The spirit laughed and said: "It is written that whatever a man does
is inscribed in his hand."

They said to him: "How could you have seen their hands? They
were under their cloaks."

The spirit laughed again and said: "Can't I see everywhere?"

Then they asked him how he had come into the young man.

The spirit said that after drowning he had had no rest in the water,
and the fish had eaten his body. His soul went out and passed into a
cow. The cow had gone wild, and her owner, a Gentile, had sold her to a
Jew. The Jew slaughtered her, and the spirit flew into the young man
who was present.

The wise men finally managed to exorcise the spirit from the young
man, and the spirit flew away.

ANONYMOUS

The Tale of the Evil Spirit
in Korets (Korzc) During the
Turmoil of War (Prague, 1665)

A transliteration of the Yiddish text into the modern Hebrew alphabet can be found in Sara Zfatman-Biller, "Tale of an Exorcism in Koretz: A New Stage in the Development of a Folk-Literary Genre," Jerusalem Studies in Jewish Folklore *2 (1982): 17–34.*

Aside from its literary, historical, and erotic interest, this verse narrative, consisting of rhymed couplets with lines of widely varying lengths, offers detailed illustrations of Jewish exorcisms (see the introduction, pages xvi through xvii).

The war indicated in the title (and barely mentioned in the story) may very well have been the Khmielnitsky uprising, which had taken place in 1648–1649, less than two decades before the publication of this text. If the author was indeed referring to those historical events, then the link between a Jewish exorcism and the Cossack pogroms occurred at a very early stage. Could the possession then have been an internalization of the massacres, whereby the exorcism drove the murderers (evil spirits) from the Jewish body? The girl is punished through no fault of her own, while in some other possessions, as in "The Possession," the story taken from The Mayse Book *(pages 59 through 60), the victim is being punished for an (often sexual) sin. Does the vulnerability of the girl's situation symbolize the helplessness of the Jews against their killers?*

This story occurred in our day,
Let the world know about it in every way.
And you can be very sure
That such wonders have never happened before.
So every man this tale can buy

And talk about miracles without a lie—
Marvels that have taken place
In our days.
Then you'll have the privilege and
The right to enter the Holy Land.
So to that let us say: Amen.

    It all happened then
In Kotelnie, a holy congregation
Of the Jewish nation,
To a pious Jew—Elye was his name.
His daughter enjoyed some fame
For being very pretty and fine.
Her deeds were as pure as the sunshine.
Mindl was her name. And no one knew
That for three years a spirit had been running through
Her body, leaving her no peace,
Causing her strange maladies.
With the first year of her agonies,
The pains got worse, the injuries—
Sometimes the spirit broke her bones.
Father and mother did weep and groan.
They couldn't find a man so wise
Who recognized the spirit's voice.
Her parents wondered about their tragedy:
What would become of this catastrophe?
They took the girl to witches and physicians.
Some said that epilepsy was causing her condition.
Others said it was a different disease.
But no one hit on the truth—if you please.
Meanwhile the unclean spirit grew day by day.
And many people did say
That the parents should take care
And stop combing the daughter's hair.
    And when the three years had advanced,
The unclean spirit showed his arrogance.
He would often wrench her heart, and soon
The awful pain would make her swoon.
Not a drop of blood in her face could be found.
And sometimes he'd turn her upside down.
He would laugh so insolently:

"Who can imitate my audacity
"When I turn her over and in?"
And her dress stuck to her skin.
Whoever saw these calamities
Had to weep so bitterly.
At times with a gaping mouth she lay on her bed,
And the spirit dashed into her head.
The girl was in such horrible pain
For the spirit hollered again and again.
Her lips never stirred,
The spirit's voice was all that could be heard.
Yet no sage and no seer could infer
Whose voice was dwelling in her.
The spirit caused her such great affliction,
Such fearful adversity beyond description.
And when Rosh ha-Shana came, the Jews
Of Kotelnie did choose
To send for Yitsik, the beadle of the holy congregation
Of Przyluka, for he was versed in exorcism and excommunication.
He could curse a spirit and cause it terror,
Fill the spirit with panic and horror.
Rabbi Yitsik gathered pure and holy men,
Respectable Jews for a minyan of ten.
To threaten the spirit with warnings dire,
To banish him—that was Yitsik's desire.
    The rabbi issued a decree:
The spirit was to give his name speedily.
"And tell me and my colleagues, too,
"Whether you're a demon or a fiend or who?
"Or are you an unclean human soul?
"I order you tell me your name and your role!"
    The spirit began to wail bitterly:
"Oh, who brought you here to heap sorrow on me?
"Why do want to know my name?
"I'll never tell you all the same."
    Rabbi Yitsik anathema did swear
If the spirit didn't reveal his name
To all the Jews who were here.
    The spirit began to shout in fear:
"Oh, how awful this anguish! To whom
"Can I lament? I'm being driven to my doom!

"I've taken over every limb and artery,
"And if I leave, the fiends will get hold of me."
    The rabbi kept threatening to do the same,
Till the spirit revealed that Yakov was his name.
But he couldn't recover. And the rabbi in his ardor
Urged and pressed him harder and harder,
The spirit begged him to stop. But the rabbi went on.
The spirit couldn't recover thereupon.
So he revealed his identity:
He was the evil spirit, the enemy.
    The girl's parents wailed in their tribulation:
"Oh! Oh! This distress is on the whole congregation!"
    They were told to take their daughter to
Pawlocz, and that was what they did do.
The head of the Jewish tribunal there began
To recite spells and prayers in order to ban
The spirit. And the rabbi uttered moans and groans
Because the spirit was breaking the girl's bones.
Sometimes he bent her back so low
Until her body looked just like a bow.
    "Help me! Help me!" she shrieked in dismay
So loudly that she could be heard far away.
"God, relieve my affliction, my tears,
"Please send some answer to my prayers!"
    There was no describing her agony
Caused by the spirit's iniquity.
And the spirit's anger and hate
Did not abate.
He held out his hand with might and main
To hit the girl on her head and her brain.
And when all the rulers everywhere
Saw her misery and sorrow there,
They sent her a miracle worker, a baal-shem
From Przemysl: His name was Avrom.
For he knew how to deal with such a case.
And God demonstrated His grace
To the girl in her terrible pain and fear.
But Rabbi Avrom saw he was getting nowhere.
So he tried to smoke out the spirit with bitter wormwood
And sulfur and fire. But it did no good.
Nothing could get the spirit down.

So Rabbi Avrom returned to his town.
For the terrible spirit would do
Whatever he wanted to.
     When people saw the girl's ordeal
They sent her to Lubar to heal.
The baal-shems pursued their goal
To expel the the spirit from the chaste soul.
That was in Little Poland during the year of the war.
The Satanic spirit grew stronger amid the uproar.
I want to write with might and main
That all our efforts were in vain.
First they tried to smoke him out.
But he devoured the fumes all about
And descended into the girl's thigh,
There he broke her leg—oh my!
He twisted her brain and turned her face about,
And his voice came roaring out.
     She raised her arms, weeping and moaning,
To God in Heaven, wailing and groaning:
"Oh, oh! I feel drunk—but not from wine!—
"Because of my torment and my pain."
     So let me tell you, gentlemen,
About the prayer that the girl recited then.
Although it's much better to see than to hear,
I'll repeat the words of her prayer:
     "Before God the King exalted and supreme."
Then she began to shout and scream:
"Almighty God!, how much longer must I
"Suffer this agony, *Eyl shadai?*
"Oh, God of Israel divine! Thou art there!
"Thou knowest I went out for a breath of air.
"Then the evil spirit flouted the Law so just,
"The Torah given to all of us.
"Now since it was the evil spirit's transgression,
"Why should I suffer for his violation?
"What sins have I committed so terribly
"That I should suffer so horribly?
"If Thou dost visit the sins of parents on future generations,
"Why should I suffer these five years of tribulations?
"Thy wrath usually abates, Thy tender mercy is revealed
"Why should I be devastated and concealed?

"Thou dost inflict Heaven's harsh decree
"On the worst sinner, yet even he
"In all his fear
"Doesn't have to suffer for more than a year.
"Thou dost have qualms.
"According to the psalm,
"Thou showest pity whatever the misdeed may be.
"So why hast Thou turned away from me?
"Am I the worst criminal?
"Why didst Thou make me drink the bitter gall?"
    After her prayer, she spoke words so wise:
She tried to curse the spirit and exorcise
Him with Holy Names and invocations
That she had heard during the conjurations.
She herself tried with all her might and main
To banish him and her pain.
She also uttered the forty-two
Letters of saintliness and purity, too,
And invoked the angels who serve God,
Blessed Be His Name, our powerful Lord.
She tried the seven letters at least
Of the Name on the breastplate of Aaron the Priest.
And also the twenty-two letters penned
By the Talmudic sage Haninah ben Teradion
In the scroll of the Law. And also the Great Name
Uttered by the high priest in Jerusalem
On the Day of Atonement, you see.
    But now let me reveal publicly
How the girl based her prayer so wise
On the tale of Isaac's sacrifice.
She began: "Lord, Lord God, merciful and gracious God!
"How long wilt Thou cover my prayer with a cloud?
"Remember, Thou didst test Abraham, our Father.
"It caused the death of Sarah, our Mother.
"Lord of the Universe, we know Thou didst say
"To Abraham: 'Bring me your only son today.'
"And Thou wast to take him although the boy
"Could have many, many offspring by and by.
"When Abraham was to do the slaughtering,
"He did not say the blessing.
"But Thou didst let the father replace

"His son with a lamb, in Thy grace.
"For it was really Thy goal
"To reveal the virtue of Abraham's soul,
"So all nations would worship Thy name and see
"That Thou art stronger than any other deity.
"And now with the evil spirit Thou dost test me.
"So that every sinful person should see
"My suffering, so he'll have the courage to repent.
"But Lord, pity me, my redeemer send.
"I've been bound up for the past five years,
"Oh, beloved God, hear my prayers.
"Great sins were committed by Sodom's men.
"But still Thou didst say: 'If I find ten
"'Righteous men, I'll forgive their sins.' But then
"Wilt Thou not find here ten righteous men
"Who will pray and fast for a bereft and desolate girl?
"For Thou keepest Israel.
"The Egyptians are a good example, for they
"Disobeyed Thee—yet for the last day
"Of Passover Thou didst ordain
"That Jews shouldn't sing Thy praises again,
"Because the Egyptians, created by Thee,
"Were drowned that same day in the Red Sea.
"And I, too, God, was created by Thee—a Jew!
"Am I worse than the Egyptians in Thy view?"
        The evil spirit heard
The girl's every last word.
Into her brain the spirit now ran
And howling and hollering, he began:
        "Why should I have to suffer
"From the things she utters—
"Words accursed and unclean?
"I really want to make her scream."
        And he started to pull out
Her hair and break her body all about.
And when we
The Holy Fellowship did see
That the girl was in terrible pain
We asked God to curse him again and again.
And we tried to smoke him out with bitter wormwood.
But it did no good.

He descended into the girl's thigh
Pitilessly, and there he did lie.
    So the girl was taken to Míropolye
To see the head rabbi that very day.
When the spirit saw him, he fell
Gravely ill,
For prior to entering the room
He had arranged the Awesome Name.
And when Rabbi Yakov began to exorcise,
The spirit moved back to the girl's thigh
Because of his terrible pain.
The girl now praised the Good Lord again.
And sang about her anguish, sang an entire hymn,
"Majestic, Threatening, and Fearful," to Him.
And when she finished, she started to pray. This is what she had to say:
    "Oh, Lord, all gates are now shut,
"But the gates of tears are not.
"And all Jews are weeping for me and hoping with passion
"That Thou wilt show me Thy great compassion.
"Lord, do it for Thy glory, and we will abide,
"So that Thy Name may be sanctified.
"Almighty God, if that is Thy decree,
"Then let me know what the end will be,
"And I lovingly will
"Receive my punishment by Thine will.
"And why should one remember the Holy Names for nothing,
"If Thou dost not build the building?"
    Now the spirit was plagued by an affliction,
And Lubar was struck by a conflagration.
My brethren fled because they did fear
That the fire would engulf them there.
Into the girl's head the boorish spirit came
And then dashed off to watch the flames.
For our great sins our work was devastated,
The girl was out of luck, and the spirit was elated
The evil spirit reveled in his celebration,
Which defied all description and narration.
    Then, on a Wednesday, the congregation
Was struck by a denunciation.
The Christians told the ruler a lie so dire:
That the girl and the spirit had started the fire.

The ruler therefore issued a decree
That the girl should be burned quite speedily
Along with the exorcists that day.
The Jews mulled, then figured out a way:
The girl was sent—that was the plan—
To Korets, to an upright man.
This man was as rich as he was wise,
Righteous and virtuous were his ways.
    And now, dear brothers, I'll tell you about
The great miracle that the Good Lord wrought.
The man was so blessed that the spirit that day
Would never have dared to disobey.
This man was our teacher, Rabbi Borukh Kat.
God granted him the honor and greatness that
He had earned. And now the whole world will hear
What the spirit confessed to the rabbi there.
The rabbi eventually did defeat and ban
The spirit. On the first day of Passover it began.
On a Sunday the rabbi came
In God's name:
    "Behold, He Who doth Israel keep
"Shall neither slumber nor sleep."
    When the rabbi entered the room, they did
What people usually do—they said:
"Welcome, Rabbi Borukh!" When the spirit heard that,
He ran into the girl's head and there he sat.
And then he spoke: "The rabbi's fame is known
"From one end of the world to the other one.
"The things I've heard so frequently
"I now with my own eyes can see.
"It's my privilege to meet such a wonderful man.
"Please sit down at my right
"And receive a blessing from me, if you might.
"It's only proper to show you my reverence."
    The rabbi responded to his deference:
"God highly praised is glorified and sanctified.
"He is our ruler and our guide.
"He is glorious and great.
"We are mere mortals—that is our fate.
"We live today, we die tomorrow.
"Our sins are punished by disaster and sorrow.

"So please do this for me.
"Give me this gift instantly.
"I now have to go to synagogue and pray.
"By the time I return, leave the girl, go away."
　　The spirit then had his say:
"My lord, I will obey.
"Perhaps you can give charity.
"That will be a great help for me.
"I will never injure you as of today."
　　Rabbi Borukh then went to pray.
And the spirit did not torment the maid
While the rabbi prayed.
Next the rabbi and the spirit had a long conversation,
But no writer could supply a full narration.
(Still, we must mention that the mighty rabbi cast
The evil spirit out at last.)
　　Rabbi Boruhk did declare:
"Please don't weaken her there,
"For we're celebrating a holiday.
"And we should eat our bread with joy today—
"The bread that we've prepared."
　　But the spirit declared:
"I now see that the fine things you say
"Will bring me too much sorrow today."
　　Rabbi Borukh retorted: "Please!
"Do it for me, leave the girl in peace.
"And I will take care of you right away
"After the holiday.
"Whatever you ask me to do—
"I promise I will do for you."
　　　"I will obey,
"I will do as you say,"
The spirit then said.
"My lord, eat your bread,
"Drink your wine—may your joy be great!"
So the rabbi went home to celebrate.
And the spirit kept still
While the rabbi ate and drank his fill.
The spirit did remain
Quiet until the rabbi came back again,
Hoping that he could expel
The evil spirit and make the girl well.

When the spirit saw the rabbi, he did say:
"For your sake I've decided to stay
"A while in this darkness. So, rabbi, to get rid of me
"You have to fast, give charity,
"And say Kaddish for me." The rabbi did retort:
"Do good and trust in the Lord.
"I will keep my promise, I will give charity
"To free you from your agony.
"For charity delivereth from death. So do right
"And deliver yourself from your plight."
     The rabbi then questioned the spirit some more:
"Slowly and not with force
"Tell me the truth and avoid shame.
"Is Yakov your real name?"
     The spirit replied: "Rabbi, all the things you say
"Will bring me a lot of sorrow today.
"Why do you ask me for my name?
"I'll tell you the truth: Yakov is my real name."
     The rabbi then asked a lot more:
"Who was it who tore
"Your soul away from you?
"And after you died, what did they do?
"Please tell me true."
     The spirit answered: "Rabbi Borukh, you'll see.
"I'll reveal the wondrous mystery.
"When I died, all around me
"The fiends did surround me.
"And with their horns they tore my soul out of me,
"Cruelly and ruthlessly.
"And before I was hurried
"To the grave and buried,
"They did tweak and twist
"Me all over—nothing was missed.
"And when finally in the grave I lay,
"The fiends immediately lugged me away.
     "To the Angel of Destruction I was sent,
"And he pronounced a brutal judgment
"For my evil deeds. I was sure that I was fated
"To go to Hell, and I felt elated.
"But in a little while I was pushed away
"From Hell, and my joy turned into dismay.
"I was handed over to fearful fiends now—

"With bizarre faces, half-dog and half-cow.
"The fiend named Ghoulhav made me tremble.
"With his face and his shape he did resemble
"A ghoul. And his goal
"Was to swallow my soul.
"He began to bite me hard.
"Then after swallowing me, he spat me far.
"Next, a powerful Angel of Destruction came to me,
"He also swallowed me speedily.
"And he also spat me far away.
    "And now a demon came my way
"And he also swallowed me.
"His face was very bizarre to see,
"He inflicted terrible pain more than once.
"He had the countenance
"Of a turtle—known in the Holy Tongue as a *tsav,*
"And what's called a *tsherepakha* by a Slav,
"And what we call a *shiltkrut* in our tongue.
"This fiend bit and wrung
"Me more than all the rest. He did cover
"My body with holes and cracks all over.
"Next he also swallowed me,
"Then he also spat me far—what agony!
    "And now another demon came along
"And joined the throng.
"His face was half-human and half-canine.
"He also bit this body and soul of mine,
"And I wept and roared in pain.
"And he also swallowed me and spat me out again,
"Treating me like a lion or a bear.
"Now all sorts of fiends were arriving there,
"And their goal
"Was to twist my body and my soul.
"They treated me as if I were living still,
"And they choked me and choked me with a will.
"Then they inflicted all kinds of brutality.
    "Next, to a stream they carried me
"And made me stand in the water there.
"Next they brought me in terrible fear
"To millstones and ground up my body and my soul.
"And then, with disaster and destruction

"They made me whole
"In reconstruction.
    "They judged me again, and their judgment was severe—
"Just as I deserved to hear.
"They hurled me back and forth from one end
"Of the earth to the other end
"For the laws I broke
"And the sins I cloaked.
"I then passed into a hog's body,
"And there I endured worse agony
"For the fiends covered the hog with gashes
"With swift fire and lightning flashes,
"Until the hog died finally.
"But my distress I couldn't flee.
"For some nine years I had to suffer.
"Then I passed into a heifer
"I thought I would find atonement now,
"For I figured a Jew would slaughter the cow,
"And I would have redemption
"Through the slaughterer's benediction.
"But my evil fate won eventually,
"For a Christian slaughtered me.
"And when I left the creature there
"I was overcome with dread and fear.
"So I ran into a cellar underground.
    "And there I was found
"By the adulteress—a wife—
"With whom I had sinned during my life.
"For she too had become a spirit like me,
"And her torment was so awful that she
"Also fled into that cellar and hid.
"Then two girls, two sisters, did
"Come—and I entered one alone.
"And the adulteress entered the other one.
"A woman for you! Long on hair but short on brains was she.
"The other girl died instantly.
"I hid in the sister until I grew
"Stronger in her every limb, through and through.
    "And now dear Rabbi Borukh, you've heard from me
"About my terrible misery.
"Isn't it better for me to remain

"In the darkness again?
"Before I leave the girl and go away
"I should tell you about my sins today.
    "I broke every law and regulation
"Listed in Jewish legislation.
"I did commit one good deed back then:
"I saved a Jew from some highwaymen.
"The angel in charge of me
"Told me to enter a pure body."
    Rabbi Borukh did retort:
"You must have faith in the Almighty Lord.
"I will do all I can do to redeem you
"With prayers, charity, and fasting too.
"Now go down to the girl's thigh slowly, without coercion."
And so, slowly, without harsh compulsion.
The spirit descended voluntarily.
Then we did see
The Holy Fellowship. The spirit felt no fright,
And so we began to deal with his might.
    First we took a huge barrel
And inserted a bottom in the middle.
Then we drilled holes in the bottom board.
And set the girl upon it.
And underneath her we burned incense,
Sulfur, and bitter wormwood so dense.
We fanned the flames, and the spirit of the incense passed
Through the holes into the evil spirit at last,
So that we weakened his strength.
    However, on that first day at length
The spirit went up to the girl's head—
And this is what he said:
    "What kind of barrel is this I see?"
    To which we replied hastily:
"We're putting the girl inside
"So that we can drive you outside."
    The spirit did reply:
"No one can force me to go down to her thigh.
"I refuse just to be mean
"And I'll shatter the barrel to smithereens."
    Rabbi Borukh said then: "You can't hide away.
"You'll have to do as we say—
"Against your will."

          So the spirit began to yell:
"Now I know that you
"Have brought this agony upon me too.
"You force yourself upon me, force your will—
"Like someone clutching someone against his will.
"And the other man hits him. That's what you
"Are doing to me too.
"You order me into the barrel so that they
"Can curse me and anathematize me today.
"But I won't obey, I won't go.
"I'll smash the girl's body from head to toe."
          The rabbi said to the spirit: "You
"Will go inside, I'll force you to.
"You can see the agony you cast."
          The rabbi forced him in at last.
The spirit had to go into the vat. And we
Sent up the incense fumes. In his great agony
The spirit ran into the girl's head, and then
We burned sulfur under his nose. And when
He saw he would have no peace, he did race
Back down to his original place.
There he tortured the girl and caused her pain
With all his might and main.
As if she were dead the girl fainted away
And for over five hours there she lay.
But we paid no heed, she wasn't dead.
          So he ruthlessly ran back into her head.
And started to shout: "You Jews shouldn't call
"Yourselves compassionate at all.
"You are cruel and ferocious in every way.
"You can see that the girl has passed away.
"None of you feels sorry for the loss."
          To which we all replied in one voice:
"Silence! We're prepared
"To give you more reason to be scared!"
          When the spirit heard that, he
Descended in his agony.
          The girl now spoke about her great misery:
"My friends, why do you hide your eyes from me?
"How long will I be judged in Hell?
"Burn me in sulfur, in fire, burn me well."
Now the girl was carried straightaway

From the barrel to her bed, and there she lay
While they went on with their invocation
According to the rules of conjuration.
    The girl screamed: "The spirit has gone from me!
"He's on the bed now—can't you see?"
    Rabbi Borukh said: "If that is the case,
"Please describe the spirit's face."
    "He's got a cricket's face, and he's hopping and
"Jumping about on my hand."
    So we intensified the imprecations
And the anathemas and the condemnations.
And we blew the shofars harder again.
    Meanwhile the girl began to complain:
"Oh, oh! He's come back, he's hidden in me!"
Our joy now turned into misery.
We tried to figure out a way
To drive the evil spirit away.
Finally we went to the synagogue—and there
We anathematized him for all to hear.
We held seven Torah scrolls,
And seven shofars did blast and roll,
And the candles kept going out.
And the spirit heard the children shout—
They yelled: "Amen!"
He heard the anathema and then
The shofars, and he began
To shake. We then went to the maid again
To see what an impact the exorcism had made.
    The girl said: "He's never been this afraid,
"Since you started the exorcism—and I
"Don't know why."
    She didn't realize the entire community
Had proceeded against him courageously.
And we, the Holy Fellowship, sent
The beadle to the spirit, and he went
To warn him that he was exorcised
And anathematized.
    We will soon get to hear
How the spirit responded to him there.
    The beadle came to him and announced:
"Now listen, the wonder workers pounced

"On you in the synagogue and exorcised you
"By blowing the shofars and snuffing the candles too.
"You've been banished and you must obey
"By leaving the girl right away.
"The cursing and the banishing
"Wipe out everything.
       "But if you don't leave her immediately
"They will send you instantly
"To the Grand Rabbinical Court, and they
"Will repeat the exorcism right away.
"They will notify all territories,
"All villages and all communities
"That they, too, must banish you then.
"And all the children will say: 'Amen!'
"You will never again find
"Serenity or peace of mind.
       "So let me give you a bit of advice:
"Obey the Holy Fellowship in a trice.
"Leave the girl and sanctify
"The Venerable and Awesome Name of the Lord on high!
"Otherwise God Himself shall exorcise you
"And anathematize you.
"But if you leave, God shall show
"His loving kindness and on you bestow,
"And as Rabbi Borukh promised, you will find
"Serenity and peace of mind."
       Now the evil spirit yelled bitterly:
"Oh, oh! Why do you force such anguish on me?!
"I would be glad to leave immediately,
"But there is someone who rules over me.
"He won't let me leave, he holds me tight
"With all his might."
       Now the girl's father did exclaim:
"Just give me his name!
"And we will banish
"Him and make him vanish."
       The spirit said: "His name is Duha."
We searched till we learned that his name was Nituha.
And when his name was revealed to us,
We thanked the Lord that He did yield to us
Intelligence and intellect for banishing

The spirit and his guardian after the warning.
The entire fellowship did gather
In the field to expel them together.
    And when we came back to the girl, she cried:
"When you were in the field, the spirit was terrified."
    Upon hearing what she had to say,
Some groups began working on him right away
In the synagogue and in her house, while
Another group went out for a while
Into the field and these men
Worked on the spirit's guardian.
That was how we weakened the spirit's power
So that he could not recover.
And on Thursday we spent half the night
Expelling him with all our might.
    But now he thought of another way
To get rid of us today.
He dashed up into the girl's head
To annul our efforts—and there he said:
    "Dear friends, if you please:
"Let me spend this night in peace.
"Put off your conjuration
"And your excommunication.
"And I will go
"As soon as the chickens start to crow."
    But we, the Holy Fellowship, did say:
"You must leave the girl right away."
    The spirit did scream and groan:
"Please—I'll leave her at dawn!
"As I've said: I will go
"When the chickens crow.
"And if I fail to keep my word,
"You can punish me in ways unheard."
    So the fellowship did confer.
The spirit would have to depart from her
Since he was filled with fear.
But because of our fasting, we couldn't stay there.
So we went home that night.
And the evil spirit felt such delight
When we were gone.
Then, on Friday morn,
We all said our prayers and immediately

We went to the girl to see
If the spirit had kept his word. But as soon
As we entered the girl's room,
The spirit began speaking then:
    "Welcome, gentlemen!"
The rabbi said: "Unclean spirit, how long will you stay?
"Won't you keep your promise today?"
    The spirit answered instantly:
"Rabbi Borukh, listen carefully.
"Make me suffer more if I am wrong,
"For I was tormented all night long.
"I saw that they would leave me no peace,
"So I had another idea, if you please.
"I told them that as soon
"As the chickens crowed, I would be gone.
"But, dear rabbi, it's not my fault, you know.
"Not a single chicken has started to crow.
"Only the rooster has crowed today.
"And so I have to stay."
    The rabbi retorted: "I hereby decree
"That you leave the girl's body speedily."
    After synagogue on Friday evening,
The spirit began speaking
To the girl's father: "Please get us
"Rabbi Borukh, for there's a lot to discuss.
"He should show me loving kindness today,
"For I am ready to go away.
"My guardian won't let me rest, and so
"Don't delay, please go."
    The father got Rabbi Borukh and brought him here.
    The spirit spoke then and there:
"Tonight I will definitely go away.
"I won't see you again as of this day.
"And that is why I sent for you,
"So you'd show me loving kindness too.
"You said: 'Whatever you ask me to do—
"'I promise I will do for you.'
"Please, your honor, do as you say.
"Bring me joy today.
"Save me from all agony,
"And I will leave the girl voluntarily."
    The rabbi answered right away:

"If you do as you say,
"Then I will do
"Whatever you want me to."
    The spirit said: "Give me your word,
"And I will do as you have heard.
"And the charity you promised me—
"Give it to the girl presently."
    The rabbi gave his word,
And when the spirit heard, He bowed to the rabbi and did as he
    should.
He went down to the girl's foot,
While the rabbi went home safe and sane.
The spirit kept still. And when
Everyone in the house was fast asleep,
The spirit from the girl did creep,
Though the girl did not know or hear
That the spirit had left her there.
    There was commotion
And there was confusion
On the Sabbath, the very next day,
Because the spirit had stolen away.
And so the congregation
Had a great celebration.
All the exorcists came,
And Rabbi Borukh did the same.
They brought the girl a Torah scroll, and then
They put talismans round her neck again.
And I, the scribe, sat with her that day,
To make sure the spirit stayed away.
    Rabbi Borukh did what he had promised he would do:
He fasted, he prayed, he said Kaddish too.
    The girl was overjoyed, for he
Helped her survive her agony.
He also found her a man to marry.
    And so, dear friends, you've now heard the story
Of how the girl did survive
Thanks to God and Rabbi Borukh, who kept her alive.
So let us enjoy the rabbi's merits and do
Such good deeds and charity too.
We will then enter the Holy Land when
The Messiah comes. And to that we say: "Amen."

Béria and Zímra

The link between Béria and Zímra (1580/1585) and Ansky's The Dybbuk is certainly tenuous, especially since the dramatist may never have read this tale—though oral versions could have filtered down through the centuries. Ansky might have read the summary published (as pointed out by Erika Timm) in Moritz Steinschneider, "Jüdisch-Deutsche Literatur" in Serapeum 1848, *380;* Serapeum 1864, *72–74.*

Nonetheless, while Ansky may have had no contact with any version of Béria and Zímra, *there are certain vital similarities between Reutlingen's story and Ansky's play. For one thing, Zímra and Khónen are both scholars—as are, indeed, the heroes of most Yiddish folk tales. Granted, Zímra is an analytical thinker well versed in the holy texts, while Khónen is a mystic who rejects the Talmud; but their learning and spirituality set both of them apart from the more physical protagonists of non-Jewish folk literature in Europe. According to Ansky,* (Collected Writings, vol. 15, 23), *non-Jewish folklore idealizes physical strength, while the physically superior character in Jewish folklore loses because he is spiritually weak. This generalization holds true for Zímra as an intellectual and spiritual hero, especially if we compare him with his more physical ancestors in Oriental literature (see Timm, cited below).*

The most crucial connection between the Old Yiddish novella and Ansky's The Dybbuk *is the shared theme of soulmates and their marriage in the afterlife. In the story, the girl dies first, in the play the boy; but each couple is ultimately united in death (a very common literary theme—I agree). Likewise, in the folk tale about the bride and groom (collected on Ansky's Ethnographic Expedition, see pages 53 through 58), it is the girl who talks the boy into committing suicide with her.*

Still, love in the afterlife differs for each couple. Béria and Zímra are wed in Paradise (Gan-Eden) and can look forward to everlasting happiness, while Khónen and Leah have to face a childless and cheerless eternity, preferable as it may be to the ultimately vulnerable position of Jews—and frustrated lovers, in Yitskhok bar Yehudah's narrative as well as the reality of pogroms and warfare depicted in the Ethnographic Expedition's folk tale and raging in the final years of Ansky's life while he was completing The Dybbuk. *From the play's ambiguity about the unblissful afterlife, we can once again infer Ansky's general ambiguity.*

A copy of the manuscript version of Béria and Zímra *was published in* Max Erik's Vegn alt-yidishn roman un novele *(Vilna: Old Yiddish Romances and Novellas, 1926). Three Yiddish versions of this tale, transliterated into the Latin alphabet, are accompanied by Erika Timm's fabulously thorough and extensive presentation and analysis:* Beria und Simra *in* Literaturwissenschaftliches Jahrbuch, *vol. 14 (1973) (Berlin: Duncker & Humblot, 1975), 1–94. In a subsequent paper, Timm cogently traces the Oriental—mainly Persian and Arabic—sources of the tale; see* Literaturwissenschaftliches Jahrbuch, *vol. 27, (Berlin: Duncker & Humblot 1986), 297–307.*

This is the true story of a girl named Béria and a boy named Zímra, who lived during the days of Hyrkanos, the viceroy. Hyrkanos was well regarded among the Jews, he was a leader of the people. Zímra, the son of Tovas and the grandson of Zímra, was very handsome and he was also very learned in the holy texts. The king loved Zímra more than anyone else who served him. Zímra had a supreme position at the royal court, and the king appointed him judge over all the people of Israel so that he might teach them the Law. The king also gave him a house in Jerusalem, near the royal castle and among the houses of the priests. Zímra presided over the tribunal of all Israel three times a year, when the Jews came for the High Holidays; and they also made burnt offerings daily.

One Rosh ha-Shana [New Year's], the king was on his throne, with his servants before him. A woman then entered with her two sons, who were quarreling over their father's legacy. You see, one son had two heads, he spoke with two mouths, and he therefore demanded a double share of the inheritance.

The king told Tovas and Zímra: "Please try this case. I want to see what kind of verdict you hand down."

They replied: "Gracious lord, father, and king, we will gladly take care of it."

The man with the two heads was brought before them, but when Tovas saw him, he was unable to pass judgment.

However, Zímra asked for a vessel filled with hot water. They brought him the hot water, and he poured it on one head of the two-headed man, whereupon the other head shrieked. Zímra said: "Why are you shrieking? I haven't done anything to you. I can see that you have only one body. So you should get only one portion of the inheritance."

The king and the entire royal court laughed happily about Zímra's wisdom and judgment.

Some time later, handsome Zímra saw beautiful Béria through her window. Béria, the daughter of Pegin, the high priest, was very modest and pious. Zímra liked her instantly, and the maiden cared for him too, for she had heard that he was very scholarly and pious. Her heart longed for him, and his heart longed for her.

Now one day, Pegin invited Tovas and his son Zímra to a banquet. Zímra was delighted and he eagerly looked forward to the evening. He said: "I am going to reveal my heart to her."

When they entered the home of the high priest, they found a delicious banquet prepared for them. The table was set with many lovely dishes and silverware—lovelier than the guests had ever seen. They were astonished. But Pegin said: "These aren't so lovely. I have something far more beautiful. Come with me."

And he took the king and Tuvas and Zímra to a small room. He had locked in his beautiful daughter, whom no man had ever seen or would see. Her beauty was indescribable, so I won't try to describe it. The high priest then said: "Do you see my treasure? Do you like it?"

They replied that they had never in their lives seen a more beautiful woman. Zímra looked at her and couldn't tear his eyes away. He was so terrified of his feelings of love that he turned pale and was unable to speak. The others noticed this and laughed at him, but said nothing. They went back to the dining room, where they got so drunk that they fell asleep.

But Zímra couldn't sleep. He was trying to figure out a way of seeing the beautiful girl even if it cost him his life. He then freely went to her room. When he opened the door, and she saw him, she stood up and welcomed him, charming and beautiful. And he thanked her modestly. She took him by the hand, and they sat down together.

He began: "There's something I'd like to discuss with all due honor and respect. And please don't take it amiss."

She said: "Dear Zímra, say anything you like. I won't take it amiss."

He said: "The instant I saw you, I fell hopelessly in love with you. I've lost my peace of mind. I beg you: If you promise to marry me, I'll get my father to proceed. He'll speak to your father and obtain his consent. I'll make sure that it happens in an honorable fashion."

She said: "Dear lord Zímra, I love you a lot more than you love me.

I can't possibly describe how deeply I love you. If God grants it, then we will bring it about."

They parted in a wonderful mood. Zímra rejoined the guests and acted as if he hadn't ruffled any surface and had fallen asleep in drunkenness. The guests thanked the high priest and took their leave. And each one went home in peace.

When Zímra came home, he fell ill. He couldn't eat or drink, he couldn't sleep, he was terribly sad. His father said to him: "Dear son, tell me why you're so sad. Tell me what's wrong."

Zímra said: "Dear father, I have to tell you how ashamed I am. The instant I saw the high priest's daughter, I fell hopelessly in love with her. I love her so much that if I don't marry her, I'll die. So, father, please talk to the high priest and ask him to let her be my wife."

Tovas said: "Dear son, hold your tongue and do not bring shame on yourself and on me. I'm certain he doesn't want her to marry into our family—I'm not pious enough. So do as I say, and get those thoughts out of your head."

Zímra said: "Dear father, let me tell you the secret. Nothing shameful has happened. When we were visiting the high priest, and everyone had fallen asleep, I secretly went to her room with all due honor and respect. And there we talked and then we pledged our troth and swore we would marry each other. I love her so much."

Tovas grasped the situation and he said: "Dear son, conduct yourself properly, and I'll see what I can do."

Zímra's father went to the four finest Jews in town and told them about his son's request. He asked them to speak to the high priest and obtain his permission, and he promised them a nice fee for their matchmaking.

The four men said: "You and your son can rest easy. We'll bring the marriage about for sure. Go and prepare the wedding."

But Tovas said: "It's too early to prepare the wedding. There's time enough even if he agrees. But I'm certain he won't."

The four community leaders went to the high priest and informed him of Tovas's and Zímra's request. The son wanted Béria's hand in marriage—Tovas would give his son a great deal of money. But Pegin, the high priest, laughed and said: "Dear leaders and good friends! I know very well that Zímra is the handsomest and most intelligent boy in this land, But I would never give him my daughter's hand—I'd rather drown her first. You have my decision. Go in peace!"

The four community leaders went back to Tovas and informed him of the high priest's decision. Tovas said: "I told you so. As for the wedding, you wanted to put the cart before the horse. I feel ashamed that I even sent you to him."

Zímra was told the news. No one could have been more miserable! His heart was ready to burst with sorrow. His father then said: "Hush, my dear son. I'll find you another bride and I'll give you twenty thousand guldens."

But Zímra was inconsolable and he said: "If I don't marry the beautiful daughter, I'll die of grief."

Seeing he had gotten nowhere with his father and the four community leaders, Zímra went to the king, for the king cared very much for him. And Zímra told the king about his desire and begged him to speak with the high priest and obtain Béria's hand in marriage for Zímra.

The king said: "I'd be glad to do it." And he sent for the high priest and told him: "I want to ask you for something, and do not refuse. Let your daughter Béria marry Zímra."

The high priest was terror-stricken and he said: "Dear king! Do you advise me to let my daughter marry into a clan that's lower than mine? All Jews will make fun of me. I can't find it within myself to do it and I won't do it! May your royal majesty do as you wish."

But the king said: "I won't force you." And so the high priest went home.

Tovas and Zímra then appeared before the king, hoping for a positive decision. But their wish did not come true. The king gave them the high priest's answer. "And so, my dear Zímra, forget about your desire. Nothing is going to happen—no matter what you do."

Zímra waited until everyone had gone to synagogue and he then went into the high priest's house. The instant Béria saw him, she let him in and welcomed him. And he began to cry.

She said: "Why are you crying?"

He said: "Because your father won't let you marry me."

She began crying, too, and she said: "God pity us!"

Zímra said: "My one true love, I want to ask you for something, and please do it for me."

She said: "Ask me for anything, and I'll do it. I know you won't ask me to do anything sinful or evil."

He said: "Please don't take any other husband but me, and I promise not to take any other wife but you."

She said: "I promise."

And so they swore their troth.

Zímra let out a deep sigh and looked at Béria. She said: "Why are you sighing?"

He said: "There's one more thing I have to ask you for, and please don't refuse. I'd like to kiss you."

She said: "You may do so."

He kissed her a thousand times and she kissed him back.

The worshipers were about to leave the synagogue. Béria and Zímra stood there and cried together.

And she said: "Dear Zímra, when you go riding with the prince, please ride past my house. I'll stand at a window so I can see you. But you won't see me unless I open the window. Every morning, when they're praying, I'll open the window and listen. At that time, you'll see me. And if I hang out a towel, then come to me."

Zímra left with a cheerful heart. Every morning after that, he rode past her window, and the two of them looked at each other.

One morning, when the prince wanted to go riding with Zímra, he said to him: "Why don't we ride outside the gates?"

Zímra said: "Fine." And so they rode out together. Now Zímra was very sad and he kept sighing. So the prince asked him: "Why are you so sad? You've always jumped with your horse, and now you're riding as if you were asleep. You have to tell me what's wrong. What's bothering you?"

Zímra said: "The high priest has a daughter, and if I don't marry her, I'll die of grief."

The prince said: "Don't worry, keep still. You have to marry her! I'll tell my father. He'll have to send for the high priest and he'll tell him to give you her hand in marriage. The high priest won't disobey my father."

Zímra and the prince rode to the castle. There the king said to the prince: "What's wrong with you? You look so grave. I think you're under the weather."

The prince said: "I'll tell you." And the prince asked his father to tell the high priest to give Zímra his daughter's hand in marriage."

The king said: "I've already asked him once, but he refused my request."

The prince then said: "I'll ask him—I'll order him. And if he disobeys again, it'll cost him his life."

The king once more sent for the high priest and told him: "I've already asked you once to give Zímra your daughter's hand in marriage. And you refused. Now I ask you again, and do not rebel!"

The high priest said: "I know that if I don't do it you'll kill me, for if a man refuses to follow the king's orders, then he's lost his life. But I still refuse no matter what happens to me. Even though Zímra is a hand-some, learned, and intelligent boy, I would rather drown my daughter than give her to him."

The king angrily said: "I'd like to have you killed for disobeying me, but I won't. Keep your daughter! I'll find another wife for Zímra."

The king then said to Zímra: "Get yourself another wife anywhere in my realm, and I'll give you a lot of money." But Zímra didn't like the idea—his thoughts were filled with beautiful Béria. He thanked the king and sorrowfully went away.

Somewhat later in Rome the pope, a very wicked man, issued a new decree concerning Jews: No Jewish woman could go to the bathhouse, no Jewish child could be circumcised, and no Jew could appear before the pope. If a Jew did try to appear before the pope, the Jew would be killed. This edict was sent out to the Jews. And the high priest in Jerusa-lem was asked to pray for the annulment of the edict.

The king and his courtiers didn't know what to do; they were terri-fied and they wondered whom they might send out to have the edict rescinded. Then the king said: "The best man for this task would be Zímra. He is wise, and his merits will help him accomplish his goal. God Blessed Be He shows the virtuous man the path he ought to take."

Everyone agreed: "Yes, Zímra is the right man!"

The king then sent for Zímra and asked him to go to the pope.

Zímra replied: "I will go if the high priest gives me his daughter's hand."

The king sent for the high priest and said to him: "I order you to give Zímra your daughter's hand if he carries out his mission, God willing."

The high priest gave his word that he would do so.

But back in his home he said to himself: "Now I'll get rid of Zímra. I'll tell him that if he goes to the pope and asks him to rescind the edict, I'll give him my daughter. The pope will kill Zímra, and I'll be rid of him."

Béria overheard this and thought to herself: "I'm going to warn him." When everybody went to synagogue, she hung out the towel. Zímra saw it and came over to her. She welcomed him very warmly and told him what her father was planning to do: "Don't let him talk you into going to the pope, otherwise you'll die and I won't be able to keep my promise to you!"

Zímra said: "If your father gives me your hand, then I'll risk my life for you."

Béria burst out crying, and Zímra said: "Conduct yourself well. The Good Lord will bring me luck, so that nothing happens to me." He said goodbye to her with tearful eyes, and she said: "Go and may God bring you luck and salvation."

When the Jews left the synagogue, the high priest took Zímra aside and told him the whole business. Zímra replied: "If you keep your word, then I'll risk my life." The high priest gave him his promise in front of witnesses, and so Zímra left and said nothing more to beautiful Béria.

The high priest said: "We've gotten rid of Zímra, he won't come back alive."

Hearing this, his daughter wept and wailed and loudly lamented when Zímra was gone, and she fasted three days and three nights every week during his absence.

The journey to Rome took a long time. Upon arriving, Zímra asked the Jews there how he could get to the pope. But they told him that the instant he appeared before the pope, he would be killed. Zímra remained silent. He had brought a lot of money, so he went to a money exchange and obtained groschens for ten guldens. Next, he went to the pope's castle and dropped a lot of these coins. The sentries let him pass while they picked up the money.

As he entered the court, many Christian counts and noblemen came toward him to ask who he was. But he dropped some money, and they picked up the coins and let him pass. Finally he reached the pope's chamber.

The pope asked him who he was. Zímra said: "I am a Jew." The pope was shocked that this Jew had walked in unharmed, and the pope's bodyguards wanted to kill him. However, the pope ordered them to let him live, but he would have the sentries killed. The pope then said: "Well, tell me, my dear Jew, what is your request? I will hear you out since God made you lucky enough to come before me unscathed."

Zímra said: "Venerable, highly praised lord! I would like to ask your honorable grace for two things, and may your grace not take it amiss and may you grant me my wishes."

The pope said: "Ask whatever you like, but nothing in regard to the Jews."

Zímra said: "I want to ask you a question about the Jews, which will be to your advantage."

The pope said: "Then ask it."

Zímra said: "Dear lord! If you had enemies, would you rather they were weak or strong?"

The pope laughed and said: "That is an odd question! If I had enemies, wouldn't I rather they were weak than strong? Now, my dear Jew, what are you aiming at and why do you ask such a foolish question?"

Zímra said: "Since you want to know, let me tell you, for I have come here for your sake. You are right, but your counselors have given you bad advice. The Jews may be your enemies, but there is no weaker or feebler nation on earth than the Jews. They are circumcised on the eighth day of their lives, and the loss of blood makes them weak. If a Jew were uncircumcised, he could kill ten Christians. Yet you have outlawed circumcision! Ten years from now your country will be full of Jews."

The pope said: "That is true. Now what is your other question?"

Zímra said: "Dear lord! If you had enemies, would you rather they were few or many?"

The pope laughed and said: "I would rather they were few than many. Tell me: What are you aiming at?"

Zímra said: "I will tell you. You have issued an order prohibiting Jewish women from going to the bathhouse. So now, four times as many Jews are being born. You see, Jewish women are so shocked by the cold water that they do not conceive. Furthermore they are not allowed to lie with their husbands. But if they do not bathe in the cold water, then they will certainly lie with their husbands, and the Jews will become as numerous as the sands by the sea and they will multiply and go to war against you and kill you."

The pope said: "Jew, you have told the truth. I have never heard a more intelligent Jew than you. I am going to reward you and let you go home in peace." He gave Zímra a great deal of money and jewels as well as an epistle rescinding his edict. The pope then ordered all the sentries to be executed for letting Zímra through, and the sentries were killed.

Zímra took leave of the pope and returned to his inn, where the Jews were waiting. He told them how he had gotten the pope to rescind the edict and he showed them the money and the epistle that the pope had given him. The Jews also wanted to give Zímra a lot of money, but he refused for he had enough. He said farewell and rode back home.

When he arrived, everyone was delighted, especially his beloved Béria. But the high priest was so dumbfounded that he nearly gave up the ghost: He had been certain that Zímra would be killed. Good Zímra showed them the epistle, and everyone was happy that the edict had been rescinded. Zímra then said to the high priest: "Please keep your promise."

But the high priest went back on his word and refused to give Zímra his daughter's hand—"even if I lose my life!"

Zímra said: "God have mercy! What good were my great efforts and the dangers I faced? I've got nothing now!" And he felt very wretched— beyond description.

In his misery, good Zímra waited until everyone was in synagogue before he went to his dear Béria. She welcomed him sweetly and beautifully with many cheerful words. He then told her that her father was going back on his promise. The two of them wept bitterly and lamented loudly, and she threw her arms around him and kissed him and she said: "Dear Zímra, God help us! I know that I'm going to die of grief!"

Zímra said: "God forbid!" And he kissed her, and she kissed him, and their kisses were so wonderful that if she hadn't already been beautiful, then she would have become beautiful now.

At this point, Zímra left.

Soon Béria died of grief. That is why you should never kiss someone when you leave him! However, Zímra didn't hear that she had died. Amid deep mourning and lamenting, Béria was properly buried.

One day Zímra appeared before the king and the prince, who received him warmly. Upon leaving the castle, Zímra ran into his father, who said: "Dear son, I'd like to ask you something. Can you keep from being terrified?"

Zímra said: "I won't be terrified!"

"You felt very wretched because the high priest refused to give you his daughter's hand. Now you'll feel even more wretched because she has died of sorrow. Don't be terrified!"

Zímra said: "Why should I be terrified? What the Good Lord does is properly done." But everyone can imagine what was in his heart!

Upon arriving home and going to his room, he wailed loudly and was so grief-stricken that he tore out his hair. His sorrow was indescribable. After lamenting, he left his room and wiped his eyes so that no one would notice. And he did that for an entire week.

Being old, the king sent for his advisors and noblemen and told them that he wanted to crown his son while he, the king, was still alive. He did so and he gave a large feast. Zímra was loved by the young king, who said to him: "My father has given me the kingdom to rule after his death. Come with me to my father, the king, and his advisors, and I will see to it that you take over the kingdom in the event of my death. Wait a short while, and then we'll ride over to the castle!"

Zímra agreed and put on beautiful clothes. He waited for a short while, but it was too long for him; time wore by too slowly. And he thought to himself: "He can catch up with me!" However, as he walked up the mountain, he grew tired, for the mountain was very high, and so he halted for a bit. All at once, he saw a beautiful horse galloping in front of him and wearing armor more beautiful than Zímra had ever seen. The horse seemed to be galloping down the mountain. Zímra though to himself: "If I could catch it, I'd ride it up the mountain."

He walked toward the horse, and the horse stood still. The instant Zímra mounted the horse, it took off, dashing over hill and dale as if it were the Devil. The horse carried Zímra to a large forest, where various herbs were growing. Next it came to a meadow, where there were many roots. The horse then halted. Zímra was glad and he dismounted in order to enjoy himself for a while. The horse galloped off and disappeared, so that Zímra had no idea what had become of it.

Nor did he know where he was. He yelled and felt wretched beyond description. He kept shouting: "Sorrow upon sorrow! Misery, how closely you've surrounded me! I have no idea what to do. I'm so far away from my father and my friends, and I don't see or hear a human being or a house or a town! Where am I and what has happened to me?"

To add to his misery, he was also very hungry. He found nothing to eat but those roots and herbs. He also drank a little water. Then he wandered through the meadow and the heath, thinking he would get back home. But the more he wandered, the more lost he got.

Eventually he came to a beautiful brook and he stepped into it for it wasn't deep. There he found a lot of precious stones, which he picked up, slipping many of them into his shirt. The brook, which was filled with jewels, flowed from Paradise. Zímra took off his shoes and walked through the water: It was harsh and strong. Upon leaving the brook, he came to a beautiful road, where he found a large rock with an inserted sword. The rock also had a wheel that kept turning and that prevented Zímra from walking any farther, for the wheel guarded the road to Paradise. But Zímra said a prayer, and the wheel stopped and let him pass.

Zímra walked on until he came to a heath bristling with sharp razors, their blades turned up. But he said a prayer to God, and the razors parted so that Zímra passed through.

Next he came to a field where a small cottage was standing. Delighted to see it, he stepped inside. There a lot of people sat eating. They looked at him and wished him "Sholom—peace." He thanked them, happy to hear that they were Jews. Zímra wanted to wash his hands and eat. But they cried: "Don't wash your hands, and make sure you touch nothing!"

He asked: "Why?"

They answered: "We are all dead, and we are neither well off nor badly off. We have to wait here for an entire year until we have redeemed our sins. Dear Zímra, pray for us! We know what you're doing here. We heard yesterday that the horse would be sent to you."

He asked them a lot of questions but they refused to say anything. So he left.

Zímra looked around—and saw his dear and lovely Béria sitting under the stairs. Shocked, he said: "Oh me, oh my! Darling Béria, what are you doing here?"

She answered: "My dear chosen Zímra! I have to sit here for another week. But if you pray for me, I can get out of here soon. Dear Zímra, I never committed any sin on earth except letting you kiss me."

He went over to her and wanted to kiss her. But she said: "Guard your life and don't touch me, or you'll die!"

He then said: "I don't know where I am or what's happened to me or where I should go. I want to kiss you—so I'll die and stay here with you."

She said: "No, not on your life! Leave me and go across the heath. That way you'll get back home."

He went away from her in deep sorrow, weeping and wailing. In the midst of the heath he ran into an old, gray-haired man with a long beard. The old man said: "Shólom aléikhem—peace be with you!"

Zímra replied: "Shólom aléikhem, Rabbi."

The old man said: "You're a stranger in these parts!"

Zímra said: "That is certainly true. I don't know where I am or where I should go. Dear Rabbi, tell me how to get home and tell me what I've done to deserve such a fate?"

The old man said: "You've committed no sin that cost Béria her life. You should go home again."

Zímra said: "Dear Rabbi, tell me who you are."

The old man said: "I am the Prophet Elijah."

Zímra said: "Dear Rabbi, bless me!"

The old man said: "I will not bless you now, I know that you have to go home again."

Zímra forgot that he hadn't prayed for Béria. When he reentered the cottage, he thought he saw a person standing with her and holding both her breasts in his hands. Zímra said: "Dear Béria, who's embracing you?"

She said: "Dear Zímra, don't be afraid! Satan is trying to lure you."

Zímra went over to his Béria, and she said: "Be careful, don't touch me until I've finished speaking."

He said: "Then please speak!"

She said: "Dear Zímra, do you want to sit on this chair or do you want to wait some more?"

He said: "I don't want to wait anymore."

She said: "Then go home and tell your father and my father: For better or worse, you want to have me. My father refused to give you my hand while I was alive, so he has to suffer because you will have me in the afterlife without silver or money. Go and pray and cleanse yourself and say goodbye to your friends. You will die on the third day. I assure you: If you touch me, you will definitely die on the third day."

He said: "I want to touch you even if it costs me my life." And he threw his arms around her and kissed her, and then she went away.

Now the old graybeard came back and he said to Zímra: "Come here, dear Zímra. I want to lead you back home and prepare you for your wedding." And he blessed Zímra. And now Zímra prayed for his dear Béria to redeem her from her place under the stairs in the cottage. His prayer was answered, and she entered radiant Paradise. And even if you don't believe me, you're still a Jew.

Next Zímra arrived home. The king was angry at him for being away for such a long time. But Zímra described everything that had happened to him and he told the king how he, Zímra, would die. The king felt very wretched about Zímra's coming death. Zímra then went to his own father and to Béria's father and told them what Béria had ordered him to say: namely, that he would die on the third day. All of Zímra's friends felt very wretched about his dying. He told them not to bury him after his death: They should place his body in the graveyard and leave him there and go home.

Zímra then prayed and cleansed himself and said goodbye to everyone. People wept and wailed so loudly that they could be heard throughout the city. The high priest also wept and wailed, for he now regretted losing his daughter.

Finally, on the third day, good, pious Zímra died—may God be gracious to him! His friends did as he had ordered them to do. They grieved and mourned beyond description. After weeping and wailing for a long time they each went home and left Zímra unburied in the graveyard.

Now the Angels Michael and Gabriel came and took him and carried him, as was only just, for Zímra had never committed any sin, and they brought him to Paradise, to his dearest Béria, and they gave the couple a beautiful wedding. God Himself gave the blessing, and the angels were the jesters and the musicians. Moses and Aaron escorted the bride and groom to the canopy. After that they all ate and drank and danced, and

King Solomon recited the Seven Blessings. A more wonderful wedding had never been celebrated in any Jewish community.

> And now you've read in this book, dear friend,
> About what great love can bring in the end!
> And so think about what
> Can come of all that.
> There are many lovely and pious Jews
> Who would very gladly choose.
> Great love, which promises luck and salvation.
> And with my salutation
> That is where I wish to end.
> May God also send us the old gray friend
> And with him the Messiah here.
> Amen—may it happen this year.

Written in the year 5340 (1580 or 1585)
I pray, the writer Yitskhok bar Yehudah of blessed memory, Reutlingen.

ANONYMOUS

The Companion in Paradise

The relevance of this story for Ansky's The Dybbuk *is the theme of true love concretized in a contractual betrothal and then violently disrupted. Unlike Ansky's couple, however, the betrothed meet again and, thanks to the virtuous Jews, are united in life rather than death. Parallel to this happy pair, the scholar and the butcher will be united as study companions in Paradise—thereby driving a wedge between the sexuality of this world and the spirituality of the next.*

The story can be found in the following manuscript: Mayse no. 117, Cod.hebr.495, Bayerische Staatsbibliothek, Munich, pp. 137r–139v). It is thought to originate from the Italian village of Rovere or Revere in the late sixteenth century.

Of the 130 stories in this manuscript, the story that follows, according to Anke Kleine (Jiddistik-Mitteilungen, no. 17, Apr. 1997, Trier) is one of many that "derive from the international fairytale tradition and whose sources are hard to pinpoint." Kleine (who provides a transliteration of the Yiddish text) traces the story back to the eleventh century—specifically to an Arabic document by a Talmudist in Kairuan, Nisim ben Jakob ben Nisim ibn Shahin (ca. 990–1062). His work, handed down in several Hebrew and then Yiddish translations, eventually migrated into German— namely, a medieval verse romance Good Gerhart *by Rudolf von Ems, who, totally christianizing the story, claims he received it orally. According to Kleine, the informant could have been Jewish; after all, other works by von Ems show his deep interest in Oriental narratives that also richly populated Jewish literature.*

Here is the story of a God-fearing scholar. This pious man fasted every day and prayed to God, Blessed Be He, asking Him who his companion in Paradise would be. The prophet Elijah then appeared to him and said: "My virtuous man, I have to tell you who your companion will be: he is a butcher in your town."

95

When the pious man heard that, he was deeply offended and he said: "Oh, dear God of the Universe, what good is it that I have studied the Torah and fasted every day and only performed good works? I have never gone four cubits without prayer thongs and fringes and the Torah, so let all the good works that I have performed be weighed against the butcher's works."

The pious man then fasted even more and did all sorts of good deeds, more than he had done before, which he knew were virtuous. He thought that Elijah had failed to tell him the truth or had perhaps been mistaken. And when the man again fasted ardently, Elijah again came to him and said:

"Why are you fasting so ardently? Didn't I tell you that the butcher is to be your companion? I am telling you the truth: you will both have the same portion of Paradise."

The pious man thought to himself: "I won't rest or relax; I'll try to find out what kind of man this butcher is. And I'll see and ask what works he has performed for him to be my companion in Paradise."

The scholar then went and found the butcher and said to him: "Dear friend, I have something private to discuss with you. Please come outside the town with me." The butcher went with him, and the pious man then said: "Dear friend, please tell me what kind of work you have done all your days?"

The butcher replied: "Dear rabbi, le me tell you. I've been a butcher all my days, and I have always donated half my income to the Biblical scholars so that they could study and to other poor people so that they could eat. And I used the other half of my income to feed myself and my family."

The pious man then said: "Dear friend, think hard. Haven't you done any other good works and practiced greater piety?"

The butcher said: "Dear rabbi, let me tell you about something that happened to me. One day I was plying my trade, when a group of Christians passed by with many prisoners. One of the prisoners was a Jewish girl, and she was loudly crying and wailing. I was very surprised: How come she was crying harder than the other prisoners? So I went over and asked her why she was crying so hard.

"And she said: 'All these people are Christians, but I'm Jewish. They captured me, and I'm afraid they might defile me and lie with me. And I'll be forced to do what I don't want to do. I'm far away from my relatives and my country and I have no one who can help me. Oh, dear God, take my soul from my body, for I would be better off dead than alive. If somebody came and killed me, I would forgive him in front of God, Praised Be He.'

"When I heard that, I felt very sorry for her. I spoke to her Christian captors and asked if I could redeem her. And that was how I redeemed the girl; I handed over all my money for her ransom and got her out of the hands of those Christians. I then raised the girl until she was old enough to marry. I went to my son and said: 'Dear son, for the sake of the Holy One, Blessed Be He, marry the girl who's living with us—you shouldn't look around for a girl with lots of money. We all know that this girl is pious. You might find a girl who's rich but not pious. You know that 'money can be earned and lost.' I talked and talked to him until he finally agreed.

"I gave them a lovely wedding and for the celebration I presented the girl with appropriate garments as I did my son, and I invited all the townsfolk to celebrate with my son and his wife. Now when they were all sitting at the table and making merry, I saw a poor boy weeping and wailing at the table. And many people were crying with him. When I saw this I took the boy to a private corner and asked him why he was crying so bitterly: 'You're making other people sad and tearful. Your grief puts me to shame. So please tell me whether you have debts that you can't pay. If so, I'll lend you the money. Or do you have some other problem? Has somebody done something to you? Tell me! If it's possible, I'll find a remedy!'

"The boy said: 'It's none of those things! It's something else!'

"So I said: 'Then what is it?'

"And he now told me that the bride had been promised to him many years ago before her capture. 'Here is our engagement contract. It was signed by two trustworthy witnesses. I've traveled through many countries, searching for her, but I couldn't find her anywhere until today.'

"When I saw that the boy was telling the truth, I went to my son: 'Dear son, you found the daughter of a rich or important man who would have given you a lot of money, but you listened to me and you would gladly marry this girl, who lives with us, and you were willing to do so for the Holy One, Blessed Be He, and for my honor. But I now understand that many years ago this girl had been promised to the boy who was crying so bitterly at our table. I have seen their engagement contract. Do me a favor and obey me again: let her marry this boy. 'Thou shalt not covet thy neighbor's wife.'

"My son then said to me: 'Dear father, I'll gladly do whatever you say.'

"So I gave the wedding for the boy and the girl, and the feast lasted for seven days. When the celebration was over, I sent the newlyweds back to their country, giving them all my money before I let them go. And so they returned to their fathers and mothers with great joy.

"Dear rabbi, that is what happened to me. I don't know of anything else that occurred." When the pious man heard the story, he was thoroughly delighted. He stood up and kissed the butcher and said to him: "After hearing your story, I can say that you deserve to be my companion in Paradise. I'd like you to be my friend, and I'm lucky to have you as a friend."

The Grave of the Bride and Groom

This folk story was gathered during Ansky's Ethnographic Expedition. Its influence on Ansky's The Dybbuk *is obvious, especially in the Liebestod of the bride and groom and the factual depiction of Khmielnítsky's butcheries. As recalled in* The Destruction of Galicia *(Collected Works, vol. 4, pt. 1, chap. 2), Ansky found a number of such alleged graves for massacred brides and grooms. In his eyes their recurrence constituted an historic legend whose truth lay precisely in its mythology:*

> Before the war, when I was traveling through Volhynia and Po-dolye, gathering folklore material, I kept hearing a very popular tale about a bride and groom: Just as they were being led to the wedding canopy, they were murdered by Khmielnítsky. In over fifteen or sixteen shtetls I was shown a small headstone near the synagogue and always told the same story about the couple. This is practically the only wide-spread tale that has come down to us from Khmielnítsky's massacres. Aiming at wiping out all Jews, the Cossacks threatened the very survival of the Jewish people, and Jews now saw themselves symbolized in the bride and groom killed just before their union and unable to carry on their family and their generation.

A possibly, if distantly, related element can be found in Yiftakh Yospe ben Naftali ha-Levi, Sefer Maase Nissim *(1696). In this collection of Yid-dish tales centering around the German town of Worms, story number 23 concerns the mysterious deaths of a Jewish bride and groom on their wed-ding night, while story number 24 describes a massacre of Jews in the same town. The two narratives are linked purely in locale and in location, but their physical proximity might be more than a coincidence: It could indi-cate a tie between the murder of newlyweds and a pogrom. Written half a century after the Khmielnítsky uprising, these stories may have been slightly influenced by those historical disasters and may also have filtered orally through the centuries.*

In many shtetls throughout Podolye and Volhynia we often find a mound next to the synagogue. Surrounded by a traditional cemetery fence, the mound is known as the Grave for the Bride and Groom. And virtually the same story has been handed down in each shtetl:

During 1648 to 1649 (5408–5409), when Bogdan Khmielnítsky and his Cossack gangs charged through Podolye and Volhynia, wiping out entire Jewish communities, two of the victims were a bride and a groom. In the midst of the wedding ceremony they were murdered, together with all the ushers and in-laws, in the synagogue courtyard. The bride and groom were buried on the very spot where they had died—right next to the synagogue. A new custom was established for every marriage taking place in the synagogue courtyard: Before standing under the wedding canopy the bride and groom, together with the in-laws, circle the anonymous grave seven times. After the ceremony the klezmers strike up a cheerful tune, while the bride and groom and all the in-laws dance around the grave, entertaining the bride and groom who lie under the mound.

Next to the Grand Synagogue of Nemirov, a headstone marks the grave of a bride and groom, and the Jews of Nemirov still talk about the following strange event of the year 1648 (5408):

One of the most prominent Jews in the town was hosting a banquet for all the poor on the day before he was to accompany his only daughter to the wedding canopy. Just as the paupers were enjoying themselves, expressing their best wishes, the Cossacks stampeded into Nemirov like savage demons. After conquering the town, they went on a barbarous rampage. The groom dashed over to rescue his fiancée, and the two of them fled through a narrow alley leading to the Grand Synagogue. A large number of Jews had taken refuge here because the building stood as solid as a fortress and was ringed by a thick wall. However, the synagogue wasn't spared. The Cossacks completely surrounded it and then stormed the wall and smashed into the building.

The bride and groom managed to escape to the nearby river. Upon finding a small fishing boat, they climbed aboard and drifted off without oars. Unfortunately, the murderers spotted them. They threw rocks at the boat, and a few of the Cossacks jumped into the water and swam after the couple, hoping to catch them alive.

When the bride saw that their pursuers were already breathing down their necks, she said to her fiancé: "You can see we're going to fall into their hands any moment now! If I were sure that they'd spare you and come after me, I'd choose to stay alive for both our sakes. But I'm terrified that they'll kill only you and not me so that they can torture me just as they always torture Jewish women whom they find attractive. I'd rather die with you than live a shameful life without you. If you truly love me, you won't refuse my wish. Let the two of us now die for the glory of God. I'd rather stay pure and plunge into these depths than fall into their unclean hands."

The groom threw his arms around the bride, and they sprang into the rushing waters.

On the third day, after the Cossacks had left Nemirov, the few Jews still alive found the bride and groom: Their bodies had washed up on the riverbank. The survivors buried them next to the synagogue, and left a mound on their grave.

On the first anniversary of their deaths, the Jews put up a headstone with the following verses in Hebrew:

Beloved infants and babies, women and men,
Dearest brides and grooms, pious souls,
They lacked nothing while they were alive,
They prepared to stand under an adorned canopy,
After their deaths the river bottom
Was too small to hold their bodies,
The victims were drowned, not slaughtered.
Only their bodies are separated,
Their souls are joined together forever.

The nineteenth day of Sivan [the third month], 5408 (1648)

Warnings and Exorcisms for Driving Out a Dybbuk

This folk tale was recorded during Ansky's Ethnographic Expedition. The structural analogies between this story and "The Tale of the Evil Spirit in Korets" are striking, even though the victim in the later folk story is a male.

There is an old Yiddish saying: "Don't question a fairy tale" (*Af a mayse fregt men nisht kin kasha*). The reason is obvious: A question and a fairy tale are absolutely complete and unrelated opposites. A question comes from the mind, from logic, from reality, while a fairy tale starts where a question leaves off, unable to go any further. A question is rooted in the head, a fairy tale in the heart. A question asks: "How is this possible?," while a fairy tale knows that nothing is impossible, that it has no boundaries. So it goes without saying that a fairy tale, which involves fantasy, cannot be asked a question, which involves reality.

The popular imagination, which creates and weaves a fairy tale in all its hues and tones, rises to the highest spheres of the holy worlds and plunges to the lowest spheres of the unclean worlds—the worlds of ghosts, demons, evil spirits, and dybbuks. In the course its wanderings, our Ethnographic Expedition managed to accumulate a rich trove of unusual tales, including stories about demons, spirits, plain devils, and especially dybbuks. The latter penetrate and occupy human bodies and refuse to leave of their own free will. Our expedition also recorded a large number of exorcism spells and Cabalistic formulas for violently driving out a stubborn dybbuk.

The story quotef below was taken from an ancient manuscript owned by Rabbi Daniel Slabodiansky of Khmélnik. At first he refused to let us copy it: He said that, according to tradition, if a man without complete faith looked into the manuscript, he could, God forbid, suffer harm. And the rabbi would feel responsible if anything happened to us, for he would be flouting the Biblical commandment that says: "Thou shalt not . . . put a stumbling block before the blind" (Lev. 19:14).

Ansky, however, kept arguing with the rabbi until he finally gave in; so I copied the entire document in the rabbi's home. I have kept the full wording of the special prayer as well as the texts of the proclamations; and on the basis of some extant notes, I have reconstructed the rest of the narrative, which goes more or less as follows:

The Tale

This happened in Khmélnik, a small shtetl in Podolye, in the Jewish year 5508 (Christian year 1748). An adolescent boy suddenly came down with the falling sickness—epilepsy. Three times a day—after morning service, early evening service, and evening service—he would collapse on the ground with his face toward the sky, pounding his fists against his chest, and, in a voice that wasn't his, confess all kinds of terrible sins and wrongs that he had supposedly once committed.

His parents took him to great physicians, Hasidic rebbes, and even conjurors (if you'll excuse my mentioning them in the same breath). But none of them could help. Within a short time the parents died of grief. The sick orphan then went out into the world, all on his own, in search of healers. Perhaps God would take pity! . . .

For the next three years the boy wandered from one Hasidic court to the next, but he found no remedy anywhere for his terrible disorder. At the end of those three years the boy, depressed and despondent, in rags and tatters, and more ill than ever, headed back to his home town, Khmélnik. Since he had no one in the world, no friend, no relative, he stayed at the poorhouse together with other paupers.

At that time a pious Jew named Sháya [Isaiah] lived in a tiny wooden cottage outside the town of Khmélnik. Knowledgeable people realized that he was a hidden saint, whose mission was to go on secret trips regarding private matters and to help Jews in distress. He therefore spent very little time at home.

Now one day, when Sháya came back to Khmélnik for the Sabbath, he happened to see the stricken boy in the midst of a seizure. The boy lay on the ground, beating his breast and shouting out his sins and crimes. Sháya halted, took a hard look, and exclaimed: "The boy has a dybbuk! I'll take the burden upon myself and I won't rest or stay silent until I exorcise the dybbuk with God's help! I'll pin my hopes on the Good Lord. He'll show me how to drive the dybbuk beyond the Moun-

tains of Darkness, to the Valley of Darkness. That way, I'll save an unhappy and rejected soul that's gone astray."

After ushering out the Sabbath, Sháya went to the town rabbi,
Shmúel, the author of *The Glory of Samuel,* and asked him to help sanctify the Lord's name and expel the dybbuk. Rabbi Shmúel, who was
familiar with Sháya and his charitable works and secret missions, agreed
to help as best he could. The rabbi authorized Sháya to do whatever he
wished in the name of the rabbinical court and in the name of the entire
congregation of Jeshurun in the holy community of Khmélnik.

The very next morning, Sháya, together with the rabbi, the judges,
and several God-fearing Jewish notables, went to the poorhouse and
formed a circle around the sick boy. Sháya then launched into his
exorcism:

"Invisible dybbuk! In the name of the rabbinical court and in the
name of the community leaders, who are now standing around you, I
hereby command you to voluntarily leave the body of Shmúel, son of
Khaim, and I hereby warn you not to cause him any harm while leaving
his body and not to injure anyone—either those who are with us here or
those who are not with us here. For our part, we promise to pray for you
so that you will be cleansed of all your sins, wrongs, and crimes, and
your soul will be purified. But if you refuse, if you fail to obey, then I
hereby warn you that I will proceed against you according to the strict
letter of the Law, with admonition, excommunication, anathema, and
even curses, and I will drive you beyond the Mountains of Darkness,
beyond all redemption.

"That is my first warning to you! See, I have warned you! I will now
repeat and then repeat once again that we will fully honor our promise
to cleanse you and save your soul. We will study the Torah for your sake,
we will pray for your sake, we will distribute charity for your sake, we
will establish the daily study of the Talmudic tractates according to the
order of the letters in your name. I myself am willing to fast an entire
year for your sake, fast daily except on the Sabbath and on holidays,
when we do not recite the Takhanun, the prayer for mercy. For an entire
year, I will recite Kaddish for you, the prayer for the dead, three times a
day. Invisible dybbuk! Heed my warning and have faith in my promise!"

All at once the boy ferociously tore away as if ready to kill everyone
there. The dybbuk's raucous laughter rang throughout the poorhouse
and his brazen voice blared and bellowed: "Ha ha ha! I laugh at you and
your warnings! As long as I'm together with the boy, I'm not afraid! You
won't intimidate me, and I won't obey you! I feel good with him and
I'll stay with him!"

The wild laughter stopped instantly, and they heard a stifled whimpering, a dull roaring, a panting: "Where should I go? Where should I live? I'm a pariah in all the worlds! No! I won't obey! I'm staying here and I won't budge!"

Sháya promptly reacted to the dybbuk's insolent words. In the poorhouse, with everyone present, he repeated his earlier admonitions six times, each time pleading with the dybbuk to leave the boy of his own free will rather than being expelled forcibly. But the dybbuk dug in his heels.

Sháya no longer waited for any response. He signaled, and the others silently filed out of the poorhouse.

When Sháya saw that he was getting nowhere with a friendly approach, he began preparing for the first conjuration, which aimed at making the dybbuk submit and obey. For the examination to be carried out by Sháya and the court they selected twenty-one truly God-fearing Jews, who spent seven days cleansing themselves in holiness and purity. They fasted every day except on the Sabbath; they kept away from their wives; they prayed with great devotion and concentration, with a special ardor as instructed by Sháya; they had three ritual baths a day after each prayer; and they were sharply cautioned to utter no profanities.

At the end of seven days, the rabbinical court was convened at the Great Synagogue in the presence of Sháya and the twenty-one truly God-fearing Jews. It was Thursday, the twenty-second day of Tevet (the fourth Jewish month, overlapping with late December and early January), in the year 5515 (Christian year 1755). They brought in the unhappy boy, took him to the platform, and bound him hand and foot with a thick rope. The judges and Sháya were likewise on the platform, as were the twenty-one purified Jews. After dividing these twenty-one men into three groups of seven men each, Sháya gave seven shofars (rams' horns) to one group and seven black candles to the second group. He then told the third group to get seven Torah scrolls from the Holy Ark.

But before they could open the Holy Ark, they heard the town rabbi weeping. He told them not to remove the Torahs until he bent over the boy, who was lying on the ground. In a voice choking with tears, the rabbi said:

"Invisible dybbuk! I, too, the town rabbi, with the might of the Torah, a power granted me by our holy congregation, do hereby give you this stern ultimatum: We will proceed against you according to the strict letter of the Law. We will show you no mercy. I therefore beg you with bitter tears to show pity to yourself. Do not force us to resort to exorcism and perhaps even anathema. I therefore beseech you and entreat you to submit. Let us refrain from dragging the sacred Torah scrolls from their permanent place in the Holy Ark not for a good deed but for cursing you and banishing you. Repent. Renounce your obstinacy so that we can avoid dishonoring the Torah scrolls. Surrender if not for our sake then out of respect for the sacred Torah scrolls, and our blessings will protect you, and our prayers to God will bring you forgiveness, absolution, and atonement. Invisible dybbuk, repent!"

And the rabbi wept loudly.

When the rabbi quieted down, the boy twisted violently. Within moments the ropes on his hands and feet burst, and he hollered in a powerful voice: "Not all the tempests in the world can drive me out, and you are incapable of remitting my sins! My sins are great and numerous—they're beyond any counting! Here I am and here I'll stay!"

They all realized that kindness would get them nowhere with this obstinate dybbuk, they would have to perform a harsh exorcism. The rabbi slowly trudged down from the platform and plodded over to the Holy Ark. He opened it with trembling hands, turned his tearful face toward the congregation, and spoke loudly to make sure everyone heard him:

"My brethren! In the name of this entire holy congregation and in the name of the rabbinical court, I hereby beg the Torah scrolls to forgive me for using them as we will now use them to expel an obstinate dybbuk who refuses to obey an order issued by the rabbinical court. God is our witness that we warned the obstinate dybbuk numerous times and pleaded with him not to force us to dishonor the sacred Torah scrolls. But, as it turns out, this is the will of the Creator of the Universe. I therefore publicly announce and proclaim that with the might of the Torah, which has been granted to me, I exempt our holy congregation from any trace of responsibility for dishonoring the Torah and I pray that the sacred Torah scrolls will forgive us. And if we are mistaken, then let God Blessed Be He preserve us from any punishment!"

Next the rabbi personally removed seven Torahs from the Holy Ark and handed them to the seven Jews, who stood there fully prepared. These seven Jews then joined him on the platform. The seven black candles were lit. Sháya gave a signal, the seven shofars blasted, all of them at once, and the first invocation began. In the silence, Sháya murmured spells, interspersing them with curses, anathemas, and conjurations. Everyone present loudly repeated the curses word for word. In between the conjurations, the shofars blasted, all seven at once.

In the midst of the blasting they suddenly heard a stifled sobbing.

The sobbing then turned into a hoarse roar, and the voice started cursing and reviling Sháya and pouring out the nastiest scorn on everyone
who was there.

Meanwhile, the final rays of sunset were fading from the tall synagogue windows. It was time for early evening prayers. Sháya ordered the
men to return the Torah scrolls to the Holy Ark, put away the shofars,
and take off their smocks. Sháya himself then went to the cantor's desk
for the prayers. Sighing bitterly, he recited the Eighteen Benedictions,
and with holy shudders the worshipers responded to each one: "Blessed
be God and blessed be His Name. Amen!"

After early evening prayers, Sháya announced that they would, God
willing, attempt a second exorcism. This time they would perform it not
in the Great Synagogue but in the old study house, and he ordered
everyone to go there once the Sabbath was done. And so after late evening prayers, the congregants scattered, "each to his own tent"—his
own affairs.

Strangely enough, the boy had started feeling a lot better after the first
exorcism. For all of Friday the dybbuk left him alone. Even on the Sabbath, when the dybbuk normally tortured him the most, the boy remained tranquil. He prayed with all the others, ate all three Sabbath
meals calmly, and managed to say grace in the company of three and
even to sleep peacefully. It was only when the Sabbath was ushered out
with the Havdala ceremony that the boy again collapsed, in the middle
of the synagogue.

They heard the dybbuk wailing feebly like a dying man, pleading:
"Pity me! Fiends and demons and devils are lurking around me! They're
going to tear me to shreds the instant I abandon this pure body. The
Angels of Destruction are gaping at me with their burning eyes! No! I
can't leave this boy's virtuous body. I'm protected here, they have no
power over me here!"

And his wailing filled the entire synagogue.

Sháya went to him, bent over him, and said very tenderly: "Invisible
dybbuk! Tell me your name and your mother's name, and I'll institute a
special prayer for you. I'll write it myself with God's help. With my
prayer I'll ask the Good Lord to shield you from the Angels of Destruction who are waiting to trap you in their nets!"

"Shmúel, the son of Rivke!" the boy sobbed and stood up.

The next afternoon, the Jews gathered at the appointed time in the old
study house. They brought the boy, bound him again hand and foot

with thick ropes, and set him on the platform with his face toward the Holy Ark. Sháya ordered them to open the Holy Ark; and while they did so, he unrolled a parchment, which contained the special prayer. During the night, he had composed it in Hebrew, writing in an elegant hand on a piece of deerskin parchment that was destined to serve as a Torah scroll. And here is the prayer as translated into Yiddish:

"Lord of the Universe, Merciful Father, Lord of Forgiveness, God our King. Thou art filled with mercy and kindness, and Thou showest grace to all Thy creatures. We come to Thee, praying to Thee and beseeching Thee to show greater mildness than demanded by the Law toward this spirit, who hath penetrated the boy, Shmúel, the son of Rivke, and doth not allow him to rest. We beg Thee, Merciful Father, to temper Thy judgment. And although he is fit to be judged and severely punished, God, grace is in Thy hands. Render mercy gratuitously unto him so that he shall not repudiate, and so that our prayer shall ascend to Thy Throne of Glory and so that Thou shalt kindly remember all his own merits and good deeds and all the merits and good deeds of his parents. And also reckon our prayers that shall ascend to Thee like incense and be pleasing to Thee like a pleasant fragrance. May they awaken Thy grace and the wellspring of Thy mercy, so that all his sins may be forgiven. Absolve him, Great God, of all the sins and wrongs that he has committed against Thee either by himself or through others, and may our prayers be reckoned by Thee as if they were his own prayers. May he be shielded and protected from all the demons and devils that lie in wait for him on all sides. Do not heed the accusers who demand that he be tried. Grant him rest and true peace. But only on condition that he shall not return to this boy and that he shall not injure any human being whether male or female. Only then shouldst Thou show him Thy vast grace, take pity on him, protect him, grant him peace and repose, and save his soul. And Thou, who mercifully hearest the prayers of Thy nation Israel, please also heed our prayers, and may our words be acceptable to Thee, our God, our Creator, and our Redeemer. Amen!"

In the silence the Jews repeated the prayer word for word and concluded with an "Amen" that filled the entire study house with a deep sigh.

Sháya turned to the boy and calmly and courteously urged him: "Shmúel, son of Rivke! Once again I promise you, in the name of the rabbinical court and in the name of the sacred congregation: If you voluntarily leave this body, we will recite the prayer that you have just heard. Recite it every single day for an entire year except on the Sabbath and on holidays, when we do not recite the Takhanun, the prayer for mercy. Furthermore we earnestly swear that we will keep our earlier promises: namely, to study the Talmud on your behalf every day and to recite psalms on your behalf for an entire year, and after every session with the Talmud I shall, God willing, recite Kaddish de Rabbanan [the prayer recited on completion of study] and I shall recite the mourners' Kaddish for an entire year! Go to your repose and do not injure anyone!"

Then they heard a weeping voice, which implored them: "Let me find another resting place in the world. I will then obey you and leave this body. I see thousands and tens of thousands of Angels of Destruction all around me; they're looking forward to the moment when I leave the boy, so that they can grab me, torture me, and rip out pieces of my flesh. How can I leave my lovely home before finding another place of refuge?"

Sháya comforted him: "Don't be afraid, Shmúel, son of Rivke; our collective prayer won't allow the fiends and destroyers to come anywhere near you. Prayers of many people are never ignored. God Blessed Be He will shield you and protect you from all the lurking demons, and He will raise your sinful soul all the way up to the Supreme Source. We are willing to wait until noon tomorrow. We will convene again at that time in this same place, this platform in this study house. And here you will publicly sanctify His Name and leave the boy's body. The Creator of the Universe will then forgive you for your sins, and you will be purified forever. But if you defy me and refuse to heed my good advice, then I warn you for the last time that I will proceed against you with all the severity of the Law, and with even greater and harsher exorcisms and anathemas that have never been heard of before. I will have to cite many names of saints. I will shake you and those who supervise you, whether above or below, so that they despotically drag you out, violently yank you out from the boy's body. You will never recover and you will be doomed both here and in the afterlife."

At noon the next day, the old study house was packed. The entire Jewish community was there—including the leaders, the magnates, the authorities. They brought in the boy and again they bound him hand and foot, and set him down on the platform opposite the Holy Ark. Sháya unrolled the parchment and read out his prayer, and in the silence the congregants repeated it word for word. Then they recited Kaddish, and Sháya yelled very loud:

"Shmúel, son of Rivke! In the name of the entire holy congregation, I am showing you greater mildness than demanded by the Law and I warn you that you must immediately leave the boy's body through his little toe. If you refuse, then I must give you this final and fearful ultimatum: Namely, that I will instantly proceed against you with admonition, excommunication, and curses such as have never been heard before and that I will hand you over to the demons forever."

The entire study house lapsed into a deathly hush, the entire congregation kept silent. All eyes were glued to the boy on the platform, all ears were avidly waiting for the response. Would the dybbuk obey? Or would he dig in his heels? Sháya leaned over, his head slightly tilted, as if straining his ears in the silence, trying to catch a whisper, a murmur from somewhere. But there was only the hush. The dybbuk had gone mute.

Sháya realized that the dybbuk refused to obey, that he was sticking to his guns. So Sháya resolutely lifted his head, straightened his body to its full length, and stretched his arms up to the heavens. His bold eyes took in the congregation as if he were solidifying his certainty that the entire Jewish community here shared his faith, that victory was on their side. His radiant face shone with the light of the seven days of Creation [a light that, according to legend, is reserved for the righteous]. His right hand then knocked on the reader's desk. In the profound hush the unexpected knock reverberated in all hearts like a remote echo from a hidden and mysterious world. Next they heard Sháya's pure voice, which was both frightening and encouraging:

"Holy congregation and rabbinical court! Since the dybbuk refuses to leave voluntarily, we must, with God's help, use force. I promise you that we will unseat the dybbuk this very day, chase him from all human settlements, and drive him beyond the wild and waste Mountains of Darkness. Snuff all the menorahs; take seven Torah scrolls, and seven men, each holding a black candle, and seven men, each holding a shofar, are to station themselves throughout the study house, and we will start our final exorcism."

The men did so, and Sháya wrapped himself in his prayer shawl. The black candles were lit, and all seven shofars at once blared through the semidarkness. Sháya's voice could be heard uttering all sorts of invocations, conjurations, excommunications. The shofars blasted seven times, and Sháya performed his exorcisms seven times. After each attempt, the terrified witnesses repeated "Amen."

Suddenly a dreadful shriek resounded throughout the study house, and they heard the dybbuk sobbing, gasping, and begging:

"Jews, have mercy, don't expel me today! I'll obey you later on! I *will* leave the boy's body. Please let me be for another twelve days and I'll leave the boy's body by any route you order me to take. Merciful children of merciful parents! Be considerate of me and pity me the way you pity this boy. I'll never ever return to the boy so long as you keep your promises. Let me add one more request: Once I leave, sit shiva for me and mourn me for the thirty days for which you would usually mourn a relative. Recite Kaddish for me not only in the Great Synagogue but also in every holy place in Khmélnik. And nullify all the anathemas leveled at me."

Sháya resolutely snapped back: "No! We will not leave until we force you out of this boy—and today!"

The dybbuk started begging again: "Have pity! I can't leave as yet—the time is not yet ripe. I still have to wait a little! Let me be—if not for twelve days then at least twelve hours. Trust me, I'll keep my word. I'll obey your orders down to the last detail! Believe me and now let me be!"

Sháya retorted: "We'll do as you ask on condition that you swear by the name of God that you will leave the boy's body in exactly twelve hours."

"Oh, I'm so miserable!" The dybbuk sobbed harder. "How can I swear since I'm not allowed to utter His Holy Name? If I were allowed to utter it, I wouldn't be terrified of the demons and devils. No! I can't swear anything, but I *will* give you my pledge: In exactly twelve hours I will voluntarily leave the boy's body."

Sháya held out his right hand, kept it aloft, and said: "I will accept your pledge. We will wait patiently for twelve hours and we have faith that you will keep your word and that you will leave the boy's body voluntarily. All we need is a signal from you when you are out."

A clear voice then said: "When you observe blood trickling from the boy's little toe and you see a small hole in one of the window panes, you will know that I am no longer among you."

Sháya lowered his arm and nodded his head to show his agreement. He ordered his assistants to return the Torah scrolls to the Holy Ark, snuff the black candles, put away the shofars, and descend from the platform with measured steps. Dusk settled on all faces. And Sháya, in his smock and his prayer shawl, stood at the reader's stand and recited the early evening prayer. After the late evening prayer, everyone headed home, and the boy was escorted back to the poorhouse.

Exactly twelve hours after the dybbuk's pledge, at dawn on Tuesday, the boy woke up with a fierce shriek, sprang from his bed, and stormed from room to room, slamming the doors behind him. The terrified residents of the poorhouse all leaped from their beds. Horrified at seeing the boy wildly scurrying around, they clustered at the window, ready to jump out. Suddenly, the boy collapsed, his voice rattling like that of a dying man. With his last drop of strength, the dybbuk shouted: "Go away from the window! I'll injure anyone blocking the window!"

They instantly heard the sound of breaking glass. A small round hole the size of a ducat appeared in the window of the eastern wall, and at the same time a thin trickle of blood came oozing from the boy's little toe.

The miracle had occurred! The dybbuk had kept his word!

The good news swept through Khmélnik like wildfire. Worshipers from all directions poured into the old study house, where the rabbis, judges, and community leaders had already arrived. They also brought along the boy. The congregation worshiped with deep ardor and recited Sháya's special prayer. The boy recited the first Kaddish, and the congregants wept tears of joy and thanked the Creator for the great miracle they had witnessed. Right after prayers, the head rabbi and the judges climbed up on the platform, and the rabbi proclaimed in a trembling but clear and loud voice:

"In the name of the holy congregation, I publicly announce and proclaim that the dybbuk Shmúel, son of Rivke, has kept his promise fully and precisely and has left us at the scheduled time. We, the local rabbinical court, therefore remove from Shmúel, son of Rivke, all the anathemas and conjurations, all the curses and excommunications that were placed upon him. From this day forward they are null and void and as worthless as the dust of the earth. Let them fall on waste fields and wild forests, and let none of them apply to him or injure him by even a hair's breadth now and evermore. Amen!"

And all the people in the synagogue repeated: "Amen!"

Next, trusted messengers went out to all the holy places in town and proclaimed the final judgment of the rabbinical court.

That same night the dybbuk appeared to the rabbi and angrily protested: "I've kept my promise to you people, I left the boy's body and didn't injure anyone. But as soon as I was out in the world, I was attacked by thousands of spirits and demons. Furthermore the Angels of Destruction created by your curses and anathemas are chasing me. I can't find any place to protect myself against them—unless I return to the boy's body. So I've come to complain to you, the town rabbi, and to ask you why you haven't kept your promise to rescind my excommunication. Please carry out the rabbinical decision immediately: Cancel the anathemas and drive away the fiends that keep harassing me nonstop."

The rabbi assured him that messengers had visited all the holy places in town and proclaimed the court's decision and publicly announced that all the curses and anathemas against the dybbuk were null and void.

But the dybbuk angrily retorted: "Your court decision has no clout because it was not made according to the Law. So it can't deprive the fiends of the control that you gave them with your exorcisms. As the Talmudic sages decided: 'The mouth that forbideth is the mouth that permiteth' [Bekhorot 36]. The person who imposes a restriction may also remove it. Sháya was the one who inflicted the anathemas, so according to the Law he himself has to cancel them with his holy lips!"

The rabbi did not hesitate. Even though it was the dead of night, he instantly dispatched beadles to wake up every single Jew and summon them all to the rabbi's own holy place. And in the darkness of the night, Sháya, together with the rabbinical court and the community leaders, went from one holy place to another, and everywhere Sháya declared that all his curses and anathemas against Shmúel, son of Rivke, were null and void and as worthless as the dust of the earth. After each proclamation, the Jews all repeated Sháya's special prayer, and the boy, who had been carried along, recited Kaddish in every holy place.

Following that night, however, the boy started losing his strength. He grew weaker and weaker every day, and eventually he couldn't move, he was totally paralyzed. It was as if the dybbuk had drained him of his very life. He also ran a very high temperature. Lying there, feverish and delirious, he kept murmuring incoherently. Often he would burst into a fearful weeping accompanied by moans and sobs.

When they saw that his life was in danger, they followed Sháya's advice and carried the invalid and his bed to the old study house. Sháya put amulets and talismans around the boy's neck, and they decided that for the thirty-day mourning period, which they had promised the dybbuk, the boy should be guarded day and night by men reciting psalms, poring over the Talmud, and so forth.

Here in the study house the boy felt better, and his fever gradually subsided. He opened his eyes and recognized the people around him. His speech became clearer and more coherent, and he improved day by day. He was still guarded day and night by Jews reciting psalms and poring over the Talmud and other holy books.

In the middle of the thirtieth night, the boy suddenly woke up and began yelling in an unnatural voice: "Help! Help! Hear, Oh Israel!" Once they calmed him, the boy sat up and explained that the dybbuk had just reappeared in the study house and had tried to approach the boy's bed, but he could get no closer than four cubits away. The dybbuk had tried with all his strength but had been unable to leap across. So he had spoken to the boy from that distance and had tried to persuade him to remove the sacred amulets and talismans. That would enable the dybbuk to penetrate him. The boy repeated the dybbuk's sweet talk:

"You know, during the more than six years I was in your body, you never once got sick, you never once had any pains. On the coldest winter days, you went around the streets barefoot and half-naked, and it didn't harm you at all. But now, ever since I left you, you've been bedridden with a tormenting illness. If you remove the amulets and talismans, I'll enter your body immediately, you'll recover completely and you'll never feel pain again!"

The sick boy continued: "I asked the dybbuk: 'Why won't you keep your word? After all, we pray for you, we're studying the Talmud according to the letters of your name, we say Kaddish for you. Don't our prayers have any power? Haven't they accomplished anything for you?' And he replied:

"'It's true that your praying, your studying, your Kaddish repetitions have made a deep impact. They've worked partly and they've cut my sufferings in half because the celestial court originally condemned me to suffer four times every day. But now, because of your efforts, I suffer only twice a day, and the torments themselves are much easier. I realize that through your prayers and Kaddish repetitions, my torments will soon stop altogether. However, the celestial court also sentenced me to spend a whole seventy years floating in the Valley of Darkness behind the Mountains of Darkness. And your prayers can't nullify that verdict. Thirty years have already worn by, but that leaves forty more, which I'll have to spend among demons and devils, under the control of Ashmedai and Lilith. I'll have to look at their horrible faces, dance their demonic dances, never have any rest or peace, and I'll be driven and driven day and night. How can I endure all those things? That's why I've come to plead with you: Take pity on me and redeem me from their hands! Let me back into your sacred body. But this time you'll let me in voluntarily, of your own free will. And I beg you to promise me that you'll never allow anyone to drive me out of your body.'"

The trembling boy then reported that the dybbuk had held out his right hand. Overwhelmed by a sudden terror, the boy had started shouting: "Help! Help! Hear, Oh Israel!" The moment the dybbuk heard those words, he vanished.

From that night on the boy started regaining his strength. The dybbuk never appeared to him again. The boy fully recovered right after the thirty days were over. He soon got married, and his wife bore him sons and daughters. And he named his first boy Shmúel in memory of Shmúel, son of Rivke.

Sháya lies buried in the old cemetery of Khmélnik. The cemetery keeper showed us his grave. By now the headstone was half-buried in the ground, and its inscription was totally rubbed off and washed off.

TSVI HIRSH KAIDANOVER

A Tale of Poznan

From: Sefer Qav ha-Yashar, *vol. 2, chap. 69 (Frankfurt-am-Main, Germany: 1706). A facsimile of the manuscript with a transliteration into the modern Hebrew alphabet can be found in Sara Zfatman,* The Marriage of a Mortal Man and a She-Demon *(Jerusalem: Akedom Press, 1987).*

While in the majority of cases the victim of a possession is female, the flip side occurs when a she-demon seduces and even marries a mortal man. The underlying distress may partly derive from anxiety about Jews who leave the Jewish fold to marry Christians. This and other sexual transgressions are certainly attacked in this story and in the next.

People should know that the mother of all the demons is named Makhles. She has whole gangs of she-demons, who appear to people in broad daylight. They adorn themselves with all kinds of gems and jewels and are very beautiful. Often they talk a man into being with them and they bear his children, who are thus half-human and half-demon. In the Holy Torah such illegitimate offspring are called *mashkhisim* (destroyers, demons of destruction). The man who mates with a female demon is punished afterwards, when she kills him, and his entire family dies out. In regard to such matters, I have written down a story about recent events.

In the holy congregation of Poznan, during the years 5441–5442 (1681–1682), there was a brick house among other brick houses in the Jewish district. Inside the house there was a lovely brick cellar, but no one could enter it, for whoever did so was harmed, and no one knew why. Once, a boy entered the cellar in broad daylight. A mere fifteen minutes later they found his corpse by the cellar door, but they couldn't tell who had killed him.

Three months later, the *khitsónim* (dissenters), the children of the half-demons, the *mashkhísim,* moved into the porch of the house. Any food placed on the stove or in the oven became full of ashes and filth; it was completely inedible. Several weeks later, the *mashkhisim* moved into the rooms. There they grabbed the tin utensils out from the cupboard and threw them down and they took the lamps and candlesticks and hurled them to the floor. When the tenants sat down to eat, the invaders tossed the food and the tablecloth on the floor, but they broke no dishes and hurt no one. However, the human occupants couldn't bear it, they had no peace day or night, and finally they all had to move out.

There was great lamenting; everyone was deeply upset that such a lovely house should be so dreadfully haunted in such a holy congregation as that of Poznan. The community leaders held council and decided to send for some renowned Gentile wizards and Christian priests, but these men failed to accomplish anything.

Next the Jews sent for a baal-shem (wonder worker) named Yoyl. He was very pious and very skillful, and the instant he arrived in Poznan he implored the demons to leave the house, for their true home was either a forest or a desert or a swamp, and no demon has the power to live among human beings. The demons replied that they had a claim to seniority in the ownerless house and they called for a judicial procedure. They would appeal to a Jewish court and prove the merits of their case. The Poznan judges and Yoyl the baal-shem entered the house and sat down in one of the rooms. There the judges heard the arguments made by the demons, who, however, remained invisible.

The demons maintained that the house in question had once been inhabited by a Jewish goldsmith who lived with a she-demon. "They had several children, and we are those children. The goldsmith loved our mother, the she-demon, he could never leave her for even an hour— they were virtually joined at the hip, and he did whatever she wanted him to do. Even when the goldsmith was in synagogue, he had to take off his prayer shawl and prayer thongs and hurry over to her. As for his real wife, he lived badly with her. She must have sensed that there was a good reason for his failure to perform his conjugal duties.

"One evening, on the first night of Passover, the goldsmith was at his seder. And when it was time to eat the afikomon [the piece of matzoh hidden for the children to steal and hold ransom], the goldsmith threw off his white linen smock and went to the demon's house, where he spent a long time.

"His legal wife also left the Passover feast and followed him in order to find out what was keeping her husband at that house. When she peered through a crack in the door, she saw a beautiful room with many candles, gold and silver vessels, and a bed decorated with gold. A naked woman was in the bed, she was very lovely, and the husband was lying with the woman, who was actually a demon. The wife was scared, too scared to say anything. So she went back home and waited until her husband returned from the demon's house.

"The wife held her tongue all that night and did nothing in regard to her husband, for she had seen that he was involved with a demoness. In the morning, she went to the town rabbi, who was known as Gaon Sheftl, the eldest of the Tribe of Levi, and she complained to him that her husband—God help us!—had been seduced by a she-demon.

"The rabbi sent for the goldsmith and ordered him to tell the truth on pain of excommunication. The goldsmith promptly confessed that a female demon had come and clung to him when he had been washing himself in a river. The rabbi then wrote some words for an amulet, which would drive the she-demon away.

"When the goldsmith lay dying, the she-demon came to him with the children he had fathered and she began to weep because he was leaving her and their offspring. She fell upon him and kissed him and coaxed him to allow her to live somewhere. The goldsmith promised to give her a cellar in his house, and then he died.

"Now for several years a war was fought in Poland, from 5408 to 5418 (1648–1658). The goldsmith died and so did all his legitimate children and all his heirs, and now there is no one to inherit the house."

The demons argued that they should inherit it.

To which the people who lived in the house replied: "We bought the house from the goldsmith's legitimate children, and you are half-demons and not part of the people of Israel." They then added that the she-demon had forced herself upon the goldsmith and compelled him to live with her.

The court decreed that the half-demons had no claim on the house, for their home was in the desert and not in a human dwelling. After this judgment was handed down, Yoyl, the baal-shem, implored the half-demons to leave the house and the cellar, and he sent them to the wild forest.

This story shows what happens to a human being who gets involved with the followers of Lilith or Makhles, the mothers of the demons: Such a man is extirpated together with his family, and they all perish. Every man should therefore be warned against going with harlots, for sometimes a she-demon appears in the guise of a harlot and mates with a man, causing him and his family to perish. Each man must therefore take care to mate only with his wife and not waste his seed. And if, willingly or not, he does waste his seed, he should immediately do penance.

ANONYMOUS

The Man Who Married a She-Demon
A Tale of the Town of Worms

*I am grateful to Erika Timm for showing me her as yet unpublished trans-
literation of this text into the Latin alphabet (Trier system). A translitera-
tion into the modern Hebrew alphabet can be found in Sara Zfatman,*
The Marriage of a Mortal Man and a She-Demon *(Jerusalem: Akedom
Press, 1987). According to Zfatman, the story was penned in Northern
Italy after 1514 (MS 12.45 Trinity College, Cambridge, fols.2y4r-31r).*

Years ago there lived a wonderful rabbi in the German town that is still
known today as Worms. It has an old Jewish community that goes back
to the generations of Jesse. The rabbi, whose name was Zalmen, was a
very rich man, and he headed a large yeshiva attended by a hundred
distinguished students, who pored over the holy books day and night.
Rabbi Zalmen had an only son, likewise distinguished, who also studied
at the yeshiva. His father and his mother loved him very much for his
good deeds.

Now when the holiday of Lag-Baomer rolls around, the students
like to have a good time. The town of Worms has a public park called
Jubilee Gardens, and people who have been here must know where it is.
On that holiday the yeshiva students, taking along the rabbi's son, went
to the park, where they played a game called hide-and-seek in our language. One boy has to lean over [and cover his eyes] while the rest
conceal themselves, and he then has to look for the others until he finds
them all. Finally, the rabbi's son was "it," and he had to lean over. The
boys all hid, and then the rabbi's son began his search. Eventually he
found everybody except for a boy named Anshel, though he kept looking and looking.

Now the park was densely wooded, and the rabbi's son hunted for
Anshel beyond the trees. Soon he came to a hollow tree, and when he

118

saw an arm sticking out, he figured it must belong to Anshel, who was evidently hidden inside the tree. The rabbi's son shouted: "Anshel, c'mon out, I've found you." But he saw that the hand did not retreat. So the rabbi's son removed a gold ring from his finger, slipped it over a finger on the hand looming from the tree, and said: "Since you won't come out of the tree, I hereby wed thee." He played his prank because he thought that the hand belonged to his friend Anshel.

As soon as the rabbi's son married the hand, it vanished with the ring. Upon seeing this, he was alarmed, for the ring was very valuable, and he was afraid of going home to his father and mother without it. When he rejoined his fellow students, he found his friend among them and he said: "Dear Anshel, please give me my ring."

Anshel replied: "I haven't seen your ring, I don't know anything about it."

The rabbi's son retorted: "I slipped it over your finger when you were hiding in that tree."

"All of our fellow students can testify that I wasn't in that tree. I hid somewhere else."

And so the ring was lost.

The boys all went back and told the rabbi the whole story, and upon hearing it, he said: "Go and bring my son home and tell him not to worry. I'm going to give him a lovelier ring." So they went to get him and brought him home. And the ring was forgotten.

A long time later, when the rabbi's son became an adult, a wonderful person, his learning was renowned far and wide. Now a leader of the Jewish community in the town of Speier sent Rabbi Zalmen an inquiry: Would the rabbi let his son marry the leader's daughter? He had heard about how good a student the boy was, and that was why he desired him for a son-in-law. The man was willing to provide a large dowry. And so the wedding took place, a joyous celebration. There were many guests at the ceremony as is customary among wealthy people, and they had a marvelous time. After the nuptials and the banquet, the groom and bride were led very festively to the bedchamber, and the door was then shut according to tradition.

No sooner did the groom lie down than he fell asleep. The bride, however, lay awake. And as she lay there, she saw someone coming to the bed: a beautiful woman dressed in gold and silk. The woman said to the bride: "You brazen hussy, why have you lain down with my husband, who married me in a tree?"

The bride retorted: "That's not true! He's my husband! I married him today, so get away from here!"

Upon hearing this, the woman strangled the bride and left her corpse next to the groom.

Past midnight, the groom awakened and he wanted to talk to his bride as is the custom. But then he saw her lying next to him dead. Terrified, he got to his feet and woke the people up. They hurried into the chamber, where they found the bride dead, and they asked him how it happened. He answered: "Unfortunately I was asleep, I don't know."

The bride was buried, and their joy turned into grief. And before everyone went home, there were many people who said that the groom had killed the bride.

So for a good three years the rabbi's son was unable to find a bride despite his great wealth and vast learning, for no father wanted to risk his daughter's life.

Eventually, however, a rich community leader, who was related to the boy, told the Rabbi of Worms: "I'll risk my daughter's life since you're my own flesh and blood. And if a terrible surprise occurred once, I hope it won't happen again."

The marriage took place, and they became man and wife. After taking them to bed, the people left, shutting the door behind them.

Once again, the groom fell asleep, while the frightened bride lay awake. And as she lay there, the beautiful woman dressed in gold came again and said to the bride: "You brazen hussy, I've already killed one girl who lay with my husband, but you weren't warned!" And she killed this bride too.

When the groom awoke, he again found his bride dead. He screamed so loudly that all the people came running. He told them: "My poor bride is dead!"

The bride was buried, and the wedding guests all left in profound grief.

For some ten years the groom stayed put, unable to find another bride. And then he reached thirty.

Now once, on the Sabbath of Repentance [between the start of the new year and the Day of Atonement], the rabbi was sitting with his wife, the rebbetsin, and the rabbi said: "Dear wife, what should we do? We have an only son and great wealth, and if he stays unmarried, all memory of us will be wiped from the face of the earth and our wealth will be divided among strangers. But what father will allow his daughter to marry our son?" And they shared their anguish and misery with each other.

The rebbetsin then said: "Dear husband, I don't think I'm mistaken: No community leader will ever allow his daughter to marry our son.

However, I know of a poor widow from an excellent family—her husband was a rabbi. She has an only child, a beautiful daughter, and they live in a poorhouse. Who knows, my dear husband? What if I go to her and offer to have our son marry the girl? Perhaps she'll be rewarded for her piety: God will see her poverty and allow her to live."

The rabbi then said to his wife: "You're right! Go and talk to the poor widow now and ask her if she'd like to have her daughter marry our son."

The boy's mother, the wealthy rebbetsin, then promptly went and knocked on the door of the poorhouse. The poor rebbetsin, upon seeing the rich one knocking, hurried over to her daughter and said: "Dear daughter, why is the wealthy rebbetsin knocking on our door?"

The daughter replied: "Dear mother, perhaps she's bringing us some food."

So they opened the door and welcomed her very courteously. They invited her to sit and they said: "Dear rebbetsin, why are you honoring us with your visit?"

The wealthy rebbetsin answered: "Let me explain why I've come here. You've probably heard what's happened to our son twice—God help us! So if it's at all possible, I'd like your daughter to marry our son. Who knows? Perhaps she'll be rewarded for her piety and will survive. It will make up for your and your daughter's poverty."

The poor rebbetsin then spoke to her daughter: "Dear daughter, you've heard what the wealthy rebbetsin has said. It's up to you, I won't force you. But I can't supply a dowry. So if you don't accept this offer, you'll remain an old maid."

Her daughter replied: "Dear mother, we're poor, that's true, and a poor person is like a dead man. I'll do it so long as the marriage contract stipulates that if I die, the rabbi will provide for you in his home for the rest of your days. If he agrees, then I'll risk my life and marry his son."

And so another wedding was set to take place.

The wealthy rebbetsin ordered lovely clothes for the poor girl. And when she put them on, she looked so beautiful that no one recognized her when she went about, and she no longer had to go begging. Now that she was a bit adorned and was lovely anyway, everyone talked about her beauty.

Few guests were invited to the wedding, which was not especially joyous, because people said: "If she stays alive, then we'll really celebrate!" They carried out the ceremony and, after the banquet, they took the groom and bride to their bed, as is the custom. The people then left and shut the door behind them. The groom fell asleep while the frightened bride lay awake.

At last, when midnight came, the bride saw a beautiful woman in splendid clothes and with golden hair approaching the bed. The woman said to the bride: "You brazen hussy, I've already killed two girls who lay with my husband! You've heard about that and yet you're risking your own life! So I'm going to kill you too!"

Upon hearing that, the bride was terrified and she said: "Dear mother, I've lived in the poorhouse all my life and I've never heard that he lost two wives. So, dear mother, he's your bridegroom. I'll get up and I'll let you lie with him."

When the beautiful she-demon heard that, she said: "Dear child, you must be rewarded for your piety, for speaking to me so piously. This is what you must do to make him your husband: He will vanish from your sight for one hour every day and come to me. So don't say a word to anyone if you value your life and if God is dear to you!"

The bride answered that no one would know but the Good Lord. And the she-demon vanished from her sight.

Less than half an hour later, the husband awoke, terrified, and quickly reached for his bride. He was overjoyed to see that she was still alive. Since it was almost dawn, the people came into the chamber and found the groom and bride still lying together. The groom's parents and the bride's mother were ecstatic, and they all had a wonderful time at the celebration. The poor girl was wealthy now, everything belonged to her. She loved her husband, and he loved her, for she was very modest.

Eventually the couple had three sons.

Now women always want to know a lot more than is useful for them. The wife lost her husband for an hour each day and she didn't know what became of him. She saw him go into the bedchamber, where he would disappear. The good woman saw her husband vanish and she thought to herself: "I'm willing to risk my neck to find out where he goes. I'm going to follow him, even if I have to risk my neck."

Noting where he had left his keys, she took them and unlocked the door. But her husband wasn't in the chamber. She searched every nook and cranny. At last, underneath the bed she found a large rock. As she spotted it, the rock moved from its place. She now saw a large hole with a ladder descending inside it. The wife thought to herself: "Dear God, should I go down? I'm sure my husband is down there."

After pondering for a long time, she finally climbed down the ladder and found herself in a large field. And in the large field she saw an elegant mansion. She entered the mansion and found an open door. She entered the room and found a table set with fine dishes and cutlery. The room had a second open door leading to another room, which she entered. And there she found her husband lying in a silken bed with the beautiful demon, their bodies enlaced. The demon lay in front, with her golden hair hanging down to the floor. Upon seeing this, the wife felt it was a shame for the golden hair to be hanging down to the floor like that. So she took a chair, put it next to the bed, and placed the hair upon it.

Then she went back the way she had come. She rolled the rock on top of the hole, locked the door, and left the keys where she had found them. And she didn't breathe a single word to anyone in the entire house.

When the demon woke up, she began screaming, loudly and bitterly, and she said: "Dear husband, I'm here and I have to die. When your dear wife was here, she touched my feet. If someone touches me, I have to die. Therefore, dear husband, since she did it out of piety, it was good for her that my beautiful hair was hanging down to the floor. You have to be rewarded. Well, dear husband, I've got the gold ring that you gave me when you married me. Take it back and go home through the hole. The hole is going to disappear, and we will be divorced forever."

He did what she told him to do and he returned home. And the hole disappeared. He also remained at home, and he said nothing to his wife, nor did his wife say anything to him.

After staying at home for three days, he gave a large banquet for the entire Jewish community. Neither his wife nor his parents knew why. The whole community ate and drank and were going to say their blessings. Thereupon the rabbi's son began: "Dear guests, before saying the blessing, let me explain why I'm giving this banquet. Dear father, here is the ring that I lost in a tree. At that time I married a demon because I thought it was the boy I was looking for. The she-demon murdered my first two brides, but now my dear wife has released me from her." And he told the entire story. And then his wife told her story and described what had happened to her, from the wedding night until his release.

And that was how the poor girl became rich and respected through her great piety and modesty.

That is why everyone should follow her example.

And that is the end of the tale of Worms.

DOV BER BEN SHMUEL

Tales of the Baal-Shem-Tov

Whether he actually lived or not, the Baal-Shem-Tov (Master of the Good Name, 1700?–1760) is credited with establishing Hasidism, a mystical movement that is still thriving among Jews today. A Hasidic sect is usually headed by a charismatic leader, a rebbe or tsaddik, whose followers circulate fantastic stories about him—much as the Idlers do in Ansky's The Dybbuk.

In 1815, In Praise of the Baal-Shem-Tov *compiled by Dov Ber ben Shmuel was published in several Hebrew, then Yiddish, editions. The book describes various deeds and miracles—which included expulsions of demons and dybbuks. These tales, like "The Gilgul" (from* The Hasidic World, *see pages 370 through 373), or Dovid L. Mekler's "The Dybbuk" (from* The Rebbe's Court, *see pages 362 through 366), at first circulated orally, in books, and in pamphlets. Printed in Hebrew or Yiddish or both, they were readily accessible, forming a powerful corpus with which Ansky was thoroughly familiar; he even adapted a number of them into prose or verse.*

How the Baal-Shem-Tov Saved a Soul

Once, the Baal-Shem-Tov was wandering about, lost in thought, for three days and three nights, without knowing where he was. Then, to his great surprise, he realized he was far from home. What did this mean? It had to mean something. Suddenly a frog came hopping up, and it was so large that the Baal-Shem-Tov didn't know what kind of creature it was. So he asked the frog: "Who are you?"

The frog answered: "I'm a Talmudic scholar and I was reborn as a frog five centuries ago. And even though Rabbi Isaac Luria of blessed memory redeemed souls, I was driven far from human beings because of my great sins."

124

The Baal-Shem-Tov asked him what he had done, and the frog answered: "First, I failed to wash my hands properly upon rising in the morning, and in the heavenly court Satan accused me of committing that sin. He was then told that my first sin would be overlooked for now, but that if he talked me into committing a second sin, both would be counted against me. However, if I did penitence for the second sin, then I would also be cleansed of the first. I was then tested with a second sin. I succumbed to temptation, and one sin led to the next—until I had committed practically every sin in the Torah. Heaven now handed down a judgment: I was not to be forgiven. Still, if I forced myself to truly repent, I would be received in Heaven. But Satan turned me into a drunkard, and so my mind had no room for repentance, and I went on sinning. Now my first sin, my failure to wash my hands properly, triggered all the other sins, and so when I died, I came back as a frog—a frog is constantly in water, where people do not come. Wherever a Jew may be, he will recite a blessing or a prayer or have a good thought, any of which can redeem a soul and make it virtuous again."

Upon hearing this story, the Baal-Shem-Tov redeemed the scholar's soul and made it virtuous again—until the frog lay dead. That was how the Baal-Shem-Tov exalted that tormented soul.

How Yóysef, the Town Preacher of Mézhibozh, Appeared to the Baal-Shem-Tov after Death

In the Baal-Shem-Tov's home there was a man named Yóysef Daytsh, and the Baal-Shem-Tov would often have him read aloud from *Eyin Yankev* [*Jacob's Source,* a popular sixteenth-century book containing homiletic passages from the Talmud, especially for ushering out the Sabbath]. Sometimes the Baal-Shem-Tov even commented on a tract in that book. And Yóysef would then continue reading.

In the middle of this reading, the town preacher came in. His name was also Yóysef, and he had died nine months earlier. He was wearing Sabbath clothes, including the hat that he had usually worn in his lifetime. The preacher said very loudly: "Good evening, Rebbe," and he walked about like a living man, even clutching his stick as he had clutched it when alive. Upon seeing him, Yóysef Daytsh was so frightened that he dropped the holy book. The Baal-Shem-Tov waved his hand over Yóysef Daytsh's face, so that he no longer saw the ghost. The Baal-Shem-Tov then said to him:

"Take a candle and stand off to the side." For two candles would always be burning in front of the Baal-Shem-Tov. He would often say that two candles were just right for the eyes—not one candle and not three.

Yóysef Daytsh took one of the candles, went off to the side, and watched the Baal-Shem-Tov conversing with the ghost for about half an hour; but he couldn't hear what they were saying. After that, the Baal-Shem-Tov summoned Yóysef Daytsh and asked him to continue reading from *Eyin Yankev*. In the midst of the reading, the Baal-Shem-Tov began reproaching Yóysef Daytsh: "Why were you frightened? You knew him when he was alive. You know he was a virtuous man, and after dying he is indeed virtuous—far more so than during his lifetime. Were you afraid he'd come to kill you?" That was what the Baal-Shem-Tov told him.

Yóysef Daytsh asked him: "Why did I deserve to see him?"

The Baal-Shem-Tov replied: "You were reading from the *Eyin Yankev*, and I was commenting on it. My words purified you and hallowed you, and that was why you saw him. If you had strengthened your mind, you would have heard what he told me and you would have asked whatever you wanted, and he would have responded. You would have gotten to know him and could often see him."

Yóysef Daytsh was very upset at failing to reach that high level. He asked the Baal-Shem-Tov: "Why did the ghost come here?"

The Baal-Shem-Tov replied: "We needed his presence, we needed an elevation."

How the Baal-Shem-Tov Extended the Life of a Dead Child.

Once, while traveling, the Baal-Shem-Tov came to a town, where he heard a proclamation telling him to stay in a certain household. When he arrived, they refused to let him in because a boy was very ill. So the Baal-Shem-Tov sent in his scribe. But the lady of the house said: "We can't let anyone in. You can see that the child is sick, and I'm very worried." And she cursed the Baal-Shem-Tov. Her husband, who could not be as rude as his wife, went out to see the Baal-Shem-Tov in his wagon: "The way things stand, there's no possibility of your staying here."

The Baal-Shem-Tov insisted, but the householder kept refusing because of his sick child. However, the Baal-Shem-Tov swore that if he stayed here, the child would live. He instantly went to the ritual bath and saw that the child was in a wretched state. It was the eve of the Sabbath. The Baal-Shem-Tov directed that no one should stay in the sick child's room: Everyone should leave. He also told his scribe to go out until he summoned him to bring wine for the Sabbath benediction.

Now the Baal-Shem-Tov remained all alone with the child. He then recited Minkhe, the late afternoon prayer, with the patient. And he kept reciting the Eighteen Benedictions until nightfall. It took a long time. The scribe, afraid that the Baal-Shem-Tov might be endangering himself while praying for the child, softly opened the door. He now heard the Baal-Shem-Tov speaking to the child's soul: "Go back into the child's body, for you will have to do so. Are you going to make a perjurer out of me?"

The scribe left, but then he couldn't stand waiting, so he softly opened the door again. He saw the Baal-Shem-Tov lying on the floor. Next the Baal-Shem-Tov stood up and said: "Yes, I told you that you'd have to go back into his body." Then he yelled: "Hersh, give me wine for the benediction."

The Baal-Shem-Tov dined there with the scribe and stayed up all night. In the morning he gave the scribe some remedies and told him what to do for the child. Meanwhile he went to synagogue and prayed.

The mother, upon seeing that her child was a little better, began weeping copiously. The scribe asked her: "Why are you crying?" To which she replied: "How can I help it? I cursed a saint." The scribe said: "Don't give it a second thought. My rebbe is a very good man, he'll forgive you."

When the Baal-Shem-Tov returned from synagogue, he likewise heard the woman weeping and he asked the scribe, who told him everything. The Baal-Shem-Tov sent a message to the woman, asking her to prepare a fine meal for ending the Sabbath. And he assured her that her child would be sitting with him at the banquet.

The boy lived for more than sixty years and he had children and a good livelihood all his days. The child's time had come to an end, but the soul went back to his body only because the Baal-Shem-Tov had sworn it would. That was why the Baal-Shem-Tov had to pray for the boy's life, his livelihood, and his children.

How the Baal-Shem-Tov Brought a Child Back to Life

A man without children kept complaining to the Baal-Shem-Tov, who assured him that he would eventually have children. As he grew older, the man kept badgering the Baal-Shem-Tov until with God's help the wife gave birth to a boy. But the baby died immediately. The husband went to the Baal-Shem-Tov and angrily shouted: "What good are your assurances that I would have children? I'd rather not have had a child at all!"

The Baal-Shem-Tov replied: "I told you that you'd have children, and I can assure you that your baby will live."

The man went home, and the child lay there without breathing. The father couldn't pester the Baal-Shem-Tov, because the Baal-Shem-Tov had assured him that his child would live. So the father went to the Baal-Shem-Tov and spoke to him in a different tone of voice: He asked whether he should prepare for the circumcision ceremony and whom he should invite. The Baal-Shem-Tov ordered the preparations and invited the *sandek* (the man who holds the baby during the circumcision). The Baal-Shem-Tov himself would suck the blood.

The child was brought into the synagogue, and when he was circumcised, no blood flowed—as if dead flesh were being cut. When it was time for the blessing, the Baal-Shem-Tov personally recited it, starting with the words: "Preserve this boy." However, the Baal-Shem-Tov spoke very slowly, drawing out the words, until the boy's spirit came back to his body: The blood spurted, and the child was alive.

How the Baal-Shem-Tov Drove Demons out of the Women's Section of the Synagogue

The women's section in the synagogue of Zbarzh was haunted by demons, who kept frightening the women until finally their section was closed down. The women then went to Rabbi Khaim of Plaskevitsh and told him the story. He thereupon visited the synagogue, where he kept wailing and studying the holy texts until he drove out the demons. The demons, however, got their revenge by harming his two children. Rabbi Khaim now sent for the Baal-Shem-Tov, who came and stayed in a separate house, where he had the two children brought to him. That night, he lay down on the table, while his scribe lay down under the table.

The demons came to the doorway and made fun of the Baal-Shem-Tov when he sang "L'kho Dodi" ("Come, Beloved," a hymn ushering in the Sabbath). He then asked his scribe: "What do you see?" And his scribe buried his face under his pillow.

Suddenly the demons headed toward the two children. The Baal-Shem-Tov shouted at the demons: "Where are you going?" To which they replied: "None of your business!" The demons weren't the least bit scared of the Baal-Shem-Tov, they made fun of him again and sang "L'kho Dodi." So the Baal-Shem-Tov did what he had to do. The demons collapsed on the floor and began pleading with him.

The Baal-Shem-Tov told them: "Go to the children and make them well again." To which the demons replied: "We can't undo what we did to them internally. We wanted to finish with them externally. That is the children's fate!"

The Baal-Shem-Tov asked the demons: "How do you manage to get into the synagogue?"

"The cantor was a fraud and his bass was a fraud. That was how we had the power to get into the synagogue. The cantor and the bass desired the women, and the women desired them. They had one another inside themselves. They fantasized about one another, and so their sin created us."

After hearing them out, the Baal-Shem-Tov sent them to a different place.

RABBI NAKHMAN OF BRASLEV (1772–1810)

A Tale of a Lost Princess

Rabbi Nakhman (1772–1810), a great-grandson of the Baal-Shem-Tov, founded a Hasidic sect that is still thriving today. Unlike the hagiographic stories about other rebbes, Nakhman's posthumous Tales, *first published in 1815 in a bilingual Hebrew-Yiddish edition, are fragmentary and hermetic allegories set in mystical times and places far from any Jewish milieu; indeed, the elusive characters are barely Jewish if at all. In* The Dybbuk, *Ansky, who was obviously familiar with Nakhman's tales, used the parable of "The Heart of the World" from "The Tale of the Seven Beggars" in* Joachim Neugroschel, Great Tales of Jewish Fantasy and the Occult, *(New York: Overlook Press, 1987). Many of Nakhman's motifs derive from Jewish folk material; "A Tale of a Lost Princess." for instance, shows similarities with the Yiddish folk story "The Girl and the Seven Geese."*

A good Yiddish edition of Nakhman's tales was put out by Shmuel H. Zetser in New York in 1929. The Yiddish version of "A Tale of a Lost Princess" omits the last five lines of the Hebrew version, so I added that five-line conclusion to my translation.

> He did speak and he said:
> On the way I told a tale,
> and whoever heard it
> felt remorse.

Once there was a king. The king had six sons and one daughter.

And his daughter was very dear to him. He loved her very much—he adored her and he greatly enjoyed playing with her.

But one day when they were together, he got angry at her and snapped: "The Devil take you!"

That night she went to her room, and in the morning no one knew where she was.

Her father, the king, was very aggrieved and he went looking for her. Now when the viceroy saw that the king was very aggrieved, he stood up and asked him for a servant and horses as well as money for expenses and he went looking for the princess everywhere.

And he looked for her for a very long time until he found her.

And now we will tell about how he looked for her and found her.

First he went all over the settlements for a long time. Next he went through deserts and through fields and forests for a long time and looked for her for a very long time.

One day, when he was in the desert, he saw a road on the side. He thought to himself: "Since I've been going through the desert for a long time without finding her, let me take this road—perhaps it will lead me to a settlement."

And he traveled for a long time.

At last he came to a castle, with many armies surrounding the castle. And the castle was very beautiful.

And the armies surrounded it in a fine order.

Now the viceroy was afraid of these armies, for they might not let him enter.

But then he thought to himself: "I'll try it." And he left his horse and walked over to the castle.

He was allowed to enter, he wasn't stopped.

And he went from room to room and he wasn't hindered. And he came to a throne room and there he saw a king in a crown, with many armies surrounding him and playing instruments for him.

And the place was very fine and beautiful. And neither the king nor anyone else asked the viceroy anything. And he saw good food there and he went over and ate. Next he lay down in a corner to see what would be happening there. And he saw: The king ordered the queen to be brought in.

And she was brought in, and there was a big to-do and a big celebration.

And bands of musicians and singers played and sang because the queen had been brought in.

And they set a chair for the queen, and she sat down next to the king.

And this was the lost princess.

And he, the viceroy, saw her and recognized her.

Then the queen looked and saw that someone was lying in the corner.

And she recognized him.

She got up from her chair and went over to him and touched him and asked him:

"Do you know me?"

He replied: "Yes, I know you. You are the princess who disappeared." And he asked her how she had come here.

"I came here because my father snapped at me: 'The Devil take you!' This is the Devil's place."

The viceroy then told her that her father was very aggrieved and had been looking for her for many years.

And he asked her: "How can I take you away from here?"

"You can't take me away from here unless you choose a place and sit there for a whole year.

"And you should long for me for a whole year, long to take me away.

"And when you have time, you should only long and wish and hope that you will take me away.

"And you should fast.

"And on the very last day of the year, you should fast and you should not sleep for a whole day and night."

And the viceroy went and did as she had said.

And at the end of the year, on the very last day, he fasted and he didn't sleep.

And he got up and went there, to the princess, in order to take her away.

But on the way he saw a tree.

And very beautiful apples grew on the tree.

And he greatly desired to eat some of the apples.

And he ate one.

No sooner had he eaten the apple than he immediately collapsed and fell sound asleep.

And he slept for a very long time.

The servant tried to wake him but couldn't wake him up.

At last, however, the viceroy did wake up.

And he asked the servant:

"Where in the world am I?"

And so he—the servant, that is—told the viceroy the whole story. And he said to him:

"You've slept for many years, and I survived by eating the fruit."

The viceroy was very aggrieved, and he went over and found the princess there.

And she was very aggrieved and she bitterly lamented:

"For the sake of one day you lost everything because you couldn't control yourself. You shouldn't have eaten the apple—that's why you lost. For if you had come on that day, you would have taken me away.

But not eating is a very difficult thing, especially on the very last day: That's when the evil spirit shows his strength. So you should choose another place and you should sit there for another year, and on the very last day you may eat, but you must not sleep. And you must not drink any wine so that you won't fall asleep. For sleep is the most important thing of all."

And he went and did as she had said.

And on the very last day of the year he started back.

On the way he saw a wellspring. And the color of the wellspring was red. And it smelled of wine.

So the viceroy asked the servant:

"Did you see? That's a wellspring. It must have water. But its color is red, and it smells of wine."

And the viceroy went over and tasted the liquid.

Whereupon he instantly collapsed and he slept for many years—seventy years.

And many armies went by with all their military equipment and with baggage convoys trailing them.

So the servant hid from the armies.

Then a carriage came, and in the carriage sat the princess.

The carriage halted next to the viceroy, and the princess stepped out and sat down next to him and recognized him. And she tried to wake him. But he couldn't be awakened.

So she began lamenting: "After so much effort and struggle and so many years of your torment and drudgery in trying to take me away— and on the one day you could take me away you lost everything."

And she wept bitterly.

Then she said:

"You and I are both to be greatly pitied. I've been here for such a long time and I can't get out."

She took a kerchief from her head and wrote on it with her tears and placed it next to him.

Then the princess stood up and sat down in her carriage and drove away.

Now the viceroy woke up.

He asked the servant: "Where am I in the world?"

The servant told him the whole story: A lot of armies, he said, had gone by, and a carriage had come, and the princess had wept over him and cried out: "You and I are both to be greatly pitied."

Meanwhile the viceroy looked and he saw the kerchief lying next to him.

He asked: "Where is this from?"

The servant answered: "She left it there and she wrote on it with tears."

The viceroy took the kerchief and held it up against the sun.

He began seeing letters of the alphabet and he read what was written there: all her lamenting and shouting.

She had also written that she was no longer in the castle, and that he should look for a gold mountain with a pearl castle: "That's where you'll find me."

The viceroy then left the servant and went looking for her on his own.

He went around for years, looking for her.

The viceroy thought to himself: "In settlements you certainly won't find a gold mountain with a pearl castle"—for he was experienced with maps. "So I'll go looking in deserts."

And he went around deserts and looked for many, many years.

At last he saw a big man whose size was anything but human.

And the man was carrying a big tree, bigger than any tree found in settlements. And he asked the viceroy: "Who are you?"

The viceroy answered:

"I am a human being."

The big man was surprised. He said:

"I've been in the desert for such a long time, and I've never seen a human being here."

The viceroy told him the whole story and said he was looking for a gold mountain with a pearl castle.

The big man answered: "None of that exists. They've filled your head with nonsense, because there's no such mountain and no such castle."

The viceroy began weeping bitterly; indeed, he wept very bitterly.

Then he said:

"They *do* exist. They must be somewhere."

And he, the strange man whom the viceroy had met, disagreed with the viceroy. He said that they had told the viceroy a nonsensical story.

But the viceroy kept arguing that it was true.

The wild man then said to him: "In my opinion it's nonsense. But since you insist, I am the lord of all animals, and for your sake I will call them all together. For they run all over the world, and perhaps one of them knows about the mountain with the castle."

He called together all the animals, big and little, and asked them.

And none of them, they answered, had seen those things.

So the wild man said to the viceroy: "You see, they told you nonsense. If you want my advice, turn back. You will find nothing. For none of those things exist in the world."

But the viceroy insisted very strongly and said: "They *must* exist."

The wild man said to the viceroy:

"I have a brother in the desert. He is the lord of all birds. Perhaps the birds know because they fly through the air. Perhaps they've seen the mountain with the castle. So go to my brother and tell him that I've sent you to him."

The viceroy went about for many, many years, looking for the brother.

He again found a very big man.

And the man was again carrying a big tree.

And this man asked him the same questions as the first man had asked.

The viceroy told him the whole story and said that the man's brother had sent him.

And the man disagreed with the viceroy, for such things, he said, did not exist.

But the viceroy insisted: "They *must* exist!"

So the man said to the viceroy:

"I am the lord of all birds. I'll call them—perhaps they know."

And he called all birds, big and little, and asked all of them.

And they answered that they knew nothing about the mountain with the castle.

The wild man then said to the viceroy:

"So you see there's no such mountain with a castle in the world. If you want my advice, turn back. For none of those things exist anywhere."

But the viceroy insisted and said that they did exist in the world.

So the second man said to the viceroy:

"You can find my brother further on in the desert. He is the lord of all winds. They run all over the world. Perhaps they know."

And the viceroy went about for many, many years, looking for the third brother.

He again found a big man

And the man was also carrying a big tree.

And he asked the viceroy the same questions.

And the viceroy told him the whole story.

The man also disagreed with him.

But the viceroy also insisted very strongly.

So the third brother said that he would help him: He would call together all the winds, and he would ask them.

And so he called them.

All the winds came.

And he asked them.

But none of them knew about the mountain with the castle.

So the third brother said to the viceroy:

"You see, you've been told nonsense."

The viceroy then began weeping bitterly and he said:

"I know that they *do* exist."

Meanwhile he saw another wind coming.

The lord of all winds was angry at the wind: "Why have you come so late? Didn't I order all winds to come? Why didn't you come with the rest?"

The wind answered: "I'm late because I had to carry a princess to a gold mountain with a pearl castle."

The viceroy was utterly delighted that he had finally located what he was looking for.

And the lord of winds asked the wind: "What is honored there? What things are greatly valued, greatly esteemed?"

The wind answered:

"Everything is greatly valued there."

So the lord of winds said to the viceroy:

"You've been looking for such a long time. You've gone to so much trouble, and you may be hindered for lack of money. So I'm going to give you a vessel: Whenever you put your hand inside it, you will take out money."

And he ordered the wind to carry the viceroy to the gold mountain.

So the tempest came and carried him.

He brought him to the gates.

Armies were standing there and they wouldn't let the viceroy enter the town.

So he put his hand inside the vessel and took out money and bribed them and he entered the town.

And the town was very beautiful.

The viceroy went to a rich man, who took him in as a boarder.

For the viceroy knew he would be spending a long time here, since it would require a lot of wisdom and a lot of intelligence to take the princess away.

He did not say how the viceroy took her away.
But in the end he did take her away.
And look at the introduction:
You shall see wondrous
allusions to the story.

RABBI NAKHMAN OF BRASLEV (1772–1810)

A Tale of a King and an Emperor

See the note at the beginning of "A Tale of a Lost Princess," page 130.

This tale, with which Ansky was familiar, features the motif of fathers promising a betrothal between their children, whereby one father breaks his word—with dire consequences—but, unlike The Dybbuk, *with a happy ending.*

Here is the story.

Once there was an emperor. The emperor had no children.

There was also a king. The king also had no children.

So the emperor set out into the world, hoping to find advice or a remedy so that he might have children.

And the king also set out into the world.

The two of them came together at an inn without knowing about one another.

The emperor saw that the other man had regal bearing. So he asked him about that, and the man revealed that he was a king.

And the king also saw that the emperor had regal bearing. So the emperor also revealed who he was.

And they told one another that they were traveling in order to have children. So they made an agreement: When they came home, and one wife bore a boy and the other a girl, they would marry the two children to each other.

The emperor then returned home and he had a daughter.

And the king returned home and he had a son.

But the king and the emperor forgot all about their agreement.

And the emperor sent his daughter away to study.

And the king also sent his son away to study.

And the children came to study with the same teacher and they fell deeply in love with one another. So they privately agreed to get married.

137

And the prince took a ring and slipped it over her finger, and in this way they became engaged.

The emperor then sent for his daughter and had her brought home.

And the king also sent for his son and had him brought home.

The emperor's daughter received marriage proposals. But she turned them all down because of her agreement with the prince.

And the prince missed her badly.

And the princess was also very sad all the time.

So the emperor took her to his courts and his palaces and showed the girl her grandeur.

But she remained as sad as ever.

And the prince missed her so badly that he fell sick. And no matter how much they asked him: "Why are you sick?," he refused to answer.

They then told his personal servant: "Perhaps you can find out what's wrong."

And he told them that he knew. For the servant had been with the prince when he had been studying with the teacher. And the servant told them why the prince was sick.

And now the king remembered his agreement with the emperor. So he went and wrote to the emperor, telling him to prepare the wedding, since the marriage had been agreed on long ago.

The emperor, however, no longer wanted the marriage. But he couldn't go back on his word. So he wrote to the king, asking him to send his son to the emperor. If the son knew how to rule countries, the emperor would let him marry his daughter.

So the king sent his son to the emperor, and the emperor tested the boy.

The emperor put the boy in a room and gave him various documents about all sorts of government business to see whether he could rule the country.

And the boy yearned to see the girl. But he couldn't see her.

One day, when he was walking past a mirror wall, he saw the girl and he fainted. So she went over to him and revived him. And she told him that she didn't want any marriage proposals because of her agreement with him.

He then said to her: "What can we do? Your father won't hear of it."

She replied that she would remain loyal to the prince. After discussing it, they decided to sail away on the sea.

And they hired a boat and sailed out on the sea.

Eventually they wanted to go ashore. And upon setting foot on dry land, they saw a forest. So they went into it.

The princess took off the ring and gave it to the prince and she lay down to sleep.

Later on, when the prince saw that she would soon awaken, he placed the ring next to her. In a while they stood up and went back to the boat.

Then the princess remembered that they had forgotten the ring. So she sent him back to get it.

He went back. But he couldn't find the place. He went to a different place, but he still couldn't find the ring.

He went from one place to the next until he lost his way entirely and was unable to return to the boat.

The princess went to look for him and she also lost her way.

The prince wandered about for a long time. And then he saw a path. He followed the path to a settlement. Once there, he had no livelihood. So he became a servant.

Meanwhile the princess, too, had been wandering for a long time. Finally she decided to sit on the beach. So she went to the sea. And there, on the shore, she found trees and fruit. So she sat down next to them.

During the day she would walk along the beach, hoping to find someone. She sustained herself with the fruit of the trees. And at night she would climb a tree to be safe from the wild beasts.

Now there happened to be a great merchant, a very great merchant, and he did business all over the world. And this merchant had an only son. The merchant himself had grown old.

One day the son said to his father: "Since you're old and I'm still young, your custodians won't entrust me with any business dealings as yet. And what will happen? You'll die, I'll remain alone, and I won't know what to do. So give me a ship with merchandise and I'll sail across the sea and get experience in doing business."

His father, the merchant, then gave him a ship with merchandise, and the son went to all sorts of countries and he sold his merchandise and bought other merchandise and he was successful.

One day, while sailing, he saw the trees where the princess was sitting. The merchant's son and his crew thought that this was a settlement. And they wanted to go ashore. As they drew close, however, they saw that these were trees, and they wanted to continue sailing.

Meanwhile the merchant's son had a good look and he saw a tree, and there was someone perched in the tree. The merchant's son wondered if he was mistaken, and he told the others who were with him. They also looked and they likewise saw a person sitting in the tree. So they decided to explore the matter.

They sent someone out in a small boat. And they kept watch to make sure he didn't get lost, so that he could reach the tree. And the messenger reached the tree and he saw that someone was perched up there. And the messenger went back and reported what he had seen.

The merchant's son then went on his own. And he saw the princess, who was sitting in the tree.

He asked her to come down. She told him that she wouldn't board the ship unless he gave her his word that he wouldn't touch her until they came home and were married according to religious law.

So he gave her his word. And she boarded the ship.

He now saw that she could play musical instruments and speak many languages, so he was delighted that she had chanced his way.

When they were approaching his town, she told him that in all fairness he ought to go home and have his father and his relatives and all his friends come to meet her because she was an important woman. And after that she would tell him who she was. For she had stipulated that he was not to ask her who she was until the wedding. And he had agreed.

And she also said to him now: "In all fairness, since you're bringing home a woman like me you should get all the sailors drunk: They should know that their merchant is marrying such a woman."

He did as she said.

He took some very fine wine that he had aboard ship and he served it to the sailors. And they got very drunk.

Then he went home to bring the news to his father and his relatives.

And the sailors went ashore drunkenly and collapsed drunkenly and lay drunkenly on the ground.

In the meantime, while the entire family was preparing to go and meet her, the princess unmoored the ship, unfurled the canvases, and sailed away. The family then came but found no one there.

The father was very angry with his son, and the son shouted: "Believe me, I brought home a ship filled with merchandise."

But they saw nothing.

The son said: "Go ask the sailors."

So the father went to ask them, but he found them drunk on the ground. The drunken sailors were dead to the world and they slept on the ground for a long time. Then they awoke. The father asked them about the ship. But they knew nothing about what had happened to them. They knew only that they had brought a ship with everything. But they didn't know where the woman was.

The merchant was very angry with his son and he drove him out of his home and told him never to show his face there again.

The son left and he began wandering all over the world.

And the princess was sailing across the sea.

Now once there was a king.

And the king built palaces for himself by the sea, for he liked building palaces on the shore because of the sea air and because of the passing ships.

And she, the princess, was sailing across the sea, and her ship drew near one of the king's palaces.

And when the king looked, he saw a ship sailing without a steersman and without people aboard. He thought he was mistaken, so he told his servants to look.

And they saw the same things as he did.

And the princess drew near the palace. She wondered what the palace might offer her. And she started turning away.

But the king sent out his men, and they brought her in, and she was taken to his chamber.

The king had no wife, he had never been able to find a match. For the one he had wanted had not wanted him, and the other way around.

And when the princess reached his chamber, she told him to swear that he wouldn't touch her until they were married according to religious law.

And the king swore that he wouldn't touch her.

And she told him it would be better if he didn't open the ship and didn't even touch it and let it be until the wedding, so that everyone could see how much merchandise she had brought, and so that no one could say he was marrying a market woman.

The king promised to do as she asked.

And the king then wrote to the rulers of all countries, inviting them to his wedding, and he built palaces for them.

And the girl asked the king to bring her eleven ladies to attend to her. And the king ordered his servants to do so, and they brought her eleven very important daughters of noblemen, and they built a separate palace for each lady.

And the princess, too, had a palace of her own.

One day she told the ladies to accompany her to the sea. They went with her and they played with her there. They would get together and play all sorts of instruments for her and spend time with her there.

And she gave them some of the wine she had on the ship. The ladies got drunk and fell on the deck and remained lying there.

And the princess went and unmoored the boat and unfurled the canvases and escaped on the ship.

And when the king and his men came back, they saw that the ship was gone. They were terrified.

And the king cried out to his men: "Don't break the news to her suddenly. She'll feel very upset after losing such a valuable ship."

For the king didn't know that she had escaped on the ship. He thought she was still in her chamber. He was also afraid she might think that the king had given the ship away.

He ordered his servants to send her one of the noble ladies-in-waiting to tell her everything in a sagacious manner.

They came to her chamber but they found no one.

And they found no one in the other chamber.

And they found no one in any of the eleven chambers.

And they saw no people anywhere.

So the king and his men decided to send her an old noblewoman at night to tell her.

And they went to her chamber and they found no one there. They were terrified.

The ladies' fathers were in the habit of exchanging letters with their daughters, and when they saw that they were sending letters but getting no letters whatsoever from their daughters, they got up and went to see them. And when they failed to find a single one of their daughters, they grew furious.

They wanted to expel the king for they were the lords of the realm. They said: "What has the king done to deserve expulsion? The king has violated the law."

They decided to dethrone him and expel him from the country. So they dethroned him and expelled him, and he went into exile.

Meanwhile the princess, who had escaped with the eleven ladies-in-waiting, was sailing on the ship.

When the ladies woke up, they continued playing as earlier, for they didn't realize the ship had left the shore. Then they said to the princess: "Let's go home."

And she answered: "Let's spend a little more time here."

Now a tempest sprang up. And the ladies said to the princess: "Let's go home."

She announced to them that the ship had long since left the shore.

They asked her why she had done that.

She said she had been afraid that the ship might be shattered by a tempest. So she had had to unmoor it and spread the sails.

And they sailed on the sea, the princess and the eleven ladies, and they played various instruments. And as they sailed, they sighted a palace. And the ladies said to her:

"Let's go to the palace."

But she refused. She said she regretted going to the other palace, the palace of the king who had wanted to marry her.

Then they saw something like a small island in the sea and they headed toward it.

And there were twelve pirates on the island. And the pirates wanted to kill them.

The princess asked: "Who is the highest among you?"

They pointed to the man in question.

She then asked him: "What do you people do?"

He replied that they were pirates.

She said to him: "We're pirates too. Except that you are pirates with your strength and we are pirates with our wisdom. For we know languages and we can play instruments. So what would you gain by killing us? Marry us instead, and you'll have wives and great riches."

And she showed them the merchandise in the ship, for the merchant's son had filled it with very great riches.

The pirates went along with what she had said, and they likewise showed their treasures and took the women around to all their places.

The men agreed not to marry the women all at the same time. Rather, the weddings would take place one at a time. Each pirate would pick a lady according to his station.

Next the princess said she would regale them with very fine wine, which she had on the ship but never used. The wine was concealed until the Good Lord sent the princess her destined husband.

And she served the pirates the wine in twelve beakers and said that each man should toast the other eleven. And the pirates drank and grew drunk and collapsed.

The princess then said to her companions: "Now each of you go and kill your bridegroom."

So they went and they killed them all.

After that, they found great riches beyond the wealth of any king. And they decided to take no copper and no silver, but only gold and diamonds.

And on their ship they threw out things that were not so valuable and they filled it with expensive things, with gold and diamonds that they had found on the island.

They also decided not to dress as women anymore. They made the sort of clothes worn by German men and, disguising themselves as men, they sailed off on the boat.

Now there was an old king. And the old king had an only son. He had his son marry and then he passed the kingdom on to him.

One day the prince said to his father that he wanted to go sailing on the sea with his wife and get her used to the sea air, just in case they ever had to escape by sea—God forbid!

And the new king and his wife and the lords of the realm sailed off on a ship. And they were all very cheerful and frolicsome. They grew so frivolous that they said they ought to take off all their clothes—the new king and the lords. And that was what they did. They stripped down to their shirts.

And they vied to see who could climb the mast. And the new king began clambering up. As he did so, who should arrive but the emperor's daughter on her ship. And she saw the ship carrying the young king and the lords of the realm.

At first she was afraid to draw near. But then she came a bit closer. And she saw that the people on that ship were frolicking about. So she knew that these were no pirates. And she drew even closer.

The princess, pointing to the young but bald king, then said to her followers: "Do you see that bald man climbing the mast? I can throw him into the water."

"How is that possible? They're still very far away from us."

She replied that she had a burning glass, with which she would throw him down.

She decided that she wouldn't do it until he reached the top of the mast. Otherwise he would fall into the ship. But if he fell from the top of the mast, he would fall into the sea.

So she waited until he reached the top. Then she took the burning glass and focused it on his head until his brain began to boil—and he fell into the sea.

When the people aboard the young king's ship saw him fall into the sea, they were up in arms. They didn't know what to do. How could they sail home? The old king would die of grief.

They decided to approach the other ship, the princess's ship. Perhaps there was a doctor aboard and he could advise them. And they drew near the other ship.

The people on the young king's ship told the ladies and the princess not to be afraid, they wouldn't harm them. And they asked: "Do you possibly have a doctor there who could advise us?"

And they told them the entire story and said that the young king had fallen into the sea. So the princess told them to get him out of the sea.

They went and found him and took him out of the sea.

The princess then felt his pulse and said: "His brain has burned."

So they went and tore open his head and they saw that the "doctor" was right. They were terrified and utterly amazed that the "doctor" was correct. So they asked her to go home with them and become the young king's doctor and enjoy great respect and honor. But she refused. She said that she was no doctor and that she just happened to know about these things.

Now the people on the young king's ship were unwilling to go home. So the two ships sailed together.

The lords of the realm wanted the young king's wife to marry the doctor, who was actually the princess in men's clothing. They thought "he" was a doctor because they saw that he was very learned. They wanted to make the doctor their king and to kill the old king.

That was what the lords of the realm wanted, but they were ashamed to tell the queen to marry a doctor.

However, the queen also greatly liked the idea of marrying the doctor. But she was afraid of the inhabitants of her country—they might not want the doctor as their king.

So they decided to throw a number of balls, where they would discuss the matter while drinking amid the festivities. And they threw a ball in each home on a different day.

When it was the "doctor's" (that is, the princess's) turn to throw a ball, she served them some of her wine. They got drunk. And amid the festivities they cried: "How wonderful it would be if the queen married the doctor."

The doctor (that is, the princess) responded: "It would certainly be wonderful, but it shouldn't be discussed in a drunken state."

The queen then said that it would be wonderful if she married the doctor, but the inhabitants of the country would have to agree.

The doctor said: "It would certainly be wonderful, but it shouldn't be discussed by drunken people."

Later, after sobering up, the lords remembered what they had said while drunk and they were ashamed in front of the queen. But then they recalled that the queen had said the same thing.

The queen likewise remembered what she had said in front of them while drunk and she was very ashamed. But then she recalled that they had said the same thing.

And so now they discussed it in a sober state. And they agreed on the marriage.

The queen got engaged to the presumed doctor (that is, the princess) and they went back to the queen's country.

And when the inhabitants saw them coming, they were very merry, for a long time had passed since the young king had sailed away, and they hadn't known where he was, and the old king had already died.

However, the inhabitants saw that the young king, who had been their king, had not come back. So they asked: "Where is our king?"

The lords of the realm told them the entire story: The young king had died, and they had taken on a new king, who had come back with them—the doctor (that is, the princess).

And the inhabitants were delighted to have a new king.

And the new king (that is, the princess) ordered a proclamation in all countries: All strangers, whether escapees or refugees, were invited to the wedding. They should not be absent and they would receive great presents.

The new king (that is, the princess) also decreed that wells be dug all around the city, so that if anyone wanted to drink, he wouldn't have to go very far, he could find a well close by.

The new king also decreed that "his" portrait be placed at every well and that guards be stationed by each portrait. And if anyone came and made a face, that is, an unhappy grimace, he should be arrested and sent to prison.

And these orders were carried out.

And all three people showed up: The first prince, who was the real fiancé of the princess, who had become king of this country; the merchant's son, who had been driven out by his father because of this princess, who had escaped with his ship and all his merchandise; and the king, who had likewise been driven out because of the princess, who had escaped from him with the eleven ladies-in-waiting.

And each of these three people recognized her face in the portrait. And they studied the portrait and recalled what they had gone through and they were very unhappy. So they were promptly arrested and sent to prison.

During the wedding, the king (that is, the princess) ordered the prisoners to be brought before "him." So all three were brought in.

And she recognized them, but they did not recognize her for she was dressed like a man. The princess then talked to them.

First she spoke to the king, who had been driven out because of her: "You, king, you were driven out because of the eleven ladies who disappeared. Here are your ladies." (For the elevens ladies were with her.) "Go home to your country and to your reign."

Next she turned to the merchant's son: "You, merchant. Your father drove you out because you lost your ship and all your merchandise. But since your money has been piling up for such a long time, you have far more wealth in the ship than before, a thousand times more." For the ship contained the great wealth that had belonged to the pirates.

"And you, prince," she said to the first prince, who was her real fiancé. "Come here. Let's go home."

And they returned home.

Amen.

AIZIK-MEYER DIK (1814–1893)

Pious Tírtse

"Pious Tírtse" was published in Warsaw in 1856. This story, which S. Ansky must have been familiar with, contains the motif of soulmates joined in the afterlife. This motif figured among the various themes that the dramatist wove into his play. See the headnote on the next story.

A lovely tale that took place in the days of King Solomon—may he rest in peace. It teaches us how our ancestors raised their children, how they arranged matches for them, and how true and loving a bride and groom were, and even more so a husband and wife.

An immense and powerful monarch was King Solomon, the son of David—May he rest in peace. King Solomon ruled over many lands and distant islands. And the Jews were very happy in his days. The Jews also settled in foreign countries, where they lived very serenely. These countries included Tyre, Spain, Arabia, and Greece, and the Jews engaged in commerce throughout the Mediterranean, as far as Gibraltar. They also sailed across the ocean, as is written in our Holy Scriptures: "And King Solomon did build a ship on the banks of the Red Sea in the land of Edom."

In his tome, *The Book of the Ritual Bath of Israel,* Menashe ben Israel says that Ophir was the original site of America but was forgotten until three centuries ago, when a great skipper named Americo gave the land of Ophir a new name: America.

Our Jews were great merchants and took long trips, on both land and sea, and, as our sages put it: "They did delight in their commerce."

And Israelites did dwell among Arabs and in the vast desert—Jews lived among Arabs and in the Sahara, which is nothing but a sandy steppe. The sand is very fine and dry, and the desert is hundreds of leagues wide and long—it is known as the sea of sand. When the wind blows, the air gets charged with sand, so that it feels as if sand were raining down from the heavens, and large hills of sand keep piling up. Pity the travelers who get caught in such a storm—they are swallowed up and buried alive and their bodies lie there for centuries and centuries without decaying, for the sand is very hot and dry. And once they are found, they look as if they have just fallen asleep.

Many such accidents have occurred, and I have talked about that in many other stories. So at this point I only wish to remind you that this sea of sand contains numerous "islands"—that is, segments of land several square leagues in area, filled with black soil and green grass and with the loveliest plants in the world. There are also very good wellsprings here and all kinds of fruit trees. People live here, and they lack for nothing. The caravans—that is, the trains of camels—haul endless amounts of merchandise across the desert and to distant countries. The travelers rest at these islands, where they purchase food and water for the rest of their journeys. In Arabic these islands are called oases. Various Arabic tribes live here, and each tribe is governed by a ruler known as the sheik.

And in these oases—In these islands many Jews have settled, and they still live there today. Like the Arabs they raise sheep, and some Jews are great merchants, who journey to distant countries in huge caravans.

In olden days, long ago, during the reign of King Solomon, in one of the oases of the tribe of Vahabites, there lived a Jew named Amihud ben Azaria of the Tribe of Zebulun. Amihud was a rich merchant with more than a hundred camels, which carried all sorts of wares to the most distant countries. He dealt in gold dust and ostrich plumes, in spices and carmine. Amihud also had a lot of male and female servants. He was very pious and decent, and his name was renowned and respected among all the Jews and Arabs who lived in those oases. If two people had a disagreement, he would preside over the case. And he sometimes even made peace between warring Arab tribes, who shed a lot of blood; they abided by his decisions for he was very popular among them and his counsel was very wise and compelling.

He had almost no children—only a daughter, who was lovelier than the roses that bloom in Sharon and more beautiful than the flowers that bloom in the valley. Her name was Tírtse. She was pious and intelligent and also an excellent housekeeper. She would usually sit at the spinning wheel with her maids, spinning and weaving or else going to the well on her own, like our Mother Rebecca (may she rest in peace).

In those times, Jewish girls had a different upbringing than today. They didn't keep shops or peddle wares. They weren't like our present daughters, who waste hours on end in front of mirrors and who get embroidery lessons but can't even patch a shirt or darn a sock. Idleness makes such a girl weak and sickly, and soon after her wedding she has to be surrounded by maids and wet nurses. No, things were different back then. Our ancient forebears taught their daughters how to be good housekeepers, as we find in the writings of King Solomon (may he rest in peace), in his chapter on a "woman of valor." He describes the right kind of wife and tells us how lucky a man is when he has one. Back then, no decent girl was ever idle. She would spin, weave, sew, and even cook just like a maidservant. She was simply more pious than they and more virtuous.

Matchmaking was also different in those times. When parents looked for a son-in-law, they would pick only a man who would keep her properly and walk in God's ways, and who came from a decent family. They didn't want an idler, who'd be a burden on them, living with his in-laws and fathering children at their expense. Nor did the parents have to travel to faraway towns in search of a bridegroom. They would always find one within their own tribe, their own clan, their own town. And divorce was rare because the husband and the wife were well acquainted by the time they married.

When Amihud was ready to give away his only child, Tírtse, he didn't have to send marriage brokers to foreign places. He had a handsome boy in his own household, a boy named Eliom, the son of a farmer called Akhiezer the Zebulonite. Akhiezer lived in an oasis some ten leagues from the wealthy merchant's home. The farmer had always been a God-fearing man. He wasn't rich, but neither was he poor. He owned enough fields, a vineyard, two hundred sheep, a hundred goats, and fifty oxen. And God had blessed him with ten sons, all of them healthy and hard-working, and they all walked in God's ways.

But when Akhiezer saw that his family was large and his income small, he hired five of his sons out to other decent people, so that the boys could make something of themselves. That was how his second oldest, Eliom, entered Amihud's household. He served him with honesty and loyalty, and God was with Eliom in everything he did.

Now Eliom did find favor in the eyes of Amihud—His employer was so pleased with him that he made him head of the staff. After that he began sending him with merchandise to distant countries. The boy became very successful, and Amihud grew to love him as much as he loved his own daughter. Eliom was very handsome and virtuous and he also found favor in the eyes of Tírtse, who loved him as much as her father did, which greatly delighted Amihud.

Now upon a certain morrow—One day, when Eliom was preparing to go on a long journey with his employer's camels, Amihud said to him: "My dear son, I'm old, I don't know when I'll die, and my daughter Tírtse has reached the age at which I have to give her a husband. So my wife and I have agreed that—if you like—you can be our son-in-law."

And these words did gladden the youth's heart—Eliom was so pleased that he hugged and kissed Amihud, and there was deep joy in the house. That night they celebrated the engagement with great fanfare, inviting the most prominent Jews and Arabs. Amihud wanted the wedding to take place that same week, but Eliom said:

"No, my dear father-in-law, first I have to notify my parents. I can't get married without them."

And Amihud said: "You're right, my boy. I'm happy to see that you care about your parents. It shows that you will also greatly respect me— and that is what I desire."

Now upon the morrow—The next day the bride had the groom put on expensive clothes that she had made with her own hands. She also gave him a precious ring with her name engraved on it and she presented him with costly gifts for his parents.

After several days of rejoicing, she ordered her servants to saddle a valuable Arab horse so that Eliom might ride out to his parents and bring them back for the wedding. Five mornings later, Eliom said goodbye to his father-in-law and his fiancée, who wept bitterly and begged him not to keep her waiting:

"Why are you crying, darling? My father lives only ten leagues from here, and my horse flies as swiftly as a bird. I'll be back in two days, and on the third day we'll be joined forever."

And Tírtse spake—Tírtse said: "You may be right, but I'm nervous, and I have a queasy feeling in my heart. I've been in love with you not just for a day or two but for a long time, and I've always prayed to God for you whenever you've traveled. But now my heart won't quiet down. I'd rather we sent out a servant to get your parents while you stayed here until the wedding—may Heaven preserve us!"

"No, my dear and darling Tírtse, I have to visit my parents myself. It won't take long. I want to be the first to tell them about my happiness. Goodbye, my precious. I'll be back. Wait for me until—"

But she broke in, though sounding as if she didn't wish to speak: "I'll wait for you even till I'm old and gray. You're the only husband in the world for me. Anyone else would be foreign."

She burst into tears and wished him a safe trip. Then she mournfully reentered the house. Her father summoned all her girlfriends so they would talk to her and while away the time. But she was very gloomy.

In the household everything was prepared for the wedding. They slaughtered a lot of sheep and they joyfully pitched a huge tent for the new couple. Tírtse spent those two days in great misery. The third day dawned, but Eliom still wasn't here.

"Oh, how awful I feel, how awful everything is! There was a storm on both nights. Oh, I don't want to talk about that—no, I don't want to be in doubt any longer. Quick, Tevye, my loyal servant! Saddle a horse and go to the oasis, to my Eliom's parents, and find out why he's taking so long. Tell him I'm awfully worried about him and scared. Tell him to come quickly—right away."

And the servant raced like an eagle. That evening he returned with the sad news: Eliom had never reached his parents, they had first learned from the servant that their son had gotten engaged. The parents had been both delighted and terrified.

"Oh, God!" Tírtse exclaimed in a tearful voice. "My heart hasn't fooled me. My Eliom is gone. He was torn to shreds by a wild beast or carried off by a storm. Or maybe he was captured by highwaymen. But I won't forget him. My grief will go on for as long as I live."

And Tírtse screamed and lamented. And her parents and her friends wept with her, and so did all the inhabitants of the oasis, both Jews and Arabs.

They sent out a hundred horsemen, they combed the entire steppe between the two oases, but Eliom was nowhere to be found.

Tírtse now removed all the jewels from her body and put on mourning and sat down in her small chamber, and for many days she and her girlfriends wept for her beloved Eliom. Her tears never dried and her lips never laughed. The world forgot all about her, as if she were dead, and her ears grew deaf to all pleasures and consolations.

Even when King Solomon (may he rest in peace) finished building the Temple, and all Jews from all countries came to Jerusalem to celebrate with song and dance, and joy was in all hearts—even then Tírtse remained in her small chamber and kept waiting for her bridegroom "like a maiden weeping for her first beloved."

Many years wore by, Tírtse's parents died, all her friends got married, and she still sat alone in her chamber, devastated, mourning, and repeating Eliom's last words to her: "Wait for me until—" And she kept repeating her answer: "Till I'm old and gray."

And she waited for her beloved as she had promised him. Her heart still nourished the hope that he would keep his promise and come back to her, for he had always been a man of his word. "No," she told herself.

"I'll stay true to him. And he'll keep his word too. If he's been captured by a savage Arab, he'll shake off his chains and come to me. Even if he's found death, that won't prevent him from keeping his promise."

And she waited and waited and tearfully peered in the direction in which her beloved had gone. King Solomon's reign had ended in its fortieth year, and his son Rehoboam had replaced him as monarch—and Eliom still didn't return. The Ten Tribes had already separated from the kingdom of the House of David, and Eliom still wasn't here. Rehoboam, king of the Ten Tribes, had already put up the two golden calves: one in the House of God and the other in the House of Justice—and Eliom still didn't show up.

And upon a certain day—One day a great storm arose in the steppe and it flung and hurled the sand about, the way a tempest throws the ocean waves. The storm toppled hill after hill and carried a great deal of sand to the oasis where Tírtse lived. And the wind also brought the body of a young man. The storm died down, and the corpse remained lying not far from Tírtse's home. A number of people clustered around the body and gazed at it, but did not recognize it. However, an old, gray-haired woman, bent with grief and old age and clutching a stick, came hobbling over. The instant she saw the corpse she recognized it.

"Oh, God! Oh, God!" she said. "What do I see? That's my Eliom. The righteous keep their word even in death."

The old woman was Tírtse, and she had recognized Eliom by the clothes that she herself had made for him. She had also recognized him by her ring. And he, too, was still the same: He looked as if he had fallen asleep.

A storm had buried him in the sand and a storm had now brought him back.

And Tírtse, who had no tears left in her eyes and no strength left to lament, lay down and put her head on his chest. And all she said was:

"God is just in all in His ways."

And she did not stand up again.

The two of them were united in one grave, which was marked by a single headstone.

AIZIK-MEYER DIK (1814–1893)

The Gílgul, or The Wandering Soul

Released by the Tsarist Censor in 1867

During the nineteenth century, the maskils—the followers of the Haskala (Jewish Enlightenment)—hated Yiddish, but realized there was no other language for addressing the Jewish masses in Eastern Europe. The enlighteners also hated irrational fiction, especially the Hasidic wonder tales; but the supernatural, which they spoofed, was a familiar terrain for their readers. One of the most ferocious, most prolific, and also most widely read authors was Aizik-Meyer Dik. His novella The Gílgul *was adapted from a Hebrew satire,* The Wandering of a Soul *(Gílgul Nefesh, 1845), penned by Yitskhok Erter (1791–1851), a highly influential author, who viewed mockery as an effective weapon of enlightenment. For A. B. Gotlober's somewhat different though equally mordant adaptation of Erter's narrative, see Joachim Neugroschel,* Great Tales of Jewish Fantasy and the Occult, *(New York: Overlook Press, 1987).*

This is a horrifying story told by a transmigrating spirit that assumed eighteen different incarnations—humans, beasts, birds, and fish—through some five centuries. Since he has not found his merited place in eternity, we should publish his story so that everyone can read it and draw a moral, thereby enabling this wandering soul to rest in peace.

A Word to the Reader

Our Holy Torah says (Deut. 18:13): "Thou shalt be perfect with the Lord our God." Rashi interprets that as follows:

"Walk with God in honesty and sincerity and do not try to prophesy. Receive with simplicity everything that happens to you."

This means that you should place all your trust in God and not try to read the future. You should pin your hopes on the Good Lord and receive everything with the simplicity of your soul. In other words, you should never say that this is the wrong time to begin something. Such is the habit of wizards and false miracle workers: They make shoddy statements merely to fool the world. Hence, the Torah says (Deut. 18:10–11): "There shall not be found among you anyone that useth divination or an observer of times, or an enchanter, or a witch, or a charmer, or a consulter with familiar spirits, or a wizard, or a necromancer."

That was what the ancient idolaters were. And in talking about Hasids, rebbes, wonder workers, and baal-shems (miracle makers), we mean only the deceivers, impostors, and wrongdoers, who pretend to be good and pious Jews, but are exactly the opposite. They bamboozle the common people, they promise that barren women will bear children, that sick men will recover by using amulets and pages torn from holy books. But the only goal of these tricksters is money. God forbid, however, that I should put down genuine rebbes and Hasids. After all, the word *Hasid* is Hebrew for "truly good and pious."

And when we talk about physicians here, we don't mean those who strive to understand the illness and the patient; we mean only those who are out for rubles. But this does not apply to *all* physicians—God forbid!

The same holds for tax collectors, including collectors of the tax on kosher meat. Our pen is aimed purely at the wicked ones, those who flout both Jewish and secular laws.

All writers in all countries, such as France and Russia, have practiced criticism—made fun, that is, of bad and false people with evil habits. But they never implied that their entire nation was wicked.

I was a physician—a surgeon. Or in plain Yiddish: a sawbones, specializing in the treatment of injuries. The town physician Knopatsky, whom people addressed as "doctor," considered himself much greater than I because he had the right to speak publicly about things he knew absolutely nothing about. Nevertheless, I could treat people just as effectively. The patients who died from my remedies could have survived no more than the ones who were killed by his prescriptions. And whenever I had to follow his advice, the patient in question was doomed.

The only difference between me and Knopatsky was that I walked to my patients while he rode in a horse-drawn coach. You see, people thought that wisdom was based on how many horses you owned: the more horses, the greater your wisdom. This doctor normally tended the rich, and so he became rich himself. In general, a dead person costs the rich a lot more than he does the poor. I, however, would visit only the poor, and they secured death for nothing.

Now one day I happened to walk past a house where a patient of mine had died—not suddenly but only after I had treated him. He had been rich, but my therapy had lasted barely two days. A great many women—neighbors and relatives and ordinary wise and pious women—were clustered around the patient, grieving. And they said to me: "He's still lying in bed, and you're silent? You call yourself a doctor? Why, you're a beggar, you're traveling on foot! Call a real physician! Call Dr. Knopatsky! He'll help all right!"

So Dr. Knopatsky came and with a doleful expression on his face he examined the patient. He then scrawled a prescription, saying that they should go to the pharmacy as fast as possible, obtain the medicine, and have the patient take it. And no sooner did he take it than he died.

Upon walking past the house after the funeral, I noticed a candle burning in the window together with a small glass of water and a small towel. The dead man's soul washed itself in the water and then dried itself with the towel. So I went over to the soul and said: "I'm delighted to see you. I truly believed I'd never meet you again in this world. You must know all kinds of secrets now, so please tell me if you know I'm not responsible for your death."

The soul replied: "Why do you ask? And if I know, will I make things right for you in this world? Or will I make things wrong for you if I say I don't know? The dead are always mute. They can't explain things to someone like you, someone who's got open eyes and open ears. That's why they can neither praise nor tarnish anyone. Only the living can bless you or curse you. So don't ask the dead, ask the living whether they hold you responsible for my death. You'll always remain free of responsibility, even if I know that it was only because of you that I passed away."

Verily I was astonished and I spake—Greatly surprised, I said: "When you were a doctor in your lifetime, what did you cure patients with if not brandy with honey and pepper added to make it tastier? I know you were a merchant. You bought and sold and borrowed, and people trusted you. Finally, after accumulating a large fortune, you told your creditors you'd lost all your money, and so you didn't repay a kopek to any of them."

The soul said: "If you really want to know what happened to me in this world, you first have to tell me how many years I lived."

I was floored by his request. "How am I supposed to know? I think that when you were sick, you told me you were seventy."

The soul responded: "It's true that I lived in that body for seventy years. But previously I spent several centuries in this world."

"What do you mean? Were you as old as Enosh or Methuselah? And besides, how can you live without a body? A soul without a body in this world—and a doctor to boot? That's the very opposite of our town physician: He's a body without a soul."

And the spirit did rejoin—The soul answered: "That's no surprise. I spent hundreds of years in this world, and like all human beings I had a body and a soul. Every time I died, the heavenly angels brought me back here in a different body—eighteen in all. My last reincarnation was as the man who just died because of your treatment."

I retorted: "You must be very wise, for you lived so many years, and each reincarnation took place in a different country. You probably understand what each person feels deep in his heart. I'd like to get on your good side so you can share some of your wisdom with me and tell me what happened to you in each reincarnation."

And the spirit did respond—The soul replied: "I'll do it because you were my doctor and you rescued me from that body, which was like a prison. Sit down and listen."

And the soul began telling me about everything it had experienced in its various bodies.

Prior to my genesis—Before I first saw the light of day as a person, my parents had had no children. My mother, who was deeply concerned about her failure to bear, wanted to consult a holy Hasidic leader and ask for help. But her husband refused to go because he didn't believe in them. So she traveled to the rebbe's court on her own. The rebbe blessed her, and she was no longer barren, while her husband, who didn't believe in the rebbe's power, remained sterile all his life.

I was a rebbe's child, and my birth was a miracle. I therefore had his nature and I grew up as a Hasid. I drank enough liquor, I left my father and mother, I eventually deserted my wife and child, and I traveled to the rebbe's court to hear his wisdom in the darkness, to snatch a sacred leftover from his plate. And the rebbe loved me for I was his kind of man. No one passed his stool as much as I did or cleansed himself as often. I splashed around so much in the ritual immersions that the whole bathhouse stank of me—far more than of other Hasids taking their ablutions.

When praying, I blared and bellowed like a wild bull, so that no one understood a single word. I never showed older people or scholars any respect or deference. When I sang the psalms, I shrieked like a savage beast. I jumped around, clapped my hands, and scurried back and forth like a lunatic. Anyone who heard me sing could have sworn that an owl and a crow were screeching from my throat. The noise spread far and wide, and I jumped on the table like a billy goat. And when my voice became hoarse and my tongue dried out, I wet my whistle with endless streams of liquor.

And it came to pass—One day, when I'd overimbibed, my innards caught fire, and an intense heat blasted from my mouth. The other Hasids surrounded me and poured an entire Red Sea down my throat— they considered that an antidote. But the masses of water failed to extinguish my fever. I burned to death, and so they delivered my eulogy.

After my soul left the Hasid's body, I turned into a frog, which jumped around like a Hasid and croaked and belched like a Hasid. But instead of liquor, I had to drink water. I was no longer a boozer, I now lived in swamps and filth. I alternated between hopping around on dry land and swimming in water. I kept moaning, groaning, and wailing, so that I deafened all ears. Every evening throughout the spring, my fellow frogs and I would gather and keep up the cacophony all night. Our voices rose and rose, and they reached the highest treetops, where the birds nested and the stork roosted. Now when the stork heard us, it came flying down and alighted in our swamp. This caused a great commotion among us, and each frog said to the next: "Just look at that bird. It's red and it's got beautiful eyes. Its legs and its beak are very long and purple, its wings are as black as coal, its neck and the rest of its plumage are snow-white."

All the frogs emerged from their holes in order to gawk at that beautiful bird. No sooner did the stork spot them than it devoured them— and myself too. Then, like a Hasid drinking liquor, it turned its mouth and its eyes toward the heavens, the better to get us down. And thanks to my Hasidism, I left the stork (which is known in Hebrew as *khasido*) and became a cantor in Poland.

And now it came to pass—When a frog becomes a cantor he's a lot happier, for a frog drinks only water and eats only soil, while a cantor sips the finest wines and liqueurs and dines on the choicest food at every wedding and every circumcision. A frog croaks for free, while a cantor won't open his mouth unless he's paid. As a cantor, I was hired sometimes for a whole year and sometimes just for a Sabbath. On one side of me stood the choir and on the other side a bass who roared like a lion. I held my hand on my cheek with my thumb squeezing my throat. Sometimes I'd warble a hymn at a cheerful party, where alcohol raised everyone's spirits; and sometimes I'd croon among girls and women dancing.

When I sang at the synagogue, my throat emitted all sorts of wild, loud, haphazard noises, and yet the place was mobbed. The people who couldn't get in surrounded the building, for they yearned to hear my voice, my trills. Rarely would a maven spend any time there. Upon hearing my very first notes, he would promptly take to his heels, exclaiming: "Only a fool can listen to a fool! He's got the voice of a frog and he shouts like a peasant—it's deafening!"

I didn't sing like a frog, though. For a frog drinks water and eats soil. But at every betrothal, at every wedding, I drank the choicest beverages and dined on the choicest delicacies. I gorged myself, I stuffed my gut like an ox, until one day I got sick. I took to my bed, and the doctor prescribed a vomitive. But I didn't want to throw up what I had thrown down into my belly. So I died.

I was now punished for misusing my holy voice for wicked ends, even singing for women and girls to make them like me, and I liked them too: I became a fish, which has no voice. I was mute and I drank water to boot—not kosher—after a lifetime as a big nosher.

Verily I did question the spirit—I asked the soul: "How come you're talking in rhymes?"

To which the soul replied: "My rhyme has its reason in every season, for when I was a cantor I would always banter. I'm used to having all the words sound alike."

The soul then went on with his story:

When the cantor did perish—When I kicked the bucket and turned into a fish, I no longer had a throat or lungs. I breathed through my cheeks, I wore scales like armor, I had fins instead of arms. I no longer had a thumb to stick under my throat. My one comfort was my big teeth, so I became a water wolf—a pike, which has very sharp teeth. I devoured a lot of worms and a lot of fish, including my own brothers, big and little children, with no distinction.

Then one fine day, I swallowed what seemed like a small worm, and it cost me my life because the worm was attached to a hook. The fisherman pulled me out of the water, took me home, and told his maid to cook me. No sooner had she thrust the knife into my belly than a voice emerged from my throat. The terrified maid shrieked bloody murder! This was no ordinary fish! Who'd ever heard of a dead fish yelling after a lifetime of silence? "The pike must be possessed by a gílgul! As sure as I'm alive, I heard the fish holler like a human being!"

The other members of the household were petrified and they consulted the rabbi: How should they deal with a fish that hollers like a human being? The rabbi perused many holy tomes and, after musing and mulling, he decreed that the fish should be buried like a normal human being.

So they dressed the fish in a winding sheet and buried it in the Jewish cemetery.

And the levy on light and on the flesh of clean animals—The tax on candles and on kosher meat was established in our country. A Jew came up with the idea and set forth a number of pertinent laws about collecting the tax. No Jew was spared. Each Jew had to cough up the money until he was broke. The inventor of that tax was a lot smarter than King Solomon (may he rest in peace). For Solomon, who spoke about trees, beasts, birds, worms, and fish, composed no more than one thousand and five songs; while the "sage" who talked about meat and candles earned a hundred thousand rubles. And these were his two children: the meat tax and the candle tax.

I call them his children because he himself fathered the task of taxation. And those two children are now the two pillars supporting the entire House of Israel. Indeed, they strengthen our religion far more than all our rabbis together. The rabbis expel and exclude and excommunicate any Jew who leaves the path of righteousness or flouts the religious laws. The tax collectors, for their part, are more pious and more devout. They never anathematize a single Jew. He can commit all the wicked deeds in the world, and they still regard him as a Jew so long as he owns up to being Jewish. He then has to fork over the meat tax like a true-blue Jew. They exempt him only if he gets baptized and no longer bears a Jewish name.

However, there is a huge difference between the meat tax and the candle tax. The latter is the right pillar and the former the left pillar. The candle tax is inflicted on anyone who's not been christened even if he doesn't keep the Sabbath, doesn't light the Sabbath candles—even if he's a pauper who has no money to buy candles with. They suck him dry, nor do they exempt widows and orphans.

As for the tax on kosher meat—it's squeezed out of all Jews unless they don't keep kosher. If a Jew twists the chicken's neck himself or can't afford to buy meat, then he won't be dunned by the tax collector.

Well, I acted the way a tax collector is supposed to act: I spared no one.

Verily I did question the spirit—I asked the soul: "Did you act according to our religious commandments? After all, the Torah stipulates that when a debtor takes collateral from a pauper, he must not enter his home: He must wait until the pauper brings out the surety to his debtor."

The soul replied: "What a bright idea! A fine figure I'd cut if I waited until he brought it out himself! I'd have to cool my heels for a whole year and catch my death of cold! Nope! My men, all of them superpious Jews with sidelocks, would charge into his house, grab the very first thing they found, and walk off with it."

Shaking my head, I asked him: "Did you break God's commandment or did you return the item by sunset as stipulated in the Torah?"

The soul replied: "Nope! I hung on to the collateral until I got paid. I was worried about the money."

"So I see you were more concerned about your money than about God. And yet you were a Jew!"

The soul responded: "I was a Jew just like all the tax collectors. They're all more concerned about their money than about God."

I asked the soul: "Are such Jews heretics—without beards or sidelocks?"

"No," replied the soul. "They've got beards and sidelocks, but none of them has a heart."

"Stop joking," I said. "No one can live without a heart."

To which the soul replied: "They have no human feelings. Their hearts are made of stone."

"If that's so," I said, "then I'm very worried about what finally became of you. Please tell me the rest of your story."

And the spirit did continue—The soul went on:

During my life as a tax collector, women learned how to weep even though they had never shed a tear in the synagogue. Those were the poor women who never pray and whose hearts are never touched by the word of God. But I taught them how to cry when I took their very last kopek.

One day, while out strolling, I felt very cheerful and self-satisfied because my work was going well. All at once I heard that the tsar was planning to abolish the kosher meat tax. The bad news was like a bullet in my heart. I had an apoplectic fit and I died on the spot.

I was buried without a funeral and without orations. And the women who had wept while I was alive now laughed because I was dead.

Needless to say, I was instantly taken to Hell. I haven't enough words in my mouth to describe what I went through there. No human mind can grasp the rewards and the punishments we receive after dying. So I really have to hold my tongue. All I can tell you is that after I suffered enough, I returned to the world as an owl. An owl can see only at night but not in the daytime, and it feeds only on mice and moles.

The publican was no longer in existence—The tax collector was gone. He had turned into a bird covered with big feathers and long hair as well as a human face with an elongated ear on each side. And my hands, which had once snatched taxes from the poor, were now wings. Since I could see only at night, I spent my days in dark places, in ruins and empty palaces, fasting from dawn to dusk. When it got pitch-black outside, I would soar into the darkness and look for food. Night was day for me, and day night. And, while flying at night, I would weep and wail if I caught nothing but a mouse. For such is an owl's nature.

The wizards and the baal-shems made quite a fuss about owls. They claimed that we were prophets, that we could predict the future. They said my wailing meant that one person was close to dying, that another was going to be killed, and so on. And when I was about to kick the bucket, I wept and wailed very noisily. Any baal-shem who heard my yammering told his followers: "Listen! This means that my enemy has died!" But he was wrong. It wasn't his enemy who had died, it was I—an owl.

And because the wizard or the baal-shem had worked a lot of magic with me, my soul came back as a human being, as a miracle-working rebbe. For a man like that, all dark things are bright and all bright things dark. As a baal-shem, I had ancient manuscripts with all sorts of remedies and antidotes. And I used them to make such marvelous things. I utilized all the duties and commandments in the Torah for enchantment. I fixed many things without praying. With amulets and Cabalistic numerology I brought husbands back to their deserted wives, and a lot of barren women conceived because of me. I got to know all the angels and devils, for I had quite an imagination. I believed that I could talk to the angels and that I alone could hear them. I felt I could raise the dead, who told me the most secretive secrets. Had I lived any longer I would have claimed to be the Messiah, and the whole world would have followed me. For they wanted me to reign over all the demons and devils.

But ere I was able to execute my horrendous desire—Before I could carry out my awful plan, my life ended. And for a terrible reason. I wanted to experiment with making myself invisible, so that I could see everyone else without being seen. I fasted and fasted, I had the correct number of three hundred and ten ritual ablutions, I conjured and conjured. Then I went outdoors, convinced that no one could see me. A Gentile passed by, and I wanted to use him for my first invisibility test. So I slapped him. And he blew up. He ran me through with his sword, and I died.

Hence—As a baal-shem I flew to Heaven, but then I was hurled back down as a mole.

"*Oh, woe is me, woe is me,*" *I pondered*—"Poor me," I thought to myself: "I was the ruler of the demons and devils, I wanted to be the

Messiah, and my soul kept rising to the higher spheres. But now I'm a mole with the face of a pig. I rummage in the soil and I burrow under the fields." And while I may have sinned by taking the Lord's name in vain for my countless spoken and written spells, I had also done many good things. I had brought peace and love to the angels and also to the demons, uniting them and preventing any discord. And now, I sat underground, distinguishing between bits of soil. My imagination had once built towers reaching to the heavens, and now I had to make do with the heaps of soil that I dug up. Once I had wanted to see without being seen, but now it was the other way around: Everyone could see me, but I could see no one. I couldn't even see the big man who came and grabbed me.

He pulled me from my den and took me home to his children, who roared with laughter at the sight of me. His wife, however, was so scared that she screamed horribly and dashed out of the room. I hit the ceiling! "Why is she so scared?" I wondered. "Maybe it's because I'm black. Why, I got you pregnant when you were barren, and you can thank me for your children." But what good were my reproaches? She wouldn't stop screaming and she wouldn't come back.

The man did hasten—The man then quickly performed his magic on me, for the Galician Jews believe that if you kill a mole with a coin, you'll get very rich. He stuck a ruble down my craw and mumbled a few words. In so doing, he elevated my soul, and I entered the body of a pregnant woman, thereby turning human again. My work, like the mole's, consisted of digging the soil. But don't think I became a farmer, plowing and sowing. God forbid! A Galician Jew is ashamed of performing that kind of labor. No, indeed, I didn't till the soil, though I did dig. In fact, I dug deeper than when I'd been a mole: I was a gravedigger.

The Temple in Jerusalem—The Temple has remained sacred for us Jews even after its destruction. We still travel there to kiss the holy place and to hug the holy stones. We remove our shoes there and touch the earth with holy trembling. And we show every Jewish corpse the same respect and reverence. After all, the body is a temple, a sanctuary for a pure soul, which is a part of God's Heaven. That's why every Jewish town has a burial society, which cleans, dresses, and buries each corpse.

If a rich man dies, they soak him for a lot of money. Part of it goes to building a fence around the cemetery in order to keep out animals. A pauper gets a winding sheet, a grave, a headstone, and so on.

I likewise joined the burial society and started out as a gravedigger. Now according to Ecclesiastes: "It is better to go to the house of mourning than to go to the house of feasting: For that is the end of all men; and the living man will take it to his heart." But don't think for a moment that I took that seriously! Don't think that I took dying to heart! Not on your life! To me, the dead all looked the same: the adults like logs and the children like chips. While families wept for their dear departed, I laughed and I poked fun at all the eulogies. I was a big boozer and gut stuffer. I guzzled liquor nonstop and I told people I drank because I couldn't stand listening to all the sorrow, all the weeping and wailing.

If ever I heard that a rich man was sick, I looked forward to his death. And when he died, I was overjoyed. I knew I'd earn my kopek, though I never got as much as I wanted. I promised to let the body lie there overnight. Once I was satisfied, I'd negotiate with the burial society to get a good location for the corpse, perhaps near the grave of a Hasidic rebbe. And I promised to use a lot of soil from the Holy Land— I said it had been taken from Mother Rachel's grave.

And if ever a pauper died, I wished that all paupers would die. What good are they?! What use are they?! In the late summer month of Elul, when Jews visit the graves of their fathers and mothers, many women would ask me where their parents were buried. I'd show them any old graves just to bilk them out of a few rubles. If they cried their eyes out and other women came over, they would say to the mourners: "Why are you crying on our father's grave?"

The first women yelled back: "What are you talking about? This is our grandfather's grave. The gravedigger personally took us here."

They went looking for me, but I hid out. Or else I'd holler: "I've got no time to chat with you!" When I was paid again, I took them to another grave. I said I'd made a mistake, and would they please accept my apologies.

I was absolved from praying and blessing, and when I said I was busy with a religious obligation, I was exempted from other ones.

The members of the burial society saw how loyal I was to them, so they made me a trustee and a treasurer. And when the kopeks slipped under my fingers, I began leading the group a bit more intelligently than earlier treasurers. "What does a pauper need a headstone for?" I said. "He's been starving to death all his life, and when he dies, they treat him like a big shot!"

Verily I did question the spirit—I asked the soul: "What did you do with the money? Did you have it paid out to his widow and children?"

The soul replied: "Nope. The burial society isn't concerned with the living. We only serve the Angel of Death."

"So what did you do with the money?"

We spent the money on dinners and banquets and borschts, so we'd be merry and cheerful all the time and not gloomy. The other members were delighted with my plan, and we feasted like there was no tomorrow. To make sure we had enough rubles, I'd charge high prices for burials. Often, when a pauper died, I'd be unavailable. His family would look for me all day long, but I wouldn't show up until evening. Then they'd have to shell out a lot of cash so that the corpse wouldn't spend the night unburied. In short, the dead were like fish in my net—a different price on each corpse. When a rich man died, we'd say that a pike had been caught, and when a poor man died, we'd say it was a minnow, and we'd be very worried.

Besides gouging so much sacred money out of people, I'd perform good deeds: I'd get even with the nonpious, newfangled Jews without beards and with short earlocks. If one of them fell into my hands, I'd really smack the hell out of his hindquarters during the ritual cleansing.

But that shortened my life. You see, I was once pounding a dead Jew who'd worn a short coat all his life. In fact, I was punching him so hard that the entire cottage resounded with the blows. He moved, he gaped at me, and then angrily got to his feet. I panicked and tried to skedaddle. But I couldn't budge, my strength was gone. So I screamed at the top of my lungs and collapsed. Everyone came running, and I died, while the dead man came to life, for he hadn't really been dead. He'd been in a state of suspended animation, and my punches had awakened him from his terrible coma. I, however, was truly dead.

And because I had mistreated the young and educated "modern" Jews and because I was an ignoramus in regard to the religious texts, Heaven decreed that I should return as a maskil, an enlightened Jew, educated and literate.

The gravedigger did perish—He kicked the bucket, and I was born to a mother and father who gave me a thorough education. I had a good mind and a fine grasp of things. My parents and my teachers pinned high hopes on me; they thought I would bring them honor and esteem in both this world and the next. My learning would enable me to represent and defend my brethren, my people, to challenge their enemies and bring justice.

Long, long ago there were many Jews—such as Isaac Abrabanal and similar men—who not only were very wise but knew a whole bunch of languages and were very pious and virtuous. They were highly respected by monarchs and often did wonderful things for the Jews.

My parents wanted the same for me. But I failed to live up to their expectations. No sooner did I begin my studies than I felt like a maskil, a savant, a philosopher, and I made fun of all our Jewish customs, our genuine sages, and their teachings. Since I regarded myself as a lot smarter than they, I cast off the yoke of our faith, the burden of the Law, and the Commandments. I wanted to become a free man, free to do all the forbidden things—fornication and other evils. I never observed the Sabbath or the Holy Days. I ate whatever I wanted—including non-kosher meat. And I ate it even on the Day of Atonement, when Jews are supposed to fast. Furthermore I never prayed, I never so much as glanced at a prayer shawl.

And that was my total erudition—to do anything I felt like. I scoffed and laughed at all Jews, I viewed them as schmucks. I was the only wise man in the world. I despised my brethren, my people—I couldn't stand the very word *Jew*. When I was among Christians, I hid my background. If there was anything bad I could do to a Jew—I did it. If there was anything bad I could say about a Jew—I said it. And if there was any money to be squeezed out of them—I squeezed. I treated my parents like garbage, I laughed at their words and their tears, for in my previous life as a gravedigger I had sneered at parents mourning dead children. I was just as scornful now. When my parents cursed me and wept about my evil deeds and my awful behavior, I would jeer at them. I was an enlightened intellectual (or so I thought), a philosopher. And they were old fools. I constantly gave in to all my passions—especially my lust for whores. As a result I caught tuberculosis and died within a short time.

I had fornicated like a dog and bitten my brethren like a dog—that is, said horrible things about Jews. I had also eaten nonkosher meat like a dog—even though the Torah says we should throw it to the dogs as their share because they didn't bark when the Jews left Egypt. But I had eaten the meat meant for dogs and I had barked like a dog. And so Heaven decreed that I should be reborn as a dog.

The maskil did pass away and was reincarnated as a canine—The maskil died and returned as a dog. Now there are different breeds of dogs, you know. One breed has woolly hair and droopy ears, and if you shave it from top to tail, it resembles a lion. It's very smart, and you can teach it anything that a dog can be taught. It stands on its hind legs and holds out its paws, just like a human beggar. It fetches anything in its jaws, including any object that you fling. And it understands whatever its master says to it. But that was not the kind of dog I was.

There is also a breed with a wide chest, a narrow belly, and bow legs. They're used for hunting and they simply whiz through the mountains like a whirlwind. But again, that was not the kind of dog I was.

There is also a breed that's small and cute. Highborn ladies hold them in their laps and feed them the finest delicacies even though they wouldn't spare a crust of bread for a pauper. But needless to say, I wasn't lucky enough to be of that breed.

To make a long story short, I was an ordinary country mutt, enormous, hideous, pitch-black, and with a rotten disposition. I spent whole days lying in the farm manure, and if anyone passed by, I would get to my feet and bark at the top of my lungs, and all the neighboring dogs would bay along with me. If anyone approached me without a stick, I would bite him and then, as he hightailed it out of there, I would chase him. But if he waved a stick at me, I would stay put. And if someone threw a rock at me, I would howl and roar and dash off with my tail between my legs and run to God knows where and hide and stop barking.

I had enough chutzpah to feel like a lion when a lion was taken past me. One lion hit me so hard that he knocked out two of my molars. That taught me a lesson. I no longer barked at people; I would bite them silently and enjoy their blood.

And in the town where I did dwell—In the shtetl I lived in there was a Hasidic rebbe, and, as is the custom, a lot of guests would gather at his court for the third and final Sabbath meal. So one Sabbath evening I trotted over, hoping to get a bone under his table. Upon reaching his place after the meal, I saw a bone with a bit of meat attached. It was in a bowl. I snatched the bone and tried to gnaw on it. But the rebbe's followers started thrashing me, attempting to dislodge the bone from my teeth and keep it for themselves, since a rebbe's leftovers are sacred to his flock. In my haste, I swallowed the bone and choked on it.

Now since I died because of holy food, I came back as a holy man with a holier-than-thou attitude—a zealot who persecuted anyone he considered less pious than himself. In other words, I had the same character as when I'd been a dog. I barked at everyone and attacked as much as I could.

There are two categories of zealots—that is, men who ardently defend sacred and other important causes. One group focuses on religion, the other on the nation. While the first group persecutes those Jews it regards as less pious, the second group, with the help of resourceful language, addresses those who have left the straight and narrow path.

When we were in our own land with our own government, these national zealots heroically defended us with swords and defeated all our enemies. Then, when we were driven from our land, they became our great protectors and champions, using their words and wise books to shield us against our enemies around the world. With their writings, they have annihilated the blood libel and other anti-Jewish lies and persuaded rulers to grant us the same freedoms and civil rights as their own nations possess. Those zealots also teach our people that we should become craftsmen and farmers and gradually acquire an education so that we may be useful citizens in this country. And in their teachings our modern sages employ skillful language and great intelligence.

The religious zealots, however, behave very differently. They don't know the meaning of compassion. If they dislike somebody, they anathematize him in this world and the next. They despise science and enlightenment. They maintain their old foolishness and add new stupidities to our pure faith. They make religious laws more and more rigorous until the entire faith becomes a terrible hardship, and the essence is forgotten over secondary matters. All their power is spent on tormenting their own brethren and vilifying enlightened and educated Jews. But protecting the Jewish nation against an enemy—that's something they won't do and can't do.

And when this religious zealotry doth adhere—And if this fanaticism is combined with arrogance, you won't find a more corrupt man in the world. For he persecutes anyone more exemplary than he himself, claiming his victim isn't pious enough. But actually, the zealot envies him for his greater qualities and virtues. And because every flaw is like a wild beast, I was transformed from a dog into a religious zealot, for a religious zealot has a dogged character.

In my dog days, I had lain in manure and wallowed in filth. And now, as a religious zealot, I loved hearing only smut: lies, gossip, slander, backbiting, back stabbing. In my dog days, I had barked at every passerby, and all the other dogs had barked with me. And now, as a religious zealot, I barked, together with my brethren, at any person approaching the gateway to enlightenment. If the person was poor and defenseless, we would excommunicate him and deprive him of his livelihood. But if he had any standing and he challenged us, we would flee to God knows where—just as I had done in my dog life whenever someone waved a stick or threw a rock at me. As a zealot, I would beg the person's forgiveness because I was scared stiff of him. But the instant I left, I would curse him, bad-mouth him, anathematize him, just as a dog, while keeping its distance, howls at the person it has scurried away from.

I didn't spare the most intelligent man. I would revile the greatest maskil, until finally one maskil bawled me out. I now realized I'd be better off holding my tongue and biting silently. That is, I would sic the common people on him, the tsar's people, and I would stand at a distance, laughing and sneering at his humiliation.

But my efforts were in vain. Any intellectual I harassed would eventually gain prestige. His name would resound far and wide; near and distant communities would hang on his every word. In the end he would become a rabbi in a large city, where important people would honor him. His honeyed words would even turn his enemies into friends. It pained me mortally, and I finally died of chagrin. For envy is one of three things that cause premature death. And because I had persecuted every intelligent man, I was reincarnated as a fox, who is the smartest of all animals and is constantly chased by hounds.

'Tis far better to be a fox than a zealot—It's better to be a fox than a fanatic, for my fanaticism had brought me nothing but shame and annoyance. My name was practically forgotten, and if ever I was mentioned then it was only as a joke. But when I was a fox, all the animal fables talked about me, and they will keep applauding my cunning till the end of time. For besides my foxy smartness, I had a human intellect, which made me the most intelligent fox in the world. I confused all the beasts and bewildered all the birds. And it still warms the cockles of my heart to remember all the tricks I played in the fields and the woods.

I recall spotting a black raven in a tree. In its beak it held a piece of cheese, which I so greatly craved. So I hunkered down at the foot of the tree and began cajoling the raven: "You're so beautiful, you heavenly bird. The whole world praises you, and all nations laud your marvelous voice. Now since I'm lucky enough to see your beauty, I'm so eager to hear you sing."

A fool believes every flatterer. So the raven opened its beak to do its warbling—and it dropped the cheese, which I devoured on the spot.

Another time, I came to a very deep well with two buckets hanging from a wheel. One bucket was down by the water, the other was at the top. I sat down in the empty bucket, descended, and drank my fill. But then I realized there was no way I could get back up again. Along came a billy goat with a long beard, a fat belly, and big horns. He stood by the well and shouted: "Oy, I want to drink! I'm so thirsty! How can I get to the water?"

No sooner did I hear him than I said: "You fool! Just climb into the top bucket and you'll come soaring down. After all, you're a lot heavier than I am. Then you can drink to your heart's content."

The fool complied. With his heavy body he clambered into the empty bucket and pulled me up as he plunged down. When I reached ground level, I climbed out, while he remained below.

Then there was the day I had a hankering for grapes I saw growing in a vineyard. I hopped and leaped, trying to snatch them, but it was no use, they were too high. Since it was extremely embarrassing to leave empty-handed, I hit on a great excuse. "Why bother?" I said. "I don't want them anyway. They're as bitter as gall and as sour as vinegar. They'll only set my teeth on edge."

Once I invited the stork to lunch. I chopped up the food, served the tiny morsels on a flat plate, and we both tucked in. But before the stork could pick up anything with his long, thin beak, my broad mouth had wolfed everything down, and the stork left with a growling stomach.

I spake unto the spirit—I said to the soul: "You're boasting too much. I happen to know that the stork got even with you. He likewise invited you to lunch. He hacked the food to pieces, served it in a cruse with a long, narrow neck, and told you to dig in. But before you could get anything out with your tongue, the stork gobbled it all up with his long beak."

The spirit did respond—The soul said:

What do you think?! Today's sages are just as silly: They love showing off their virtues and hiding their defects. Now the stupidity of having a long tail—which we smart foxes have—cost me my life. You see, one day I ran into some hunters with their hounds. They chased me across fields and woods, until the hounds were exhausted and confused. I hid in a hole amid rocks, and the dogs were about to leave empty-jawed. But unfortunately my long tail stuck out. They spotted me, pounced on me, and killed me.

And since my death brought no salvation, I became a spirit. I haunted roads and fields, terrifying all the travelers. I growled like a bear or howled like a wolf or roared like a lion, and sometimes I floated like a will-o'-the-wisp over bogs and swamps, scaring people away.

Just as my tail had been my undoing, it now brought me luck. You see, a Hasidic Jew bought my fur from the hunters and made a lining for his rebbe's coat, using my tail as the collar. And the instant the collar touched the rebbe's neck, I was privileged to become a human being again, a baal-shem—as cunning and conniving as a fox.

I did not abandon my earlier character: I had led people astray, floating about the fields and woods, shining at night, making people think there was an inn nearby. And I was no different as a rebbe, I was a misleader of lots of people. And just as I had imitated different animals, I now yelled my way through psalms, and everyone who heard my shouting called me holy and hallowed. This meant that my prayers went straight to Heaven, and if I blessed someone, then he was truly blessed.

People would come to me from the four corners of the world. I hoodwinked them all like a cunning fox, bleeding them dry. For there are more than enough suckers, and suckers were all I needed. They were my best sheep, I fleeced them thoroughly and made a mint. I can still remember all the advice I gave them.

One day, while traveling to visit all my flocks and pull the wool over their eyes, I stopped off at an inn. My followers told the innkeeper: "Prepare properly, for a man of God has come here. Cook some decent dishes and serve enough wine and schnapps."

Knowing that a rebbe never paid, the innkeeper replied: "I don't have any meat or oats or hay, and there's no place to spend the night."

When I heard that, I thought to myself: "I've got to do something nasty to him. Otherwise no one will respect me."

Upon noticing the innkeeper's baby, I sneaked over and thrust a grain of barley into his anus. Then I stole back to my room, lay down on my bed, and told my Hasids: "Let's rest a while. The innkeeper will be punished for the way he's treating us."

I drifted off, and no sooner had I closed my eyes than the baby started bawling like a lunatic. His mother tried to nurse him, she rocked him and sang to him. But the baby kept screaming nonstop. He couldn't be quieted and eventually he bawled himself hoarse. The terrified parents thought he was possessed or damaged by an evil eye. Rushing into my room, they exclaimed: "We beg you, divine man! Save our baby from dying!"

I hollered at them: "Get away from me, you evil people! You atheists! I can't stand the sight of you!"

The father fell to his knees, pleading with me to forgive him, imploring me to bless his baby. He promised me a huge amount of money, for the baby was their only child. So I gave in. I stood up, washed my hands, and went to the baby. I placed my right hand on his head and blessed him, while I slipped my left hand under his behind and pulled out the barley seed. The baby soon calmed down and fell asleep.

The news of this "great miracle" spread through all the Jewish communities, growing more and more miraculous with each retelling. They even said that I had struggled with the Angel of Death and taken away his knife—everyone had witnessed it. Other people claimed that I had snatched the child's soul from the Devil's hands and put it back in the child's body. My reputation grew throughout the country, so more and more Jews came to be blessed by me and to see me working my wonders. They made me very rich.

Whenever I traveled, I was welcomed by all the innkeepers. They served me the finest dishes and gave me nice tidy donations. I worked all sorts of miracles, increasing my fame.

In time I built myself a palatial mansion with a silver throne, on which I had the following words engraved in Hebrew: "David, King of Israel, Lives Eternal"—the same phrase that King David had engraved on his gold throne. In the adjoining room, which I named the Messiah's Room, I had a big, expensive table lined with chairs. That was where the Messiah would sit surrounded by all his saints. I indicated the seat of each prophet and each rebbe.

Everyone believed me as if they had seen it with their own eyes, and they brought me costly presents to decorate the room: diamonds, utensils of gold and silver, and so on. I pretended to be very wise. I took from some people, but not from others, thereby creating envy and hatred. People beseeched me, they vehemently exhorted me to accept their gifts and place them in the Messiah's Room. I had no choice, and so I acquired great wealth.

Verily I did question the spirit—I asked the soul: "I'm sure that many of your prophecies didn't pan out, so couldn't your followers have easily seen that you were a swindler?"

And the spirit did respond—The soul replied:

You have no idea how badly a sucker wants to be suckered! If a prophecy doesn't come true, then the sucker comes up with his own excuse for the rebbe. No matter what, the rebbe is always right. If a man I blessed then suffered a great misfortune, the fools said it was his own fault, he was a sinner, which was why the blessing had turned into a curse. So how could you blame our rebbe? And if my predictions didn't work out, my followers were astonished, but they simply held their tongues.

Hearken unto me, I will recount thee a tale—Listen, I'm gonna tell you a story:

Once, when the winter had gotten off to a rainy start, a man came to me and said: "Holy Rebbe, pray for me, pray for the rain to turn into snow and frost on the roads."

I asked him: "Why do you need winter so badly?"

And he answered: "Dear Rebbe, I've got a government contract to supply grain to the army, which is a long distance from here, a month away. I was paid an advance of fifty thousand rubles. So I need to have a sleigh path."

I asked the man: "What are you called, and what is your mother's name? I'll pray for you, and your wish will be fulfilled."

He told me his and his mother's names and he also gave me five hundred rubles. Then he left in a cheerful mood.

Well, day after day wore by, but not a single snowflake appeared. So the man came to me and complained very loudly: "Divine man! Where is the snow I bought from you?"

I told him to give it a few more days. He waited for a week, but the rain wouldn't stop, and no snow fell. So he came to me once again and complained loudly: "Oy vey, Rebbe! You have no idea how miserable I'll be if the road is bad. I won't be able to deliver my grain on time, I'll go broke and die in prison."

"You have no choice," I replied. "You have to run away. Major changes have taken place in Heaven. They've fired the angel of snow and replaced him with the angel of rain. That's why it's raining now instead of snowing. And you can tell I'm right if you consult the almanac, which predicts frost and snow for this time."

Well, I've described one trick. Now let me tell you another story, which you'll enjoy a whole lot. You'll see how a smart guy like me gets out of a jam.

My own child once fell ill, and my wife tearfully begged me to pray for him. "Don't worry," I comforted her. "Our child will definitely recover."

My wife went off full of hope, but then the sickness got worse. She tearfully came back to me, I promised her that our child would be healed and I paid a rabbinical fee. A few days later, she came to me again and cried out: "Husband, don't wait another moment! Raise a rumpus in Heaven—our child is dying!"

"Don't worry," I answered. "I've already told you several times that our child will definitely survive."

That very same day my wife came to me, wringing her hands and weeping loudly. Our child had died.

Dumbstruck, I sat there, and my Hasids clustered around me. I yelled: "What's happened to me!? Don't I have a single friend among the angels? Couldn't they have warned me? Do what you like with my child—I haven't lost hope. I don't know if he's dead, Heaven hasn't told me so. I don't want to hear about it from any of you!"

The child was buried, but I didn't tear my coat, I didn't go to the funeral, I didn't mourn for the traditional seven days, I didn't grieve. After a while, however, I was sitting among my followers, explicating the Torah, filling their heads with all sorts of nonsense, as we normally do. All at once, I burst into tears and shrieked at the top of my lungs: "Oh, God! My child has died! I just received the bad tiding from Heaven!"

I took off my shoes and sat down for the seven days of mourning. My Hasids all gaped at me in astonishment and truly believed that I was a miracle worker.

I spake unto the spirit—I told the soul: "You call your Hasids sheep. But they're really cows, turkeys, asses!"

And the spirit did respond—The soul replied:

If only all Jews were such asses. That's what the rebbes have been craving for such a long time. Do you think we can live off the intelligent Jews? Those enlightened people don't believe in our miracles, they laugh and poke fun at us, and they turn a deaf ear to any talk of the supernatural. That was why I hated their guts and why I persecuted them all my life. I sicced my drunken followers on them, and they inflicted all sorts of torments. And the more the Hasids act like asses in unison, the better and finer and more useful they are for their spiritual leaders. That's why thousands upon thousands gather together on the Sabbath and on Holy Days, especially on Rosh ha-Shana (New Year's), on the eighth day of the Feast of Tabernacles, and on Simhath Torah (the Festival of the Torah). And the rebbe looks like a prince among his legions.

Now once, on the eighth night of the Feast of Tabernacles, we were making the circular procession with the Torah scrolls, singing and springing, and I was dancing and prancing like a billy goat. I was drunk as a lord and I sang out: "Abraham rejoices in our rejoicing about the Torah!" Then I yelled: "Make way for the martyrs who'll soon be coming to me in the prayer house and celebrating the Torah with me!" And I bawled in Hebrew: "Let us rejoice in our Torah! Long live Abraham our Father!" And, in his honor, I filled my sanctification cup and drained it.

Now a great miracle appeared to me. I saw the entire synagogue whirling around. Terrified, I collapsed and shouted: "I beg you, my martyrs, my dear guests! Come to my place! We'll celebrate there! We'll talk about our Jews!"

I returned to my home, where I locked and bolted the door, while my followers cried: "There's no rebbe like our rebbe! There's no saint like our saint! For he is very great in the next world! Remember! The Patriarchs have left their thrones in Paradise and come to his synagogue to celebrate with our rebbe! We personally saw him talking to them and dancing with them! He addressed each of them by name and invited them to his home to confer with them about the Messiah. Our rebbe will conquer the guardian angels and he will overcome all our enemies and the Devil and grind them into dust."

My followers were talking about supernatural things when in ran a boy, who shouted at his father: "Daddy, I went to make number two and I found the rebbe's corpse lying there!" The horrified Hasids went to see for themselves and found my holy body lying in human feces under my window.

A great lament resounded: "Because of our sins, our rebbe has perished. Because of our vices, the Devil wrestled him down and threw him out the window!"

But actually I had never wrestled with the Devil. After guzzling too much liquor, I had gone home to sober up. I felt sick to my stomach, so I stuck my head out the window in order to throw up. I got dizzy because my window was on the second landing; I fell out and broke my neck.

Now since I had treated all my followers like asses, I was transformed into a donkey.

Verily, the tsaddik did perish—The rebbe died, and I became a donkey. I transported heavy loads. In my previous incarnation, I had had a very easy time of it and put all my burdens on my foolish devotees. I had dined on all sorts of delicacies and lived like a prince in wonderful mansions, which I had built with my followers' money. But now I was forced to eat thorns and nettles and lie on the dung next to the stable. And rather than flying through the heavens like a free bird, I had to trudge very slowly on the ground. I was beaten a lot by my owner and constantly laughed at by all the beasts and cattle.

Nevertheless, I had my pride. And when all the beasts and cattle assembled to find a king, I wanted to be their ruler. To avoid being recognized, I slipped into a lion's skin, scaring the hell out of them. But then the instant I opened my mouth, they recognized me, and I dashed away with my tail between my legs.

Another time, I was ridden by a lunatic who claimed to be the Messiah. So many people went running after him that the news reached the king, who was infuriated. He ordered his soldiers to shoot this fraud, and they killed both him and me.

Having had the privilege of being sat on by a saint, I again came back as a human being. I, the ass, was now a doctor, a wise doctor, who was as respected as a rebbe, but who was actually as dumb as a donkey.

Verily I spake—I said to the soul: "I'm truly sorry to hear that after many lives as various animals you became a doctor who was as dumb as a donkey. Honestly, what kind of fool would take a prescription from you?"

The soul answered: "Shut up! Don't pity me. I realize you're saying that only because you're afraid I'll return as a doctor and steal your patients. But there's no cause for alarm. Don't forget that I was a doctor before you were even born. I was so proficient that they venerated me like a rebbe, a sage. I reigned supreme, but I had the brains of a donkey."

"I don't understand," I told the soul. "How could you be a donkey and yet have a fine reputation?"

"I was a liar and an impostor. But now that I'm a spirit, I swear I'll tell you the truth and nothing but the truth. You see, I knew as little about medicine as a donkey does, and yet I did a good job, for people trusted me with their lives, they feared and respected me. You may find it hard to grasp, but remember: I'd been a fox once and also a dog. So I knew how to cover up my ignorance with the cunning and falseness of a fox and to attack other doctors with the nastiness of a dog."

"I don't get it," I said. "How can a man combine two opposites? How can he possibly be as smart as a fox and as dumb as a donkey?"

To which the soul responded: "You're mistaken. A fox isn't smart, he's cunning. He's false, conniving, and corrupt—whereas the foundation of wisdom is truth and intelligence. Just be a little more patient. Let me talk, and I'll explain everything. Then you'll catch my drift."

The science of medicine—The science of doctoring is very profound and mysterious. The wisest men have failed to plumb its depths because it involves all the disciplines in the world. You have to know physics, mathematics, mechanics, psychology, and hundreds of other fields, without which you can't start to grasp even a glimmer of medicine. So until people thoroughly master all these areas, the science of medicine remains beyond their comprehension. Granted, in our time people have come a long way in all other domains, such as chemistry. They've figured out what every substance is composed of. They can transform water into fire, air into water, and so forth. But they still don't know what constitutes the life of any creature—that is, how and why it lives. No human being can create an ear of corn, much less a fly.

Now it's self-evident that until we can understand how a creature or a plant lives, much less how we can make one, we can't understand how to prolong a human life. We can't know how many kinds of death there are in the world since a person can die for a million different reasons beyond our ken. And equally obscure are the early symptoms of any illness, so that we're unable to nip it in the bud. Nor do we have the means to cure all diseases. As for the remedies we use, we didn't find them with our intelligence; we developed them by chance, through centuries of trial and error.

So we can't really call medicine a science as yet, since we use treatments without knowing why they work. We heal purely on the basis of experience, and that's something even an unintelligent man can do. So if a man boasts that he has an exhaustive knowledge of medicine and can cure the sick because he's brilliant and knows the source of life, then he's bound to harm a lot more people than he helps with his quackery. His pen is more destructive than a sharp sword, and his prescriptions are poisonous. His victims are more numerous than locusts. A smart doctor doesn't crow about his wisdom. Only a fool sees himself as a great physician. If a doctor brags about his prowess, then that should tell you he's an ass.

And so, as a doctor, I was an arrogant donkey. In my student days, I made fun of my professors, I cut classes, I spent all my time running after a beautiful cook, a beautiful seamstress, a beautiful flower maker. I'd swear I'd marry each one and make her a doctor's wife if she gave me all her money.

I spake—I said to the soul: "Stop gabbing already! I believe you, I really believe you were as dumb as a donkey. But I'd like to know how you came to be so lucky as a doctor and why your prescriptions were so effective."

The spirit did rejoin—The soul answered:

I'm surprised at you—you're a doctor yourself! You're always dealing with people and yet you aren't acquainted with the character of the masses, the common folk. They judge someone purely by his appearance—that is, the elegance of his clothes, the splendor of his home, his table, his servants, the value of his furniture. If a man is as dumb as a donkey, all he has to do is dress opulently and swagger through the streets—and ordinary people will regard him as a great sage. I had already inferred that, and so I knew how to gain their esteem.

The great Greek physician Hippocrates wrote a book crammed with treatments for all diseases. But I penned a better and more useful tome, filled with advice on how doctors should conduct themselves and earn their livelihood. The great sage Pythagoras named his book *Golden Parables*. But his title is misleading. Parables aren't made of gold, they simply moralize. They contain wisdom—and that's all. My book could be called *Golden Advice*, for it teaches even the stupidest ass how he can make a mint as a doctor.

I'll read you a few chapters, and you'll no longer be surprised that I was so fortunate. Just listen and you'll strike it rich. Now that I'm dead I feel no envy.

Golden Advice

First of all, you should dust your hair with white powder and tie a small pillow to your belly. Then the masses will say: "This man must really be a great doctor, for his hair has turned gray from all his studying and his belly must be stuffed with all knowledge."

Second, put a skull on your desk and a stillborn embryo in a jar of alcohol on your windowsill. Any visitor will be thunderstruck by your vast wisdom.

Third, buy a huge number of books, bind them all in red with gilt spines, line them up in a bookcase with glass doors, and never read them so long as you live. The public will see them and think that you're a great scholar.

Fourth, pawn whatever you must and buy beautiful horses. The loan shark may skin you alive, but get yourself a fancy coach. You can wipe out an entire town, but if your coach and horses are at your door, you'll be treated like a VIP and a great professor.

Fifth, when you visit a patient, don't ask about his illness. Instead, scrutinize the people standing around him and you'll readily figure out what to do. When leaving, tell them the situation is very serious, and you fear the worst. That way, no matter what happens to the patient, you'll maintain your prestige. If he dies, they'll say the doctor predicted it, he's an expert. But if the patient survives, they'll think that you can resurrect the dead. And the whole world will beat a path to your door!

Sixth, you ought to know that paupers don't seek medical help until they're dangerously ill, so healing them is very difficult. It's wisest to ignore them altogether. If a poor patient recovers, you won't make anything. And if he dies, you'll be blamed. When a pauper consults you, snap at him in a nasty and arrogant tone. He'll feel intimidated and he'll flee to the back of beyond.

Seventh, you should announce office hours for free treatment of the poor. That way, you'll be mobbed daily at those scheduled times, and people will say: "He's a genius, it's impossible to get to see him." Pick out patients with a little money, take them into your office, discuss their illness, write a prescription, and squeeze out as much cash as you can. Then, as they leave, tell the rest of the paupers: "It's very late. Come back tomorrow."

Eighth, always bad-mouth other doctors. Rip them to shreds. If there's another doctor in your town, and he's a great scholar who always reads newspapers and travelogues, grind him underfoot. Tell people: "What a quack! When he tends a patient, his mind is somewhere else.

He's thinking about what's happening in Holland and what the British Parliament is debating, and he doesn't have the foggiest idea about what's wrong with the patient." If your town has a young doctor, then say: "Some doctor! An inexperienced pipsqueak! He's going to dispatch ten thousand patients before he cures a single one!" And if the doctor is old, then say: "Some doctor! He's blind and deaf, and his methods are ancient! He can't tell his ass from his elbow!"

Ninth, when a doctor calls in other doctors to discuss treatment, you should scowl and sneer to make the other doctors realize that you're the superior physician. And to make it even clearer, you should bluntly tell him: "Believe me! You botched it! Your patient's more dead than alive! And you've gotten away with it!" The others will regard him as a quack and praise you to the skies. If the patient eventually succumbs, they'll blame the first doctor. And if he survives, you'll bask in all the glory.

Tenth, when the first doctor objects to your method, then stick to your guns, even if he's right. That way, people won't notice you haven't got a clue. Once the patient is at death's door and just about hopeless, you can start caving a little. No matter what happens, you'll be the hero. If the patient dies, you can blame the first doctor. And if he lives, you can say it's because they took your advice.

And with these regulations—By sticking to those rules, I led a good life as a doctor. My fellow citizens saw me as the greatest medical expert in the world, as a second Hippocrates. Not summoning me to a sick person was considered a major sin. If I wasn't asked to treat someone and he died, there was a great clamor in town. I know I killed countless people—more than the hairs on my head. Yet no one said a word. I accumulated an enormous fortune and enjoyed tremendous prestige— like a cabinet minister. In fact, I *was* a minister serving the king of deadly fear: the Angel of Death. Once I started rolling through the streets in my ministerial carriage in order to kill patients, Satan stopped wielding his knife, for the pen I used for prescriptions murdered a lot more people than his sharp blade.

And verily, as I became long in the tooth—As I grew old, my practice widened, and I started really curing people. This infuriated the Angel of Death, and he took my life.

And now, since I had exulted in the title of doctor, I was sentenced to return as a turkey, which always preens itself because it's very stupid. I strutted and gobbled all day long and I had a very nasty disposition. My claws were red, and my head was blue. I spread my tail like a wheel and lowered my wings to the ground like curtains. If anyone so much as whistled, I shrieked. And whenever I saw a red creature, I would fly into a rage, attack it, and try to peck out its eyes. In short, I flaunted all my stupidities just as earlier I had arrogantly covered up all my failings. But instead of commanding universal respect, I was now teased and ridiculed by all the children. And it went on until I grew very fat.

At this point, a Hasidic rebbe bought me. I was slaughtered and then served up as a good dinner. The rebbe licked my bones clean, thereby elevating my soul: I was reborn as a human being, who had nothing elevating about him. He had some kind of pedigree and was as proud of it as a turkey—that is, I was totally full of myself.

Hast thou ever set eyes—Have you ever seen an Arabian horse? No other horse is as swift and beautiful and as loyal to its master. These horses, which mate only among themselves, produce offspring with the same excellent features. They're strong and swift and beautiful and they command high prices. That's why their bloodline is carefully guarded—like that of the major human families. Each horse has its pedigree document, which, signed by reliable witnesses, indicates the horse's name, its dam and sire, and its date of birth. Such horses are called thoroughbreds, and great princes and kings pay thousands of rubles to hire these studs for their mares. The children of rabbis are likewise thoroughbreds, and rich Jews pay through the nose to get a pedigree for a son-in-law.

Verily I did question the spirit—I asked the soul: "Do all these children become rabbis just as the offspring of genuine Arabian horses are all purebred?"

The soul replied: "No. In this respect, they can't be compared to Arabian horses. The bridegroom can be a scholar, and his children morons. Or the rabbi's daughter can be a beauty, and her children a horror show. The rich Jew pays only for a pedigree marriage and not just for practical reasons. That's why all rabbinical children are very proud. And that's the only thing they inherit from their parents.

"I myself was a mangy, scurvy fool, a dunce. But both my parents were descended from rabbis, so I was conceited and arrogant. I spent all day wandering around the house, my arms akimbo, my belly sticking out, and I kept telling myself: 'Who can hold a candle to me?'

"I regarded any man without a rabbinical background as a worm. I couldn't understand how someone like that could even live. I warned my children to avoid such people for they were impure, and it was shameful to talk to them. If any of those nonrabbinicals tried to marry into our dynasty, I would weigh his family tree against mine, and if I found more rabbis in mine, the suitor would have to pay dearly. And if his ancestry included no rabbis, then he had to cough up a fortune."

I spake—I said to the soul: "I'm amazed that you could let such impure nonrabbinicals into your family!"

The spirit did rejoin—The soul answered: "You must know that gold and silver purify bastards and make up for all defects. A man can be an oaf, a boor, an imbecile, a scoundrel—but if he's got money, he'll get prestige and power, and everyone will adore him the way the Jews fleeing Egypt worshiped the Golden Calf. Polish Jews are boastful about pedigree or money, and if—Heaven forfend—someone has both, then you can't even breathe the same air. The sky is too low for him and the world too narrow."

I spake to the spirit—I said: "Judging by your grandiose manner, I'd say you had both virtues: wealth and ancestry."

The spirit replied: "Right you are! I had money and pedigree, and I profited from both. With my money I did business, and because of my 'rabbinical' position I acquired prominent matches."

I did inquire—I asked the soul: "Why didn't you become a rabbi like your forebears?"

He answered: "I've already told you that all I inherited from my parents was their pride. As a boy I even studied the Talmud at the Jewish elementary school, but I didn't understand a single word."

I thereupon did inquire—I then asked the soul: "How come your parents had you study something you couldn't grasp? Why didn't they let you learn secular subjects, useful things—say, a trade, reading, writing, arithmetic, languages?"

To which the spirit did respond—The soul said: "You're joking! People with our ancestry would never let their offspring learn such stupid workaday things—God forbid! It would have been shameful for them if their children didn't remain in school, studying the Talmud, until they got married and then so long as the bride and groom lived with her family."

I spake further—I then said: "I don't understand how a man can devote years to such impractical stuff. What good is it? All he can learn is how to cheat people. Any business he engages in must be neglected and ruined, and his wife's dowry melts away very quickly."

The spirit thereupon did rejoin—The spirit answered: "You're right! My business went under in a short time, I lost my wealth during my first year of marriage, and yet I remained rich."

Verily I was astonished—I was very surprised! But he explained it all: "When I saw I was about to go bankrupt, I borrowed several thousand rubles and I announced—"

No sooner did my ears hearken to those very words—The instant I heard that, I recalled that I had recently treated this man. So I asked him to tell me about his death. And he replied: "I died the way my parents died. I fell ill like any man and I summoned doctors. They wrote prescriptions, I took the medicines, and I died. You must be acquainted with my disease, since you treated me too."

I thereupon did inquire—I asked the soul: "Are your wanderings over?"

He replied: "I only know what's happened to me in the past. I haven't the foggiest clue about the future. I could easily be reborn as a worm or some other small, unclean creature, which would humble me for my arrogance."

To which I did rejoin—I asked the soul: "How can you be saved from further wanderings?"

The spirit answered: "My salvation is solely in your hands. You have to copy down my entire story and publish it, so that all its readers can become better human beings. The Hasid will stop his desecrations. He will stop running to the rebbe and abandoning his wife and children. Cantors will stop violating their melodies. The tax collectors will stop fleecing the Jews. The gravediggers will stop bilking people and putting corpses to shame. And the begrudger who makes himself God's spokesman will stop persecuting others in God's name, for God Himself will right each wrong. And the miracle worker will admit to his followers that he is a mere trickster. And the doctor will no longer insult other doctors or deceive his patients. And a man of fine ancestry will realize that the essence of a human being resides in his virtues and fine qualities; without them a man is worthless—no matter how excellent his forebears. He will stop preening himself like a turkey and he will accept a son-in-law who may have poor parents but who can support himself and his wife.

"Once all those people are redeemed, I can rest in peace and I will never have to be reincarnated yet again."

I thereupon did warrant—I promised to do as he wished. I said: "You've been born in eighteen different bodies. So tell me, when did you first come down from Heaven?"

The spirit replied: "That was five hundred years ago."

"And how much time," I went on, "passed from your first human birth to your death in your fifth incarnation as a tax collector?"

The spirit answered: "That was about two hundred years."

"Well, then the calculations don't work out," I said. "Five hundred years ago you were born as a Hasid who took a ritual bath and then went to see his rebbe. And yet three hundred years ago you were already a tax collector. Everyone knows that the Baal-Shem-Tov lived only about a century ago, and the meat and candle taxes were introduced only some fifty years ago."

Now the spirit did commence—The spirit started making fun of me: "I see I'm dealing with a thinker, an investigator, a master calculator. You ponder everything and you weigh everything meticulously. You know who you are when you conduct yourself like that in all your dealings. You're an atheist, a heretic! Good God! You can see that a spirit is talking to you! You're nitpicking and you're asking questions that only an idiot like you would come up with! And you don't believe what a spirit says! Had I known that you're an infidel, I would never have started talking to you! But now it's too late! I've told you everything! Don't let it go to waste! Do what I've told you to do. Maybe it'll be my salvation. Write down my story and print it and then distribute it. Jews will read it and believe it. I know them—they're not rational. They'll accept anything a spirit tells them. That will truly be my salvation!"

And I did carry out—I did what the spirit had asked me to do: I wrote down his story and I published it.

SHOLEM ALEICHEM (1859–1916)

The Haunted Tailor

(Taken from an ancient chronicle and tweaked and polished)

The novella was originally penned in 1900. My translation is based on the text in Alle Verk fun Sholem-Aleikhem *(New York: Folks-Fond, 1919).*

This is one of Sholem Aleichem's few outings into the supernatural— whether serious or comical. Using satire, a lethal weapon of the Jewish Enlightenment, he depicts a world of baleful superstition, with traditional religious life crumbling amid dehumanizing poverty and rigid convention. While Ansky, despite the sarcasm in some of his writings, could at least sympathize with a few of his traditional characters, Sholem Aleichem revels bitterly here in the ignorance and humiliation of these haunted Jews, who outdo one another in stupidity, trickery, and self-delusion.

Mocking the traditional art of storytelling, the author, in the wake of writers like A.-M. Dik, begins countless paragraphs with a fancy Hebrew phrase that is then repeated in workaday Yiddish. As the reader can see, I have rendered those Hebrew phrases with lofty rhetoric and in italics to contrast them with the more colloquial diction.

Chapter One

There dwelt a man in the town of Zlodeyevke—That is, a man lived in Zlodeyevke, a shtetl located near Mzepevke, not far from Khaplapovitsh and Kozodoyevke, between Yampoli and Stritsh, on the very road you take from Pishi-Yabele, through Petshi-Khvost through Tetretvets, and from there to Yehupets. And his name was Shímmen-Élye—but he was nicknamed Shímmen-Élye-Hear-Our-Voice, because when he prayed at the synagogue, he was in the habit of shouting, yelling, chanting, and warbling at the top of his lungs.

And this man plied the sartorial trade—not, that is, haute couture (Heaven forfend!): He did not copy the creations in what's known as fashion journals. Rather, he was a patch tailor—a great expert, that is, in sewing a patch. Indeed he could darn a hole so skillfully that you couldn't even detect it, and he could turn any piece of apparel inside out and revamp it thoroughly—making old clothes brand-new. He could, for instance, transform an ancient overcoat into a kaftan, a kaftan into a pair of trousers, the trousers into a jacket, and the jacket into something entirely different. And don't think for even one moment that this is a piece of cake! Shímmen-Élye-Hear-Our-Voice was a virtuoso—one of a kind. And since Zlodeyevke was a dirt-poor shtetl, where ordering new clothes was no everyday affair, people thought the world of him.

He had one flaw, however. He couldn't get along with the affluent Jews; he loved poking his nose into public affairs and sticking up for the poor—he railed quite openly against the community do-gooders and he slung mud at the tax collector, calling him a money milker, a blood-sucker, an ogre. And as for the rabbis and the kosher butchers, who were in cahoots with the tax collector, Shímmen-Élye called them a gang of robbers, swindlers, killers, muggers, murderers—Goddamn their hides and their fathers' and forefathers' hides all the way back to Abraham's father, Terah, and to Uncle Ishmael to boot!

Among the craftsmen and in their guilds, Shímmen-Élye-Hear-Our-Voice was regarded as a maven in religion—that is, an authority on rabbinic literature and Jewish subjects. For he would spout Biblical verses and whole passages from the Gemara and the Midrash, none of which made the least bit of sense: *Thy nation. . . . I, unworthy man. . . . I will make merry and celebrate. . . . Today the world is being destroyed. . . . And the children in her womb struggled with one another. . . . It was Thou who didst create the sun and the moon. . . . As it is written in the Bible. . . .* No matter what the occasion, he always had a Hebrew or Aramaic phrase at his fingertips. And his voice was quite a piece of work, though a bit too shrill and gurgly. But he was adept at all the variations of all the liturgical melodies and he knew all the prayers by heart. He was passionate about being the prayer leader and he was the shammes (warden) of the tailors' little synagogue. He could swallow harsh insults, especially on Simhath Torah, the holiday commemorating the completion of the year's reading of the Torah; on that day, it was considered a great honor to lead the congregants in the verses beginning "Unto Thee it was shown"—an honor that was auctioned off.

Shímmen-Élye-Hear-Our-Voice had been bitterly poor—one might almost say destitute—all the days of his life; but he never let it get him down. "On the contrary," he said. "The poorer you get, the more you live it up; the hungrier you get, the louder you sing. As the Talmud says:

May poverty among the children of Israel be like a beautiful bridle for a white horse. . . ." (This "quotation" was really a mishmash of Hebrew, Aramaic, and Ukrainian.)

In a word: Shímmen-Élye was the kind of person who is called "poor but happy." He was short and ugly, bristling all over with pins and needles and sporting bits of cotton in his black, curly hair. He had a wispy goatee, a slightly mashed nose, a slightly cracked lower lip, and big black eyes that were forever smiling. He would always caper rather than walk and he would always hum a song: *Today the world is being destroyed*—but don't worry!"

And he did bear sons and daughters—And he had lots of kids of various heights—mostly girls, some of whom were fully grown.

And the name of his consort—His wife was known as Tsíppe-Béyle-Réyze, and she was his antipode, that is, his exact opposite: tall, ruddy, and robust—a Jewish Cossack. On the very first day, right after the wedding, she had gotten him in her clutches and she never let go. He may have mended pants, but she wore them—she was the man of the house, not he. Shímmen-Élye was greatly in awe of her. She'd start in on him with her big mouth, and he'd shake and shudder. And sometimes, in private, if things went that way, she would even give him a sound smack, and he'd stand for it lying down and jokingly recite a Biblical verse:

"*Today the world is being destroyed*—but don't worry! The Holy Torah says: *And he—the man, that is—shall rule over thee*—be in charge, that is. What's done is done! And not all the kings of East and West can do a damn thing about it!"

Now it came to pass, something happened. One summer day Tsíppe-Béyle-Réyze came back from the market with her basket, flung down her purchases (the garlic bulb and the few parsnips and potatoes), and angrily snapped:

"Damn this whole business! I'm sick and tired of racking my brain day after day after day, trying to figure out what to make for lunch. You've got to be a genius! Noodles and beans again and noodles and beans once again!—may God forgive me for my words! Now take that Nekhome-Brokhe, for instance! What a pauper, what a beggar, what a down-and-outer, what a charity case—and she's got to have a goat! And how come? Because she's got a husband—Leyzer-Shloyme. Okay, he's a tailor, but he's still a man! Well, a goat would be something! With a goat in the house you can get a glass of milk for the kids. You can cook kasha with milk occasionally, you can provide lunch, you can have a solid supper. Now and then you can enjoy a pitcher of sour milk, a piece of cheese, a pat of butter—what sheer delight!"

"I'm afraid you're so right," said Shímmen-Élye calmly. "There's an explanation in the Midrash: *Every Jew hath a share of Paradise.* This means that every Jew deserves to have a goat, as it says in the Bible. . . . "

"What good is your Bible verse?!" screamed Tsíppe-Béyle-Réyze. "I say 'goat,' and he gives me a quote! I'll give you a quote that'll quote up your eyes! He feeds me Bible verses—my wonderful breadwinner, my shlimazl! Do you hear? I'd swap your entire Torah for a milky borscht!"

Tsíppe-Béyle-Réyze dropped these and similar hints several times a day, and they grew so broad and blatant that Shímmen-Élye finally promised her a goat—he gave her his word of honor. She could sleep easy: Shímmen-Élye would get her a goat, with God's help! The crucial thing was: Faith! *Today the world is being destroyed*—but don't worry!

From then on, Shímmen-Élye pinched penny after penny. He denied himself a lot of basic necessities and he pawned his Sabbath kaftan to pay for their weekly needs and to scrape up a ruble or two. Eventually it was decided that he should take the cash and head for Kozodoyevke to buy a goat. Why Kozodoyevke? There were two reasons. First of all, Kozodoyevke was renowned for its goats, as its name alone can tell you: for, translated into Yiddish, it means "milkable goat." And second of all, Tsíppe-Béyle-Réyze had heard from a neighbor, whom she hadn't talked to in years, that she, the neighbor, had heard from her sister, who not so long ago had visited her from Kozodoyevke, that in that town there was a schoolmaster nicknamed Khaim-Khone the Sage because he was actually a moron; and this teacher had a wife known as Temme-Gitl the Mute because she always talked a blue streak. Now this Temme-Gitl the Mute had two nanny goats, both of them milkers. So the question was: Why did she need *two* goats—and both of them milkers at that? Would it be a great misfortune, by God, if she had only one? There are tons of Jews who—praise the Lord—don't own even half a goat. And what if they don't? Will it kill them?

"You're so right!" Shímmen-Élye told his wife. "That's an old lament, as it says in the Bible: *Askakurde dbarbante*—!"

"Not again!" his wife cut in. "Another Biblical verse! I say 'goat,' and he gives me a quote! You'd do better to go to that schoolmaster in Kozodoyevke and tell him this: 'We've heard that you've got two goats and that both of them are milkers. What do you need two milkable goats for? You need them like a hole in the head! If you're thinking of selling one—then sell it to me! What do you care?' That's what you should tell them—get it?"

"I get it. You think I don't get it?" said Shímmen-Élye. "With my money am I supposed to beg them? Money can buy you everything!

Gold and silver make even pigs clean. Things are bad only if there's no money, God forbid. The Talmud says: *A pauper is like a corpse.* Which Rashi interprets as follows: *If there's no bread, go to bed!* Without fingers you can't give someone the fig. As it is written in the Bible: *Askakurde dbarbante d'hungry*—!"

"Another Biblical quote and still another! My head is quoting! You can drop dead!" said Tsíppe-Béyle-Réyze, cursing him and damning him. And she drummed it into his head for the one hundredth time: He should start with the schoolmaster—it might work. "You think he won't want to? Why shouldn't he want to? What does he need two goats for, and both of them milkers to boot? There are Jews who—praise the Lord—don't own even half a goat. And what if they don't? Will it kill them? . . ."

And so on and so forth. The same, only more so.

Chapter Two

And there was light. At the crack of dawn, our tailor woke up, stood up, said his prayers, took his stick and his strap, and got off to a safe start on foot.

It was Sunday—a fine, bright, clear, warm day in summer. It had been a long time since Shímmen-Élye had experienced such a wonderful, beautiful day. It had been a long time since Shímmen-Élye had wandered across the fields in the open air. It had been a long time since his eyes had seen such a green, spic-and-span forest, such a lovely green carpet, such meadows sprinkled with flowers in all colors. It had been a long time since his ears had heard the twittering of birds, the fluttering of tiny couples. It had been a long time since his nose had smelled the deep fragrance of green grass, of fresh soil.

Shímmen-Élye-Hear-Our-Voice had spent his whole life in a different world; his eyes had always seen utterly different images: a dark hole, a stove by the door, pokers and shovels, and a brimming slop pail; near the stove, near the slop bucket, a bed made of three small planks; on the bed, a litter of kids (Heaven preserve us), each smaller than the next, half-naked, fully barefoot, unwashed, and constantly hungry. . . . His ears always heard completely different voices: "Mama, bread! Mama, roll! Mama, eat!" And, drowning out all their voices, the voice of Tsíppe-Béyle-Réyze:

"Eat? The worms should eat you, God forbid—you and that father of yours, that shlimazl, God forbid! You can all go to Hell, God forbid, you and him!" And other such sweet blandishments!

His nose was accustomed to very different smells: the smell of damp walls that turned wet in winter and moldy in summer; the smell of sourdough with bran, of onions and cabbage, wet clay, scraped fish and guts; the smell of old clothes hissing under a hot iron, in a dense cloud of steam and charcoal fumes. . . .

Escaping briefly from that poor, bleak, gloomy world to this new, free, shiny, fragrant brightness, our Shímmen-Élye felt like a man who jumps naked into the sea on a hot summer day. The water carries him, the waves lap and lollop against him, he dives, he dives, he inhales deeply, filling his lungs with air. It's revitalizing, it's truly Paradise! . . .

"Now why, for instance, should it bother God," wondered Shímmen-Élye, "why should it bother God if every working man came out here, to the open fields, and enjoyed a little of God's world every day, or at least once a week? Ah, what a world, what a world!"

And Shímmen-Élye began chanting softly and interpreting in his way: "God, Thou hast created Thy world on the other side of town. . . . Thou hast chosen us Jews to live over there, in Zlodeyevke, squeezed together, cheek by jowl. . . . And Thou hast given us. . . . Ah, Thou hast given us sorrow and suffering and poverty and ague with compound interest, *in Thy merrrrrrcyy.* . . ."

Shímmen-Élye kept crooning to himself, and he felt an urge to drop down right where he was, in the field, on the green grass, and enjoy a wee bit of God's world. But then he remembered he had a chore to perform and he said to himself: "*This is as far as we read on the Sabbath before Passover!* You've done enough singing, Shímmen-Élye. *Enter a different world!* Stride, brother, stride! You can rest up, God willing, at the Oak Tavern. It's run by your blood relative, Dodi. You can get a schnapps out of him any time—as it says in the Bible: *Studying the Torah is more important than anything else! . . .* A drop or two is better than anything else. . . ."

And Shímmen-Élye-Hear-Our-Voice strode on.

Chapter Three

Midway along the road—Exactly halfway between Zlodeyevke and Kozodoyevke there was a rustic inn called the Oak Tavern. And this tavern exerted an irresistible force. It was a magnet, drawing in all the draymen and all the travelers going from one shtetl to the other. You just had to stop at the Oak Tavern, if only for a minute or two! This mystery has never been solved. Some people say that Dodi, the tavernkeeper, was a very charming and hospitable man—if you had the money, that is, you could get a proper schnapps and the finest snacks. And other people say that Dodi was one of those men known as fortune tellers or prophets: They never deal with stolen goods themselves, but they seem awfully chummy with all the infamous robbers. However, since no one knew anything concrete, it was better to hold your tongue. . . .

Dodi was a rough-hewn man, fat and hairy, with a huge belly and a bulbous nose, and with the voice of the Wild Ox that will be eaten by the righteous when the Messiah comes. He didn't, as they say, have a care in the world. He made money hand over fist and he also owned cattle. An aging widower, he was alone in the world. He was uneducated in religious practices: He couldn't tell a penitential prayer from the Passover Hagaddah or from the grace said after a meal. That's why Shímmen-Élye, the tailor, was ashamed of Dodi. As a prayer leader and synagogue warden, he didn't like being related to an ignoramus. . . . And Dodi, for his part, was ashamed of being related to a tailor, a "patcher." Each was embarrassed by the other. Nevertheless, Dodi welcomed him with open arms whenever he saw him, simply because he was more scared of Shímmen-Élye's sharp tongue than of the man himself.

"Ah, a patron, a patron! So how've you been, Shímmen-Élye? How's your Tsíppe-Béyle-Réyze? How are the kids?"

"Well, *What are we, what are our sufferings?*," the tailor replied with a Biblical verse as was his wont. "We're as well as can be expected. *Some shall perish in the turmoil, some in epidemics.* Sometimes we're better, sometimes we're worse—so long as we've got our health. The Bible says: *Askakurde d'barbante d'hungry dkarnosse.* And how are *you,* my dear kinsman? What's been happening in your neck of the woods? *We recall the fish dishes.* I can still remember your dumplings last year and the bit of schnapps—that's the most important thing with you. After all, you don't like reading a holy book. *Why do the heathen rage?* A prayer is meaningless to you! Oh, Dodi, Dodi! If your father, Uncle Gedalye-Volf—may he rest in peace!—were to return from the grave now and have a look at his dear Dodi living in the countryside among a lot of goys—if you'll pardon my mentioning them in the same breath!—then he'd die all over again. Oh my, what a father you had, Dodi! What a good, pious Jew he was! If he'll excuse my saying so: He drank from a dark cup. . . . In short: *There is no man who doth not carry a burden.* No matter what you talk about, you're heading for the grave. . . . Give me a drop of schnapps. As Rabbi Pimpom says in the Talmud: *Pawn your coat and wet your whistle!*"

"Already? You're getting a head start with your Tail-Mud," said Dodi, serving him a jigger of schnapps. "I'd rather hear about where you're riding to."

"I'm not riding," said Shímmen-Élye, gulping down his drink. "I'm walking. As it says in the Paeans: *They have legs but they cannot stride.* If you've got feet, you can walk. . . ."

"If that's the case," said Dodi, "then tell me, old pal: Where are you walking to?"

"I'm walking," said Shímmen-Élye and drained a second jigger. "I'm walking to Kozodoyevke to deal in goats. As it says in the Bible: *Thou shalt purchase goats.* . . ."

"Goats?" Dodi asked him in surprise. "Since when does a Jew, a tailor deal in goats?"

"Well, I say 'goats,' "replied Shímmen-Élye, "but I really mean '*a* goat.' Maybe God'll send a decent goat my way, you know. Nothing too expensive. That is, I personally wouldn't be buying a goat. But my wife, Tsíppe-Béyle-Réyze—long may she live!—you know how bullheaded she can be. Well, she's dug in her heels once and for all! *What a lament!* She wants a goat! And you know that a man has to obey his wife. It says so explicitly in *Astonishing Sermons,* doesn't it? Do you remember the passage?"

"You're more familiar with these things," said Dodi, "than me. You know that I . . . that I haven't a clue about all that stuff. But there's one thing I don't understand, my dear cousin: Since when are you a goat?"

"*It was Thou who didst create the sun and the moon!*" snapped Shímmen-Élye. "Since when is a tavernkeeper a maven in regard to high-quality prayer books? Nevertheless, when the Passover seder comes around, you manage to reel off the 'bless-my-soul' psalm with God's help before you put on your prayer shawl. And on the Day of Atonement you recite, as is proper: *This is my sacrificial offering; take it instead of my life.* Huh? Isn't that so?"

Dodi got the jab. Biting his lip, he mused: "Just you wait, you lousy little patcher! You're too much of an eager beaver today. And you're showing off your learning too much today! I'm gonna get you a goat that'll really get your goat!"

And Shímmen-Élye ordered another jigger of that bitter drop that is a panacea for all ills.

I cannot tell a lie: Shímmen-Élye enjoyed a shot or two of schnapps, but he was no drunkard—Heaven forfend! When did he have the money anyway? Though he did have one failing: No sooner did he drain one schnapps than he had to have another. And these two jiggers were enough to leave him tipsy and cheery; his cheeks were flushed, his eyes were shiny, and his tongue—his tongue loosened and started wagging nonstop.

"You're talking shop," said Shímmen-Élye. "Our guild, scissors and iron. Our nation, God's own nation, has a fine quality: Every Jew wants glory, and glory, as you say, is gory. . . . Any old cobbler wants to rule the roost—even if the roost is just a slop bucket. Brothers, I say: *I am not worthy of all these honors.* . . . I need them like a hole in the head. Get yourselves a shoemaker. *I do not desire thy wit and I do not desire thy bit.* Thanks but no thanks for the honor. I don't want any headaches! To which they say: 'Nonsense. If the guild decides on something, then there's nothing you can do.' So I say: 'As it says in the Bible: *If they put the royal mantle on thy shoulders, then rule thou over us!*' You get your headaches and you're the warden. . . . But hush! I'm talking too much. I've totally forgotten that a goat is waiting for me. *The day is still large.* The day doesn't stand still! Good day, Dodi. *Be thou strong, be thou strong, and strengthen thyself.* Be well and strong and make dumplings!"

"Don't forget," said the tavernkeeper. "On the way back, God willing, drop in again, for Heaven's sake."

"God willing, God willing. I can't promise, but I'll try!" replied Shímmen-Élye. "What can I tell you? I'm only flesh and blood. As they say: 'A man's a man and a duck's a duck.' Just prepare a nice jigger of schnapps, Dodi, and a nice snack—and we'll toast my wonderful deal— the way we should. Our nation, scissors and iron, God's own nation!"

Chapter Four

And Simon-Elijah did leave the oaken edifice, Shímmen-Élye-Hear-Our-Voice left the Oak Tavern quite drunk and cheerful, *and he did arrive,* he reached Kozodoyevke safe and sane. And there he began asking where he could find Khaim-Khone the Sage, who had a wife named Temme-Gitl the Mute and two milkable goats. He didn't have to do much asking, for this wasn't exactly one of your Mediterranean metropolises, where you can easily lose your way, God help us! At first sight, the whole shtetl of Kozodoyevke lies open before you as if on a silver platter. Here are the butcher shops with the butchers, the butchers' assistants, and the butchers' dogs. Here is the marketplace, where the women make their rounds in their socks, going from one Christian vendor to the next, feeling the poultry:

"Listen," they ask the Ukrainian peasant woman. "How much for the hen?"

"Hen? This ain't no hen—it's a rooster!"

"So it's a rooster—big deal! How much for the hen?"

Two steps further there's the synagogue courtyard, where old women sit over small troughs, hawking pears, beans, and sunflower seeds; where schoolmasters force-feed their charges; where children shout; and goats, goats galore, caper about, munch the straw on the roofs, or squat on the ground with their smoothened little beards, sun-bathing and chewing their cuds. And over there is the bathhouse with its sooty walls. And there is the river, its surface covered with greenery like the fir branches topping the tabernacles at Sukkoth, while the water is filled with leeches and croaking frogs. The river glows in the sun, glitter-ing like a diamond and stinking like there's no tomorrow. . . . And on the opposite riverbank there is nothing but earth and Heaven—and no more Kozodoyevke!

When the tailor entered Khaim-Khone the Sage's home, he found him working. Wrapped in a huge prayer shawl and sporting a pointed yarmulke, he was singsonging at the top of his lungs, enlightening the children about "Bovo Kamo," the "first section" of the Talmudic order that deals with "damages." Alternating the Aramaic phrases with literal Yiddish renderings, he yodeled: *This goat . . . which sighted some manner of food . . . on top of the barrel . . . this goat pounced . . . on the food—*"

"*Good morning to you—dekhitu dekufu demakhtu!*" cried Shímmen-Élye-Hear-Our-Voice, half in Aramaic and half in a garbled parroting of that language. He then translated his gobbledygook into plain Yiddish:

"May you, Rabbi, and your pupils have a wonderful morning! As I hear, you are poring over a subject about which I have gone to the trouble of coming to see your spouse, Temme-Gitl—namely, a goat. Now if it were up to me, I wouldn't buy a goat. But my wife (long may she live!), I mean Tsíppe-Béyle-Réyze—she's dug in her heels once and for all. *What a lament!* She wants a goat! And you know that a man has to obey his wife. It says so explicitly in the Talmud: *Askakurde dbarbante d'hungry dkarnosse.* . . . Why are you looking at me so strangely. *Look not at the glass, look at the flask.* This means: Don't disparage me for being a simple worker, a craftsman. You've probably heard about me. I'm Shím-men-Élye, the sartorial tailor, from the holy congregation of Zlodeyevke. I'm a member of the guild and the warden of our little synagogue—though I need all that like a hole in the head. 'Thanks but no thanks for the honor,' I tell them, 'and I don't want any headaches!' To which they say: 'Nonsense! If the guild decides on something, then there's nothing you can do.' So I say, 'As it says in the Bible: *If they put the royal mantle on thy shoulders, then rule over us!*' You get your headaches and you're the warden. . . . Oh, dear! I've been talking so much that I nearly forgot to say hello properly. How do you do, Rabbi!? How do you do, children, *sacred sheep, worms, insects, brats, rascals, and serpents!* You should only want to dance as much as you want to study—isn't that so, children? Haven't I hit the nail on the head? . . ."

Upon hearing all this verbiage, the pupils started pinching one another under the table and cracking up. They were absolutely delighted by this visitor. How wonderful it would be if God sent them such guests frequently! But Khaim-Khone the Sage was unhappy: He hated being interrupted. So he called in his wife, Temme-Gitl, and he and his pupils went back to the goat that had pounced on the food, and they all chanted vociferously, alternating Aramaic and Yiddish as usual:

"*Thereupon Rabbu ruled . . . that the goat had to pay . . . for the food and . . . for the full damage . . . done to the barrel. . . .*"

Shímmen-Élye-Hear-Our-Voice realized he'd get nothing out of the schoolmaster, so he turned to his wife. And while the schoolmaster was teaching his pupils about the Talmudic goat, Shímmen-Élye the tailor conversed with Temme-Gitl about *her* goat.

"As you see me, I'm a craftsman," said Shímmen-Élye the tailor. "You've probably heard about me. I'm Shímmen-Élye, the sartorial tailor, from the holy congregation of Zlodeyevke. I am a member of the guild and the warden of the tailors' little synagogue. Though I need it like a hole in the head. *I do not desire your wit and I do not desire your bit.* Thanks but no thanks for the headaches, and I don't want any honors! . . .

"I've actually come here to see you about one of your goats. Now if it were up to me, I wouldn't buy a goat. But my wife (long may she live!), I mean Tsíppe-Béyle-Réyze—she's dug in her heels once and for all. *What a lament!* She wants a goat! And you know that a man has to obey his wife. It says so explicitly in the Talmud. . . ."

Temme-Gitl, a short woman with a small, bean-shaped nose, which she kept wiping with two fingers, listened for a moment or two, then broke in:

"So you've come to me to buy one of my goats? Well then, let me tell you, my dear man: First of all, I have no intention of selling a goat, because if I really think about it, why should I? For money? What's money? Money is round—money rolls away, but a goat remains a goat. Especially a goat like this one. And is she really a goat? She's no goat, she's a mother! And she's so easy to milk—Heaven preserve us! What a milker! And then the food she eats! Does she eat anything at all? A smidgen of bran once a day, plus a tuft of straw from the synagogue roof. . . .

"But okay! If the money's right, I'll think about it. Money is—how would you put it?—a tempter. For money I can buy another goat, even though a goat like my goat is hard to find. And is she really a goat? She's no goat, she's a mother! But hush! What good are words? I'll bring in the goat, and you can see for yourself! . . ."

Temme-Gitl hurried off, came back with the goat, and showed her visitor a pitcher of milk that she had gotten from the goat that day.

At the sight of the milk, the tailor's mouth began to water, and he exclaimed: "Tell me, my dear lady, what is your price? That is, *how many virtues?* . . . How much do you think I'd have to fork over for this goat? If the price isn't right, then I'm not buying. And do you know why? First of all, because I need a goat like a h-h-hole in the head. But since my wife (long may she live!), I mean Tsíppe-Béyle-Réyze—has dug in her heels once and for all. *What a la*—!"

"What do you mean?" Temme-Gitl interrupted him in the middle of "lament" and wiped her little nose. "What's your price? Let's have it? I can tell you one thing—do you hear? No matter how much you paid, you'd be getting a *metsíya,* a bargain! And do you know why? If you buy my goat, you'll have a goat—"

"C'mon already," the tailor broke in. "That's exactly why I want to buy her—because she's a goat and not a viper. Besides, if it were up to me, I wouldn't buy a goat—I need it like ninety-nine holes in the head. But since my wife (long may she live!), I mean Tsíppe-Béyle-Réyze—has dug in her heels once and for all, *what a la*—!"

"C'mon already," Temme-Gitl broke in, "I'm telling you!"—and again she started touting the virtues of her goat. But the tailor wouldn't let her go on, he broke in, and they kept interrupting one another until their arguments coalesced into one, turning into a mishmash, a borscht with buckwheat and noodles: "A goat? A mother, not a goat! . . . I wouldn't buy a goat . . . a smidgen of bran . . . she dug in her heels once and for all, what a lament . . . money is round . . . easy to milk—Heaven preserve us! . . . I mean Tsíppe-Béyle-Réyze . . . does she eat anything at all? . . . once and for all, what a lament . . . plus a bit of straw from the roof of the synagogue . . . a man has to obey his wife . . . a goat? A mother, not a goat! . . ."

"Are you two gonna stop goating already?!" the teacher broke in and then he faced his wife: "Didn't you hear me? We're in the middle of a Talmudic discussion about restitution for damages, and you two are carrying on: 'Goat-goat! Goat-goat!' Make up your mind! Sell them the goat or don't sell them the goat! Goat-goat! Goat-goat! My head's goating me already!"

"Right!" cried Shímmen-Élye. "Where there is learning, there is wisdom! Make up your mind. Why talk a lot? *Mine is the silver and mine is the gold*—my money, your merchandise. Just say three things: a word and two more and we can toast our wonderful deal. As it is written in the holiday prayer book: *Mekhaspes mepatspetsim,* which means—"

"What do I need your meaning for?" said Temme-Gitl quietly. "Just tell me what you'll pay for my goat!" She arched her body like a kitten and wiped her lips to and fro.

"That's neither here nor there!" replied Shímmen-Élye just as quietly. "Why should I do the talking? What kind of a talker am I? *Ye shall not harden your hearts!* I see I've been wasting my time. I guess I won't get your goat today! Sorry to bother you!" And Shímmen-Élye headed toward the door and seemed about to leave.

"C'mon, c'mon!" said Temme-Gitl, grabbing his sleeve. "Why the hurry? Is the river on fire? Make up your mind! Didn't you start a conversation about a goat?"

To make a long story short, the schoolmaster's wife told him *her* price, the tailor told her *his* price. She lowered a little, he raised a little, a ruble down, a ruble up—and they finally came to terms. Shímmen-Élye counted out the cash and strapped the goat, while Temme-Gitl spit on the money for good luck and wished the tailor success and prosperity. She kept mumbling to herself, her eyes darting back and forth between the money and the goat, as she saw the tailor out, pelting him with her blessings:

"Go in good health and continue in good health and enjoy the goat in good health, and may God grant that she remain as she was here—no worse, and there's no limit on getting better. I hope she keeps on and on with you and keeps giving milk and more milk and never stops giving milk! . . ."

"Amen! Likewise, I'm sure!" said the tailor. He tried to go through the doorway, but the goat wouldn't hear of it. She lowered her horns, dug in her back heels, bleated at the top of her lungs, and trilled like a young cantor at his first performance: "Mehehehehe, my wrongs! Mehehehehe, my sins!" as if asking: "Where are you dragging me to?"

Now Khaim-Khone the Sage stood up in all his self-assurance and, with his whip, he helped to get the goat out of the house. And the gang of pupils did their share, addressing the goat in Ukrainian:

"Hey, goat! Goat! Goat, get going!"

And the tailor took off.

Chapter Five

And she did refuse—And she—the goat, that is—did not want to go to Zlodeyevke with the tailor . . . not for all the straw in China! She pulled at the strap with might and main! But it didn't help. Shímmen-Élye yanked her along and explained that all her twisting and bleating and kicking against the pricks were futile:

"It is written: *Thou livest against thy will.* Like it or not, you're forced to live in exile—no one's asking your opinion. Once—in the good old days—I was a free spirit, too, a fine young boy, an elegant lad in a waistcoat and good shoes that creaked and squeaked. What did I lack? A headache? God told me: *Get thee out of thy homeland!* Crawl into the trap, Shímmen-Élye! Marry Tsíppe-Béyle-Réyze! Have kids! Suffer all your days and years! *That is why thou wast created*—that's why you're a tailor!"

Such were the arguments that Shímmen-Élye leveled against the goat as he hurried along, almost running. A warm breeze blew apart the tails of his patched-up kaftan, sneaked into his earlocks, and stroked his goatee. The gust brought his nose the pleasant scents of mint, camomile, and other herbs and wildflowers; but his nose wasn't accustomed to these spicy fragrances. He was so enraptured that he began reciting the Incense Prayer, *Pitim-haktoyres,* crooning through the list very nicely, in a beautiful melody: "Balsam and clove, resin and frankincense" and all the other spices. Then he girded his loins to reel off late afternoon prayers in the cantorial mode, but in a different style! All of a sudden, somebody (who knows from where? It must have been the Devil, the Tempter) whispered mysteriously into Shímmen-Élye's ear:

"Just listen, Shímmen-Élye, you fool! Why sing your heart out on an empty stomach? Night is just around the corner, and your mouth hasn't tasted a thing today aside from two jiggers of schnapps! Besides, you gave your relative your sacred word of honor that on the way back, God willing, you'd drop by for a snack. A promise is a promise! If you shoot your mouth off, you'll shoot yourself in the foot!"

And Shímmen-Élye zoomed through the Eighteen Benedictions, whizzed through the supplications, and blissfully strode into the Oak Tavern:

"Good evening to you, my dear kinsman Dodi. I've got great news. *With Laban did I dwell.* I bought a goat, a goat, I tell you, from Goatland, a goat! You can check her out and give me your expert opinion— you're something of a scholar, after all! And now guess: *How many plagues struck them in Egypt?*—How much do you think I paid?"

Dodi cupped his eyes to shield them against the sun, which was setting in a golden streak on the edge of the sky. After studying the goat like a great maven, he appraised her at twice the sum that the tailor had paid. Shímmen-Élye was so overjoyed that he slapped Dodi on the back!

"Dodi, my dearest friend! I wish you health! *Thou art right—it is as thou hast said!*—This time you missed the mark! May we live happily ever after!"

The tavernkeeper pursed his lips and shook his head wordlessly. "Hm, hm, hm!" he muttered as if to say: "What a metsíya—highway robbery!"

And Shímmen-Élye's head tilted to one side, and his bent middle finger touched his vest as if he were zipping out a needle in order to thread it quickly.

"Well, Dodi, what do you say? God's own nation? Are we good businessmen or what?! Ha? Just wait and see her get milked—knock on wood! You'll kick the bucket on the spot!"

"I'd rather *you* kicked the bucket yourself!" Dodi exclaimed.

"Amen, and likewise, I'm sure!" said Shímmen-Élye. "If I'm really a welcome guest here, Dodi, then please take my goat and put her up somewhere in your stable, so nobody'll steal her—God forbid! Meanwhile I'll say my evening prayers. I already did my afternoon prayers on the road. And next, we'll recite a blessing over a drink and also have a bite to eat, of course. As it is written in the Book of Esther: '*One doth not chase the unchaste'*—you don't dance before a meal. Is that written in Esther or not?"

"What's the difference?" said Dodi. "If you say it is, then it is. You're the learned Jew here."

After finishing the evening prayer and, as is traditional, spitting after the final words, the tailor said to the tavernkeeper:

"If the pain of pregnancy is really that awful, then we can also say: *Let me swallow, I pray thee, some of that pottage!*—Please pour me something from that green bottle, and let's each have a drop of schnapps and be healthy. Health is the basis of wisdom, as we say in our daily prayers: *Cause us to lie down in peace.* . . . "

After a schnapps and a snack, our tailor began talking a blue streak: about Zlodeyevke, about the congregants, about synagogue matters, the guild, tailoring, scissors and iron, God's own nation. And he also railed and ranted against Zlodeyevke's synagogue officials and the wealthy men and their "order." He swore that his name wasn't Shímmen-Élye if the best solution was not be to ship them all off to "Siburier." . . .

"Do you hear, Dodi?" he said, finishing off his sermon with a Biblical verse, as was his wont: "*A pit will open up and they will be swallered up*—the Hell with them and their fathers and mothers!—I mean our do-gooders! . . . All they know how to do is suck blood and fleece the poor and skin them alive! I earn three rubles a week, and I have to give them a quarter ruble every week, you hear? But what can I do? Still, I ain't the kind of fool who rushes in where angels fear to tread! What's that you say? Let others take care of them! *May Jonah come!*—their time will come! Never mind! They haven't signed a contract with God! My wife Tsíppe-Béyle-Réyze—long may she live!—says I'm a shlimazl, a moron, a jerk, because if I only wanted to, I could show them who's boss. . . . But who's going to pay any attention to a woman? Don't I have a mind of my own? Our Holy Torah says explicitly: *Vehu yimshol bkho*—*and he shall rule thee.* . . . Do you get the drift of those words? They're as sweet as sugar. Just listen, we'll go through them word for word. *Vehu*—*and he*—that is, the husband; *yimshol*—*shall rule*—that is, wear the pants. But where were we? *Once thou hast begun to fall, thou shalt fall and continue to fall*—You've begun filling my glass, so fill 'er up again, as the Bible says: *Askakurde dbarbante.* . . ."

As Shímmen-Élye prattled away, his tongue grew heavier, his eyelids more leaden, until he finally leaned against the wall to catch forty winks. His head dangled, his arms were crossed over his chest, and three fingers held his goatee: he looked for all the world like a man thoroughly engrossed in the deepest ponderings. If he hadn't been whistling through his nose, rattling through his throat, and puffing through his teeth (ts-ts-ts), no one on God's green earth would have suspected him of being asleep. And even though he was dead to the world, his brain was still busily working away, and he dreamed he was at home in his workshop. Spread out on the table before him was an item of clothing that was difficult to pinpoint. I could say it was a pair of trousers—but then where was the crotch? No trace of a thigh? I could say it was some kind of undershirt—but then why were the sleeves that long? So just what was it? I can only infer that it was neither one nor the other, no undershirt and no trousers. Then what in the world was it? It had to be something! . . . Shímmen-Élye turned it over: It was simply a kaftan! And what a kaftan! Brand-new, smooth, satiny. Never in his life had he held such a kaftan under his needle! But that was none of his concern. Taking the knife from his vest pocket, he looked for a seam and prepared to undo the kaftan. But luckily, Tsíppe-Béyle-Réyze burst in at that very moment and started cursing him and damning him.

"They should cut up your belly, your guts—you shlimazl, you green cucumber, you fine bean! Can't you see? That's your Sabbath kaftan, damn it! I had it made with my own money—the money I saved by keeping a goat! . . ."

And Shímmen-Élye remembered that he now owned a goat—with God's help—and his heart swelled. Never in his life had he seen so many pitchers of milk! So many hunks of cheese! And butter, whole bowls of butter! Plus cream, buttermilk, and sour milk, all nicely clotted. And reams and reams of butter cookies and milky crackers baked in butter and strewn with cinnamon and brown sugar. And the fragrance, the fragrance! Then all at once a nasty smell, a familiar smell—ugh! He felt something crawling over his neck, behind his collar and under his ear and across his face, and something tickled him, and a stench filled his nose. . . . He groped for it and clutched a bedbug in his fingers. . . . He opened one eye, then the other eye; he glanced at the window—oy vey! What a horror! What an ordeal! It was already dawn!

"*It was Thou who didst create the sun and the moon!* A nice nap!" Shímmen-Élye muttered to himself and shrugged. He woke the tavernkeeper, hurried into the courtyard, opened the stable door, attached the strap to the goat, and dashed away like a bat out of Hell—like a man who's afraid he's going to miss goodness knows what! . . .

Chapter Six

And the consort—Shímmen-Élye's wife, Tsíppe-Béyle-Réyze, couldn't understand why her husband was staying out for such a very long time. She began wondering whether he'd had an accident—God forbid! Maybe highwaymen had waylaid him, grabbed his few rubles, killed him, and dumped his corpse in some ditch. Since the corpse wouldn't be found, she'd remain—God forbid!—an agunah, a deserted wife, with so many children—Heaven preserve them! . . . She'd have no choice but to drown them and herself in the river—it shouldn't happen to your worst enemy! These and similar thoughts, alas, whirled through her mind that night, and she couldn't get a wink of sleep.

When the first cockadoodle-doo ushered in the new day, she jumped into her dress, went outside, and sat down on the threshold to look out for her husband. Perhaps God would take pity, and the tailor would show up. "That's what happens when a shlimazl goes away!" she thought to herself, planning to give him the proper welcome that he so richly deserved! But when she finally spotted him and saw the goat walking behind him, attached by the strap, her heart filled with joy, and she spoke to him amiably:

"What took you so long, my little canary, my poppy-seed bagel? I already figured you were dead and buried—God forbid!—my gem of a husband!—or that you'd had some kind of accident—God preserve us!"

Shímmen-Élye put his belt back on and led the goat to the porch and, to take his mind off his wife's tongue, he began nattering away:

"Now listen, wife! I bought a goat—a goat from Goatland, a goat that never even goated our forefathers! Our local housewives should only get whipped for all the years that they never even *dreamed* about such a goat! She eats nothing—at most a smidgen of bran once a day, plus a bit of straw from the roof of the synagogue! And she gives milk—Heaven preserve her!—like a cow! She can be milked twice a day. I personally saw a full bucket of milk—I wish I could see so much good stuff with you! And is she really a goat? She's no goat, she's a mother! That's what she says—I mean Temme-Gitl. A metsíya—highway robbery, damn it! She drove a hard bargain, but I managed to push her down to six and a half rubles. How long do you think I had to haggle before we came to terms? Basically, she didn't want to sell a goat—I barely got her to agree. I nagged her all night. . . ."

While he was talking, Tsíppe-Béyle-Réyze was thinking: "Nekhome-Brokhe—she can go straight to Hell! She thinks she's the only lady around here, she's the only one with a goat, and nobody else. I'm scared her eyes'll pop out when she sees Shímmen-Élye's wife owns a goat, too. And Khaye-Meyte? They act like good sisters. God Almighty! They should only suffer half the stuff they wish on me!"

Those were her thoughts as she heated the oven and began preparing buckwheat noodles for breakfast, while Shímmen-Élye wrapped himself in his prayer shawl, put on his prayer thongs, and stood there praying with all his heart and soul—he hadn't prayed so ardently for a long time! He chanted the hallelujahs, which open and close so many prayers; he crooned like a great cantor, snapped his fingers—and his singing woke up all the children. When their mother told them that their father had brought home a goat, and that they'd be cooking noodles in milk, the children were beside themselves with glee. They jumped off the beds in their shirts and joined hands and danced. And they sang a ditty that they had only just composed:

A goat, a goat, a little goat!
Daddy brought home a little goat!
The goat will give us gobs of milk!
And Mommy will make nooo—dles, too! . . .

Watching the children singing and dancing, Shímmen-Élye felt utterly ecstatic "Poor kids!" he thought. "Starving for a little milk. But don't worry, you'll be full today, God willing. . . . You'll be getting a glass of milk every day and buckwheat with milk, and milk for tea. . . . A goat is a blessing for you! What do I care about Fishl the kosher-meat tax collector?! I'll thumb my nose at him! He won't give you any meat, just bones. Let him choke on his bones! What do I need his meat when I've got milk?—knock on wood! Meat for shabbes? For shabbes you buy fish. Who says a Jew has to eat meat? I haven't seen that carved in stone. . . . If all Jews listened to me, they would buy goats. Then our tax collector would cut a fine figure with his belly! . . . The Hell with him and the Hell with all his ancestors!"

Those were Shímmen-Élye's thoughts as he rolled up his prayer thongs. He washed his hands, recited the bread blessing, and girded his loins for the milk banquet. Suddenly the door opened and in walked Tsíppe-Béyle-Réyze, clutching an empty pot and blazing crimson with rage—and a hailstorm of curses and swearwords came rattling down on Shímmen-Élye's head! Those weren't curses—rocks were raining from the sky, fire and brimstone were pouring from Tsíppe-Béyle-Réyze's mouth:

"The ground should only vomit up that drunkard father of yours and swallow you instead! You should only turn into a stone, a bone! You should be burned with all the fires of Hell! You should be shot with a musket! Hung and drowned, grilled and roasted, sliced up and chopped up! Just go and see what kind of goat you brought home—you robber, you murderer, you heretic! You can go straight to Hell and smash your head and your arms and your legs—oh, dear God, sweet, kind, loyal Father!"

Shímmen-Élye didn't wait to hear the rest. He straightened out his yarmulke and went to have a look at the disaster that had befallen him.

When he saw the lovely creature tied to the door jamb and nonchalantly chewing her cud, he halted in a daze, at a loss. What should he do? Where should he go? He stood there, mulling and mulling, until he muttered to himself: "*I wish to die with the Philistines!* Goddamn that school driller and his wife and all their ancestors! They think they've found someone to pull their monkey business on! I'll give them the business, all right—something they'll never forget! He looked like such a nobody—that school driller, he acted like he had no head for business. And then he pulls this on me! That was why the pupils were giggling when the schoolmaster sent me off with the goat and his wife kept congratulating me on all the milk I'd be getting. I'll teach them to milk people! I'll milk out their Goddamn life's blood—those sanctimonious bastards! Those Goddamn milkers! . . ."

Such were Shímmen-Élye-Hear-Our-Voice's thoughts as he started out for Kozodoyevke. He planned to curse the living daylights out of them for all they were worth!

As he trudged past the Oak Tavern, he spotted the tavernkeeper with his pipe in his teeth and our tailor burst out laughing though he was still far away. "What are you celebrating?" asked Dodi. "What are you laughing about?" "Please have a look for yourself—then maybe you'll laugh too?" said the tailor and he laughed more raucuously as if ten demons were tickling him. "Well, Dodi, how do you like my disaster? *All men are abandoned.* . . . When crap happens, it happens to me! Do you get it? Boy, did I ever get cursed at by my wife—long may she live!—I mean Tsíppe-Béyle-Réyze. *With a chariot and steeds!* In bloody detail on a silver platter! And on an empty stomach, to boot! But I'll pay them back with interest—that schoolmaster and his wife! You can figure I won't take it lying down! *An eye for an eye!* A slap for a slap! I hate it when people try to pull monkey business on me! Well, for now, Dodi, give me a shot of booze for my aching heart—I need to wet my whistle so I can have the strength to talk and so my soul won't go the way of all flesh. . . . L'chayim, Dodi, we have to stay true to our Jewish faith— that's the main thing. As it is written in the Bible: *Today the world is being destroyed*—but don't worry! You can be sure I'll make them face the music all right! I'll teach them to pull their monkey business on our guild, scissors and iron, our nation, God's own nation!"

"Who told you it was monkey business?" asked the tavernkeeper quite naïvely and puffed on his pipe. "Couldn't it have been just a simple misunderstanding?"

Shímmen-Élye practically exploded!

"That's a non-sekidor! What are you talking about? Do you know what you're talking about? All I did was go there to buy a goat and I called a spud a spud, like Jacob asking for Rachel. I plainly said: A nanny goat! So what the hell are you talking about?! . . ."

Dodi puffed on his pipe, shrugged his shoulders, and held out his arms as if saying: "I'm as innocent as a newborn lamb!"

And Shímmen-Élye grabbed the goat and got back on the road to Kozodoyevke. *And his wrath did blaze up in him*—he was boiling!

Chapter Seven

And the educator. . . . And the teacher plied his trade—that is, he sat there, force-feeding his pupils. He was still on the topic of damages, and the children's yelling could be heard across the entire synagogue courtyard as they followed each Talmudic phrase with a literal translation into Yiddish:

"*Keshokhshokh bisnuvoh*—it wagged its tail, the cow—*veshovrohes*— and it shattered the pitcher—"

"*To Israel and to the Teachers and to their disciples*—Good morning, sir, to you and your disciples!" said Shímmen-Élye. "Can I interrupt you for a minute? Don't worry, the cow won't jump over the moon, and the pitcher won't become whole again. So who cares? You really pulled a fast one on me—a nice bit of monkey business—but so what?! *I love it when I am heeded*—I hate monkey business! You've probably heard the story—haven't you?—about the two Jews sitting on the top bench of the shvits on the eve of Sabbath? One says to the other: 'Here's my whisk broom—give my back a good scrubbing.' So the other guy scrubs him so hard that he breaks the skin and draws blood. So the scrubbed guy says to him: 'Now look! If you wanted to settle accounts with me up here on the top bench, while I was lying naked, and you had a whisk broom—then let it be, you did right. But if this was just monkey business, then I have to tell you: I don't much care for this kind of monkey business.'"

"What's the moral of your parable?" asked the teacher, removing his spectacles and using them to scratch his ear.

"The moral," said Shímmen-Élye, "is aimed at you and the lovely goat that you palmed off on me by mistake—that is, for a laugh! But with a laugh like that you can truly split your gut! Don't think you're dealing with some dumb needle-and-threader! I am Shímmen-Élye, tailor of the holy congregation of Zlodeyevke, member of the guild and warden of the tailors' little synagogue, scissors and iron, our nation, God's own nation!"

At those last words Shímmen-Élye practically leaped into the air. The teacher put his spectacles back on and stared at the tailor the way you gape at a delirious babbler—and the entire class laughed so hard they nearly had kittens.

"*Why hast thou done evil to this nation?*—Why are you glaring at me like a nasty wedding clown?" the tailor snapped angrily. "I come to you and buy a goat—and you sneak in the Devil knows what instead!"

"You don't like my nanny goat?" the teacher asked naïvely.

"Nanny goat, you say? If that's a nanny goat, then you're governor of the province!"

The entire class roared with laughter, and in walked Temme-Gitl the Mute. And now the pandemonium really broke loose. Shímmen-Élye talked, and Temme-Gitl talked louder, the teacher sat and stared, and the pupils laughed. The tailor and the teacher's wife kept talking away until she finally lost her temper. She grabbed the tailor's hand and dragged him off.

"C'mon, let's go to the rabbi! People should see the way a Zlodeyevke tailor harrasses us! What horrible slander!"

"Fine with me!" said Shímmen-Élye. "Let them see the way supposedly decent Jews—a religion teacher and his wife no less—trap a stranger and cheat the living daylights out of him! As it says in the Long Prayer: *Darn it all!* And you come along, too, dear teacher!" Shímmen-Élye said to the schoolmaster. Khaim-Khone put on his plush cap over his yarmulke, and they agreed that all four of them would go to the rabbi: the tailor, the teacher's wife, the teacher, and the goat.

When the foursome arrived at the rabbi's home, they found him in a calico housecoat, wiping his hands, and very slowly reciting the prayer that follows the response to a call of nature. He fervently drew out every single word, dwelling on it and emphasizing it: "Heeee hooo haaaath creeee-aaaated. . . ."

And after dotting every last *I* and crossing every last *T*, he lifted the tails of his robe and settled in his chair, which had no seat, just ancient, shiny, shaky arms and legs like an old man's old teeth, which should have fallen out long ago but miraculously hang in.

After listening to both sides, neither of which let the other speak, the rabbi sent for his assistant and the kosher slaughterer as well as the other most prominent congregationists, the Seven Benefactors of the Town. When all were present, the rabbi addressed the following words to the tailor:

"If you please, tell your story again from start to finish, and then she will tell her story."

Shímmen-Élye the tailor was not too lazy to repeat and rerepeat the same story as sure as he was Shímmen-Élye, the sartorial tailor, of the holy congregation of Zlodeyevke, a member of the guild and the warden of the little synagogue—even though he argued with them: "*I am not worthy of all these calamities,* I need them like a hole in the head. *I do not desire your wit and I do not desire your bit.* Get your slaps and be the warden. Thanks but no thanks for the slaps, and I don't want any honors! So they say: '*If they put the royal mantle on thy shoulders, then rule thou over us!* You should get slaps and you should be the warden. . . .'"

To make a long story short: He had come here, to Kozodoyevke, to buy a goat—that is, he personally wouldn't have bought a goat, he needed a goat like ninety-nine holes in the head. However, he had a wife—long may she live!—her name was Tsíppe-Béyle-Réyze—and she hadn't given him any peace—*What a lament!* She wanted a goat! And you know that a man has to obey his wife. So he had gone to Khaim-Khone the Talmud teacher, and they had haggled over a goat. *For Rachel thy doubter:* over a goat! In the end, he had forked over the rubles, and they had palmed off—the Devil only knows what—it was monkey business, that's what it was! And he, Shímmen-Élye, he hated monkey business. You've heard the story—haven't you?—about the two Jews in the shvits on the eve of Sabbath? . . .

And Shímmen-Élye the tailor told the parable of the bathhouse once again, and the rabbi and the rabbi's assistants and the Seven Benefactors of the Town all laughed.

"Well, we have listened to one side," said the rabbi. "Now let us hear the other side."

So Khaim-Khone the Sage got to his feet, straightened out his hat on his yarmulke, and began in Hebrew: "*Listen to me, gentlemen.*" Then he switched to Yiddish. "This is the story of what happened—the full story:

"I was sitting and teaching my pupils, yes, sitting, and I was teaching the order on damages, "Bovo Kamo"—yes, "Bovo Kamo." And in walks that man from Zlodeyevke, that man, and he says he's from Zlodeyevke, from Zlodeyevke he says, and he says good day, he says, and he tells me this whole story, he tells me he's a Zlodeyevker, that is, from Zlodeyevke, he is—and he has a wife, he has, and her name is Tsíppe-Béyle-Réyze—yes, that's her name, yes, that's it—isn't it?"

The teacher leaned toward the tailor, and the tailor, who'd been clutching his goatee all this time, stood there with his eyes shut, his yarmulke slightly askew, and rocked, and said in his manner:

"*It is true and can exist and is correct!* She has all three names— Tsíppe and Béyle and Réyze. That's the name she was given and that's the name she's gone by ever since I've known her these past thirty years or so. But let's hear what else you have to say, my friend. Just don't stray from the subject! Stick to the topic at hand—*about the first and about the last!* Tell us what I said and what you said. As King Solomon says: '*There is nothing new under the sun*'—which means: Cunning never helps."

"I don't know from nothin', I don't!" said the frightened teacher and pointed to his wife. "She was the one who talked to him, she was the one who haggled with him—she! I don't know from nothin', I don't!"

"Now," said the rabbi, "let's listen to what she has to say."

The rabbi pointed his finger at the teacher's wife, and she, Temme-Gitl the Mute, wiped her lips, propped herself on one hand, and with her other hand she began gesticulating—swiftly, nonstop, and with a blazing face.

"Just listen to me, Jews, this is what happened:

"Now this man, this Zlodeyevke tailor, that is—no offense, but he's . . . he's either a lunatic or a drunkard or who knows what?! Have you ever heard the likes of it? A Jew comes to me, comes all the way from Zlodeyevke, and leeches on to me and won't let go and nags me to sell him a goat, I had two—and he reels off some megillah about how he wouldn't buy a goat, he needs it like a ho-ho-hole in the head, but he's got a wife—her name's Tsíppe-Béyle-Réyze—she's dug in her heels once and for all—a goat! And a husband, he says, has to obey his wife. Do you understand what he's talking about? So I says: What's it to me? If you want to buy a goat from me, I'll sell you one—that is, I really wouldn't sell a goat for all the money in the world. What's money, after all? Money is round, it rolls away. Money rolls away, but a goat remains a goat, especially a goat like this one. And is she really a goat? She's no goat, she's a mother! And she's so easy to milk—Heaven preserve us! What a milker! And then the food she eats! Does she eat anything at all? A smidgen of bran once a day, plus a bit of straw from the roof of the synagogue. . . .

"But after thinking about it, I figured: 'I've got two goats—Heaven protect us!—and money is a tempter.' To make a long story short: My husband—long may he live—got involved and we agreed on a price. Guess how much? It shouldn't happen to my worst enemies—Lord in Heaven! And I handed over the goat! May all my near and dear have such a goat! And is she really a goat? She's no goat, she's a mother! And now the tailor's slandering us, he says she's no nanny goat! You know what? There she is. Give me a bucket please, and I'll milk her before your very eyes!"

Temme-Gitl borrowed the rebbetsin's milk bucket and she milked the goat before their very eyes, and showed the full bucket to each person in turn: first, of course, the rabbi and the judges, then the Seven Benefactors of the Town, and finally the rest of those present. And a turmoil broke out in the room, a Heaven-shattering bedlam!

One person said: "The tailor should be fined—he should treat us all to a round of drinks!" And someone else said: "A fine ain't enough—we should confiscate the goat!" A third person said: "No, the goat is a goat. Let the tailor live happily ever after with her in wealth and honor. We should treat him to a few good whacks and then kick him out with his goat—and they can go straight to Hell!"

Seeing this turn of events, Shímmen-Élye very slowly inched toward the door and skedaddled.

Chapter Eight

And the tailor did lift his feet—He made a run for it with the goat and raced toward Zlodeyevke like a man fleeing a fire. He peered around to make sure he wasn't being followed—God forbid!—and he thanked the Good Lord that he had escaped *for free and without payment of silver*—unscathed, unslapped. . . .

Upon passing the Oak Tavern, he thought to himself: "You won't get the truth out of me, Goddamm it!" And he didn't say a word to Dodi about what had happened.

"Well, what's been going on?" asked Dodi, feigning curiosity.

"What do you think, Tsíppe-Béyle-Réyze, old pal?" replied Shímmen-Élye. "People respect me! No one pulls any monkey business on me, *for I am a man and not a leper!* I wasn't born yesterday. I just opened my holy mouth and tested the teacher's knowledge of the Torah, and it turned out that I know the Commentaries and interpretations better than he does. . . . Well, to make a long story short: they asked me to forgive them and they gave me the nanny goat I had paid for. Here she is. Please watch her for a moment. As it is written in the Bible: '*Take the creatures and give me the wealth*'—Take the goat and give me a shot of schnapps."

"Not only is he full of himself, but he's a liar too!" thought the tavernkeeper. "I should play the same trick on him again and then hear what else he has to say." Out loud he said to the tailor: "I've got something special for you, Shímmen-Élye, a jigger of old cherry brandy, if you'd care for some."

"From the wine that will be sipped by the righteous when the Messiah comes!" said Shímmen-Élye, licking his lips. "Don't mind if I do. Pour me a little. Let a conna-sewer express his opinion. I know you serve a good glass of cherry brandy, but *not every man is a liar*—I mean, not every man is a maven."

The very first glassful loosened our tailor's tongue, and he said to the tavernkeeper: "Now listen, my dear cousin, you weren't born yesterday, by God, and you deal with lots of different people. Tell me honestly, do you believe in magic? In illusion?"

"What do you mean?" asked Dodi, playing the innocent.

"I mean," said Shímmen-Élye, "a dybbuk, a hobgoblin, a devil, a gílgul—a wandering soul? . . ."

"Why do you ask?" said Dodi, making a naïve face and puffing on his pipe.

"No special reason," said Shímmen-Élye-Hear-Our-Voice, and he kept talking about gílgul possessions, about witches and wizards, demons and devils, imps, trolls, and werewolves. Dodi pretended to be all ears as he puffed on his pipe. Finally, he spat and said to the tailor:

"You know what, Shímmen-Élye? Tonight I'm gonna be too scared to fall asleep. Frankly, I've always been afraid of ghosts. But starting today, I'm gonna believe in gílguls and also trolls. . . ."

"What choice do you have?" asked the tailor. "Try not to believe in them. Let a real live imp visit you and start playing his proper tricks—he'll capsize a trough of borscht, pour out your water, drain all your pitchers, smash all your pots, tie the fringes of your prayer shawl into knots, toss a cat into your bed, and the cat'll lie on your chest and it'll feel like it weighs half a ton, and you won't be able to move. And when you get up, the cat'll peer right into your eyes like a sinful human being. . . ."

"Enough! Enough!" said the tavernkeeper. He spat for safety's sake and waved his hands around. "Enough with stories like that in the evening!"

"Well, good night, then, Dodi. Please forgive me for troubling you a little. You know it's not my fault. As it is written in the Bible: '*There were no words*'—Granny ain't got enough worries. . . . Good night!"

Chapter Nine

When the tailor did arrive—When he came home, he was furious and he wanted to read his wife the riot act for all she was worth; but he made every effort to control himself: "Oh well, a woman's a woman. Forget it!" And for the sake of peace, he told his wife an appealing lie:

"Listen, Tsíppe-Béyle-Réyze, old pal. People do respect me, it seems. Never mind what I did to the teacher and his wife—we can forget it. I really gave it to them, but good! Furthermore, I dragged them off to the rabbi, and the rabbi ordered them to pay a fine. Because if a man like Shímmen-Élye comes to buy a goat from them, they should feel greatly honored, because this Shímmen-Élye, says the rabbi, is a big shot who—"

But Tsíppe-Béyle-Réyze didn't want to hear any more of the praises heaped on her husband. She couldn't wait to see the genuine nanny goat that he had brought home. She grabbed a pot and hurried to milk the goat. Before long, though, she came dashing in, unable to say a word, for she was dumbstruck. She seized Shímmen-Élye from behind (pardon me!), clutched his collar, gave him three solid right hooks, and threw him out together with the lovely goat: "Go to Hell, go straight to Hell, Goddamm it!"

The tailor, remaining outside with the lovely goat, was promptly surrounded by a cluster of men, women, and children. They listened to the miracles reported by Shímmen-Élye: This goat, which he held on to by his belt, was a nanny goat only in Kozodoyevke—that was the only place she could be milked in, the only place she gave milk in. But the instant they arrived here, she stopped being a nanny goat. . . . Shímmen-Élye swore on a stack of Bibles and by all that was holy—one can believe an apostate—that he himself, with his own eyes, had personally seen her getting milked in the rabbi's home, and she had filled up a whole bucket.

A lot of people stopped, scrutinized the goat very earnestly, asked to hear the story over and over again, and were very astonished. . . . A few laughed, poked fun, made cracks, while others shook their heads, spat, and said: "A fine goat! If she's a goat, then I'm a rabbi's wife."

"So then what is she?"

"A gílgul—a wandering soul! Can't you see it's a gílgul? The goat's possessed."

The word *gílgul* was snatched up by the entire crowd. They told all sorts of tales about gílguls—possessions that had occurred here in Zlodeyevke, in Kozodoyevke, in Yampeli, in Pishi-Yabede, in Khaplapovitsh, in Petshi-Khvost, and all over the world! Who didn't know the story of Leyzer-Volf's horse, which they had taken outside the town, slaughtered, and buried in a winding-sheet? Or, for instance, who hadn't heard about the quarter chicken, which had started moving its wing when it was served at the Sabbath dinner? . . . And similar true stories.

When Shímmen-Élye stood up to walk on, he was honorably escorted by a whole regiment of schoolboys, who yelled after him: "Hurray for Shímmen-Élye-Hear-Our-Voice! Hurray for the milking tailor!"

The crowd roared with laughter.

Shímmen-Élye took this to heart. Bad enough that he had suffered this misfortune, but now they were jeering at him in the bargain! He went to his guild with the goat and raised a hue and cry: "C'mon! Why keep quiet?" He told the whole story of how he'd been taken for a ride in Kozodoyevke and he showed them the goat. . . . They instantly sent for schnapps and in the end they decided to go to the rabbi, the rabbi's assistants, and the Seven Benefactors of the Town: They would holler at them, move Heaven and earth. What?! Who had ever heard of such an outrage?! Grab a poor man, a tailor, bamboozle him out of his last few rubles by selling him a bogus goat and then palming off—the Devil only knew what—on him. And then poking fun at him—and twice in the bargain! Something like this had never happened even in Sodom!

And the guild members went to the rabbi, the rabbi's assistants, and the Seven Benefactors of the Town and hollered at them and moved

Heaven and earth: "What?! Who has ever heard of such an outrage?! Grab a poor man, a tailor, bamboozle him out of his last few rubles by selling him a bogus goat and then palming off—the Devil only knows what—on him. And then making fun of him—and twice in the bargain! Something like this has never happened even in Sodom!"

And the rabbi, his assistants, and the Seven Benefactors of the Town listened to the complaint and had a meeting at the rabbi's home that very night, and they resolved to compose a proper letter on the spot to the Kozodoyevke rabbis, rabbis' assistants, and Seven Benefactors of the Town. And the Zlodeyevke rabbis, rabbis' assistants, and Seven Benefactors of the Town sat down and composed a letter in a very lovely and elegant Hebrew rhetoric to the Kozodoyevke rabbis, rabbis' assistants, and Seven Benefactors of the Town. And here is the exact wording of the letter as translated into an equally elegant Yiddish:

> To the Venerable Rabbis, Rabbis' Assistants, Sages, Geniuses, Dignitaries, the Pillars of the World, on Whom the entire House of Israel is founded:
>
> Peace be unto you all and peace be unto all Jews of the holy congregation of Kozodoyevke, and may all that is good rest upon their heads. Amen.
>
> *Our ears have heard*—It has come to our attention that a great wrong was perpetrated on one of our citizens, Shímmen-Élye, known as Shímmen-Élye-Hear-Our-Voice, son of Bendit-Leyb-Khaim. To wit: Two of your people, the schoolmaster Khaim-Khone and his consort Temme-Gitl (long may she live!), did exert cunning to swindle our tailor of money, namely six and one half silver rubles, which sum they then put in their vessels and they did lick their lips and they said: "We have not committed any injustice!" But that is no way for Jews to behave!
>
> All of us who have affixed our names here below can testify that this tailor is a poor worker who has many offspring and who earns an honest livelihood through his great drudgery, and King David said long ago in Psalms: "*When thou eatest the labor of thy hands, happy shalt thou be, and it shall be well with thee.*" Which our sages interpret as follows: "Happy in this world and well in the next world."
>
> We therefore request that you promptly investigate what has been perpetrated, and may your judgment shine forth like the sun, and you should hand down one of these two verdicts: Either the schoolmaster and his consort should return the full amount of his money to the tailor or else they should give him his female goat, which he purchased, since the goat that he brought home is not a female! This can be attested to by the entire town, which can swear to this according to the laws of the Torah.

And let peace be unto Jews, for as our sages have said: "There is nothing more blessed among Jews than peace. Peace be unto you, peace unto Jews who are far away and unto Jews who are near. Peace be unto all Jews! Amen."

Written by us, your humble servants, for whom your little finger is thicker than our loins.

Respectfully,
The Rabbi, son of the Rabbi (of blessed memory), and the Rabbi, son of the Rabbi (of blessed memory), and Borekh Kaftan, Zorekh Gizzard, Fishl Trash, Khaim Squeal, Nisl Stalk, Mottl Peel, Yeshue-Heshl Gutgut

Chapter Ten

And during those nocturnal hours—That night the moon shone and it peered down at Zlodeyevke, on its dark, ramshackle cottages, which lie squashed together, without yards, without trees, without fences. At night the town looks like a cemetery, an old cemetery, with old gravestones, many of which are genuflecting and many of which would have collapsed long ago if they weren't propped up on blocks. And even though the air is not exactly splendid, and the smells from the marketplace and the synagogue courtyard are not exactly enticing, and the dust is as thick and as high as a wall—nevertheless all the inhabitants came out like cockroaches from their holes: men and women, oldsters and toddlers—to "catch a breath of air" after the hot, sultry day. They plopped down on their thresholds to chitchat a little, enjoy some small talk, or simply gaze up at the sky and study the face of the moon and the gazillions of stars, which you couldn't possibly count even if you had a mind like Solomon's!

That night, Shímmen-Élye, trying to avoid the pranksters, wandered through the back streets, alone except for the gem he had bought in Kozodoyevke. He had planned to start out for Kozodoyevke at daybreak, but meanwhile he had sneaked into the tavern run by Hodel, the Excise Lady, in order to drown his troubles in a shot of schnapps. He also wanted to get some things off his chest, ask her advice, and discuss the calamity that had struck him.

Hodel was a widow who "thought like a man." She was pallsy-wallsy with all the government officials and chummy with all the craftsmen in town. Why was she nicknamed the Excise Lady? Well, way back when, she had been a very pretty girl, a beauty, and a filthy rich excise man once spotted her taking some geese to the kosher slaughterer. The excise man stopped her and asked: "My girl, who's your father?"

She blushed, laughed, and scooted away, and from then on they called her the Excise Lady. Others say that the excise man then visited her home, spoke to her father, Nakhmiye Trash, and asked for her hand as is, with no dowry, and he even offered to pay her father a certain amount. They were already preparing for the engagement ceremony when the townsfolk started gossiping about her, and because of those rumors the engagement was canceled. Later on, she was quietly married off to some shlimazl, an epileptic. But she refused to attend her own wedding, she wept profusely, and the whole shtetl wept. They said she was still crazy about the excise man, and someone wrote a ditty, which is still sung today by the girls and women in Zlodeyevke. The ditty starts as follows:

It was midnight,
The moon was shining
And Hodel sat by the door,
Where she was pining. . . .

And it ends as follows:

I love you so much,
My darling, I do.
I simply can't live,
Can't live without you.

That was Hodel the Excise Lady, and it was to her that our tailor poured out his bitter heart. He told her everything that was burdening his mind and he asked for her advice: What should he do? "What should I do? You're sort of like what King David says in the Song of Songs: *Black am I yet beautiful. . . .* Some women are beautiful, some are brainy, but you're both. So give me some advice: What should I do?"

"What should you do?" said Hodel and spat. "Can't you see that it's a gílgul? The goat's possessed. Why keep a white elephant? Kick the goat out—it can go to Hell. If you don't kick it out, you might suffer the same fate, God forbid, as my Aunt Pearl, who's gone on to a better world."

"What happened?" asked Shímmen-Élye, terrified.

"What happened?" said Hodel with a sigh. "My Aunt Pearl—may she rest in peace!—was a decent and pious woman. In my family everyone's decent. . . . But here in this crappy Zlodeyevke—I hope it burns to a crisp!—people like to talk behind other people's backs and ruin their reputations, whereas to your face they kiss your butt—cuddle-wuddle. Well, to make a long story short: One day, when my Aunt Pearl—may she rest in peace!—went to the marketplace, she happened to spot a ball of cotton yarn on the ground. She says to herself: 'A ball of cotton yarn—that's something I could use.' So she bends down and picks it up.

Then she walks on. But the ball of yarn jumps into her face and falls on the ground. So she bends down once again and picks it up, and the ball jumps into her face again and falls on the ground. So she mulls about it, then spits on the ball of yarn (the hell with it!), and she's about to go home. She looks at the ball—and it's rolling after her! She tries to run—and the ball of yarn just rolls faster. To make a long story short: The poor thing comes home with one foot in the grave and then she faints dead away. She was sick for something like a year. So now how do you explain it? What do you think? Well? Can you guess?"

"Hmm! *All are beloved, all chosen*—women are all cut from the same cloth!" said Shímmen-Élye. "Those are old wives' tales, haunted mills, figments, fancies, fantasies. If we listened to all the gobbledygook that women babble, we'd be scared of our own shadows. As it is written in the Bible: '*Women are foolish*—women are geese!' But so what?! *Today the world is being destroyed*—but don't worry! A good night to you."

And Shímmen-Élye the tailor went back out. The night was spangled with stars. The moon was sailing through wispy clouds, which looked like high, dark, silvery mountains. With half its face the moon peered down at the shtetl of Zlodeyevke, which was sound asleep. A few householders who were scared of bedbugs had taken their bedding outdoors and pulled their yellow sheets up over their heads. They were snoring their hearts out while dreaming the sweetest dreams. They dreamed about raking in a wad of cash at the county fair, making a mint, netting a nice bit of change; they dreamed about a lenient landowner, about a successful deal, about a piece of bread, about an honorable livelihood—about honor in general. Very diverse dreams!

Not a living soul was to be seen in the street, not a peep was to be heard. Even the butchers' dogs, after barking their lungs out all day long, were curled up between the blocks, burying their muzzles in their paws—and shush! Now and then, a dog would let out a muffled growl when he dreamed about a bone that other dogs were drooling over or about a fly meandering into his ear and whispering a secret. And every so often, a foolish bug would flit through with outspread wings, hovering and circling, humming like the string of a bass—"Mmmmmmmmmm!"—then drop to the ground and fade out. . . .

As for the town watchman, who usually made the nightly rounds of the shops, rattling with his two sticks—rattle, rattle! Rattle, rattle!—he had apparently gotten sloshed on purpose. For he was leaning against a wall, fast asleep. . . .

And in this silent darkness, Shímmen-Élye the tailor was wandering through the entire town all by his lonesome, not knowing whether to walk, whether to stand, whether to sit. . . . And he roamed and roved, softly murmuring to himself: *"A dog came and ate the little goat.* But it didn't cause Granny any worries, she simply bought herself a horse. Let wrack and ruin come to the goat! A goat?" And he launched into the Passover song: *"This is the kiiiiiid, the little kiiiiiid, my father bought for two zuzim"*—a song that tells us that no sin goes unpunished!

He burst out laughing and was startled by his own laughter. Meanwhile he sauntered past the Cold Synagogue, which was renowned for its ghosts: Every Sabbath night they would come and pray there, wearing white smocks and prayer shawls. The tailor thought he heard a crooning—"Ooooooh!"—like the wind gusting into a flue on a winter night. . . . Shímmen-Élye edged away from the Cold Synagogue and turned into the Christian street. Suddenly he heard a voice: "Pstsss!" It was a hoot owl perching way up high on the church spire. . . . The tailor felt terribly gloomy, frightened, in mortal peril. But he pulled himself together, screwed up his courage, and wanted to recite some Biblical verse—the kind you recite at night. Except he couldn't remember the verse, it had flown away!

And as bad luck would have it, all sorts of fearful images crossed his mind—memories of friends who had long since passed on to the True World. And he recalled all kinds of horrifying stories that he had heard in the course of his life: stories about devils, about ghosts and demons in the guise of calves, tales about trolls scurrying around as if on wheels, about werewolves who strode on their hands, about creatures with only one eye . . . and stories about the living dead, who wear shrouds as they wander through the World of Chaos between here and the afterlife. . . .

Shímmen-Élye was convinced that his goat was no goat but actually possessed by a gílgul or a demon that was about to stick out a tongue seven yards long or flap its wings and let out a whoop that would shake the entire town: "Cockadoodle-doo!" The tailor's head was bursting. So he halted and loosened his belt. He wanted to get rid of his white elephant. But what good did it do? The handsome fellow dug in his heels: He didn't want to leave the tailor for even a minute! Shímmen-Élye tried to take a few steps—and the goat followed him. The tailor turned to the right, and the goat turned to the right. The tailor turned to the left, and the goat turned to the left.

"Help!" shouted Shímmen-Élye in a strange voice and scurried away! And as he scurried, it was as if someone were chasing him and bleating in a goatish falsetto, talking to him like a human being and chanting to him like a cantor: *"God who granteth death and life giveth death and bringeth resurrection."*

Chapter Eleven

Came the dawn—In the morning, when men got up and went to pray, women took off for the marketplace, and girls to tend the herds, they found Shímmen-Élye the tailor sitting on the ground. Next to him, with its feet tucked in, sat the lovely goat, chewing its cud and wagging its goatee. People walked over to the tailor, spoke to him—but he didn't say a word, he merely sat and stared like a clay golem. . . . Soon he was surrounded by a throng, a crowd, with people hurrying up from all over the shtetl—talk, turmoil, tumult, all the way up to Heaven: "Shímmen-Élye's goat. . . . Hear-Our-Voice. . . . Gílgul. . . . Demon. . . . Were-wolf. . . . Devil. . . . Disguised. . . . Led. . . . Riding all night long. . . . Tortured. . . . Tortured to death. . . ."

Enough lies started making the rounds: The tailor had ridden—each and every person claimed he had seen it with his own eyes. . . .

"Who rode on who?" asked one man, sticking his head into the throng. "Shímmen-Élye on the goat or the goat on Shímmen-Élye?"

The crowd roared with laughter!

"Shame on you for laughing like that!" cried a craftsman. "Men with beards! With wives! With kids! You ought to be totally ashamed of yourselves! Did you gather here just to laugh?! Can't you see what an awful condition the tailor's in? He's got one foot in the grave! We should get him home and call the doctor! Don't just stand there laughing your heads off! You can all go to Hell—you and your dads and your dads' dads!!!"

Those words came shooting out like cannonballs, and the crowd stopped laughing. One man hustled off to get water, another to call Yudl the healer. A few Jews picked up the patient—pardon me!—carried him to his home, and put him to bed. Soon Yudl the healer came hurrying over with all the tools of his trade and launched into his "great rescue action." He applied leeches and cupping glasses, then opened a vein and drew oceans of blood.

"The more blood we draw," said Yudl, "the better, because all sicknesses—may we be spared!—come from the inside, from the humors." That was how Yudl the healer explained the "science of medicine," and he promised to drop by again that evening—God willing!

Tsíppe-Béyle-Réyze took just one look at her husband—that miserable shlimazl—lying there on the wobbly sofa, under piles of rags, babbling feverishly, incoherently, with his eyes rolled up, his lips parched—and she began wringing her hands, banging her head against the wall, and lamenting and yammering in a chant that is usually reserved for mourning the dead.

"Oy, gevalt! Oy, gevalt! I've been struck down by thunder—a huuuge thunderbolt. Hooooow can you leaeaeaeave me with my little chiiiiiiildren?! . . ."

And the children, naked and barefoot—poor things!—clustered around the wretched mother and helped her to weep. The older children wept silently, hiding their faces, swallowing their tears; while the smaller ones, who didn't have a clue as to what was going on, simply bawled their eyes out, the longer, the louder. And the youngest tot, a three-year-old boy with bow legs and a careworn little face, nestled against his mother with his bloated belly, his hands squeezing his head, and wailed: "Mama, wanna eaeaeat!!!"

All these different noises joined into a medley that no outsider could endure. Anyone who stepped into the tailor's home would promptly flee in bewilderment, with a bleeding heart and a shattered mind. And when he was asked: "How's Shímmen-Élye getting on?" the man would wave his hand as if saying: "Oy vey! Oy vey!"

Several women, close neighbors, with tearful faces and reddened noses, remained inside the house the whole time. They peered straight into Tsíppe-Béyle-Réyze's eyes, making bizarre grimaces and nodding their heads as if saying: "Oy vey, Tsíppe-Béyle-Réyze, you poor dear!

Truly a miracle! For fifty years Shímmen-Élye-Hear-Our-Voice had been living in Zlodeyevke like a worm, mired in poverty, obscurity, and destitution. No one had ever talked about him, no one had ever known what sort of person he was. But now that he had fallen ill, people suddenly recognized all his virtues. They suddenly realized that Shímmen-Élye was a rare, a good, a pious soul, a great philanthropist—that is: He squeezed money out of the rich and gave it to the poor. For their sake he quarreled with the entire town, fought bloody fights, and he would share his last bite of food with others—and they praised his qualities on and on and extolled the poor tailor as if delivering a eulogy. Just about the whole town came to pay their respects and they did everything in their power to keep him from dying before his time—Heaven forbid!

Chapter Twelve

And the artisans did congregate—The workers of the town of Zlodeyevke got together at the home of Hodel the Excise Lady. They guzzled schnapps, yelled, hollered, raised a rumpus, made mischief, cursed the rich—behind their backs, of course—and dragged them through the mud!

"Zlodeyevke—a nice town! The Hell with it! Why do our rich people hold their tongues? Hope they rot! Each one of 'em wallows in our blood, and nobody defends us against injustice! Where does our community coffer get money from? From us—that's who! And when they need cash for a plight, a quandary, a kosher butcher, or a bathhouse—who do they skin alive? Us—that's who! Why are you silent, fellow Jews? Let's go to the rabbis, the judges, and the Seven Benefactors of the Town and settle their hash! What kind of Godforsaken world is this where a whole family gets slaughtered?! *Come, let us hold council!!!"*

And the brethren of the Labor Guild of Upright Jews stormed over to the rabbi and raised Cain. Whereupon the rabbi read them the response, which the drayman had only just delivered from the Kozodoyevke rabbis, judges, and the Seven Benefactors of the Town.

This is what the letter said:

> To the venerable Rabbis, Judges, Famous Sages:
> May mountains bring peace to the gold chandeliers of the holy congregation of Zlodeyevke. Amen.
> The very instant we received your words, which were like honey on our lips, we all instantaneously assembled and meticulously investigated the matter, and our finding was that one of our members has been the object of unjust suspicion. We can only conclude that that tailor of yours is a wicked man. He has borne false witness, which has led to slander between two communities. He deserves to be fined! We the undersigned can testify and swear an oath that the goat is a milker—if only all Jewish goats could be such good milkers! Do not listen to the tailor's megillah! Pay no heed to the words of the corrupt; may mouths that spew lies be stopped up.
> Peace be with you and peace be with all Jews now and forever and ever.
> Thus speak your younger brethren, who wallow in the dust at your feet.
> Respectfully, Rabbi, son of Rabbi (may he rest in peace). . . .
>   And respectfully, Rabbi, son of Rabbi (may he rest in peace). . . .
>   And respectfully, Henekh Gullet, Yekusíel Pitchfork, Shepsl Potato, Fishl Ducky, Beryl Schnapps, Leyb Sieve, Eli Buttonhole

When the rabbi finished reading this letter to the workers, they got even angrier: "Aha! Those Kozodoyevke wise guys! Making fun of us!? We'll teach them to disrespect us! Scissors and iron, our nation, God's own nation! . . ."

And they instantly convened another meeting and sent for schnapps. And they decided to take the lovely goat, head straight for Ko-

zodoyevke, and wipe out the teacher and the school and the entire
town!

The thought was father to the deed! No sooner said than done! The
group got some sixty members together, sixty workers: tailors, cobblers,
carpenters, blacksmiths, slaughterers, woodchoppers—warriors, young
guys, all of them equally tough, armed to the teeth: a wooden yardstick,
a flatiron, a boot last, a hatchet, or even a hammer. A few simply bran-
dished various kitchen utensils: a grate, a rolling pin, a carving knife.

They agreed to invade Kozodoyevke on the spot—*to kill, to annihilate, to exterminate*—"once and for all!" said the brethren. "*May I die
with the Philistines!* Let them die—and that'll be that!"

"Quiet, friends!" cried a member of the Labor Guild of Upright
Jews. "You're all set to fight, you're armed to the teeth, but '*where is the
lamb?*'—what's happened to the goat?"

"That's right! Where's the gílgul gone off to?"

"Escaped!"

"That gílgul is no fool! Damn it! Where could it have escaped to?"

"Probably home to the teacher—that's pretty obvious!"

"You're crazy! You're talking like a jackass!"

"Jackass yourself! Where else could it have run to?"

Well, to make a long story short: What good was all the arguing. You
can holler your lungs out—*the lad was not there.* . . . The goat was
gone! . . .

Chapter Thirteen

For now. . . . We're leaving the haunted tailor, who is wrestling with the
Angel of Death; we're leaving the Labor Guild, which is preparing for
battle; and we're joining the gílgul—that is, the goat.

When the gílgul observed the hullabaloo exploding in the shtetl, it
thought to itself: What was in it for the gílgul? Why bother sticking with
the tailor and getting dragged all over the place by that shlimazl and
starving to death? It would be better to head for the hills and run as far
as its legs could carry it! So long as the gílgul didn't become a bum and
a beggar!

And our pal skedaddled like a lunatic, didn't even feel the ground
underfoot, respected nothing and no one, leaped over men and women,
wreaked havoc and mayhem in the marketplace, and put lives at risk! It
knocked over tables of rolls and crackers, troughs of sour cherries and
currants; it sprang over pots and glassware, which dove, plunged, and
shattered—bangety-bang! The market women shrieked in terror: "Who

is that? . . . A shlimazl! . . . A goat! . . . A creature! . . . A gílgul! . . . Oy, gevalt! . . . What a mess! . . . Where is it? . . . There it is! . . . Grab it! . . . Grab it now! . . . Grab it! . . ."

A whole gang of men with their coats pulled up and women with their skirts hiked up (pardon my French!) scampered off after the intruder, crashing into one another. A lost cause. Our pal now knew what freedom was and it dashed off as far as its legs could carry it.

And the miserable tailor? . . . The reader will ask: "What may we conclude from that? . . . What is the meaning and the moral of the story?" Don't badger me, friends! The ending was not a happy one. The beginning of the story was very cheerful, and it ended like most cheerful stories: very sad, alas! . . .

And since you know the author of the story, since you know that he's not the melancholy type, that he hates woeful tales and prefers humorous tales, and since you know him, you know that he hates moral tales, and that preachy sermons aren't his cup of tea—the author therefore takes leave of you, laughing and joking, and wishes that you Jews, indeed all human beings, should laugh more than you cry. Laughing is good for you—doctors prescribe laughter.

YITSIK LEYBESH PERETZ (1852–1915)

The Baal-Shem-Tov Arranges a Marriage

Dedicated to Ansky, the Collector

The Yiddish text of this story, penned much earlier, can be found in Y. L. Peretz: Di Verk fun Y. L. Peretz, vol. 7 (New York: Faerlag Yidish, 1920): 101–122.

Fascinated by Jewish folklore, Peretz, like so many other Yiddish and Hebrew authors, relied on many popular sources—including the vast reservoir of Hasidic narratives. This story lies within the tradition of Hasidic hagiography. The tie with Ansky (aside from Peretz's dedication to his close friend) is the motif of soulmates finally united. In this case they come together thanks to the arduous quest of the boy's father. But in so many other Yiddish folk tales and modern fairy tales, the boy or the girl or both go on an onerous odyssey and suffer through endless tribulations until their victory.

In a Polish shtetl on the banks of the Bug River there lived a couple whom the Good Lord had not blessed with children. Yet neither the husband, Shmúel, nor the wife, Mirl, would have ever so much as dreamed of getting a divorce, and their otherwise sunny life went on and on.

The town never gossiped about it nor did the Jewish court force the issue. People knew that "his soul cleaved unto hers" and vice versa: The two were virtually joined at the hip, devoted to each other body and soul, and any mention of divorce would have slashed them like a slaughtering knife.

On the other hand, Shmúel, a merchant dealing with Danzig, was extremely lucky in his business. And people knew when his good luck had begun, where it came from, and what it was based on.

It was before Shmúel struck it rich, before Mirl stood at the front of the women's section in the synagogue, before she wore diamond ear-

221

rings. At that time he dealt in a little lumber, tying two or three rafts to another merchant's large transport. Shmúel and his wife lived in a tiny cottage propped on wooden stilts and sporting a thatched roof.

Now one Friday afternoon, before the start of Sabbath, the Baal-Shem-Tov was riding home through the shtetl and—talk about luck!—an axle broke in his wagon right in front of Shmúel's cottage. Shmúel and Mirl came out and took the Baal-Shem-Tov in without even realizing who he was—they mistook him for an ordinary Jew! They sent for a wheelwright to fix the axle, but it was already too close to sunset, and so the Baal-Shem-Tov stayed for Sabbath. Shmúel had always been a hospitable man, and Mirl likewise had a mild eye and a generous heart for guests. So from that moment on, not surprisingly, fortune smiled on them. The Baal-Shem-Tov got into the habit of visiting the couple whenever he drove through the shtetl, and their luck became brighter and brighter.

Year after year Shmúel sent more and more rafts down to Danzig, added more and more pearls to Mirl's necklace, and more and more rooms to their cottage, with two rooms set aside for their great guest, the Baal-Shem-Tov. The thatched roof was replaced by shingles, and the cottage became a house—their cup ran over! The house was always teeming with merchants. And once the snow had melted, a minyan of shippers easily got together from the neighboring Jewish shtetls and—please excuse my mentioning them in the same breath—more and more Christian rafters from the surrounding countryside. Shmúel's storerooms were bursting, while beams and thresholds were lugged to the riverbanks. And the billfold in Shmúel's inside coat pocket grew thicker and thicker.

The biggest floods had no effect on Shmúel's logs, the strongest winds never blasted them apart. And even if a shipment was sent out late, even if winter started early, the rafts would somehow steer themselves through the ice floes and arrive safe and sound. . . . And our Shmúel kept buying larger and larger forests. He enjoyed great prestige, his place in the synagogue was at the eastern wall, while Mirl stood in the first row of the women's section, right by the grating. And whenever the Baal-Shem-Tov came to their home, he and Shmúel would spend hours in private conversation.

It was all very mysterious. What did Shmúel talk about with the Baal-Shem-Tov? His business perhaps. . . . Shmúel wasn't much of a Talmudic scholar, nor did he know anything about the Cabala. . . . So why didn't he ask the Baal-Shem-Tov for children?

People were certain that if Shmúel dropped even the slightest hint, the Baal-Shem-Tov wouldn't turn him down. Blessing Shmúel would be no big deal. So what was going on? People figured that Shmúel was so up to his ears in business that he forget about such things—and people were rankled: What was wrong? He was no spring chicken, and there was no telling when God might call. Innuendoes were uttered. In the marketplace, or at synagogue during the brief recess between afternoon and evening prayers, a friend might grab him by the lapel and ask: "So what's it all about?" Shmúel would hold his tongue and extricate himself with a strangely gloomy smile or else he would change the subject. The friend would come home and shake his head: "Oh, boy! Some people! . . ."

Upon hearing this, the wives would exclaim, "It's outrageous!" and they would confront Mirl in the women's section during prayers, or at an entertainment the day after a wedding, or during holiday greetings, and they would ask her: "What's it all about?" Fine, a man was a man, he was preoccupied, he'd forget his head if it wasn't screwed on. But she, Mirl! And the women pointed out that nobody lived forever, and that a woman wasn't young forever and her husband wouldn't be attracted to her forever. And the later he came to his senses, the more difficult it would be for her. But Mirl would emulate her husband: She would hold her tongue and smile or change the subject. . . .

And there were good reasons why she held her tongue and smiled— she knew what she meant to her husband: She was a "pot with a lid." But she *was* a woman, after all, and it tugged at her heart: a baby, a little boy, a male heir who would say Kaddish when his parents died. And the tugging became an aching, a yearning for a child, and she, too, began wondering more and more: How had her Shmúel become such a materialist, discussing business all the time with the Baal-Shem-Tov, talking about unimportant stuff and neglecting what really mattered?

For her part she could really do without the pearls and the earrings, the headband and the bodice, and all the jewelry he bought her—more of it and more expensive every year. . . . She truly loved her husband, he was worth more to her than ten sons; but she didn't want to leave this world like a pale shadow, she longed to be a mother. . . .

Mirl planned to talk to him, in a pleasant way, as she could. . . . But no opportunity arose, and you couldn't just bring it up out the blue.

Now one day, when Shmúel would be returning from *shakres* (morning prayers), Mirl was preparing breakfast. As she happened to pass the mirror, she glanced at her reflection: She looked different from yesterday or the day before yesterday. Then she took a closer look. Time hadn't stopped: Her face was no longer so fresh, her eyes were no longer so shiny, and wrinkles were forming under her eyes. . . . She sighed and felt melancholy as she left the mirror and sat down at the table, lost in thought.

Shmúel came home with the bag containing his prayer shawl and prayer thongs and, as usual, said: "Good morning!"

Mirl, instead of rising to meet him, mumbled: "Good morning," and she didn't even smile. "Breakfast's ready," she said in a strange voice.

A bit worried, he asked: "Is something wrong, Mirl?"

Instead of answering, she lowered her eyes.

"Never mind," he thought to himself. After washing his hands, he sat down at the table. His wife barely touched her food.

"Mirl?"

She didn't look at him. Her eyes closed and tears came running down her cheeks. "It's not so simple," Shmúel thought. He got up, stepped over to her chair, raised his hand, and was about to stroke the ribbon in her hair. But she shook him off: "Leave me alone."

She got to her feet, hurried over to the couch, and threw herself down, with her face to the wall. Shmúel halted in the middle of the room, puzzled and afraid to approach her. He wasn't used to such behavior and didn't know what it meant: "Mirl, are you sick? Should I send for the doctor? Tell me. . . . I know there's something wrong."

Mirl rolled over, almost angry: "And you don't know what's wrong with me? Isn't the same thing wrong with you?" She burst out crying: "How can a man be so crazy about business? How can a man be so money-mad?"

Shmúel was amazed: "Who? Me?"

"Who else? Me?" She then turned away and complained virtually to the wall: "How can a man be so money-mad? How can his greed gain so much control over him? . . . The Baal-Shem-Tov visits you, you're privileged—you spend hours cooped up with him, and you could ask him something, you certainly could. But you don't even mention the most important thing. . . . Time doesn't stop. . . . A silent, empty house. . . . No trace of a child. . . . And what do you ask for? Money and more money. Business is all you talk about. Your lumber, your rafts. . . ."

Shmúel rubbed his forehead: The penny had dropped.

He walked over, sat down next to Mirl, took her hand, and said: "You know, Mirl, I've never said a word to the holy Baal-Shem-Tov about my business."

Mirl sat up, her mouth gaping.

"Do you believe me, Mirl? I swear it's true—my word of honor."

She believed him. Shmúel's word was as solid as a brick building. "Then what do you two talk about?"

"I have to tell you," replied Shmúel. "We talk about other people's business. I do ask him for things, but for other people, not for me! You know that our shtetl is poor, there are few ways of earning a living, and there's no lack of illness and misfortune, God help us. One man wants to marry off his daughter, another wants this, still another wants that. . . ."

Mirl's eyes lit up with pride in her Shmúel. "So that's the kind of person you are," she stammered, leaning her head on his chest—then moving it away again. "But I still want a child."

"That's up to God, Mirl."

"That's why there's a Baal-Shem-Tov."

"I don't want to pester him with things like that."

"You have to!"

"I have to?"

"Because I want it. Your Mirl wants it."

And on and on it went. . . . And the two of them were so engrossed, so busy with one another and what they were talking about that they didn't hear somebody driving up at their gate, entering their vestibule. . . . And suddenly the door opened: It was the Baal-Shem-Tov himself, in the flesh. Now, of course, they had to tell him what was going on.

The Baal-Shem-Tov asked Mirl in his sweet and sorrowful voice: "Do you really want a child?"

Shmúel, upset, looked at her. And she said: "I want a child, Rebbe, I want one! And he wants one too." She pointed at Shmúel.

"Aha! And you want one too, Shmúel?" The Baal-Shem-Tov's face lit up with his smile. "Well, let's go into the study." And that was where they went. Shmúel followed the Baal-Shem-Tov and shut the door behind him. Mirl, her heart pounding with fear and joy, tiptoed over and—she couldn't help it—she quietly opened the door a crack. She couldn't help it at all!—she pressed her ear to that crack and eavesdropped on their conversation. She heard the Baal-Shem-Tov sit down and ask her husband to sit; then the visitor said:

"You have to know, Shmúel, that Heaven sent me only one blessing for you. With the power of that blessing I made you rich. But if you want children, you'll have to give up your wealth."

"I'm sorry, Rebbe, but I've never desired wealth."

"My dear Shmúel." Mirl's heart pounded with joy.

The Baal-Shem-Tov went on: "If you lose your wealth, you'll have nothing but poverty."

"Then poverty it is!" Shmúel insisted, and Mirl's heart beat faster behind the door.

"Poverty means begging."

"So what, Rebbe."

"You might even go without the barest necessities—God forbid!—and you'll have to literally hold out your hand for alms."

"I'll make the best of it."

Mirl's heart skipped a beat: Her Shmúel would—God help us!—hold out his hand for help from other people.

"You and your wife might lack even a single crust of bread—God forbid!"

Shmúel began trembling. . . . His Mirl!

"Are you willing?" asked the Baal-Shem-Tov.

Mirl forgot herself and burst into the study: "He's willing, Rebbe, he's willing."

"Really?" the Baal-Shem-Tov asked Shmúel. "Even if you become a homeless wanderer, a 'fugitive and vagabond in the earth'?"

"If Mirl is willing!"

"I'm willing, I'm willing!"

"Then so be it!" The Baal-Shem-Tov stood up and comforted them: "Until God takes pity on you."

And so it was.

Before a year passed, they had a baby in a cradle, a boy. "And he shines," said Mirl and everyone else, "like the sun. God protect him from the evil eye."

And the child thrived and grew. He endured measles and chicken pox and kept growing. . . . From the cradle to the abecedarian, from the abecedarian to the Talmud teacher, from the Talmud teacher to the study house. The boy was a child prodigy growing up, the pride and joy of his parents, of his community, of the entire world. They named him Dóvid—both grandfathers were named Dóvid. And as Dóvid grew, Shmúel's business faltered. The wheel of fortune turned completely.

It had begun at the circumcision party. The lumber was already floating down the Vistula, and the couple's home was filled with distinguished guests, with joy and glee: "Mazel tov! Mazel tov!" The godfather was handing back the baby so that he could be brought in to the mother, when someone tapped on the window and then came through the door. Bad news from the river: "A wind tore up the rafts, and the current carried off the lumber. Not a single log has survived."

Shmúel looked up at the heavens and quoted Job: "The Lord giveth, the Lord taketh away!"

"Blessed be His name!" the mother added from her room.

Shmúel tried to cheer up the petrified guests: "There's still a bit of timber in the forest, and some people owe me a little money. L'chayim, friends, let's drink!"

But in a short time his debtors were likewise impoverished—he couldn't get a penny out of them. All he had left was a patch of forest.

When the boy's first schoolday came, Shmúel wrapped him in a prayer shawl and carried him off to the *kheder*, the Jewish elementary school. Mirl stood at the window, peering after them, her proud and joyous face pressed against the pane. She was no longer quite the same Mirl, but her eyes were shining!

As Shmúel carried Dóvid through the marketplace, he ran into an acquaintance, a forest supervisor, whom he greeted. The man stopped him: "Something awful's happened, Shmúel, awful. . . . It's horrible. . . ."

"What is it?" Shmúel figured something had happened to the man.

"It rained," said the man, "and it rained. The roads are full of pits and holes, and whatever's left of the highway is twisted and covered with scattered lumber and smashed wheels and axles. The trees are rotting, and so are yours, Shmúel."

Shmúel came home in a bleak mood. But Mirl wouldn't throw in the towel: "You know what, Shmúel? Sell my jewels and what little silver we have and start a new business. Why don't you try grain?"

And try it he did. He now dealt in a little wheat, a little rye, slowly, cautiously. He saw that luck had turned its back on him. He certainly didn't dare play with water anymore.

Meanwhile Dóvid began studying the Five Books of Moses. The parents forgot about their troubles and celebrated: a party, a banquet! They had to put on the dog: "If you pinch a cheek," goes the Yiddish proverb, "it'll turn red." Mirl set the table with all sorts of goodies— more than they could afford. And around the table sat the community bigwigs. Dóvid stood on the table, facing his scholarly examiner, who had his hand on the boy's head: "What are you studying, Dóvid?"

Just as Dóvid was about to answer, the house darkened, the sky was overcast, a black cloud came racing in, a gale came roaring as if ripping loose from a chain . . . and hail came pummeling down, shattering the windows.

Of Shmúel's meager grain, which he had purchased on the stalk, nothing remained—a bare smidgen of straw for the landowner.

But it wasn't the end of the world. They still had a home, and their neighbor, a Gentile, had an eye on it. They sold him their house, rented an apartment from him with an attached shop, and started a dry goods business. And so the torment dragged on for a couple of years. Then came a new reason to celebrate—the bar mitzvah: Dóvid wore prayer thongs for the first time and was to give the traditional sermon. He stood on the platform in the synagogue. All eyes were glued to the boy. Behind the curtain of the women's section, Mirl trembled at the thought of something bad happening. But Dóvid's voice was intoxicating. How beautiful it was—

All at once a Jew burst into the synagogue: "Fire! Shmúel, your store's on fire!"

The church bell clanged. Gentiles with pails and hatchets scurried over to save the house. But Shmúel was left without a home or a store.

They made the best of it. An apartment could be found. Shmúel began wandering the streets, looking for work. Now and then he would do a little brokering or carry a message. Mirl likewise had to lower herself, finding bargains in the marketplace—eggs, a fat chicken—and re-selling them to her neighbors. She then sank even lower—filling orders for housewives and delivering the food to their homes. The poor, rag-gedy thing was mortified—but her eyes were radiant with pride, and so were Shmúel's, despite his drudgery.

Dóvid kept growing—knock on wood!—and he was already perus-ing the sacred books in the study house. He made a name for himself—a prodigy, a genius among geniuses. And a gentle boy, a pious boy. Mothers blessed him, and matchmakers beat a path to his door. In fact, a broker who arranged marriages between people in different cities and counties came with an offer from the head of the Jewish community of Berdítshev. This prospective father-in-law, a learned and wealthy man from an excellent family, even sent a Jewish judge to examine the boy. The judge, a venerable oldster with big spectacles and a long, white beard, was a tad disoriented. It was the eve of the new moon, and Mirl served the banquet: She had dug up a herring and some white bread. After the ceremony of washing their hands, the guest, Shmúel, and Dóvid sat down at the table. Mirl stood by the stove, eagerly waiting. She didn't have the nerve to share a meal with such an eminent Jew. And now the judge wiped his mouth. Shmúel handed him a volume of the Talmud, and the judge opened it and moved closer to Dóvid:

"Do you know this?"

"I know it," Dóvid's voice rang out.

"Look through it again."

"I don't have to. . . ."

Shmúel glanced at Mirl. She blushed and responded with the shadow of a smile. The judge took back the tome and asked a Talmudic question, a very knotty problem. Mirl had faith in her son. He ran his hand over his smooth forehead, his face reddened, his eyes glowed, and a sweet smile flickered on his lips. Then he opened his dear little mouth—a silvery chime would now be resounding. But all that came out was a puff of air. Dóvid had lost his voice!

Poverty was endurable—granted. But this certainly wasn't foreseen in the contract. Since the Baal-Shem-Tov hadn't come by in a while, Shmúel took his wife and his son to see him and discuss the matter: What kind of dismal proviso was this?

The Baal-Shem-Tov smiled. "That's the way," he said, "it has to be until . . . the time comes." And he told them to do as follows: Mirl, whose guest he had been so often, should remain with him as his daughter's guest. She would lack for nothing—God help us. Dóvid should also remain and study in the Baal-Shem-Tov's own study house: "For now, he can study without a voice." When they heard the words *for now*, they breathed a sigh of relief.

"And you," the Baal-Shem-Tov turned to Shmúel, "will have to be a homeless wanderer for a time. You lost your good luck in the water, so you'll have to recover it from the water. Follow the river downstream. From one Jewish community to the next. And listen, Shmúel: If you come to a community that's heard of me, that knows my name and knows the meaning of 'Baal-Shem-Tov,' keep wandering. But if you find a place where they gape and gawk and haven't a clue as to who and what I am, that's where your good luck will be restored."

And he prodded him: "Get going, Shmúel! Didn't I say you'd become a beggar? Make yourself a bag, take a stick, and go! Follow the Bug, then the Vistula," he added and returned to his study.

When the Baal-Shem-Tov tells you to do something, you do it; you say goodbye.

Mirl remained in the Baal-Shem-Tov's home as his daughter's guest. Dóvid sat in the study house and pored over the sacred texts, speechless "for now." And Shmúel went and slung a beggar's bag over his shoulder, and began trudging along the riverbank.

And on he trudged. And in any community he came to, the Baal-Shem-Tov was renowned—for curing the sick, blessing couples with children, and putting unfortunates back on their feet. He was the talk of each town; all tongues praised the Baal-Shem-Tov and never tired of praising him.

When Shmúel reached the Vistula, he began trudging along its banks. And more of the same: It wasn't easy finding a place where no one had ever heard of the Baal-Shem-Tov. His fame had reached even the most out-of-the-way hamlet. Shmúel trudged and trudged, until he reached a border. He had no passport, but the Baal-Shem-Tov had told him to wander. So Shmúel sneaked across, arriving safe and sound. He kept trudging on the other side of the border, his bones aching, his swollen legs buckling. He wasn't discouraged, he had to restore his good luck and Dóvid's voice.

One Friday, late in the day, he arrived in a German city, where he wound up in a narrow alley. His legs could carry him no farther. So he leaned against a wall and gazed up at the sky: God in Heaven, where was there a bathhouse here? Where was there a synagogue? And where would Shmúel celebrate the Sabbath? At that very instant, a window opened in the house across the road, and a German Jew, an old man, stuck his head out. Despite his beard and yarmulke, he had the face of a real German Jew. His beard was nicely groomed, and his yarmulke wasn't the round kind that Shmúel was used to: This one had an angular shape—a German yarmulke.

Shmúel trembled: The man was sure to yell at him for standing there, for leaning against the wall. But the man wasn't angry. He shouted something in German, but with a Jewish flavor, coming from a Jewish heart: "*Sind Sie Jude?* [Are you Jewish?]"

Shmúel nodded. "What a question!" he thought to himself.

"Then please come over!"

Shmúel veered across the road. A door opened, and a servant emerged and told Shmúel that the master asked him to come upstairs. The servant took the visitor up a waxed and carpeted stairway. Shmúel walked on tiptoe, afraid of leaving traces. When they reached the next floor, the German, with a German woman behind him, was already standing there, in the doorway.

The German held out his hand to Shmúel: "*Shólem-aléikhem* [Peace be with you]." It sounded almost German.

And the woman said in German: "A guest in the house, and God is in the house."

Their voices weren't very cheery, but these people seemed truly hospitable. They led Shmúel into the parlor and offered him some appetizers. The servant, who had left, now came back and announced: "It's ready!"

It turned out that a bath was ready for Shmúel. He went in, scrubbed himself thoroughly for the Sabbath, went out, dried off with towels, and was about to put his clothes back on. He peered around: Where were they? The servant had taken them along. . . . They had been replaced by a fresh shirt, a *talles-kotn* [ritual undergarment], and everything else. He took the shirt and the *talles-kotn* from the chair but hesitated in regard to the other garments: Could they be linsey-woolsey—which was forbidden?

But now his host knocked on the door: "*Mein Herr,* please hurry. It's time to usher in the Sabbath." Again his voice sounded very tense.

But they were going to usher in the Sabbath: Shmúel forgot all about his fear of linsey-woolsey. He got dressed, and they went to pray: a German synagogue, but no organ; a chancel, but no women. . . . And the men prayed—in a German manner, but from the *Sidur* (the *Daily Prayer Book*). Upon coming home, they recited *Shólem aléikhem,* the prayer welcoming Queen Sabbath and the angels escorting her. Then they spoke the blessing over the wine. . . . And a set table—may it happen to all Jews. The silver candelabras and the utensils and all kinds of crystal and glassware were glittering and shimmering. During the meal, the participants crooned Sabbath songs, and during grace the hostess also read from the *Sidur* and likewise blessed. The daughter—Shmúel just noticed her—a girl of about fifteen, also joined in the blessing. After the meal, they showed the visitor to the guest room. Never in his life had he seen such a bed.

As he drifted off, he wondered: "How can that be? So much wealth and not a single smile on their faces? It's Sabbath, and when they forget themselves a bit, they sigh—he and she and the daughter." But then Shmúel was overcome by sleep.

In the morning they went to synagogue, and after lunch Shmúel took a nap in the guest room.

"Would you like a volume of midroshim?" asked his host.

"Yes, please."

The host handed it to him. Shmúel opened the book, but he was distracted: He kept wondering what was wrong with the German, until he finally dozed off.

It was the same during *shaleshudes* [the final Sabbath meal], and when they were ushering out the Sabbath. After that, the Germans became gloomier. They remained silent; and if they did utter a word, it sounded as if it were coming from a grave. Well, Shmúel couldn't ask—a guest doesn't poke in his nose. But he did have his thoughts, and when the wife and the daughter left, Shmúel tapped the husband:

"Tell me, my friend, do you know the Baal-Shem-Tov?"

"Whom?"

Shmúel enunciated more clearly: "The Baal-Shem-Tov!"

"What business is he in?"

Shmúel's heart pounded joyfully. And the German said: "I've never heard of that firm!" He then added: "Totally unknown!"

Shmúel cheerfully jumped to his feet: "That man is no firm, he doesn't have a business—God forbid!"

But Shmúel saw that his host wasn't listening. The German sat deep in his armchair, lost in thought, staring vacantly.

"The poor man must have a lot to be sad about," Shmúel figured. He then tiptoed to the guest room and flung himself down on the bed. But he couldn't sleep. He lay there until very late at night. The street grew more and more silent until it was utterly hushed. The streetlights were snuffed. In the dark stillness Shmúel heard the woman softly murmur to her husband that it was time they turned in. Then the daughter came too.

The German apparently didn't stir. The mother and the girl stood or sat near him. They began to murmur and sigh very softly. . . .

All at once the girl burst out crying and left the room. The mother likewise burst out crying and followed her. And the father—he groaned! Then he stood up: "Oh, God! Oh, God! Oh, dear God!" And he followed the others.

Shmúel decided to have a talk with the German before moving on. As it says in Proverbs [12:25]: "Heaviness in the heart of man maketh it stoop; but a good word maketh it glad." If you feel sad, unburden yourself. And Shmúel fell asleep.

In the morning he was about to say goodbye when they invited him to stay for breakfast. Once the mother and the daughter were gone, Shmúel wanted to have his talk with the host. But you can't just burst in—so he tried a more subtle approach: "Tell me, my friend, have you really never heard of the Baal-Shem-Tov?"

Again the German replied: "I've never heard of that firm. It's totally unknown here."

"I see!" said Shmúel with a lighter heart. "He's not a firm, my friend, he's a Jew."

"A Jew?" the German asked, with a bit more interest, knitting his brow perhaps for the first time.

"A Jew!" Shmúel repeated. "A man of learning, a virtuous, God-fearing man, a man who does good deeds, a heavenly man—"

"What?"

"A man of God!"

"Oh?" the German replied, a bit skeptical and about to plunge further into his melancholy.

"I have to move on, my friend," said Shmúel.

"Oh. Are you in a hurry?"

"I'd like to say goodbye."

"Oh. . . ." The German held out his hand; he also wanted to call his wife and his daughter.

"Please don't make a fuss, my friend," said Shmúel. "Don't be offended, but I'd like to ask you for something."

"Ah, yes. . . . Very gladly. . . . Please forgive me for overlooking it. That's the way I am, alas." And he reached into his pocket.

"No, no. That's not what I mean. I want to ask you for something else. You *are* a Jew!"

"Body and soul!"

"So am I. Please tell me what's wrong with you."

The German was dumbfounded. Shmúel leaped in: "Something is bothering you spiritually—you, your wife, and your daughter. Tell me what it is. Open your heart to a Jew. Sometimes a Jew can help another Jew. Ignore my poverty."

"It's not that," the German replied. "It's just that no one can help us." He then went on: "We've been to the greatest doctors . . . the greatest professors. . . ."

"A *khalás*—God forbid?" asked Shmúel, using the Hebrew word for "sickness."

"What?"

"An illness?"

"A disease. . . . Yes, a mysterious disease. . . . A calamity—"

"There's someone," Shmúel broke in, "who can help you."

"Yes, the Good Lord!"

"On his behalf: the Baal-Shem-Tov!"

The German listened closely, and Shmúel told him about the Baal-Shem-Tov, about his great miracles. The German's heart swelled and swelled, his face gradually brightened, his eyes shone clearer and clearer, and he soaked up Shmúel's words like a sponge, asking whenever he didn't understand something—soaked them up like a wonderful thing, a glad tiding. . . .

"Listen to me," Shmúel concluded. "I don't want to, I mustn't know which of you is ill. But listen to me: Tell your servant to hitch up a wagon, and let's go to the Baal-Shem-Tov."

The German wavered. Then after a while: "Yes. . . . But I have to speak to my wife and my daughter."

Shmúel joyfully cried out: "Put your right foot forward, speak to them, and God will help."

However, all women are apparently the same: The wife had been standing behind the door. At the right moment, she came in, followed by the daughter. She then said that they ought to try it.

A few hours later, the wagon was ready. They climbed in, and the horse galloped off. They stopped only at the border, where they spent a long time since Shmúel had no passport.

While they're waiting to cross the border, let's see what's been happening with the Baal-Shem-Tov.

The Baal-Shem-Tov was sitting in his study, all smiles. He said to his assistant: "Go get me Yóyne the tailor." And the assistant brought him. "Tell me, Yóyne," said the Baal-Shem-Tov, "can you take a man's measurements without his knowing it?"

"Goodness, that's what I do with you, Rebbe. When your daughter—long may she live—asks me to sew something for you, I come and size you up."

"Can you also do it for women?"

"It's all the same to me, Rebbe."

"Would you do something for me?"

"Anything in the world, Rebbe!"

"Fine. Now there's a woman staying in my home. . . ."

"Aha! You mean Mirl, Rebbe."

"Yes, and her son Dóvid is studying in my study house. Please take their measurements with your eyes."

"What kind of clothes do you want me to make?"

"Dóvid is going to get engaged, Yóyne. So he needs clothes, and so does his mother—elegant clothes."

"What sorts of materials, Rebbe?"

"Use the best, and charge it to me, Yóyne."

"Fine, Rebbe."

"But the clothes must be ready exactly one month from today."

"Not an hour later, Rebbe."

One evening, exactly one month later, the tailor brought the clothes. The Baal-Shem-Tov said to his daughter, who was sitting with him: "Take these clothes to Mirl and have her put them on. Tell her I said so. And she is not to leave, she is to wait in your room until she's summoned."

The daughter didn't utter a single word. She took the clothes and walked out.

"And you," the Baal-Shem-Tov told the beadle, "take these clothes to Dóvid at the study house. Tell him I said so. He should wash himself, then put them on, and come and wait with his mother until I summon them." The beadle was about to leave. "Next," the Baal-Shem-Tov went on, "you are to immediately summon our neighbor, the judge, and also the scribe, and then gather a minyan. Now step on it!"

Soon all these men showed up, and the Baal-Shem-Tov asked them to be seated. He then told the beadle to have the daughter prepare a snack. "What kind of snack, Rebbe?"

"The kind served at an engagement party, a prestigious engagement."

The beadle came back a short time later. "It's ready!"

"Now bring in candles, more candles." And as the beadle brought in candelabras with candles and set them up on the table, a wagon halted at the front door. Shmúel and the German with his wife and daughter climbed out and came into the house.

The Baal-Shem-Tov stood up: "Good day, Avróm!" And he shook the German's hand. "Welcome, ladies! Please have a seat!" Surprised and confused, they sat down—the mother and the daughter at a separate table, of course.

"And now, my German friend," the Baal-Shem-Tov smiled. "I can tell by your eyes that you already have faith in me. First tell us how you became rich. And you, Shmúel—why don't you open the door a little?" The Baal-Shem-Tov smiled at him. "A crack. Your wife Mirl is sitting there, and she likes to eavesdrop."

Shmúel obeyed gladly, and Avróm, the German, spoke in German, but they understood him.

Years ago, he had been very poor. He had had a tiny bit of money, but he was afraid to start a business. One summer night, he was so worried that he couldn't sleep. Then someone tapped on his window. . . . Slipping out of bed quietly to avoid waking his wife, Avróm opened the window. The visitor was an acquaintance who lived outside the town, at the mouth of the river. The man said: "A flood's brought in some lumber. Peasants have salvaged it, and you can buy it for a song!"

"Do you hear?" the Baal-Shem-Tov said to Shmúel, who was still standing by the door. "That was your lumber!"

"I hear, Rebbe, I hear," Shmúel replied, still lingering by the door crack.

The German felt he had to justify his conduct, he pointed out that legally such flotsam and jetsam were considered ownerless. And he told of how little he had paid for the wood . . . and how much he had earned on it—a nice, tidy sum.

"And money," the Baal-Shem-Tov broke in, "breeds more money. . . . And soon you had a daughter, a beautiful girl—a golden girl, as you people put it. Does she have a fiancé?"

"That, godly man," said the German, wringing his hands, "is my misfortune. She can't get engaged!"

"Why not?"

His daughter, the German explained, had been offered the best and finest matches, but she had contracted a disease. The instant she met a prospective husband, she got sick, nauseous, and if she wasn't taken away immediately, she would pass out. "You can see how fresh and healthy she is, godly man, but the moment she sets eyes on a suitor— she faints.

"I've taken her to the best doctors, the greatest professors—"

"Really?" the Baal-Shem-Tov broke in with a smile. "Is that your entire affliction? And I, my German friend Avróm, will introduce her to a prospective fiancé. Not only will she not faint or get nauseous, but she'll run to him with open arms! Shmúel, bring in your wife and your son."

Mirl didn't lose a second, she hurried in and stood next to her husband as if chained to the spot. She was followed by Dóvid. . . . The boy and the girl exchanged glances and were scared and turned pale and then red. They involuntarily took a few steps toward each other, then halted, bewildered, embarrassed. They tore their eyes away from one another and looked down in confusion.

"Well, girl?" asked the Baal-Shem-Tov. "You don't feel sick? You want this man as your fiancé?"

Trembling, she nodded her head.

"And you, Dóvid, do you want this girl as your bride?" The Baal-Shem-Tov ordered him: "Answer me, Dóvid.

Dóvid answered decisively: "Yes, Rebbe."

"And you will also," said the Baal-Shem-Tov, "give a sermon. Scribe, write out the engagement contract."

The Baal-Shem-Tov had the contract stipulate that Avróm, the German, would give the bride and groom all his wealth as a dowry and that her parents and his parents would live with their children for the rest of their lives.

DER NISTER (Pinkhas Kahanovitch, 1884–1950)

The Hermit and the Little Goat

The original Yiddish texts of this and the next story, "Demons," can be found in Der Nister's Gedakht, (Berlin: Jüdischer Literarischer Verlag, 1922).

This author was one of the few Yiddish writers to depict a positive, indeed lyrical, though often eerie, demonology bristling with tales within tales. His gentle, humorous, even ironic prose is rhythmic, with many internal rhymes, following a long Yiddish tradition of splicing rhymes into prose stories. While Der Nister's macabre and melodic universe may be the exact opposite of Ansky's mournful tragedy, the two authors converged on several points: Neither believed in the supernatural, yet both, like Péretz, drew on Jewish mysticism in an effort to create or re-create an ethnic past as the basis for a sense of peoplehood.

It was a bright and frosty winter night, moon and stars in the sky, snow, bedded snow, in the fields, and no sound from the paths, no horse and sleigh, no bell from the way, just field and peace, peace and snow far and wide.

In a circle of straw, with a candle in the middle, sat "those people": Mocker, Prankster, and Fiend. Sitting, hunched over their legs, their scrawny bodies rummaged by cold, waiting for something and watching out, and meanwhile without work, watching and hushing. All at once, Mocker said:

"Demons, listen: Moon is staring, moon is disturbing, and snow is far and wide, and no one will ride, and demon has no work, and there are no human traces, no one striding, no one driving, no bell to be heard. One has to ponder: Am I Mocker if I don't hit on something?! . . ."

"Something, . . ." said Prankster.

"True enough," Fiend helped. "And so?"

And Mocker waited for a while. But then suddenly he rose, got to his feet, his face toward the field, pondered quickly, and then left the circle and—whoosh and whoosh: field and feet, feet and field, and faded on the far horizon.

Hush. Minutes passed, and became the past. . . . And Mocker resurfaced on the horizon, and came and came and fast and fast, and wasn't alone and wasn't on foot: Mocker was riding a ram. Lying on the ram with arms and legs, holding on with his feet round the belly, his hands on the beard. Hurrying, scurrying to the circle. And Mocker dismounted from the ram, grabbed him by the horn, led him to the circle, settled down, stroked him, caught his breath, and said:

"Ram, ram, billy goat, don't you hear a bell remote? Don't you know how far our lady's found, our lady in command and crowned, casting spells on pregnant wives, on women in labor, caressing kitties, rousing mothers from their sleep, haunting them with daunting dreams: dream water and dream floods, dream flares and dream fires—our old witch?"

The ram twisted his head around, banged his horns into the ground:

Yes, he knew: He was sent to bring her there, bring the witch by her hair, how one wished and when one wished, winter night, moon still and bright, snow-white and steppe-light: "Demons, sirs, your graces, let me leave the circle spaces. I have a word, I have a spell, billy goat and billy smell, if I don't bring them right away, from the river or the bridge, if I don't bring them straightaway, from the forest or the field, or the dovecote and its hole, I'll suffer the demons' penalty, I'll be hanged by my goatee. . . ."

The demons heard out the ram, then exchanged glances for a while as if conferring with their eyes; and after mulling, they decided: They would let out the goat to get the witch. . . .

So Prankster took hold of the ram's horn and led him out of the circle: "Go."

"And you," the ram turned and said to Prankster, "wait."

And Prankster turned back to his cronies and sat down on the edge of the circle of straw, and he cuddled up and he huddled with his legs, and together with the others he started waiting in silence and patience.

Still and bright the moon shone over their heads, limpid and lucid it shone into the circle, and through the pure and nightly winter sky it floated amid the stars. Golden moon dust drifted into the floating, and the moon was ringed by a huge, white halo and it was escorted on its voyage by over-stars and under-stars.

Silence. Moonlit night and field at night. . . .

Suddenly—and from behind the moon, from its high and radiant height, the witch came riding on a long broom: Down from higher, down from higher, and nigher and nigher, and on her broom she joined the circle of demons. Catching her breath after coming from sky and night and height, she turned to Mocker:

"Mocker, why have you called me? And why have you hassled my night and my flight?"

And Mocker replied: "Gracious witch, things are gloomy, and demons—I and Prankster and Fiend—are without work."

"Well, so what do you want?"

"A tale, dear witch, a word, about something you've seen, about something you've heard. . . ."

"For instance?"

"Anything but mockery."

"And you, Prankster?"

"Anything but pranks."

And Fiend added: "Something good that ends in fiendish evil."

And the witch began:

The Witch's Tale

In a fierce and faraway forest there once lived a hermit. Year in, year out, he'd feed on grass and seeds and he'd drink water from the nearby hidden well in the wood. For years he was cut off from community—sitting in the wood, in the cave—and so the hermit grew wild and woolly, and he looked like a wild beast with a human face.

And sometimes the bear and sometimes the wolf would run into him among the trees, stop in the midst, wait for a while and not stir, and stare at him and stare, and then silently and with animal awe allow him to pass.

A wild forest kid found his way to the hermit and lived with him in the cave. Ate from his hand, slept by his side, spent each day, spent each night, went with him on each walk through the woods. The hermit shared his world with that single chaste and silent creature: talked and talked himself out, told her all there was to tell—and expressed and entrusted his pure morning truths and evening thoughts.

And sometimes on a summer afternoon, in the forest, amid trees and leaves, the hermit would be sitting on the ground, and the goat standing at his side. . . . And the hermit would take her head in his hands, turn her face toward him for a long, long time, smiling and staring näively into the kid's wild, pure, and artless eyes, and then he would stammer in the meager remains of his language, stare and stammer:

"Little goat, little goat, my little goat. . . ."

A year went by, then two: half of each day kneeling to pray, inside his cave, inside the forest, praying for everything outside the forest, sharing his few words and pure thoughts purely with the goat. . . .

Once—it was a summer day. And the hermit had walked quite far from the cave and wandered through the woods. As is done now and then: silent and wistful, from tree to tree, from place to place, till he entered an unfamiliar thicket. And as he observed the alien region and was about to turn around and double back—all at once, a man appeared before him as if spirited from the ground. And with mute and commanding eyes, the man had a look and then had his say:

"Hermit, they're calling?"

"Who?"

"No answer."

"Where?"

And the man turned his silent and alien back and signaled to the hermit to follow him. . . .

Looking back for a time, the hermit in his thoughts said goodbye to cave, to forest, and to his goat, and then faced forward and, with no questions and as if with no will, fully devoted, he followed the man. They walked and walked an hour and two, and the man never looked back all the while, spoke no word to the hermit, but went his way, straight and certain, and with a will and assurance the man led him along, from place to place, from silent wood to silent wood, where human beings never tread, just earth and roots, silent earth in woods, deep woods.

But then the twilight came settling in. The sunbeams were slanting into the woods. Silent and golden strips of sunlight wandered far among the trees and lay there lengthy, and the woods were so pleasant and peaceful. And the man and the hermit went deeper and deeper. And now the woods grew stiller and darker. The golden strips of sunlight slowly, slowly slipped away. A sigh was heaved in the woods, and the woods became silent. Stillness in the forest, evening in the forest, and in the stillness someone appeared to the man and the hermit: a dwarf. Small and cold and quiet, with a cold eunuch face, he sauntered along, his hands in his pockets, his cap pulled up on his brow and down on his nape, and he leisurely strolled between the trees.

The man halted before him and asked: "Dwarf, from where?"

"From constantly," came the response.

"And where to?"

"Where everyone always. . . ."

"And why so cheerful?"

"There's a reason why."

"And why is that, Dwarf?"

"Wanderers wander and walkers walk, fools seek and saints pray, hermits fast and wizards speak spells—Dwarf knows all that, he knows."

"Knows what?"

"That there is a mountain, in the mountain a cave, on the cave there's a rock, on the rock there's a seal. . . ."

"And in the cave?"

"In the cave—a scroll, and it says in the scroll that. . . ."

"That?"

"That joy in the wings, and eagle in the clouds, eyes in the head, and distance before the eyes, and truth—not far and not wide. . . ."

"And where?"

"Truth in the earth."

"Truth?"

"Yes, truth is the kernel. . . ."

"And the place?"

"Is a secret."

"And who knows about it?"

"This person's . . . goat!"

And the dwarf pointed at the hermit and, cold and small and close to the ground, with his hands in his pockets, he calmly went his way.

The man then turned back toward the hermit and said:

"Hermit, listen. It's falling on you, they're calling on you: You must track down Goat, find the kernel, and frazzle the dwarf's peace and quiet. . . . But look: Beware of advice, steer clear of encounters. . . . Your will is your foe, your hurry your seducer, chance your friend, and patience is what loves you. . . . And the bird will be your guide. . . ."

Said his say and turned away, toward where Dwarf had appeared, the man went that way and disappeared.

Silently the evening thickened. Grasses and silent grasses, branches and higher branches, leaves and trees were suspended in silence as if in the air—no stirring, no rustle, no bird, no chirp of a bird, and no motion. The forest stopped breathing, and still and dark the night settled in: And it found the hermit, still and barefoot, and from the holy to the Holy of Holies, kneeling in late afternoon prayers in the peaceful woods.

The hermit knelt and prayed:

"Lord of the forest and of late afternoon prayers in the forest, show me my paths. . . . Send me my little goat—my guardian and my companion. . . . And protect me from blunders, from temptations and afflic-

tions. . . . And let me hear the voice of the bird—my destined guide. . . .
Let the sign be now in the woods and the peace of the woods. . . ."

After he prayed he stayed on his knees. The woods were already
stiller and darker, waiting with trees and grass for a ripe time. And a
voice was heard, from the woods, from the depths, from evening, and
from silence, a bird burst out:

"Chirp and chirp—thanks for today, joy for tomorrow, the sun is
dipping, the sun will be rising, and light in Heaven and food on earth
and woods to shield the nests and the birds. . . . And Hermit, you:
Don't fret, stay here, stay for the night, and early tomorrow—all will be
clear at sunrise, and be safe and calmly stay, the bird will never abandon
you."

After singing his song, he flapped his wings softly and didn't stay
and flew away.

The hermit then stood up from kneeling and peered about for a
place to sleep and calmly and slowly looked and chose, silently lay down
and stretched out.

Safely and soundly the hermit slept all that night, and in the morning, when the sun was high in the sky, the first golden ray shone down
on the forest, on the hermit's face, warmed him and waited, woke him
and warmed him, and finally—good and loyal and lustrous—it awakened him in the morning. And when the hermit opened his eyes, he
suddenly and surprisingly found his little goat in his lap. Close to him
and silent with him, the goat was there with open eyes, a morning creature, peering devotedly into the hermit's eyes and waiting as if for long,
since the crack of dawn, waiting for the hermit to get up. And the hermit sat up with a start and, loving and happy, he hugged her, caressed
her: Goat, little goat, the little goat's come. . . .

The bird was already waiting among the leaves, waiting for the hermit, and the bird now started to twitter: "Chirp and chirp—and everything's clear, the day is new, the faith is fair, the bird gave his word
yesterday, he honors his promise, he keeps his pledge, he does not deceive. And now get up and now get going. . . ."

The hermit got up from his sleeping place and free and early and
with faith and through woods he went his way.

And the hermit went on, woods in and woods out, from thicket to
thicket, with Goat at his side, with Goat as his sidekick, from place to
place, and no end to the woods and no term to the trees.

And a while wore by. And the hermit spent no night where he
walked all day, barefoot and ragged. He strode whole days over silent
soil, he made his way through soft leaves in decay on the ground and

past dry branches and, still and wistful, unwilling and unwillful, he frightened the forest snakes. Hares and squirrels heard the footfalls and perked up their ears and hid in the trees or behind the trees; frightened, they looked and they listened and suddenly skipped and leaped and vanished among the trees and the branches.

And Hermit and Goat walked on and on, at times together, at times in single file, saying no word, exchanging no glances, detaching themselves—each absorbed in himself, forgetting the other. And the bird forgot about them too: Throughout that time he never reminded them of the way—not in the morning and not in the evening; he never appeared on any tree, he never awoke them for the day, never comforted them for the night, and throughout that time he greeted them never and hailed them not. . . . Gloomy and with no guide they forgot about the way and the goal, they trudged at random and with no remembrance and no longer looked for any way out.

But then once—it was a hushed and budding forest morning. The sun had just come into the woods. And soon after starting out, the hermit and the goat reached a free and open space, surrounded by forest and clear of trees and covered over with high, green grass. There they halted and looked around, and alien and unfamiliar, they joyfully gazed at the open space. And as they stood there, from the woods, from the opposite side, came the dwarf and headed toward them. . . . Drew near and asked the hermit a question:

"Hermit, where to with your little goat?"

To which the hermit pensively replied:

"Where to? To where I am called. . . ."

"And why so gloomy?"

"The way is unknown. And the bird won't come."

The dwarf then walked up close to the hermit and glared up at him, into his eyes, and said: "Hermit, you fool! The bird is dead. It's no use your waiting! . . ."

"Well?"

"Believe the dwarf, the woods are the dwarf's and the woods are a witness: The man's a seducer, the man's in disguise. It's Mocker at work, it's Prankster; he taunted, he thought he could come between you and Dwarf in the forest. Their work didn't work! Spit and know!" And now Dwarf came even closer and glared even harder into Hermit's eyes: "Know that even if your bird were still alive, Dwarf has a net, for little and big, and countless servants who do his bidding, at his beck and call for any errands—the bird is gone, the bird is dead!"

"And so?"

"Just look!"

And the hermit raised his eyes and saw: The empty place was replaced by a beautiful palace. In the morning and in the shine of the morning, and with an entrance and windows. . . . And the courtyard and the palace and all the wings of the palace rested in the morning, standing, and with peace and quiet made ready for guests. The palace was hushed, and cleared and prepared was the courtyard, and clean and empty, and resounding with emptiness. And ready and open was the small gate. . . . And the dwarf showed the hermit the gate and he leisurely and benevolently said:

"Go in!"

The hermit wanted to obey the dwarf right away, step into the courtyard right away, enter the palace right away, and rest his limbs after the long journey and its fatigue. . . . Instead he stood and stood, as if mulling and musing. . . . But suddenly he recalled the man's warning before his departure: "Steer clear of encounters." And all at once he forcefully wheeled around and swiftly and intensely looked around for the little goat. Upon spotting her he took hold of her horn and said:

"Little Goat, c'mon. . . . We aren't fated to rest here."

At that instant, the bird emerged from the woods, the deep woods, flew past the hermit, past his eyes. Swift and swift, on wings away and into the woods across the clearing. . . . And when the hermit turned back to the dwarf, no trace was left of Dwarf or palace: The space was once again clear and bare and surrounded by woods and covered with high grass. . . .

Blithe and buoyant, the hermit then walked into the opposite woods, and brisk and bright he heard the morning song of the bird:

"Chirp and chirp—fine and fine, the first time and fully forth. The same will be the second time, the same must be the third time, then. . . . And steadily the little goat, and behind the hand the little goat, and you will stave temptations off. And one and so and two and three, and you will walk along the way and in the end the way that's true. . . . Hermit, walk and keep on walking, and Bird will keep his mind on you."

Sang his song and disappeared.

Alert and alive the hermit then set out again. Brisk and bright, he kept humming all the way, stopping every now and then, and from the ground and from under his feet he picked a forest flower and held it to his nose. And he kept remembering Little Goat: Whenever she lagged behind, the hermit turned his head and waited for her—let her emerge from among the trees, catch up with the hermit, hurry over to him, and gratefully and cheerfully the hermit gazed at her, and caressed and caressed her:

"Yes, Little Goat, Little Goat. . . . Yes, fine Little Goat. . . ."

And one more day wore by and two and three. . . . And it was day in the woods and it was night in the woods. Hermit and Goat again grew silent and sad, and they trudged through the trees, hushed and disheartened, out and in, in and out, and deeper and deeper, and again the bird forgot about the wanderers. . . . This time the hermit lost heart and spirit; as he walked he looked more fatigued, more forsaken, his venture seemed emptier and sillier; more obstacles and temptations came his way, appeared to him, and dry and innocent forest branches hanging from trees impeded him and peeved him and pestered him.

The hermit grew impatient with the goat as well. He had been walking ahead of her, never looking back at her, never soothing her, never heeding her: If things are fine, they're fine, if not, then let it be. . . . And little goat felt it too: She had never caught the hermit's eye. Poor and silent, she had lagged far behind, dispirited and innocent, feeling somewhat guilty and leaving the hermit in his ill humor, in his rotten mood.

Until one evening. . . . Worn and weary, after wandering for a long and empty day, the hermit made his way to a place for the night, where he lay down and wanted to sleep. But the moment he closed his eyes, he heard a sound not so far off: On the ground, among the forest leaves, something was rooting, was raking and rummaging, trying to emerge. From the earth, silently, stealthily, cautiously, two gnomes stole out and settled on the edge of their entrance. . . . Silently. For several minutes they sat it silence. But then one gnome turned to the other and asked:

"Don't you know, gnome, what's happening with our people? Have you heard any news?"

"I've heard," the second one replied.

"What?"

"People are laughing."

"At what?"

"Someone's telling a tale."

"A tale?"

"Yes, about a fool who looked for the fool. . . . They said that if he found him, he'd make him happy: The fool is rich, the fool is good, and he's wallowing in wealth. . . . So he went to look for him. . . ."

"And?"

"He roamed the world, he explored every land, visited all brainy people, sages gave him advice. But nothing came of anything: He never found the fool."

"That's a parable, little man. And the moral?"

"For a long time now a hermit's been wandering through the forest. . . . A man called him, a bird promised him, he's seeking the kernel. . . ."

"And?"

"There's also a tale about the kernel. . . . Our people tell it:

"Once upon a time there was a gnome. One day he heard about Heaven. And so he wanted to go to Heaven. He asked our king, and our king handed him over to his eagle. The eagle then flew off with the gnome. The eagle flew and flew around . . . and until the present, until today, we haven't heard any word from the gnome. . . . It is said that the gnome wants to return. . . . He realizes he'll never get to Heaven."

"Why not?"

"Heaven, man, is just an invention."

"And the moral?"

"The moral, gnome, is the kernel."

"And what, gnome, would you tell the hermit?"

"I would tell him: Rich are cellars, treasuries of gold are there. You are richer than they. From one end of the world to the other there's nothing to seek, you're already there. Don't wander, don't seek. . . ."

The gnome was done, and for a few minutes they both sat in silence by their pit. But then more rummaging could be heard in the fallen leaves. The two gnomes bent over the edge of the pit, made a place to go back down. First one gnome went down, then the other, they covered up and silently vanished. . . .

Hushed and dusky, the sky peeped through the trees. In the woods no wind and no waft of a wind. The trees stood as if made of stone—no twig swayed, no leaf stirred. Everything in the woods prepared for sleep, falling silent before falling asleep.

The hermit lay with open eyes, thinking to himself: "And, Hermit, what if Gnome is right? And what if this were only a spell, bewitchment and bedazzlement? . . ." The hermit was already ready and about to turn back to the goat and say: "Goat-fool! We're being fooled!" But then for a while he mused and held back, and he recalled the man's warning: "Steer clear of advice." At that moment, leaves rustled in a nearby tree— the bird came flying and it sang its song:

"Evening, evening, when everything rests, when everyone receives the reward for the day—the reward is reaped in the bosom of night. But not by one man: He lies forsaken and not rewarded and not indulged and not comforted, he is not remembered with a single word—forgotten he alone. Yet this you should know: He is not overlooked, there is an eye, it watches him. He must believe and he must consider: He is loved, he is being tested, and he was chosen for this test, to be awake, to wake at night, and gaze at the stars, the constellations—he envies them not for he's not their equal. . . . Chirp and chirp—and you, Hermit, should also believe, and never heed what enemies say, and what befalls you on the way befalls anyone who is tested, for stumbling, for stopping—it's sent by the lower pit . . . And you, Hermit, must strengthen yourself, to prepare yourself, for the final test, it will take place, in good time. . . . You will then think: "It's over for me, no help for me from anywhere, and all the ends have come.' Don't worry, don't worry! You must remember that the bird won't forget you. . . ."

The bird was done singing, and silently and without a rustle and without a bustle of his wings he vanished somewhere from the tree.

Calm and relieved, the hermit now lay in his sleeping place and thought about the bird's relieving words, and then he turned on one side, closed his eyes, and, buoyed and braced, he fell asleep.

That way the hermit passed the second test, and then also the third.

And for the last time the bird had forgotten about the hermit for a while, and the hermit and the goat had been roaming and roving—with no road and no goal, with no help and no hope, neglected and dejected and unremembered and with no encounters whatsoever. Then one day, a hot day, the hermit lay down in the woods, and worn and weary, with no thought and no strength, he fell asleep. Nor did he know how long he slept—a day and a night, or two days and two nights. But in his sleep, in its midst, he felt a hand touching him, and nocturnally and fervently it started waking him. . . .

And when the hermit opened his eyes, it was night in the forest. The woods were filled with dreadful darkness and uneasiness: Something cold was blowing high in the trees, something was rustling, something was happening in the darkness—but the hermit saw nothing: no tree and no root, no glow and no afterglow, not near him, not around him, not anywhere. All he could feel was someone standing over him and awakening him.

"Who is it?"

"The spirit of the forest."

"What do you need?"

"Soon there will be a storm in the woods."

"And?"

"Come with me, I'll protect you."

"What about the goat?"

"The goat has gone astray. . . . Come. . . ."

"I'm not coming. . . ."

And the hermit lay down on the ground and waited. . . .

For a minute or two the spirit was silent and pensive. And then he got the goat and held her horn and handed her over to the hermit in the darkness: "Hold her."

"And you," he said to the hermit, "sit down."

And in the darkness the spirit knelt before the hermit and took him upon his beastly body, his black and hairy hide.

And the forest rustled: Trees in the darkness, woods and winds, and something was happening, something was preparing. And the hermit on the spirit of the forest rode deeper and deeper into the woods, deeper into the darkness, deeper into the din, all the while holding the horn of the goat and not letting go. . . .

The rustling in the woods became a rumbling, became a roar: Earth and trees and forest winds blasted and bellowed, bellowed and blasted. And suddenly—a bolt of lightning lit up the woods, a crackling and kindling, a flash and a flame—and for a minute the forest and all its darkness stood out against an infernal fire. . . . The hermit shuddered and let go of the goat. At that instant the spirit of the forest disappeared from beneath the hermit. And all at once and in the midst, the hermit was standing on the ground. . . . For a minute the lightning was followed by silence—and then all of a sudden. . . .

A cheerful and radiant palace loomed in front of the hermit, with an entrance and with windows and light in the windows. And shapes emerged at the windows: women upon women and heads by heads, younger ones, older ones, dressed and exposed, with flesh and charm, with wine and smiles and with heads of young men among them. . . .

A nocturnal banquet was taking place. . . .

All the revelers rushed to the windows, charming and cheerful, gregarious and hospitable, waving to the wanderer.

Tired and exalted, nocturnal and dismal, a weary music came wafting from the radiant rooms, fusing with flesh and with night and with light. And the music spread out through the inside walls and the palace walls and into the woods and among the trees. . . .

The revelers beckoned and called to the hermit, and the hermit stood below and, forlorn, he looked up at the windows. But then fast and fleet a door flew open on a higher floor, and a young woman in silk came rustling down the stairs, toward the hermit, and she was beguiling and bewitching, with the scent of spices and with female flesh, and taking him on and summoning him up:

"With me. . . . Join us. . . ."

The hermit didn't stir from the spot and, more confused, he peered up at the windows; he didn't move, he stammered: "Little Goat, Little Goat. . . ."

Then all at once the night palace was snuffed, and the young woman next to him disappeared. And the hermit stood there, in a deeper darkness, in a stronger storm, in a wilder wind. . . . And suddenly, a deluge descended from the heavens and from the gloom: Earth and sky, air and trees were turned into a torrent. Endlessly it poured on him and lashed at him, upon his head and from all sides, and wet and cold, forlorn and baffled, the hermit stood in the midst, in the middle, alone in the darkness. . . .

The palace and the young woman appeared again and called him again—but the hermit paid no heed. Then everything kept changing quickly: palace brightness and rainy darkness, rainy darkness and palace brightness. . . . Once and twice and thrice—but the hermit resisted yet again.

And when the hermit opened his eyes after night and bedazzlement, it was already broad daylight. The hermit was standing outside the forest, with the goat snuggling at his side. A broad, bright field stretched ahead of the hermit, and a long, trodden morning way ran through the field and into the distance. . . .

And at the edge of the woods the bird appeared in a tree and he sang:

"Chirp and chirp—fine and fine, resisted temptation, and that's good. Now go out on a new road to seek happiness, with the holy your goal, to the kernel blessed. . . . As of today I will guide you no more, you will be led by the man in the moon, ask him every night, and he will show you the right way, I hear, and you heed him. . . . And now—bless you, with your destined goat, your companion on the way to happiness. . . ."

In the morning the hermit then left the woods, free and early, taking the straight, the distant, the trodden way, and refreshed and renewed he walked toward the broad and open field, while constantly looking back at the forest, finding it further and further away.

At midday, when the sun was midway in the sky, and bright and broad the field remained, the hermit saw something lying far, far away in the field. Toward it he went—walking and walking, drawing closer. And when he arrived, he saw a man upon the ground, a wanderer lying near a well in the midst of the field, resting up from the day and the way. The hermit then stooped down to the man, sat down and asked him:

"Where from?"

Calmly and slowly the wanderer peered at him and then replied: "Far from here."

"And where to?"

"Much farther from here. . . ."

"For what?"

"For the ancient loss."

"Who has lost what?"

"The whole world—a kernel. . . ."

"Should we go together?"

"No."

"Why not?"

"It's a tradition . . . from the famous elder."

"Namely?"

"The ways are holy, the wayfarers holier, blessed is the walk and more blessed the walking, and walking means . . . alone."

"But our goal is one?"

"Yes, our goal is one, but the wanderers differ. . . . And if we seek separately, we will find—in shape and in form . . . and each in his way— his world and his kernel. . . .

"And the well?"

"That is the heritage well, from generation to generation, from wanderer to wanderer, our mirror and our eyesight. . . ."

And at these words, the wanderer got up, went to the well, stood there wordless for a while, bent over the edge, and wordless and wistful stared down. . . . And the hermit also got up and also went to the well and stood on the opposite side. He let his eyes down into the water and calmly and slowly and deeply stared. . . . For a while the wanderer and the hermit peered into water and also at each other. But soon each forgot about the other, and each was absorbed in his water image and in his thoughts. . . . Silently they stood there, on and on, each unnoticed by the other. And when the hermit awoke from his thoughts, he no longer found the wanderer in the water. . . . And when he looked up and into the field, the wanderer was far, far away, and with his stick in his hand and his knapsack on his back, he was trudging along the long, straight way toward the horizon   The hermit then summoned the goat from the well, glanced once again at the wanderer, and then took off along his way and into his day. . . .

Vast and alone lay the field in the day. Alone and only with the goat, the hermit walked along—silent and pensive, field in, field out, from sky to sky, and till the evening, till the sun started dipping and dropped in the west.

Silently the night edged in from the east. Darker and darker grew the field behind the hermit and in silence and sorrow it peered at him as he went his way. And the hermit was lost in thought and he didn't remember the day, and he forgot about a place to sleep, he just kept walking, till the night settled in. . . .

And when the hermit abruptly halted on his way, peered around the field and the darkness, looked but found no place for sleeping, he suddenly gazed back at the way behind him and saw: At the end of the sky and roundabout from the sky, a round moon, a field moon, was shining, and in the moon, the man in the moon. . . .

Straight from there the moon man gazed at the hermit, watched and watched him from far away and calmly, with the calm of his eyes, waiting for him, and wordlessly waiting. . . . Silent and waiting, lay the vast, huge field, Heaven and earth were nocturnally wordless, and in Heaven the man and on earth the hermit—facing each other, waiting and waiting it out.

And now the moon man spoke: "Hermit, you've been put in my power, so I have to provide for you today, now that you're standing and waiting. . . . And in the night you're a stranger, in the night there is a ruler, just go out on all the ways, walk on the earth, with your head in the sky. . . . Look back at the past way, and I'll light your way through the field and I'll show you a cottage and a place for sleeping tonight. . . . And look: Just stay there a while and do not stir without my knowing. Settle there with Little Goat, and take care of the goat until I come, to summon you and command you in the nights, in a time, when I must. . . . And now go. . . ."

The hermit turned to the moon man and obeyed him, silently looked at the field and the evening and entered the distant and luminous night. . . .

Fuller and higher the moon rose upward behind the hermit, glossier and shinier, farther and bigger it grew, softer and brighter it drifted upward, and golden and airy it sowed its glow in the field and on the road through the field. . . .

All evening long, the hermit never looked back, never turned round, all that time he felt only the moon and the moon man behind him. Guarded and brightened by them, he walked and walked, until late at night in the field he stumbled upon a ruin. . . . For a while the hermit looked back at the moon man, grateful and wordlessly grateful for himself and for Goat, he gazed at the moon man, and then he turned toward the ruin, he found a door and he stepped inside. . . .

The hermit settled down in the ruin. Slowly and deliberately he scanned and studied it to see what was needed for himself and for Goat, prepared for a long time and a long while, slowly, slowly grew used to the place and the surroundings of the place, and so from day to day he became more and more a resident of the ruin. Quiet and certain, the hermit waited for assurance by the moon man, and meanwhile, every evening and every morning, he knelt in long and silent prayers, in the field and in the ruin, and prayed and prayed. And after prayers, he would take the goat into the morning, go sometimes near and sometimes far, wander about, seeking herbs and kernels, and sometimes for a day, and sometimes longer, he would gather food and bring it back.

And the hermit took care of the goat, never let her out of sight, never let her roam far alone, but always stayed with her all the while and all the time.

Evening. Silently the sun would set in the field, earth and sky lay vast and empty in the evening. The hermit would sit on the ruin's threshold, silently and wistfully staring and staring at the setting sun, and suddenly remember Goat. . . . Startled he would scrutinize his surroundings, then find her lying at his side, then caress her: silent and satisfied, he would gaze and gaze into her eyes, and eventually bend over and tell her: "Goat, Goat, and what will happen when we find the kernel?. . ." Pure and trusting, the goat would peer into the hermit's eyes, and honest and open, she would not look away. . . .

And the sun would set, the field and its surroundings would grow still, and the hermit would get up from the threshold, first let in the goat, then cross the threshold himself, shut the door, and prepare for the night and for bed in the ruin.

Sometimes at night, when the ruin was dark and still, the sleeping hermit would dream:

> Settlement . . . and in the settlement—doors and stables open-ing. . . . The animals released for the day and for grazing. . . . And the horses neighing, and the cows mooing and the bulls bellowing, and the sheep and the goats bleating. . . . And the shepherd is al-ready in the village. . . . And now the doors are opening up—and he hears a knocking. . . .
>
> "Who's there?"
> "The shepherd."
> "What do you want?"
> "Your goat for the herd. . . ."
> "Hold on. . . ."

The hermit then got up with his sleep and his dream, trudged blind and groggy toward the door, opened up and saw: Ohh, no, it was only a dream. . . . It was nighttime still. . . . The hermit then went back in, lay down next to the goat, couldn't sleep, lay next to the goat, talked to her, and talked until broad daylight. . . .

And it was summer when the hermit arrived in that field and at that ruin. And then—very slowly and imperceptibly—the summer began to shift away. Tardy and drowsy the sun rose each morning, and it set at twilight, early and weary. And the fall shifted forward, closer and closer. . . . And during those silent autumn nights, the hermit would stay in the moonlit field; for hours, long hours, and all night long, and all through the night he would peer at Moonman, peer and probe: Perhaps the time had already come. . . . And perhaps he should start out now, in the autumn and on his path. . . . And the man in the moon would peer back at him for a long time, direct and indifferent, silent, never saying a word, and not yes and not no. . . .

So the hermit understood that the time was not ripe, and he prepared his ruin for the autumn, shut himself in, locked himself in, against rainy days and rainy nights, stayed inside and sat indoors with the goat.

And out of doors and in the field, the rain began, cold and gloomy, slow and steady, heavier and heavier. And that was how the days wore by: rain today, rain tomorrow, and constant and consistent—daytime, nighttime, sky and dark clouds, dark clouds and fields.

And there were nights when the hermit sat by the tiny fire in the tiny stove, peering and pondering, and the little goat lay at his feet, and the hermit kept caressing the goat. . . . Tranquil and thoughtful and unaware of himself—stroking her head, stroking her back, to and fro, to and fro, slowly and slowly running his hand over her hair. . . .

And that was how the fall wore by: a day and a day, a week and a week, a month and more. . . . And one night, the hermit was sitting by the fire, lost in thought—when all at once and suddenly, a wind and a downpour blasted into the door, blasted and tore:

"Hermit, why are you sitting?"

The hermit was startled and he got to his feet and, surprised, he listened to the outside and to the field. He stood and he stood. . . . And then, since nobody opened the door, he sat down once more, settled down by the fire, and returned to his silent evening thoughts. Then the wind blasted the door once more:

"Hermit, why are you sitting?"

And this time the hermit stood up more swiftly and, more startled than before, he gaped at the door. A third blast came, and now the door

opened, and on the threshold a wanderer appeared. Drenched and drip-
ping, nocturnal and all wrapped up, the wanderer stood at the threshold
a while, silent and gazing about and not stirring from his spot. . . . After
several minutes, the wanderer walked into the room and walked over to
a corner, took his sack from his back, put his stick in the corner, undid
his belt, removed his outer clothes, and on his own, not asking, but
acting as if in his own domain, he prepared a place to spend the
night. . . .

The hermit stood there all this time, staring at the wanderer, waiting
for his words. Meanwhile, as the wanderer prepared his place, he said to
the hermit:

"Hermit, sleep. . . ."

"Who are you?"

"The envoy."

"To where at a time like this?"

"On a mission."

"From whom?"

"From God, the Messenger."

"And what will you say?"

At those words the wanderer turned away, said nothing, lay down,
stretched out, covered himself, and fell asleep. Pensive, the hermit stood
and stood by the wanderer's bed; alien and distant he gazed at the wanderer's lying, at his body, and at last the hermit left and lay down too.

Dreams upon dreams, something was turning and tangling in the
hermit's sleep—field and kernel and snow upon fields. . . . And snow
was bedded there and kernel was lying there. . . . And the hermit grew
cold in his sleep, tossing and turning and rummaging all through the
night. And in the morning, when the hermit opened his eyes to the day
in the ruin and peered about, there was no trace of the wanderer's place
or the wanderer. . . . The hermit felt the coldness and emptiness of a
winter morning. The ruin was brighter than usual. And gray and frosty,
the window peered—overnight the first snow had been poured on the
world and the winter. . . .

And the winter came and the winter settled in.

Snow on snow and white field on white field. . . . And blizzards
blasted under the heavens, and winds filled the fields and the vast fields,
whirling and having something to do, entire days, dawns and dusks,
under horizons, raging and sweeping and sweeping back, and jumbling,
and once more, and preparing more than wintry fields for the winter.
And the ground grew dry and hard and resonant, and a soft, young snow

settled on the soil and bedded down, and far and wide, and for miles and months. . . . The hermit's ruin stood all alone, in the middle of the field, covered and buried, snowed in and forlorn, barely peeping from the ground.

For days on end the hermit and the goat sat in the ruin, spent their evenings silent and wintry, by the stove, seldom, seldom speaking at all, seldom glancing at one another, even more seldom leaving the ruin. Winds and blizzards swept across the fields, frost and cold ruled under the sky, and the hermit spent silent hours standing at the small and blasted window, peering and peering out, lingering and listening—and the field was blasted and the winter was buried, no bell and no sleigh, no passer and no passerby, and no human foot. . . .

And then one night—it was a frosty, moonlit winter night, and the hermit, after sitting so long in the room, stepped outside the door but stepped no farther, stopped in surprise. . . . Beyond the door, high in the heavens, as if waiting and prepared, the moon drifted, full and bright, and in the moon—the man in the moon. The man looked down at the hermit and then said:

"Hermit, at this time, in this place—tomorrow. . . ."

Hushed, the hermit stood and stood, facing the man in the moon, asking nothing, asking no question, and finally, not catching on, he turned and stepped back inside the ruin.

The night wore away, and the day followed suit, and the next night, at the scheduled time, the hermit stepped outside, stood in the scheduled place, and fixed his eyes on the man in the moon, and the man said to him:

"Hermit, not far in the field, in a cave in the field, there lives a witch. . . . And in the witch's cave, in her home, there is a servant, her hand, her right hand at all times. And tomorrow the servant will be captured by demons, he will plead for his freedom, he will buy his way out, he will send them to the witch. . . . And wicked is she and clever is she: And the witch will serve them, she will buy her dear servant's way out, pay the demons with a story, and at its end it will happen there, in the same place where the demons sit . . . when demons know! . . . And Hermit, hear: Where straw lies, on snow in the field, a circle of straw, and a small candle burns, a candle in the middle—seek there, that's where you'll find what you've long been seeking. . . . And then hear: Prepare for the journey and blessed be and farewell, and tomorrow you will have the sign, it will come to you, the servant will call, and you will be led by love—your little goat is promised you. . . ."

The hermit heard him out, then silent and for the last time he said farewell with his eyes, said farewell to the man in the moon, took another look, stepped back, turned, and reentered the ruin.

And the night went away, and the morning came that day. The moment the hermit had lit a candle in the ruin at dusk, he saw that the goat had come suddenly leaping out of her corner; next she had stood for a while like a statue, and then, stimulated and agitated, started roaming around the room—from place to place, from wall to wall, sometimes stopping by a wall, leaning against the door, rubbing her body against it, and then tearing herself and pacing once more. Every so often, she would suddenly go over to the hermit, mutely beseeching, expecting something from him and—not waiting for it but tense, impatient, and dissatisfied—she continued roaming around the room. Once and twice—and more and more all the time, muter and muter, more and more pitiful, not understood and finding no place.

The hermit kept watching her all the while—from place to place, around the room and in all the corners, surprised—and this morning he didn't recognize and didn't understand his poor and usually silent little goat:

"Little Goat, Little Goat, what's wrong, Little Goat?"

And the little goat wouldn't rest, she kept going and going, an hour and an hour. Her lashes grew cloudy and gray, and lost and awkward she lumbered through the ruin, pleading with the ground and the floor, with the ceiling and the corners, studying them and smelling them. And at last—weakened and not understood, the goat trudged over to the door, hard and silent, and stuck out her head, and silently waited at the door. . . . She stood for an hour, long and longer, keeping her head straight, in one position, waiting and waiting and listening.

And now midnight came and suddenly—there was a knock at the door. . . . It was the witch's servant knocking for the hermit: "Hermit, it's time!"

Hastily and intensely, the goat returned the knocking: "We're coming!" And then the goat turned to the hermit: "Hermit, come!"

The hermit promptly gathered his kit and kaboodle, put the sack on his back and took hold of the stick, gave the ruin a final and hurried glance, and then opened the door and stepped outside. . . .

And the instant they closed the door behind them and looked at the field, they saw: High and under the height of the heavens, under the moon and under its shine, an old and shriveled witch came riding on a broomstick, and then from her height, from the shine on the field, and beyond the snow, beyond the vast snow, beyond the distant horizon—she disappeared. . . .

The goat then turned to the hermit, her head in the place where the witch had vanished, and the goat and the hermit, saved and elated, struck off on their path. . . .

And the goat ran ahead, every so often digging her head and her feet into the snow, waiting impatiently for the hermit, standing up straight and resuming her running, ahead and onward, dashing and calling, calling and dashing, for an hour, and two, and three, running and running, and suddenly. . . .

And the witch had been telling her tale for a very long time, and here she broke off in the midst of the tale, holding her tongue and gazing and gazing at the distant horizon. . . . The demons felt this, terrified, and they peered around in disbelief and nervously and hastily they sensed a bad ending. So they awoke the witch from her trance: "Well, well, witch, what about the ending?"

"I'll get there, I'll get there. . . ." And more silently and more distantly the witch peered at the horizon. And suddenly. . . .

And all at once the witch pulled herself together, got to her feet, and in a strange voice, with her body and intensity, she yelled: "Friends, you're sitting on it!" And then louder: "Demons, the hermit is coming!"

A yank, and the demons got to their feet, frightened and fearing, each on his own: swiftly and without looking about they headed toward a special side of the field. . . . The witch soon straddled her broom and soared back to the moon and to the shine of the moon. And the circle of straw and the candle in the circle remained alone in the field. . . .

And the hermit came to his kernel.

DER NISTER (Pinkhas Kahanovitch, 1884–1950)

Demons

See the note introducing "The Hermit and the Little Goat," page 237.

Demon, you're old."

"Yes, little demon, true."

Two demons were lying one night somewhere in a gloomy grotto, in a wild wood. It was dark, it was raining. So they snuggled together, huddled together, the younger one's hands in the older one's fur, slowly and easily stroking his hair and scratching in between, and finally reaching the bare, dry skin, touching it, and having his say:

"You're old, demon."

"Yes, little demon, true."

"What will become of you?"

"My flesh will be flayed and my hide will be made into a drum."

"And until the flaying?"

"I'll be put in a corner by a witch or a wizard, and behind some stove, and young devils, big and small, will come and ask about my time and my age and ask me for tales."

"And you, demon?"

"And I'll tell them tales."

"Let me ask first: Tell me a tale."

The older demon played hard to get, wavering a while as if not wanting to do it. But the youngster poked his slender fingertip under the oldster's skin and ribs and spurred him on: "Well, demon, well? Don't play the fool!" So the oldster demon gave in and began

The Demon's Tale

It happened when I was young. My hooves and my horns were still sharp and my legs served me well—in winds and on fields, on hills and in valleys, wherever they had to. Now one night I was given an order: to go to a forest and wait on its edge, on its fringe. I was needed there, for some kind of task. . . .

So off I went. And when I arrived I found a young devil. He was already abiding there, awaiting me, and then when he saw me he said: "A man will soon come riding through, from the forest, from its depths. We have to lead him away, have to lead him astray. . . ."

And that was what happened. Soon we heard a wagon coming from the forest, a man drove the horses, urging them on, rousting and roaring from the depths. So we went through the woods, along the path, jumped into its width, leaping and loping and rolling around, atop one another and over each other, I on him and he on me, and hocus-pocus—and when the man had reached us and reached our where-abouts, the woods and the path turned and twisted, and the horses abruptly halted; the shaft and the wagon collided with something and came to a stop. And now there was no road and no route, just trees by trees and trees around trees, and the wagon was stuck, and the horses were spooked, in the woods, in the midst.

Petrified and unprepared, the man sprang down from the wagon, toward the horses and toward their faces, he stood before them and before their fright, until they were free of their terror and horror, until they recovered and surrendered to him once again in their horsey way. Upon seeing this, we—my companion and I—headed toward the horses and toward their backsides, both at one time, suddenly terrifying them with our terror flies. Hastily and more hurriedly, they yanked themselves up, from their shafts and harnesses, and, wild and bewildered, they wrenched themselves out of the hands of the man. He let them go, he let them leave—the horses and the entanglement.

The man then walked a short distance away and looked around: Where was he now, where was he caught, and where could he get out? He stood and stood, he looked and looked. And then we, my devil and I, from a distance and from a path, we turned up in human guise. One by one, silent and barefoot, the two humans arrived in the forest, in the evening, the way people walk through the woods, never speaking, and the way people turn up suddenly—that was how they arrived, ap-proached, needing to pass the man and pass his place. The man waited for them, and when they reached him, he turned to them and said:

"Good evening, people." Did they know? He had just gone astray from the way. Could they possibly help him and show him the right way? . . .

They could indeed, why shouldn't they?

And how far was it from here to there?

Oh my, not far at all! He should follow them, they were going there, it wasn't far from here. . . . The man believed them and followed them, the passersby, silently, walking behind them, behind their backs, never saying a word, hushing and trusting—and after those men got the man away from his place and from his horses and wagon and walked with him for a while, the path abruptly came to an end, and so they halted and lingered and looked about in surprise: What was this, where were they, and just how had they gotten here? And when the man stood behind them and behind their backs, he felt giddy and dizzy, and in the distance, the distance of trees, he spotted a glowing cottage, and the two men were gone.

In the cottage sat a shriveled crone with a sieve and feathers; the other, her husband, the forest warden, lay on the stove, covered up, dead to the world, sleeping his forest-warden sleep in the evening. . . .

And the man headed toward the cottage, and when he arrived, he tapped on the window.

"Open, good people!"

The crone came over to open the door and she met him in the doorway. He stood there, squinting because of the light; then he looked at the ceiling and then at the floor, and then at the walls, and all around, and at last he said:

"There's something I don't grasp, don't grasp about being here."

"What?" the crone asked aloud.

"Suspicious," the man stammered.

"Of what and of whom?"

"I don't even know."

"What are you talking about?"

"I don't know. . . . I went astray from the way and encountered two men, and I asked them for help, and they guided me, but then they were gone. Then I spotted your cottage, I don't understand. . . ."

"And what would you want?"

"What would I want? Perhaps someone could clear things up and show me the way to my way? . . ."

"Show you the way?" the crone asked, and she went back to her place, picked up the sieve, and turned to the stove, "Old man, listen. A man has gone astray, we must show him the way. Climb down. . . ."

The old man opened his eyes, threw off his covers, lifted his head, peered down at the room and at the man, slowly eyed them for a while. Then he climbed down, slipped into his fur, walked over to the door, and said to the man:

"Come. . . ."

And as the man stood by the door, before he even crossed the threshold, the light in the cottage went out, the ceiling above and the walls around were gone. The man was outdoors, in the forest, standing by a wet and mossy well with four walls, and then, holding on to the well, he aimed his spit at one of the walls, at its dampness and wetness.

"Tfoo!" The man spit into the well and hastily sprang away.

"Don't spit!" a voice called out and a head turned up.

"What do you mean?" the man asked the head.

"I mean that you're now in our might and our main."

"And what will happen?"

"You'll do as we say."

"And what will you say?"

"First of all: You'll climb into the well."

"I don't want to."

"Grab him!" the devil yelled at me, his assistant. "Grab him!"

And before the man could even start to turn and defend himself, I grabbed his legs from behind and splash!—he suddenly flew into the well. . . .

After plunging down and splashing down, the man caught his breath, and when he came to, when he recovered from his terror and anger, he obstinately glared at the devil and proudly and scornfully asked him:

"What now?"

"There's an udder on a cow. And if someone doesn't give, then someone else simply takes, and you are in our power now."

"I've already heard that."

"Fine." And the devil now turned away from the man and toward one of the well walls and knocked upon it. A door promptly opened to a filthy corridor, a long and nocturnal corridor, and on the ceiling and in the middle a lamp was burning, a dim and dusty lamp, dimly lighting the walls and the corridor, which was lined with closed and locked and silent doors. . . . The devil went over to one of the doors, knocked upon it, whereupon it opened. The devil sent the man in first, then ushered me in and told me to follow the man, then the devil brought up the rear, and at last we arrived at that house. And there we met in a tavern, in a small roadside tavern.

There was nothing in the tavern: no person and no furniture—aside from a couple of chairs and tables in the middle and by the walls, and these chairs and tables were all set and ready, and unoccupied and lit in a tavernly manner, waiting for someone to come by and come over. So we sat down at one of the tables. The devil then knocked, and a waiter appeared, a silent waiter, all prepared to wait on us, and he came over to the chair and to the devil, with a cordial and a courteous bow, standing there, hanging on the devil's every word, waiting for an order.

"Wine!" the devil exclaimed. And the waiter withdrew.

A few minutes, and the waiter returned with bottles and glasses, put them on our table, set them precisely and exactly and fittingly, then stepped aside and with respect and devotion went on waiting for our wishes and wants.

The devil took one of the bottles: first he filled the man's glass, then he filled mine, and finally filling his own, he stood up and held his glass toward me and then toward the man, saying almost nothing, yet commanding, demanding:

"Let's drink!" And the man didn't refuse. The devil then filled the glasses again—and the man obeyed.

And when the man drained his glass a third time, you could see that he had altered, had changed, his face seemed replaced, he had turned milder, mellower, was soothed and softened in his forgetting and regretting; and then he stood up and stepped over to the devil, and cheerily and merrily, slapping him on the back, he said:

"Oh, devils, devils, it's not so bad, devils! . . ."

"What's not so bad?" the devil asked with a smirk.

"Being a devil!" the man replied.

"Should we swap with each other?"

"Ah!" The man was glad and he agreed: "With the greatest pleasure—I'm ready and rearing, and promptly and quickly!"

The devil had been waiting and waiting for this, and the instant he heard those very words, he sprang up from his chair and stepped over to the man, and saying nothing and speaking nothing, he peeled off his hide and pulled off his horns and put them on the man. Then he swiftly took off his hooves and removed the man's shoes and exchanged them; and he hurried and hastened, and by putting those things on the man, he transferred his power to him, speaking with spells, whispering with lips: Let him do as he would, let him do what he could, and good luck and good health. . . .

When all was donned and all was done, the devil pushed the man at bay to view him at a distance away, and the devil stepped back and sized him up and down from head to foot, and the devil was elated and delighted, was thrilled and enthralled. And this way and that way and well and good and good and well: "And just as I'm a devil and you're a man, and just the way we're both. . . . And now, man, let's celebrate!"

And the devil then waved at the waiter and gave him an order, and the waiter opened a door to a hall, and the hall was massive and mighty, and it smelled of tavern bareness and emptiness, and from somewhere there came a light, which lit up the hall, the bare, massive hall with the empty walls.

And devil and man, with transposed appearances, walked into the middle of the hall, and then the devil waved at me and gave me an order; and swift and quick and lickety-split, I sped around the walls and across the floor, everywhere and wherever needed, I knocked on the walls. Doors then opened, small doors and big doors, overdoors and underdoors, by the ceiling and on the floor. And—souls appeared: first little ones and human ones, little squirrels and little beasts, twisting and struggling, from the walls, the straight walls, mobs of brutes and masses of beasts, plunging in and pouring in, and banking on and building on themselves and their own, their own approaching and arriving; and after them, older ones arrived: larger ones and more earnest ones, cooler ones and calmer ones, through doors and through holes in the doors, slowly stopping, and in clusters and in crews, an enormous population, all with horns and all with tails, all of them haughty as proper for them, and all unhurried as befitting them—and they kept coming, a mob and a mass, and suddenly a vast and dusty herd, chockful and jam-packed, dense and hairy—they came dashing in, leaving space for those that followed and . . . maids came racing and rushing, strange and varied, licentious and disheveled, with lewd gestures and rude women, in derisive gangs and gaggles—and the devil and his band, with demons and with cymbals, with devils and with rattling and clattering.

And the devil gave another order: "A table! Bring a table and place it in the hall, in the middle. The man wants to climb on top of the table, the man wants to demonstrate something. . . ."

Upon hearing the devil's last few words, the bewildered man moved to the side, trying to blend into the crowd; but the devil blocked his way, impeded his path, urged him on and fueled his desire: "Don't worry, man, and don't be ashamed, there's no one to be concerned about. Everything will be fine, and the end will be good."

The table had already been lugged into the hall. Meanwhile the merry and clamorous crowd waited and entertained itself, species with species, creature with creature—each cluster speaking its language, doing its doings, big with big, and little with little, hustling and bustling. And when everything was ready and the table in place—up jumped the imp, raring and clownish, free and frolicking, sprang toward the man, held out his hand, called to him, raised him up, helped him to rise, and the man willy-nilly got on the table, and briefly hesitating and abashedly waiting for the noise to be fading, he turned to the crowd:

"My friends, you must know I'm a simple soul, I've never appeared before an audience or a congregation, but I've entered your jurisdiction, and I've swapped with the imp and with his fur, and so I have to do as you say, I'm ready to obey. . . . Give me your demands and commands, and I'll do what I can and show my compliance."

"His shame! Let him show his shame!" the crowd shouted as one.

"What do you mean?" the man asked.

"He should spit in his own face, spit in his own features!"

"That won't work, imps!"

"And why not?"

"A man can't do that, his mouth is in his face."

"Then *we* will do it, *we* will spit!" The imps dashed to the table and on the table.

"Halt!" shouted the imp who stood on the table with the man, confronted the imps, held out his arms to shield the man. "Halt. Stick to the point and demand what's possible."

"Let him out of his hide. . . . Let him turn out his inside, let's see his innards, his lungs and liver. . . ."

"He can't. You can't get out of your skin!" the imp shouted.

The crowd shouted for the third and last time: "Let him show himself, his own self, his humanness and humanity. Let him show what a human can do and may do."

"Good!" the man agreed.

And he stood up straight and agreed and nodded his head, and he waited a while, on the table a while, till the shouting was eased, till the crowd was appeased, and when they grew still and waited for him, and each imp raised his head, the man then said:

"Imps, if you wish to see a man himself and his own self, what a man can achieve and attain, you have to grant him freedom fully, put yourself in his domain and do whatever he orders you. And you should swear to him, for one and for all, swear by the community and by all that's holy and by all your horns and otherwise not."

"What does that mean?" the imps were surprised and they did not grasp, they came running up and were angry too, and they looked at each other and questioned each other: "What does that mean? He swear by us and we swear to him? And who forces us and how are we safe?"

"I will swear to you," the man tried to calm them.

"By what?" asked the imps.

"By myself and by all that's human."

"It's false and it's flesh!"

"Then by what?"

"By those horns of yours: You wear them now, you use them now, so you have their strength, you must swear by their length. And if they are desecrated and your oath is violated, you will never leave this place alive."

"Fine!" And the man agreed again.

Then the demons began to come up and collect: first little with little, hugging the ground; then along the edges all around, the bigger ones—little with little and big with bigger—and in the hall they formed a huge, a fearful, silent circle of demons and oaths. The imp on the table reigned on the circle and over it, held his hands out over it, and whispered and spoke a spell; and, holding his hands out and speaking his spell, he uttered the oath, on the circle and the demons, on the demons and the circle, the oath and its harshness, the oath and its solemnity.

"And now, *you!*" After the swearing, a voice was heard from the circle, addressing the man and the imp.

No demons went over, they stayed in the circle, in their earlier sequence; they stood where they were and with their oath; they saw how still and strange the imp and the man were on the table together, putting head and head together as if agreed and arranged, pointed head and pointed head, both bodies receding and retreating, leaning over and touching only with heads, taking upon themselves only from above and what behooved them, only from below and from the demons—from everyone for safeguarding.

And when the man and the imp raised their heads at long last and went their separate ways, the man, smiling and sunny, turned to the crowd and said: "And now, imps, let's forget about the oath and get down to business. I propose that you bring a mirror. Set it up on the wall across from me, and everyone turn and look at the glass, and I and I alone will appear before you and before the glass and place before your eyes what you have agreed on and wished for and discussed, and what was decided and I stipulate one thing: no word and no gesture, just seeing and silence."

"Fine."

Two servants were sent, and they started out, and they passed through the door of a side room, where they spent several minutes, and then the door reopened, and the crowd made way, a wide way, for them, as they brought in a mirror to the site determined by the man; and taking a look, the whole congregation turned to the mirror and to the reflection.

And the room grew dark and dusky and darker, its light waning and fading.

The crowd was nearly in total night, standing together, with the man over them and on the table, and the demons exchanged glances with the man in the mirror and then waited for him; but the man took his time, he had time to take: And engrossed and enthralled he looked back into the mirror. And suddenly—the man was aroused from looking and from waiting and waiting, and he vaguely waved his hand, and something unclear whisked across the mirror, and the demons saw:

The mirror abruptly turned dim and gray, the color of water, and nothing was visible. The grayness was stirring and scattering, it kept shifting and switching, it kept turning and twitching. Something was happening in the mirror, and all at once it was night in the mirror, dark and as dark as the sea, black and as black as pitch, and high up a lantern showed up, red and flickering, and terrifying as if warning of deadly danger it lit up a path, a long and nightly path, a lengthy and upward path. Then a man emerged on the path, a wayfarer walked and his way was far, a dusty and woeful wanderer, he walked and then he went, verging on vanishing from sight and from the skyline. And just as the wanderer, remote and minute, seemed like a speck—all at once on his route of return, the earth opened up in the middle, revealing a cave; and from the cave and from its depth a head stuck out and slowly and slowly from behind and below it began to rise.

It was an old and gray and broken imp.

And up he came, the imp, the old imp, and stood and at the edge of the cave he peered and peered and he slowly peered his fill, around and about, at the field and at all corners of the field; and then, when he finally spotted the man, far away, on the horizon, he cupped one hand on his mouth and howled and shouted very loud: "Man there, man there! Turn around and come back!"

The man heard the voice from afar, so he turned around and peered back for a bit, till he sighted the imp; he stood there some minutes, waiting and wondering, and then, as if deciding, he headed back toward the imp. And when he arrived, the imp said to him:

"Man, I've been watching and watching you, I've seen you in long nights, I know who you are, I want to propose something. I have a daughter, a beauty, and as things go among us, and I'm quite old, I want her to have children, I want to have grandchildren, to hold them and love them, and you have no children, and you want some but you won't have them, but you will with her—so come with me. . . ."

"And who am I?"

"The essential one."

"Well?"

"I am proposing my daughter for you."

"And for her?"

"All qualities and all possibilities of imps and generations: your world on them and your mastery over them and—once again—a daughter, an exceptional one."

"And the children?" the man asked.

"Are yours," the imp answered. "I won't make demands, I won't give them commands. Let them become human and belong to all humanness."

"And what will you get out of them?"

"I—the privilege."

"Privilege of what?

"Of seeing them and loving them."

"Then I'll go with you—and let it be a demon."

And the cave from which the imp had emerged now opened up, and the man went in first and the imp after him. And now the cave and the depth appeared to the demons in the hall, and then the mirror showed something else, and the demons saw:

Rich and full of ease, with an upper floor and a lower floor, stood a night palace in a large space, a nightly and a silent place, and lights were lighting in all its windows, and all around there were stairs and doors. So the imp and the man went to one of the doors and they opened it and entered a corridor, long and linear, silent and resounding, and lined with more doors. They went on to a door and they knocked and they waited, and then on the other side of a room, a door opened, and they saw:

Silent, nocturnal, and before going to bed, the demon's young daughter knelt in the middle of the room, facing the bed and the head of the bed, where a nightly, idolatrous lamp was burning. She knelt there, her eyes on the tiny flame, her hands over her head, and she kept staring there in her demon prayer. . . .

And silently the imp, her father, came in and he dropped down and knelt behind her, and he, too, knelt for a while in front of the light and the lamp. Then he stood up and silently and respectfully he aroused his daughter from kneeling and praying:

"Daughter, hey, daughter."

"What is it, father?"

"I've brought you your spouse."

And the imp's daughter got up and went to the door and stood on the side, and in the corridor, where the man was waiting, she looked and she saw him, saw him standing and waiting. Then she turned to her father and said: "Let him come in, father."

And the man came in and talked with the imp and the daughter came in and they stood in the room. For a while they gazed at one another and held their tongues. And then, when the imp had done his duty, he turned toward the door, as if out of place and not in his place, and silently, and as it needed to be, he went his way and he went away. The door then moved on its own, and slowly, slowly, and softly, for the marriage, it shut and it locked from the inside.

"What's that? What does it mean?" shouted the imps, who stood in the hall and in the mirror saw it all.

"What does it mean? What does it prove? And who gave him the right?" The imps raved and ranted and turned to one another and asked one another.

"He's laughing at us!" A voice from the crowd was heard by the crowd.

"Damn his eyes: He's laughing at us!" cried the voice and all the demons in the hall. And they turned toward the man and with hands and fingers, with faces and anger, they headed toward him—damn his eyes!

"Keep calm, imps, and remember what we agreed."

"What was it?"

"To hear and to hush."

"We can't."

"You must."

"How come?"

"You swore!"

"Right." The imps recalled their oath, they backed down and backed off from the man.

"Right." They agreed with each other and with the man, they exchanged glances and they had no choice, they fell silent. . . .

"And now, imps, to the mirror!" And the man kept holding his arms out toward the wall and toward the mirror.

The imps gathered together and held their tongues and stood in a circle, gazing where the man had pointed, and as before, this is what they saw:

The glass in the mirror once again altered its aspect and appearance, gaining a dimness and sparseness, a graying and blurring. Spots arose and random spots, they appeared and disappeared, came and went, floated and befuddled, and finally stopped and came out with something:

The night palace emerged from behind the cave, with light and ease, with upper apartments and with doors and windows, and materialized as if for the first time: with night and surrounded by night, with radiance and palatialness. And the old imp turned up in a window, beaming and with a baby in his hands; satisfied and full of pride and joy he carried the boy to the window and showed him to the outside world. . . .

The baby didn't want, didn't wish for the window, he was drawn to something else. All at once, in front of the demons, the palace turned around and disappeared, and silent and alone one of its rooms appeared, with walls and with a void, with furnishings and an interior. And the old imp, holding the baby, stood at the center, the baby drawing him toward one of the walls. And when the old imp with the baby moved toward that wall, the baby tapped it, and with his other hand he dragged the old imp along by his horn.

"Right here, grandfather, this is where you should show yourself."

And the old imp hesitated and wanted to evade the request, so he drew back his head and his horn, bending the baby's body to the side. But the baby held him tight, held back his twisting and bending, and so the old imp smiled broadly and did what he did:

He pushed a small table over to the wall to which the baby was drawn, then he put the baby on the table and had it gaze straight at the wall and he stationed himself in back of the baby. . . . After several minutes of the child sitting still and not turning around, the old imp peered and peered at a point and then started to talk and to speak, with his eyes and his eyesight far away, to muse and to speak, and speaking at random, till he finally raised his hand to the wall. . . . And all of a sudden the wall disappeared before him and the baby, and the wall was replaced by a void and a vacuum, and the child and the demons and the demons and the child met face to face and came very close:

"Grandfather!" cried the youngster, hurtling back and falling into the oldster's lap. "Who is that?"

"Don't be scared, baby, it's nothing."

"What about his horns?"

"They are bewitched."

And with the baby afraid and lying in the old imp's lap, some time wore by, and all that time the old imp kept stroking the baby's head and words of comfort he said, and so: Slowly and slowly the baby kept lifting his head more and more, raising it higher and higher, and finally— calmly he got up from his grandfather, from his lap, and more freely and more firmly the child looked around the hall and the demons, and he still held onto the old imp's horn, pulling him down, peering with him at the hall and the demons, and the baby asked:

"And who are those people, grandfather?"

"Those are demons, baby."

"And what do you have to do with them?"

"Nothing."

"And what about your horns?"

"Just rags and bones, and no might, no control."

"And what are they doing there, the demons?"

"They're not doing, they're done to."

"Who's doing it?"

The imp held out his hand and he wanted to point at the man standing above and over the demons. But at that very moment, the man noticed the imp and his gesture, and it wasn't worth it, and he motioned to him that it wasn't allowed. So the imp pulled back, turning his hand from where it mustn't be, and, stammering and randomly, he answered the child:

"Who? Him?"

"Boy, broker of sins!" All the imps jumped up and cried out together after a long and silent watching.

"Old stench! Rotten bones!" They charged forward, eyes flooding with blood and fists bulging with veins. "Kill him! Kill the bastard!" And from the circle they charged toward the mirror and toward the baby in the mirror.

However, the man promptly waved at the wall and at the mirror in the middle of the hall, and the imp and the baby promptly disappeared, and when the imps reached their goal, with arms and with hands, with eyes shot with fury, all they found was a blank and ordinary mirror, and only they themselves and their furious faces were mirrored in the mirror. . . .

"Where are they? Where have they gone?" The imps charged back to their tables, to the man, who was above them, and whom they questioned.

"Shush, demons!" the man from above ordered the throng. "Shush!"

"We already knew, we already expected it—who brought him here and who entrusted him with the matter?" they asked in their oath and their weakness and in the man and his upper hand.

"Who brought him here? Let him stand trial, call him to account!"

"*I* brought him here!" said the imp who had traded places with the man and introduced him to the demons and who now presented himself and appeared on the table. "Demons, calm down. It's not nice, it's not nice in front of the man. He will laugh and say: 'There's no unity among demons.' A break appeared in the demons' wall, releasing their hosts one by one, in single file. So hear me out: The man showed us one of our own, an old and smelly one, an ugly and senile one. He betrayed our trust, he abandoned us, he sabotaged our senses, he passed his daughter off as a human, which makes him hideous and odious, which makes him depraved, and depraved was his conduct, and dismal is his luck—for sure! But we have to see, but we have to mull and grasp the matter. So I propose: Let us stay as we were, and let the man show us what happens next, let him show what he can do and what an imp can achieve; and we will ponder, and we will confer and consult and reach a resolution."

Having heard out the imp, all the demons agreed. They mused for a while, exchanging glimpses, exchanging glances in silent assent. When the imp saw that they were prepared and approving, he didn't ask them, he gestured toward the man, he motioned and he pointed at the mirror: "Go on, man!"

And the demons gathered after their frenzy and after their fury and they thronged before the table and before the mirror, and wordless and soundless they entered the circle and whatever would happen in the circle.

And the man showed them: And for the third time the mirror changed and shifted and turned gray, appearing and disappearing, in the night and with stars, in the sun and with spots, uncovering and covering, fading and waning, dulling and dimming, on and on, till an image came on:

It was dawn and in that palace. The man and his demon wife emerged in their bedchamber, a night lamp still burning on the ceiling; dark and shielded, halfway and twilit, the pale and outside day was starting to seep through cracks and shutters. The man and his wife had just gotten up from their sleep, and they should have left their room by now, but they lingered on, doing nothing, yet very busy, and so, doing nothing, they refused to end the night and their togetherness.

And the man went over to his maiden, halted before her, put his hands on her shoulders, gazed into her eyes for a while and again, gazed with dawnish love, in silence and the silence of after-night; and the maiden gazed back, bashful and thankful, sated and standing opposite him, allowed and permitted, looking and looking forward, her shoulders in his hands. The man then took her head in his hands, silently drew her body to his, and she yielded, silent and satisfied, she submitted to her beloved, went and was loved, embraced and brimming with happiness, waiting, silent and happy, for him and for what was to happen.

"What is it, my love?" she said.

"You should earn your dawnish love."

"Well?"

"Let me ask you." And the man took and led the maiden to the bed, the nocturnal bed, wordless and soundless, and he pointed at a place on the edge. She sat down, and he next to her, and he took her hand in his and he said to her:

"Let me ask you, you must know: How does a human free himself from a demon and from demons and from being abducted?"

"With love and your way, my beloved," she replied.

"What do you mean?"

"Men should come to the demons' daughters and give them love— love them, desire them, they yearn for them and for their love."

"Then what will be?"

"In the end the demons will appear in the world, in the day, the bright day, they will come before men, with bag and baggage, and with wives and children, and with a congregation, and whatever a congregation possesses—they will fall at their feet and say:

"'We have seen that we cannot hold out, we have no strength and no chance; so we have come up and come to you, we surrender to you, do with us what you will—make us woodchoppers and water carriers: We will serve in every way and hear and obey.'"

"And who told you about that?"

"My father."

"That's in the end, for after and later. . . . And for now and before that time is ripe: Now that a man is in demons' hands, how can he be freed?"

"We know."

"I beg you: Open up a wall to the world of the demons, in the dawn and in the lower pit. Show them to me, them and their places of night and seduction, and free a man, any man at all."

"Done."

And the maiden got up and stood up from being with her man and from sitting with him, and she walked away, and, as if experienced and accustomed, she went to a wall and stood before it, with her face toward the wall and her back to the man, and she waited a while, standing and speaking. Then the wall opened up, and the man and the maiden peered at the demons in the hall, and the demons at them.

And the man with the maiden in the chamber saw that over the demons in the hall the abducted man was standing on his night-and-magic table, worn and weary, spent and sallow. Horns and hide were slipping aside from his head and his body, loosening and lessening, begging for day and for rest from the night and the performance, from the playing and the clown.

And the maiden's man saw and grasped the man's situation, and silently and unnoticed by the demons he signaled the man: Let him wait and stay calm—he knew about him, he was working for him, he saw where he was. . . .

And then the man went to his maiden and once more put his hand on her shoulder, and she looked at him lovingly and ready to serve him, devoted and dedicated. And her husband's eyes smiled, and silently he pointed at the man there, the abducted man:

"Him."

"You found your way to me at the right time."

"What do you mean, my love?"

"We know: It is our job and we do what we must."

And off she hurried, satisfied and with a loving smile, and playing and promising at the threshold, she turned toward her husband, her human spouse, who resented her leaving him all alone, who begrudged her the time of her leaving him alone, and swearing with love and assurance that she would fulfill his request, that she soon would return, bringing back whatever was needed.

And silently they waited, the man in the chamber here and the demons in the hall there, they waited for the woman of the palace, waited a minute and another minute. And soon the door opened again, and silently, from the other side, the woman appeared in the silence, crossed the threshold, and entered the chamber.

And the demons in the hall and in the hush saw the woman standing there at the entrance, clutching something quiet and covered, walking, cheerful and happy with what she carried, walking toward her husband and to her beloved, halting in front of him, holding it for him:

"Here you are!"

The demons, standing together in the hall, were queasy and uneasy, so they turned to one another, hasty and hurried, conferring together, perceiving the matter with bewildered eyes, exchanging glances and wondering: "What's going to be, what's going to happen?"

"Slut!" one demon blurted and bellowed.

"Flesh and sluts!" the rest broke in with hands and with fingers, and they all charged forward and yelled at the woman: "Slut! Take it away, remove it from our view! That is your death!"

"I don't want to!" the maiden spitefully snapped back in their faces. She stood with her husband and uncovered what she was clutching.

"Cockadoodle-doo!" The terrified rooster on the woman's hands suddenly spread his wings and crowed: "Cockadoodle-doo!"

"Hold him! Grab him!" The devils suddenly turned toward their man and toward the table and, hands on hands and fists on fists, they headed toward him and hurled themselves at him: "Hold him! Death to him!"

But at that instant, in the mirror and in the glass of the mirror, a hole emerged, the size of a human, and the maiden's husband appeared, and he waved at the man and he signaled him: Faster!

And the man, the abducted one, suddenly jumped into the congregation and leaped over the heads of the demons, toward the mirror and the hole that had formed. And a hand arose from the other side, the now empty side, and the hand pulled him and his entire body across to that other side.

"Hold him! Grab him!" the demons chased after him and after his disappearance, and one over the other, and one atop the other they charged into the mirror. "Death to him, turmoil, he'll tell about our shame! . . ."

"I certainly will!" the man, already redeemed and far away, yelled from the other side. "I certainly will! I'll expose your shame and—"

The demons no longer heard the man and his voice so far away. Beaten and foolish, they stopped at the mirror and at the hole and with hands abated and with powerless anger, they were ashamed of themselves and their charge and they stood there, disappointed.

"What about the man?"

"The man kept his word and he told it all."

And so the demon ended his tale.

SROL VÁKSER (1892–1919)

Seven Days from Now
and The Final Tear

The author died in a pogrom, and these two stories were published post-humously in twin journals based in Berlin: Milgroym *3 (1923): 35–39 (Yiddish), and* Rimon *3 (1923): 35–38 (Hebrew).*

Depicting amorous sadomasochism in an extreme form of the fairy tale, Srol Vákser plugs into a folklore tradition that puts a heavy price on the attainment of erotic wishes: Lovers in such narratives suffer the worst ordeals before being reunited—perhaps in death. That is the link to Ansky, who, gathering Jewish folklore, might have unearthed similar harsh fanta-sies. He was certainly familiar with them in the heritage of Yiddish litera-ture (by Rabbi Nakhman and others).

Seven Days from Now

A princess had a handsome slave who polished her tiny slippers every morning. She thought about him, knowing that he was in love with her. But the slave was proud in regard to his love and he concealed it deep in his soul like a precious treasure.

Now one spring morning, when the east was turning rosy and paint-ing the awakening heavens purple, and God's world was beautiful, was fresh and green, the shoe polisher was intoxicated by the dewy air, the sweet scents of garden flowers, and the fragrances of the green meadows. In the black luster of her slippers, he saw an image of his beloved, he saw his silken fantasy, and he doubted whether he could resist temptation: He would have to reveal his sacred secret to the princess.

Treating her slippers like holy objects, he put them in a holy place, and then raised his arms to God and swore:

"If my tongue reveals my feelings to the princess, I will rip it out. If my eyes lust for her beauty, I will gouge them out. If my right hand touches the princess, I will chop it off, and if my left hand touches her, I will burn it off in fire!"

However, the slave did not know that the princess was standing on the other side of the door, as pale and nude as the morning star, and that she trembled as she listened to his oath word for word.

Daylight came, and the princess was already awake. Silken morning breezes had awakened her earlier than usual, awakened her with the sweetest sounds plucked from the finest harp strings. And she sat there, light and cheerful with the morning, waiting for the slave.

And when he brought in the polished slippers, the princess gazed at him with smiling eyes, archly pursed her silken lips, and said: "Does the slave even know that he is a handsome boy? . . ."

The slave bowed down to the ground and bashfully replied: "Your slave knows that the princess has a handsome fiancé."

"My fiancé doesn't know how to love," the princess complained in a sorrowful tone.

The slave gave the princess a pitying look, not daring to say a word.

Since it was unsuitable for a slave to pity a princess, she dismissed him.

The second morning came, and the slave again brought in the polished slippers.

The princess looked at him with kind eyes and said in a soft, sweet voice that she knew the slave's secret: He was in love with her.

"God," he proudly replied, "does not prohibit even a slave from loving."

It didn't bother her, the princess said. Let the slave love her, she even enjoyed it.

It was not for her enjoyment, the slave said, that he loved her.

This angered the princess, and she dismissed the slave.

The third day came, and the princess looked pityingly at the shoe polisher, pursed her silken lips, and said that she knew that the slave kissed her slippers every day, wept and prayed to them.

He didn't soil them, the slave explained.

Let him soil them, the princess said leniently, so long as he kept sanctifying them, weeping and praying to them.

"I'm no idolater!" said the slave, lowering his eyes.

Then why had he been praying to the slippers?

He said he didn't know.

The princess was offended and she dismissed him. And on the fourth day, the princess was already looking at the slave her eyes filled with promise. And she knew, she said, that the slave wanted to bring her fresh flowers every day.

And the slave proudly explained: "God does not prohibit a slave from having a will."

It didn't bother her, said the princess. Let him bring fresh flowers every morning. She would even show them to her fiancé and boast about them.

"It's all the same to me," the slave stammered. This annoyed the princess, and she dismissed him.

On the fifth day the princess was confused and nervous. And when the slave brought her the slippers but brought no flowers, she yelled at him, ordering him to bring her flowers on the spot!

He was her slave, he replied, kneeling, and he would carry out her orders on the spot. . . .

But the princess snapped that she would throw the flowers at her fiancé's feet. . . .

The slave kept silent.

Wouldn't it bother him, she asked slyly and roguishly, if his flowers were scattered under her fiancé's feet?

The flowers would be hers, not his, the slave proudly replied, so it was all the same to him.

The princess was deeply offended and she dismissed him.

Now came the night before the sixth day—a dense, sleepless night. The princess felt tormented, bored, waiting impatiently for the slave to come in, and she was determined once and for all to extract the forbidden love from the proud slave's heart.

Her strength ebbed as she waited, and before the morning star appeared, she rang her bell, and the startled slave came running in. He hadn't polished her slippers yet, but he did bring her the flowers.

And the princess looked at him with charming eyes, pursed her silken lips, and asked whether these were the flowers of his love.

"No!" the slave replied, self-assured.

"Where are they—those flowers?"

Instead of replying, the slave tore out his tongue right in front of the princess.

The princess was furious. She dismissed the slave and suffered mortal anguish. She jumped about as if poisoned, mangled, and almost went berserk.

She then told her fiancé that he should not dare to visit her until she summoned him. Meanwhile she forbade him to come that evening.

And the night before the seventh day, she was out of her mind, a sea of passion was seething in her heart, and her brain was boiling like a cauldron. The pillows burned beneath her, and her eyes spewed fire. Her fists were clenched like iron, and she gnashed her teeth.

She had to defeat him, she yelled, she *would* defeat him. Otherwise she would kill herself!

And her loud ringing at midnight frightened the slave, and he burst into her bedroom without her slippers and without the flowers.

The princess sprang from her bed as wild as a demon, ripped off her nightgown, stood naked by the burning fireplace, and lecherously shouted: "Look and lust for me!"

The slave instantly gouged out his eyes. The princess then coiled around his body like a serpent and shouted wildly: "Hug me!"

But the slave pushed her away with his right hand, which his left hand instantly chopped off.

The princess threw herself on the slave like a wild beast and dragged him to her bed with all her strength.

The slave fought and fought the princess with the help of his left hand until he finally threw her down and ran away and crashed into the fireplace, where he burned off his left hand.

From then on the slave was mute, blind, and without hands. The princess broke off her engagement and she polished the slave's boots every morning.

The Final Tear

This is the story of a happy prince who loved a haughty princess.

"If you'll love me until my dying day," said the princess, "then I'm willing to be your bride."

So the prince swore by all that was holy that he would love her until her dying day.

Then the princess asked how he would prove his love.

"I will have you ride," said the prince, his face radiant with happiness, "in gold carriages with gilded wheels and with ardent steeds hung with diamonds and brilliants. I will take you to crystal palaces with marble rooms, I will seat you on marble chairs, I will lay purple runners under your feet, and adorn you with the costliest pearls and corals, and dress you only in silk and plush. I will find the most wondrous birds in the world, pluck their loveliest feathers, and weave them for you into a crown set with emeralds and sapphires. I will have your body rubbed with the most fragrant oils. You will drink the best wines and bathe in milk and honey."

"No, that is not how you will prove your love," the princess haughtily replied.

And the prince's eyes burst into thousands of flames of happiness and he continued speaking:

"I will take you to kings and emperors, to the grandest balls, in magic and splendor. For years and years we will soar like eagles over mountains of gold and rivers of silver. We will arrive in the farthest lands and seek out the deserts and islands most out of the way. Your happiness will drown out the sounds of the steppes, of the waves, and the roar of the storms, and you will confide the secret of your life to the mysterious hush of the calm horizon. I will take you to the wealthiest world and the natural nooks, and underneath the most beautiful sky, woven from gold and silver dreams, I will build you a pyramid of roses and other flowers. From the high and mighty top, amid the purest clouds, you will shine for me like a godly dream, and a golden sun with silver rays will kiss your head as it pours out its glory."

"That is not how you will prove your love!" said the princess.

"Well, then I will bring you the most remarkable singers and players and world-famous dancers, bring the tenderest trills of the sweetest, noblest throats and the very finest chords of the most ancient and most modern and most miraculous violins, and immortal hymns will be created for you, and the most magical birds will tell you legends of paradise. . . ."

"That is not," said the princess, "how you will prove your love!"

"I will constantly pamper you, caress you, kiss you, cherish you, love you. With a prayer on pure lips together with the morning star, I will kneel at your feet; at nightfall I will lock the door to your bedroom with seven silver locks and guard your bed with a gold spear, protect your peace and count every breath you take. . . ."

"That is not how you will prove your love!" the princess said again.

"Day and night I will suck vital juice from your pure eyes, draw purple thoughts from your roselike cheeks, finely carve my fate upon your marble forehead, and pour out the purest desires upon your breasts. . . ."

"No, that is not how you will prove your love!"

"If you like," said the prince, "I will live happily as I have been living until now, laugh and delight with Heaven and earth, dance with mountains and valleys, play in fields and forests, and sing love songs to you, as cherubs sing to God. And if not, I will happily give you my life, I will thrust a fiery lance into my heart, fall dead at your feet, and my blood will bear witness to my love!"

"My soulmate must be a priest, not a sacrifice!" the haughty princess replied.

"Then," the happy prince cried out, "I will bring you a bloodstained slaughtering knife that has slashed the throats of my brother and my sister, and the knife will bear witness to my love!"

"The sacrifice is not enough to make you my priest!" the princess replied.

"Then," the happy prince wildly cried out, "I will place my father's crowned head at your feet!"

"That's meager!" the haughty princess said.

"I will give you a gift—my mother's heart!" the happy prince insanely cried out.

"That's meager!" the haughty princess said.

"Then," the happy prince breathlessly cried out, "I will abandon my large kingdom, betray my subjects, and change my holy faith!"

"That's meager!"

"Then I'll kill you!" he tyrannically cried out.

"That's enough," the princess finally replied. "I will anoint you as my high priest, to be consecrated with my own blood." But then she said: "Tell me: Do you have loyal tears to repay my love? Does your heart possess the great grief to ransom my death? For the man I choose for visiting the inner sanctum of my temple, the man I permit to enter my Holy of Holies even once—he must bear my holiness within himself for the rest of his life, and my fire must not go out, must burn forever in his heart."

"No," the happy prince replied, "I don't know what tears are and I don't know what grief is. I have never known suffering or fathomed grief. Never have my ears caught a moan, never have my eyes spotted a tear. Whenever the wind was weeping outside, they sang me cheerful songs in my chambers; whenever the heavens were covered with black clouds, and darkness was ruling the world, they closed the doors and the shutters and they lit up my home with magical light. I don't know where grief is."

"Grief," said the princess, "accompanies love, and loyalty is recognized through suffering. They give taste to life. If you possess no grief, you will not know the taste of love. If you do not know suffering, you cannot know my heart. Because only deep sufferings give birth to tears, and only a loyal tear pays for love."

"And I have no tears!" said the prince, forlorn.

"Happy prince," said the haughty princess, "a person must have tears, tears!"

"What should I do," asked the happy prince, "to make you my bride?"

"Go and search for the source of love and draw from it, and then I will be your bride."

The happy prince stood by the golden gates of love, he knocked and said: "Open up, you gates of love, and let the happy prince come in! I am a happy man in the world, I have already drunk from all the beakers of delight, and now I want to enjoy your treasures."

The gates of love opened immediately, and a pure cherub with small, crystal-white wings flew over to the prince and said with a friendly smile: "Blessed are you who have come to us—we have been waiting for you. We saw that you were happy in life. You have strength, power, beauty, wealth, and honor, but you possess nothing of our treasures. So come to us. Our gates are open for both happy and unhappy people—bless you for coming to us."

The prince walked through purple and gilded rooms lined with mirrors until he reached an enchanted chamber. A chamber with no walls, floor, or ceiling, with only pure skies drifting above and below. Seven golden suns shone above and seven silver moons shone below. And the prince walked, or rather floated, toward the lord of love. And the lord of love blazed on a glowing throne, and small, airy seraphs danced around him. In his right hand he held youth, in his left hand a harp, while at his feet old age was kneeling and begging for a bit . . . of love. Eternity shone in his eyes, and grief rested on his forehead.

"Come here," said the lord of love to the happy prince, and beams of light radiated from his lips toward the sky. "Tell me your desire, and I will fulfill it."

"I am in love," said the happy prince, "with a haughty princess. She demands tears from me, but I am unable to shed tears because I'm a happy man and I possess no tears."

The lord of love gave an order—the upper and the lower heavens burst into lightning bolts, and a small, airy seraph left and brought back seven loyal tears, pure, warm tears drawn from the treasure of grief, and the seraph poured them into the happy prince's heart and said:

"Now your heart has seven pure, warm, and loyal tears. They will be your wealth for the seven loves that nest in your heart: love for your brother and sister, love for your father and mother, love for your kingdom, your people, and your faith. And now for your final love, the strongest of all, your love for the princess. Every love has its tear in you and its pain, and you will feel pain for your love when you shed your tear. It will fade and vanish like a dream! . . ."

Cheerfully the happy prince came to the haughty princess with the news that he now had seven hot, pure, loyal tears in his heart. Now he was worthy of her love.

"Yes, now I will give you my love," replied the princess, "after you fulfill my desire."

"Ask me for anything," said the happy prince, "and I will do whatever you desire of me!"

"Bring me a blood-smeared slaughtering knife that has slashed your brother's and your sister's throats!"

Oh, it was hard for the happy prince to slash his brother's and his sister's throat, but love carried the day and it heroically passed the first ordeal.

Then the first tear came loose from the happy prince's heart. The tear burned in his breast, it throttled his throat, it flamed in his eyes. He had to let go of the tear for strong and great was the pain, yet he held the tear back with might and main because it was too hard for him to forget his love for his brother and sister.

"Shed your tear," the haughty princess commanded, "and forget your love for your brother and sister!"

While shedding the tear, the happy prince moaned for the first time in his life. Within seconds, a black grief pressed his heart, and the poison of life surged in his blood.

But then his heart felt lighter and he forgot his love for his brother and sister like a dream—love with its sweet grief.

"Now," the haughty princess commanded, "lay your father's crowned head at my feet!"

Hard as it was for the happy prince to do such a cruel deed, the emperor's crowned head soon rolled at the haughty princess's feet.

And the second tear came loose from the prince's heart.

The tear bored through his heart, throttled his throat, and cut his eyes like gold. And the prince, who loved his father so much, absolutely refused to shed the tear.

But the haughty princess gave him an order, and he had to shed the tear like a hero.

"Bring me your mother's heart as a gift!"

Oh, that was something he couldn't do! His mother loved him so very much! . . . But the princess had such power over him, her words had such a sway over him, that he brought her his mother's heart as a gift.

And the loveliest tear came loose from the happy prince's heart. The tear burned in his breast like the fires of Hell, shattered his brain, poisoned his blood, and he could not shed the tear. For it's impossible to forget your love for your mother. You take it along into the grave!

But the haughty princess wanted him to shed this tear too, and shed it he did with unusual strength.

"Now," the haughty princess commanded, "abandon your kingdom, betray your subjects, and change your faith."

A man who had murdered his brother and sister, his father and mother, could easily abandon his kingdom, betray his subjects, and change his faith.

"And now," the haughty princess commanded, "kill *me!* And do not dare shed the tear of your final love, your love for me!"

That was the final ordeal.

The happy prince passed it with great strength. He killed the haughty princess, and he still has the final tear.

The happy prince has long since forgotten his sister and his brother, his father, his mother, his kingdom, his subjects, his faith—but he remembers his princess.

The final tear keeps burning his heart, its fire throttles his throat, it cuts his eyes, but he holds it back, he holds the tear back.

And whoever sees the prince says: "That is the happy prince, he guards the final tear."

S. ANSKY (1863–1920)

The Ghost Writer,
or Letters from the Beyond

The final Yiddish text, Briv fun yener Velt, *is to be found in S. Ansky,* Gezamelte Shriften, *vol. 8 (Warsaw: Farlag An-Sky, 1928): 83–119.*

Mótke Khabád, one of several renowned Ashkenazi jesters, supposedly lived from 1820 to 1880. Whether or not this funnyman ever existed, Ansky drew on his sarcastic persona to ridicule both traditionalism and anti-traditionalism in the modern Jewish world. While part of the audience of Ansky's The Dybbuk *may have been steeped in what the Enlightenment considered superstition, the fusion of folk material and satire in* The Ghost Writer *exposes the author's contradictory relationship to Jewish life. This is also hinted at in the choice of his literary form, an epistolary humoresque, which was introduced by Yóysef Perl (1773–1839) in his nasty anti-Hasidic novel* The Revealer of Secrets *(his Hebrew version was published in 1819, his Yiddish version in 1937). As in Ashmedai, Ansky offers a very detailed panorama of popular Jewish belief, treating it with both tenderness and derision.*

A Packet of Missives from Mótke Khabád (R.I.P.) to Shlemiel, commonly known as the liar—May His Light Shine

Letter One

To My Friend, Our Charming, Our Prominent and Eminent
Teacher and Master, Rabbi Shlemiel, May His Light Shine:
My dear Shlemiel!

Evil tongues have spread a rumor that you don't, alas, tell the whole truth and nothing but—that is, you stretch it ever so slightly—Heaven preserve us! As a result, somebody or other might question whether these letters really come from me. And so I find it necessary to clarify how I manage to send my letters from our True World, the World of the Beyond, to you in the World of Chaos. In this way, I hope to prevent our Jewish brethren from sinning—Heaven forfend—by nurturing doubt and distrust. And so on.

We all know that ever since the first days of Creation it has been very difficult to obtain any facts whatsoever about anything happening in Our World and especially in Gehenna. Only the saintly author of *The Beginning of Wisdom,* the Hasid, the prodigy, the Cabalist, Elye, son of Moyshe, succeeded in penetrating the deepest secrets of the True World and describing all the Seven Halls of Gehenna from start to finish.

The revelations in *The Beginning of Wisdom* caused a harrowing turmoil in all the worlds. They undertook the harshest investigations to determine who had exposed the secrets of Gehenna to that genius. In the end, many of the biggest fiends and demons were dismissed from their positions. From then on, there were no more links between the two worlds. Demons tremble at the very thought of uttering even a peep about the things that happen among them. Nor can we learn anything from the Celestial Advocates, because they are strip-searched prior to being released to your world. The saints in Paradise could, indeed, transmit something to you when they appear in your dreams; but they're terrible cowards—poor things—and they're even more scared of Sammael [Satan] than the demons are. Well, and as for the wicked, there's nothing to say: Escaping from a boiling cauldron ins't as easy as it sounds. And that's why you earthlings haven't received one scrap of information from here all this time.

But now, radical changes have occurred in the True World. During the past few years, Gehenna has admitted young Jews—a strange new gang of reel-'em-off souls! They're such wild beasts that they resist even the most horrible tortures. With the most fearful chutzpah they laugh their heads off at the most terrible punishments, and they simply say: "Wow, don't that beat all! Back in the World of Chaos we experienced the most gruesome agonies—and compared with that your inflictions are child's play!"

And no matter how devious and devilish the sufferings that Sammael and his advisors dreamt up, he could get nowhere with this new gang—the results were nil. Finally, a cunning demon spoke up. In his youth he had been a Celestial Advocate, but had then converted to demonhood. He now gave Sammael some down-to-earth advice: Send those diehards back to your world and let them endure its punishments.

And it's really helped! The instant they threaten to ship one of those arrogant creeps back to life, to the World of Chaos, and they even show him the place he'll wind up in, he starts acting like butter wouldn't melt in his mouth and he swears he'll be pious and virtuous so long as he can remain in Hell.

Sammael came up with another great idea: He had the walls of Gehenna covered with pictures of the worst tortures perpetrated in your world. Those images are so terrifying to the sinners in the boiling cauldrons that they shed rivers of tears in their great pain and pity. Sammael also introduced a new custom: Every morning, in all Seven Halls of Gehenna, the demons read aloud the news bulletins about all the events in your world. The impact in Hell is so overwhelming that other demons can't stand it and they stop up their ears.

Yet despite all that, there are some reel-'em-off guys with so much courage that they dig in their heels and remain indifferent to the dire warnings. In the end they are given their due and sent to the Devil—or rather to your World of Chaos.

One of these wild beasts is bringing you my letter, dear friend Shlemiel. Needless to say, it wasn't easy getting to him. But don't forget: I *am* Mótke Khabád, after all! I charmed him so thoroughly with a few quips that he took the letter along. I must warn you, though, dear friend Shlemiel: Don't enter into any further relations with him, don't put him up, and don't store any package for him. You might, Heaven forfend, be committing a sin and you'll lose your world and the next. God willing, another reel-'em-off traveler will bring you my next letter—a detailed account of how I passed on to the Great Beyond and how I'm resting in my peace.

Your Friend,
Mótke Khabád (R.I.P.)

Letter Two

To My Friend, Our Venerable, Our Charming, Our Prominent and Eminent Teacher and Master, Rabbi Shlemiel, May His Light Shine:
And now, my friend Shlemiel, I will minutely describe everything that has happened to me from the moment of my demise until today.

First of all, I must tell you that I am resting in my peace, thanks to the Good Lord. To tell the truth, I never expected Hell to be so peaceful. I remember very distinctly lying on the ground, while my better half, Treyne, was mourning me and yelling hoarsely: "You shall rest there in peace!!" I mentally laughed at her and thought to myself: "What a silly woman!! What kind of rest can I look forward to? The instant I arrive, I'll encounter the Dumah, the Guardian Angel of the Dead, after which

I'll be beaten by evil spirits. Next I'll enter Gehenna with all its tortures!"

But looking back, I now realize my better half was right. Do you understand, Shlemiel? I'm resting. I swear on a stack of Bibles: I would never have dreamt that a Jew could possibly have such a restful Hell as I now do. Think about it! Throughout my life, from the changing table to the final ablution table, I was a homeless wanderer, afraid of everything and everyone. I was scared of my parents, scared of the rebbe, the evil spirit, Hell, afraid of ghosts and demons, afraid of goys young and old, afraid of Jews, afraid of the authorities, afraid of evil decrees, persecutions, defamations, pogroms—not to mention my anxieties about my paltry income. But that's over and done with! All my worries, all my fear and trembling were whisked away.

Mulling over these things, I realized that all my terror came from a single source—the fact that the body is tied to the soul. Neither per se has anything to tremble about. Alas! Now what does a Jewish body need? Does it need pleasures? All it needs is a little peace of mind. If it looks for some income, it does so not for its own sake, Heaven forfend, but to keep body and soul together. And the soul certainly needs nothing—it can barely deal with the burden of a Jew's hundred daily blessings. . . . But since body and soul are joined, they both tremble: The soul fears that the body may get harmed—and the body fears that the soul, God forbid, may stumble and be stained.

Now that my soul and my body have gone their separate ways, both are very content. My body is lying in its apartment like an aristocrat without a care in the world. One can't say that the apartment is particularly spacious or luxurious. But, knock on wood, there's a bit of leg room, elbow room, and wiggle room. And if you take a close look, you'll see that this apartment is no poorer, no darker, no damper, no colder than the apartments I had in your amiable little world. Furthermore, just consider the true value of this apartment: It's all mine, it's eternal, and I don't have to worry about the rent! Imagine the pleasure of owning my own terra firma (in plain Yiddish: my own spread) in my own name—and I'm sure that even the government itself won't evict me.

And that's not all! Imagine the sheer delight of knowing that no one will tear my shroud from my body, no one will slash my innards out of my belly or shove nails into my eyes! Needless to say, a human being is a sinner, and at times the body may mutter that it's not content because the worms are making it a little uneasy. But that's a trifle, of course. What Jewish body is not accustomed to being worm-eaten?! And what worms at that!

Well, and as for the soul, it, too, is reborn. Imagine throwing off such a heavy yoke as a Jewish body! And now the soul struts around Hell like an aristocrat, and no one prevents it from going where it wants to. No one asks it for a pass, for a birth certificate, for a residence permit. No one even asks the soul what special house of worship (in plain Yiddish: labor-union synagogue) it belongs to or what prayer style it practices. Granted, at times the soul may feel faint if not a bit queasy because there's no one to argue with about "approaches" (in plain Yiddish: pogroms), quarrel with, start a new fraternal organization with. How does the saying go? Nothing's perfect.

Incidentally, I hope we can launch a new movement in Hell. If we do, the place will be so good, beyond our wildest dreams.

Your Friend,
Mótke Khabád (R.I.P.)

Postscript: I still haven't written you a word about what I promised to tell you about. Let it wait till my next letter.

Letter Three

To My Friend, Our Venerable, Our Prominent and Eminent Teacher and Master, Rabbi Shlemiel, May His Light Shine:

First of all, I will now describe for you the exact cause of my demise.

I can state without the least exaggeration that I had a very fine and noble death—may the same be said about you someday, dear friend Shlemiel. For one thing, I had the special honor of passing away right during the Days of Awe, a few days before Rosh ha-Shana! You can't imagine how easy and almost cheery it is to perish at that time. It can't be compared with the ordeal of dying during the Three Weeks before the Ninth of Ab [the anniversary of the Destruction of the Temple]— not to mention the Nine Days between the first and the tenth of Ab, when Jews abstain from meat and wine. During the Days of Awe you feel so tangibly that the Resurrection is just around the corner. You're certain that you'll be dead only briefly, that the Messiah is due any moment. A new world of justice and goodness is about to start, and Sammael and his covens of demons will fall through the earth. Dying at a time like that is nearly as easy as taking a short stroll.

The very opposite of that is dying during the Nine Days, when all minds are absorbed in the Destruction of the Temple, all hearts are bereaved and grieving, and all ears are filled with the dismal strains of dirges and the Book of Lamentations. It feels as if the entire planet, God forbid, is in Sammael's hands, as if the Messiah will never come and no corpse will ever arise from its grave. A human being is shortsighted, alas, as shortsighted as a chicken.

Needless to say, I didn't die a truly easy death—nowadays, that's quite rare. But I swear on a stack of Bibles that I was very close to it. My soul slipped out of me as quickly and lightly as a hair from a glass of milk—I barely noticed it. At first I was a little scared of the agony of dying. I knew from our holy books that even quiet and decent Jews can often suffer a harsh and painful demise, that some Jews go through a long and drawn-out struggle with the Angel of Death—they are bashed and thrashed so horribly that they reach the True World without a vestige of human appearance. Others languish dreadfully because the Angel of Death doesn't know how to approach them or what sin to get all riled up about. So he keeps them in a lengthy stupor, which is a lot worse than the tortures of Hell.

I can't say that I yielded to the Angel of Death in a friendly way. Quite the contrary! I, too, wrestled with him long and hard—like a hero. However, I wrestled not with my hands but with words and arguments. I proved to him that he was a dolt, an ignorant clod, and that his efforts to grab my soul were in violation of Jewish law. I tell you, Shlemiel: He practically kicked the bucket himself! I very, very nearly beat him at his own game! In the end, he did get my soul but only by flouting our religious laws—and I fully intend to lodge a complaint with the Celestial Council of Justice. I don't know if it can help much, but it *will* humiliate him—and that's the main thing.

Now I can't say that the Angel of Death was a surprise guest. I had been expecting him since Purim. You see, at Purim a large group of Hasids gathered in our synagogue, and we were living it up. We danced, we sang, we sermonized, we quipped. I was there, too, of course, and I pulled off more pranks than anyone else. I figured that at Purim you can't, as we say, distinguish between cursing Haman and blessing Mordecai—anything goes! I can say anything I like! And since I was in high spirits, I ridiculed everything and even poked a little fun at the Good Lord and His ministering angels. Suddenly I felt a jab in my heart and I thought to myself: "Now you're in for it, Mótke!" And indeed I was!

The next day, I started feeling that things around me weren't so great, that the Angel of Death was coming my way. I kept faltering, stumbling. Sometimes when I was lost in thought, I clearly heard all kinds of demons flying and circling overhead. I noticed that members of the burial society were walking around my home far too often and sometimes even coming in—by mistake, supposedly, or with a flimsy excuse.

Once I even dreamt about the Dumah, the angel that carries the dead to the afterlife. He asked me in Hebrew: "What is thy name?"

Luckily I wasn't scared. I promptly told him my name, and he skedaddled.

But it was a bad omen, and so I began preparing in time. I made out a will, sewed a couple of fine shrouds, and bought a copy of *Crossing the Jabbok* [the collection of prayers recited by a dying person or by his survivors]. In short, I girded my loins. Nor did I have a long wait. Upon reciting the third penitential prayer, I was just about to head for synagogue when I heard a knock at the door. I looked up—and speak of the Devil! There, facing me, was the Angel of Death with his gang of guardian angels. . . .

But here I have to break off—otherwise I'll miss my messenger to your World of Chaos.

Your Friend,
Mótke Khabád (R.I.P.)

Letter Four

To My Friend, Our Venerable, Our Charming, Our Prominent and Eminent Teacher and Master, Rabbi Shlemiel, May His Light Shine:

My previous missive broke off with the Angel of Death coming into my home.

One look and I instantly recognized him. But I wasn't the least bit frightened. The holy books tell us that anyone who so much as glances at him is filled with fear and trembling. But I tell you, Shlemiel, that's a load of garbage. He's an angel like any other angel and he acts very refined, far more refined than, say, the Dumah. (What more do you need? When the Angel of Death takes your soul, he addresses you in the polite form!) All the terror is inspired by his having a thousand eyes. But I swear on a stack of Bibles that it's nothing. Granted, at first sight you feel a little wobbly about so many eyes. But when you peer at them more closely, you promptly realize that for all his thousand eyes he doesn't see more or farther than an ordinary angel with one eye. The reason is that he may see a thousand things simultaneously but he can't do more than one thing at a time. For as we all know, even an angel can't be in two places at once. As a result, the Angel of Death often gets confused and doesn't know what to tackle first. I'm certain that people would be less afraid of him, if they could easily give him the slip—and they can do it precisely because of his thousand eyes.

No sooner had he crossed the threshold than he commanded: "Mótke Khabád! Prepare for your demise! In twenty-four seconds I will claim your soul!"

I was not overly enthused by his order and I replied: "Hush! Don't be in such a hurry! Haste makes waste! That's unheard of—twenty-four seconds!"

"This is a celestial decree!" he retorted.

"Big deal," I said. "So it's a celestial decree! Where's the fire? I've seen a lot of decrees that weren't carried out for years."

"Those are a different brand of decree!" he answered. "The ones I carry out have to be obeyed within twenty-four seconds."

"Now tell me, Angel of Death," I went on. "What sins of mine would deserve such a dire punishment?"

"Your fine quips about the Lord and His ministering angels!"

"What quips? The ones at Purim?"

"The ones at Purim, yes, the ones at Purim!" He smirked. "See? You're quite well versed in your own mischief!"

"But at Purim," I argued, "there's no prohibition against making quips, singing, poking fun at whatever we like. It's clearly written that at Purim we should reach a level at which we can't distinguish between cursing Haman and blessing Mordecai! So what are you complaining about? Wouldn't you do better to check out who stayed home at Purim in peace and quiet? Even the finest and most pious congregants—not only Hasids but even anti-Hasids—painted the town red on both Purim and the day after. Whole minyans charged through the streets, belting out songs, and youngsters carried flags like at Simhath Torah [the festival of the Torah]. And now out of the clear blue sky—we're being condemned for having a good time!"

"You just don't understand the ways of the Lord and His ministering angels!"

"I do understand," I shot back. "but I don't find this very just!"

The Angel of Death agreed: "It's *not* very just."

"Now wait a moment!" I yelled. "It's not only unjust, it's against Jewish law. How can I possibly be judged for my sins in the middle of the year? It's outrageous! I sinned on Purim, and I'll be judged during the Days of Awe. It'll be signed on Rosh ha-Shana, sealed on Yom Kippur, the Day of Atonement, and delivered on Hoshana Rabbah [the seventh day of the Feast of Tabernacles, when every person's fate for the coming year is irrevocably determined in Heaven]. It will all be executed in due form. When I'm condemned at that time, you can come for my soul. And now, if you'll be so kind as to leave, goodbye and good luck!"

The Angel of Death gaped at me and burst out laughing. "You must have been sitting behind the stove all this time and never cracked a holy book. Don't you know there's been a new ruling about judgments? Waiting from one Yom Kippur to the next takes too long. According to the new regulation, every guardian angel has the right to hand down a fateful sentence at any hour and any second."

I was boiling. "Does that mean without a trial and without a judge?" I shouted furiously.

"What are you talking about?" the Angel of Death retorted. "The sentence is recorded on parchment in the style of all legal verdicts."

"What do I care about the parchment and the style," I yelled, "if the judgment is a miscarriage of justice."

"Well, so it's a miscarriage of justice! Who cares?!" he calmly stated and drew out his kosher slaughtering knife. . . .

But now I have to break off. I've just been told that Hérshel of Ostropólye, our famous jester, is hovering nearby and he's going to tell a joke about the Queen of Sheba's muzzles. I've got to float over and hear it.

> Your Friend,
> Mótke Khabád (R.I.P.)

Letter Five

To My Friend, Our Venerable, Our Charming, Our Prominent and Eminent Teacher and Master, Rabbi Shlemiel, May His Light Shine:
On this day I can continue the story of my debate with the Angel of Death.

After compelling him to admit that a decree from a guardian angel cannot be compared to a verdict handed down by the Celestial Council of Justice, I went on: "How can you, Angel of Death, maintain that the sentence must be carried out immediately if the Celestial Council can still rescind it?"

"It certainly *can,*" replied the Angel of Death, "but it doesn't poke its nose into such matters."

"What do you mean it doesn't poke its nose?" I cried. "It's duty-bound to poke its nose. Doesn't the prayer book clearly say: 'Repentance, prayer, and charity will avert the evil decree'? C'mon! Has that been erased? Or has it been quibbled away?"

"It hasn't been erased and it hasn't been quibbled away," my visitor replied coolly. "Nevertheless, all your remedies are a waste of breath—about as useful as cupping-glasses for a dead man!"

"Are you ever mistaken!" I dug in my heels. "You're not going to make me believe that a good prayer can't avert a decree! C'mon now—a prayer? Don't you know what beautiful prayers we Jews have? For instance—" (I recited the opening lines in Hebrew, then translated them into Yiddish.) "'Thou dost not wish the mortal man to die, Thou wishest him to return to Thy paths and live.' Plus you mustn't forget we have such excellent prayer leaders—they can set the world on its ear. Why don't we ask our prayer leader to pray?! Then you'll see—"

"Shush!" the Angel of Death stopped me. "Simmer down! I know that you Jews have lofty prayers and excellent prayer leaders. But that's all good for the Days of Awe, when the Celestial Council gathers under God's Throne of Glory and passes judgments. A group of defenders stands to the right and bevies of accusers stand to the left. Every prayer is accepted, every letter, every dot. A decree, however, is a horse of a different color. Your prayer will rise to Heaven, but by the time it arrives, by the time it's received, by the time it's answered, you'll have torn up a few lovely winding sheets—"

"Well, fine, so maybe you're right," I broke in. "But what about charity? Why won't charity help me? I'm a pauper, but what won't a man do to keep body and soul together? I'll pawn the last shirt off my back and use the money to redeem my soul."

"You've got a hell of a lot of chutzpah!" the Angel of Death guffawed. "My knife's at your throat, and you want to buy your way out with a pauper's shirt! You fool! If you want charity to stave off a decree that's to be carried out in twenty-four seconds, you'd better have a mound of rubles, a mint! Even then, of course, I won't release you. The only thing that's in my power is to put you in a coma. That'll give your wife time to measure the graveyard—and to leave no stone unturned. After that, I'll grab your soul anyway."

"Shush! Don't try to frighten me with a fortune!" I cried. "No ancestor of mine ever set eyes on that much cash, and neither have I. But don't forget that we have rich Jews—thank the Lord!—moneybags, a Rothschild. For them, a mound of rubles is a drop in the bucket!"

"And you really think they're going to bail you out?"

"Of course they will," I explained. "Is Rothschild ignorant of Jewish law? Doesn't he know he's obliged to redeem an endangered Jewish soul? I'm sure he hasn't forgotten that all Jews are brothers and he'll fork over the cash the instant I ask him. So please hold back for a moment. I'll just go over to him and get my booty."

"You're wasting your time!" cried the Angel of Death. "I'm quite familiar with the wealthy Jews—Heaven preserve us! I can assure you: Not one of them will shell out a single kopek to have me release a Jewish jokester. They'd sooner help a goy who reels off psalms than a Jew who pokes fun at everything."

"Well, then I guess that leaves repentance," I exclaimed. "So let me repent." And beating my breast, I launched into the Yom Kippur confession—a sin for each letter of the alphabet.

"Spare me your repentance!" The Angel of Death stopped me. "Nothing will help you, no breast-beating, no strenuous efforts—you haven't got a prayer! We've introduced a different brand of repentance. If you want to block the decree, bring me your children, your relatives, your friends, and confess *their* sins. Once I get my hands on all of them, I'll see about letting you live for a few more seconds."

"Go to Hell with your repentance, Angel of Death!" I shouted angrily.

"I'll go there anyway!" he replied. "First, though, I need to take your soul. . . ."

But now I have to break off. It's Friday night, the Sabbath has already begun, and they're locking the gates of Hell. God willing, I'll write you a week from now about what happened next.

Your Friend,
Mótke Khabád (R.I.P.)

Letter Six

To My Friend, Our Venerable, Our Charming, Our Prominent and Eminent Teacher and Master, Rabbi Shlemiel, May His Light Shine:

Now I'll go on with the story of my debate with the Angel of Death.

When I saw that I was in bad straits, that his knife was at my throat, I hit on a new strategy.

"You said," I began, "that my sentence is written on parchment and in the style of all legal verdicts? Why don't you let me see it?"

"With the greatest pleasure," he replied and handed me the parchment.

Taking a look, I exclaimed: "How is this possible? It says here that you've been sent to claim the soul of Mótke, the son of Zélik the Hasid in Vilna. So then why have you come to me?"

He was surprised. "What do you mean: Why have I come to you? Where else should I have gone? You're Mótke, the son of Zélik the Hasid in Vilna!"

"A load of nonsense!" I firmly avowed. "I'm not Mótke, I'm not the son of Zélik, I'm not a Hasid, and I'm not from Vilna."

"Well, then, who are you?"

"I'm Alter, the son of Khaim of Dubróvno! And if you don't believe me, I can show you my birth certificate!"

"Oh, now the dear Jewish tricks are starting!" the Angel of Death shouted angrily. "Aliases! Phony birth certificates!"

"Go prove it's phony!" I retorted coldly.

He blew up. "How pleasurable dealing with Jews! You just yelled about Jewish law, you boiled over, you made a racket—and now you're coming up with a phony name and a phony birth certificate! Is that according to Jewish law?"

"Stop noodging the life out of me!" I broke in. "Law—shmaw! I don't want to debate you and I don't have time for a chat! Just go away with my blessings and find your Mótke Khabád the Jester, and leave me alone—I'm Alter. And I really don't have time, you're gonna make me late for synagogue."

I reached out to get my prayer shawl and my prayer thongs, which were on the wall. But the Angel of Death stopped me:

"Not so fast, Alter, son of Khaim!" he said fiercely. "Don't imagine you've wriggled out of my clutches! We're not as stupid as you think— we've found a remedy for aliases and phony birth certificates. So tell me. What do people call you? What's your name?"

"Alter, son of Khaim of Dubróvno."

"Very fine," he calmly responded, searching his breast pocket. He then pulled out a parchment and handed it to me.

"Here you are: a verdict made out for Alter, son of Khaim! Happy now?"

I checked the document and nearly fainted. "How is this possible?" I yelled.

"It's very possible! And quite simple! We prepare decrees in advance for all the names in the world. That way there won't be any hindrance to any decree. Get it?"

"Oy, do I ever!" I answered with a bitter sigh.

"Well, if you understand, then quit stalling! Hand over your soul! You've got only a few seconds left!"

With a heavy heart I argued: "What do you mean only a few seconds? What can I do with such a tight deadline? I barely have time to confess, and when will I say goodbye to my wife and kids? When will I bless them?"

"In an emergency," said the hard-hearted angel, "one can dispense with goodbyes."

"C'mon! It's the last time!" I exclaimed.

He tried to calm me down. "Why the last time? Your wife and kids are gonna visit your grave."

"A fine place to meet in—a cemetery! I'll be six feet under—how can I see those dear faces?"

"Why do you have to see their faces? What do you care? You'll hear their weeping and wailing. That way you'll be able to picture their faces."

"Damn it!" I went on. "How can you have the heart to cut a Jew off from his family, from his wife and kids, from teaching, from everything?! You're no Cossack, God forbid!"

"The way you Jews carry on!" he snapped. "When I claim a young soul, people holler at the top of their lungs: 'How is this possible?! What cruelty! Little tots! Schoolchildren!' And if I approach an older Jew, people complain: 'His wife, his children, his grandchildren!' So do tell me: Whose fault is it that you've lived so long? If you'd died in your youth, you'd have spared yourself the trouble of dying in your old age."

"'Oh, better had he never been born,'" I quoted in Hebrew. Sighing deeply, I burst into tears.

Apparently, this touched the Angel of Death a tad and he softened his tone. "Fool! Why are you crying? I tell you, you won't even feel your soul leaving you. Just consider what your soul is hanging by. A thread! Don't forget: I'm an expert! If you hadn't been carrying on, I would have polished you off long ago, and you'd be as free as a bird. . . ."

Sharpening his knife, he added: "Yesterday I went to an elderly teacher to claim his soul. When he saw me, he wailed, grabbed his *Crossing the Jabbok*, and screamed 'Help!' And when I got down to business, it turned out he didn't have the strength to die. So I gave him a little vim, a little vigor, to enable his tormented soul to leave."

At these words, the Angel of Death grabbed my throat and held out his knife. . . .

I have to break off. God willing, I'll go on with my story next week.

Your Friend,
Mótke Khabád (R.I.P.)

Letter Seven

To My Friend, Our Venerable, Our Charming, Our Prominent and Eminent Teacher and Master, Rabbi Shlemiel, May His Light Shine:

As my last letter explained, the Angel of Death was about to polish me off. He grabbed my throat and raised his knife, but I clutched his arm and cried out: "One more second! I have something very important to tell you."

"What now? More arguments?" he replied. "That's enough! I don't have all day!"

"No arguments. I only want to ask you about something that concerns you."

The Angel of Death let go of my throat and withdrew his knife: "Well, ask away. But make it snappy! No flowery rhetoric, no long-winded megillah! Get to the point!"

"You see, Angel of Death," I began, "I don't know whether I'll ever set eyes on you again. So before we part company, I'd like to find out if what they say about you in our World of Chaos is true."

"What do they say about me?" he exclaimed brusquely. "C'mon, c'mon. Tell me, let's have it!"

When I saw that my words had made an impression on the Angel of Death, I cried:

"It's fine saying: 'Tell me!' But my throat's dry. Please wait a while. I'll start at the beginning. Let me wet my whistle with a warm drink. Then I'll tell you."

"Are you crazy? Have you lost your mind?" he broke in. "How can you drink after confession? Have you forgotten that you're not allowed to eat or drink between confession and death?"

I sighed. "You're right, I forgot! Well, so listen to what I have to tell you. But you have to promise you won't be offended by anything I say."

He smirked. "I've got a thick skin."

"People say," I went on, "that you married when you were young, and your wife turned out to be a shrew. . . ."

"What do you mean 'shrew'? . . ." said the Angel of Death, slightly embarrassed, lowering all his thousand eyes. "She was no such thing. . . . She was a bit—how can I put it?—a wee bit high-strung. . . . A wee bit temperamental. . . ."

"They also say that eventually you couldn't stand her anymore and so you ran off to the ends of the earth."

"A blatant lie!" he cried out. "I never ran away. We merely separated, and I went to the ends of the earth to rest up a little. The climate there is very fine. . . ."

"Well, be that as it may, you did separate. She was left pregnant and she bore a son, and he grew up to be a shlimazl. When he pressed you to get him some kind of livelihood, you told him to be a doctor and you said that whenever he visits a sick person, he should always first check your whereabouts. If you're standing at the head of the bed, he should say that the case is hopeless and he should not accept any amount of money for treating the patient. But if you're standing at the foot of the bed, he can be confident that no matter what kind of remedy he prescribes, the patient will recover.

"Your son followed your advice and he acquired a reputation as the greatest doctor. Now one day the king's only daughter fell ill, and the king's messengers proclaimed in all countries that the man who cured the princess would receive half the kingdom and the daughter's hand in marriage. However, if someone tried and failed, he would lose his head. When your son heard this, he went to the king and volunteered to heal the princess. But when they took him into her room, he saw you standing by her head. He started begging you to leave. But no matter how much he pleaded, you refused to budge. Then all at once your son cried: 'Papa, Mama's coming!' And you dashed away."

The Angel of Death listened with downcast eyes and then softly murmured: "The story is basically true, but I didn't dash away. I simply didn't want to see her again, so I spit three times to ward off the evil eye and I walked away."

"I assumed you didn't run," I went along with him. "I figured you spit three times and then walked away. But aside from that, is the story true?"

"If only it weren't," he sighed, "but it's as true as true can be."

"Tell me," I continued. "I've heard that your spouse is nearby, within arm's reach, and that she might walk in at any moment. Wouldn't it be better if you didn't lose another second? Spit three times and walk away before it's too late?"

"Many thanks for your friendly advice," he smirked bitterly. "But I can put your anxieties at ease. I no longer mind running into her. We've made peace."

I was surprised. "How come?"

"It's simple," he said. "Our son's been making a good living for us. You see, when he cured the princess, the king welshed on his promise. He didn't let her marry my son and he didn't give him half his kingdom, but he did make him an assistant to a minister, a kind of head baker. So my son gave up medicine and began dealing in grain. His mother moved in with him, and it turned out that deep down she was still in love with me. She advised her son to lighten my work load in my twilight years. She knew that my hardest chore was to claim a peasant's soul, so she told our son to allocate grain to hungry peasants, thereby preparing their souls so that they'd meekly leave their bodies. And that's what he did. As a result, my work in the countryside became almost as easy as in the Jewish shtetls. What a simple job—I swear on a stack of Bibles. Before I even got to a peasant's home, he was already stretched out with an open mouth, ready to hand over his little goyish soul. And so my missus and I made peace."

"So that's the deal?" I said. "Well, can you tell me who lightens your job when it comes to claiming souls from hearts—?"

I didn't have time to finish my question. All at once, I felt something like a yawn coursing through all my limbs, my eyes grew radiant as if scores of menorahs were burning in them, and my ears were filled with the blaring of rams' horns. I smelled a potent odor of incense, and my mouth tasted gall—what the Bible [Num. 5:22] calls "the water that induces the spell." I sneezed good and hard—and that was that! . . . I was sliced in two. My body lay on the floor while my soul floated through my shelves of sacred tomes and tried to find a way out of the house. . . .

In my next letter I'll describe what happened to my soul right after my demise.

Your Friend,
Mótke Khabád (R.I.P.)

Letter Eight

To My Friend, Our Venerable, Our Charming, Our Prominent and Eminent Teacher and Master, Rabbi Shlemiel, May His Light Shine:
The instant my soul left my body, the room felt dark and cramped, dirty and dreary. My soul began rising to the highest heavens, to the sun and the stars, to God's luminous Throne of Glory. But when my soul looked down at my body, it felt a profound grief.

I can't boast about having been a daredevil or a madcap during my lifetime. I was a quiet and moderate Jewish funnyman. Nevertheless, I had some of the features of a warrior, a hero. If anyone so much as aimed at slapping me, I would instantly stick out my elbow. If anyone beat me, I would cry and sometimes even holler. If anyone tickled me with feathers, I would demonstrate my anger and even respond with a curse. And—pardon my French—if ever I itched, I would scratch myself. Granted, none of this involved any great courage, but my reactions were fully human.

And now all at once, my body lay there deaf and dumb, helpless, senseless, motionless. All it was good for was to support a fence. Gazing anxiously at its poor partner, my soul lingered in the room, until my body was given a decent burial. Meanwhile my soul heard all the lamentations of my widow and my fatherless children, of kinsfolk and whimperers. My soul heard all the pleas that were made to it and it memorized the list: whom to intercede for, whom to see in the True World, and what injustices to bemoan. And when my body was placed in the coffin and carried out, my soul flew after it.

Like a whizzing arrow, my soul flew straight up to the Throne of Glory with malice and vehemence. It lugged an entire Jewish life, a dark and bitter one, full of grief and shame, deprivation and persecution. It hauled along a mountain of complaints and questions. It toted whole wineskins of unwept tears, piles of sighs, rivers of boiling blood. My soul zoomed all the faster to reach the seventh heaven and, angry and frightened, to dump all these things at the foot of the Throne of Glory and to shout at God: "Look what's happening in your world!"

And my soul was sure that this would raise a rumpus in all the heavens, trigger a turmoil in all the worlds, and all the angels and seraphs in command of your World of Chaos would be called to account, a dead reckoning. And the sacred words of the Yom Kippur prayer, "And We Will Declare Thy Might," would come true: "And the angels will start to hasten and they shall tremble and shudder and they shall say: 'Now the Day of Judgment is come to recall their deeds for judgment, for in Thine eyes no one will be righteous in the Law.'"

My soul rose higher and higher. The earth below was far, far away, tiny and gloomy, like a greasy prayer shawl. The void in the center was the ocean. Towns looked like peas, countries like leaves torn from branches, rivers like the fringes of a prayer shawl.

For a brief time, my soul flew alone. But soon it was surrounded by whole bunches of companions—higher, lower, on all sides, likewise soaring toward the Throne of Glory—young and old, ugly and beautiful, clean and filthy. They, too, were full of grief and anger, with bundles of complaints. Next, whole legions of angels showed up, speeding along with prayers, sighs, moans, amens, pious thoughts, repentances, and all sorts of good deeds. Next came dark and savage hordes of devils and diabolical accusers, viciously guffawing, dragging bad resolutions, obscenities, sinful actions, cunning smirks and hateful glances. And among them, without angels or devils, there were poor wretches, like leaves blasted from trees: blessings and curses, oaths and anathemas, blood and tears and sweat, mute glimpses of Heaven from sufferers, quiet sobs from the lips of languishing children. And terrible, muffled, interrupted shouts from all over the earth—choking on blood.

And the higher my soul flew, the denser and smaller the space around it became, the louder, shriller, and stormier the noise and commotion. Everything was boiling and seething. Everyone was milling, suffocating, and struggling upward arduously and painfully as if clambering out of pitch. After a while my soul was squeezed and squashed among millions and billions of angels, accusers, souls, repentances, prayers, moans, yells, tears, and all kinds of deeds, writhing, wrenching—the racket stunning all the heavens.

"Veer off to the side, toward Hell!" came a soft, muffled voice. "Otherwise you're doomed!"

My soul looked and saw a small, young angel next to it—confused, with tattered wings, and carrying a child's languishing soul.

"Is there no way I can get up to the seventh heaven?" that soul asked the angel.

"Not for all the tea in China!" replied the angel. "Just look up! Do you see clear, radiant heavens? Do you think the seven heavens are all there is up there? Well, you're wrong. There are countless heavens, and new ones are created every day. And do you know from what they're created? From us. From everyone anxiously writhing and wrenching to get to the Throne of Glory. Every day and every hour, multitudes like thick clouds come from the earth, and because their numbers are enormous they're unable to get through, and they're crushed and stiffened—and made into a new heaven."

My terrified soul began shaking. All its senses were fading. But it forced itself, swerved aside—and a second later it was floating in a place where there was nothing, no time and no space, no up and no down, no light and no dark. This was Hell.

In my ninth letter I'll describe what happened next.

Your Friend,

Mótke Khabád (R.I.P.)

Letter Nine

To My Friend, Our Venerable, Our Charming, Our Prominent and Eminent Teacher and Master, Rabbi Shlemiel, May His Light Shine:

I realize, my friend Shlemiel, that you're all set to ask me a boggling question: With my body lying six feet under and my soul being purged in Hell, who is the "I" who is writing to you under the name of Mótke Khabád?

My answer is as follows: It stands to reason that after the parting of my body and my soul, there is no I. Yet the I remains. It consists entirely of the tiny knot that kept body and soul together in life and that only got unknotted in death but did not vanish. This knot, which is neither spiritual nor physical, has senses from the body as well as from the soul. It sees and feels and comprehends them both; and albeit on the outside, neither here nor there, it constantly feels both here and there, it's deep in the ground and far in Hell, and it maintains a spark of unity between body and soul, keeping alive their hope for the Resurrection.

I must confess that during my lifetime my soul and my body never got along with each other. There was no love lost between them and no rapport—they were often at loggerheads. My soul, which was always absorbed in spiritual matters, regarded my body as a crude thing, as mindless flesh, which only does what it's told and goes where it's led, and which, with all its coarse senses, is no higher or nobler than a soulless beast. And my body, though always obeying the commands of my soul, would give itself airs and would hit the roof, claiming that it was the big toiler, that my soul had sentenced it to hard labor, all the labors of Pharaoh, while my soul itself lounged in the innermost rooms like an aristocrat, issuing orders and indulging in empty thoughts and dreams. However, *I* suffered more than either of them from all that feuding—*I*, that is, the little knot that kept body and soul together.

And now that I've separated from them and they've parted company, their bond has not, as I've said, been totally severed. My body may be crushed under a mound of soil, every last particle rotting, chewed and chomped by all kinds of big and little worms. Nevertheless, it has one of the soul's senses, it recalls the whereabouts of its shredded remains and is full of unconscious desire for the Resurrection. And far as my soul may have flown from my body, it remembers my body and constantly sees it with its spiritual eyes and understands everything my body is going through. My soul sees every worm that gnaws its flesh, sees every stripe inflicted by the lashes of the demons, every gash left by the nails of the demons, by their red-hot tongs, by their torture instruments. The soul understands and tries to hit on some way that the body could elude these torments, could drive away the scorpions, shake off the worms, could twist hard enough to heave away the mound of soil quashing it and keeping it in utter darkness. And in that darkness the soul spends the entire period of its purging.

For a long time I couldn't grasp what this purging was all about in Hell's antechamber, where there are no cauldrons of pitch and brimstone and no demons or Angels of Destruction. The soul flits about, unhampered, and no one calls it to account; its eyes can even pierce all the heavens, right up to the Throne of Glory, and it can see both Paradise and the Seven Halls of Gehenna. But now that I've thoroughly studied the matter, I understand the point of the purging in the antechamber to Gehenna

To see everything, grasp and fathom everything, to be able to produce the finest explanations, to forge the greatest plans, to rebuild and tear down whole worlds mentally, but without having any substance of one's own, without having the possibility of even moving a feather under a corpse's nose, of mashing even a smelly worm that sucks its way into a helpless body—an existence like that is worse than Hell, worse than the traditional whipping in the grave. That is the most atrocious purging! That is the antechamber to Hell!

Your Friend,
Mótke Khabád (R.I.P.)

Letter Ten

To My Friend, Our Venerable, Our Charming, Our Prominent and Eminent Teacher and Master, Rabbi Shlemiel, May His Light Shine:
Yesterday I felt like taking a stroll and catching a glimpse of Hell. I had been girding my loins for a long time. But since I didn't have much of a desire to go, I kept putting it off. The antechamber is filled with such a rapt and deathly hush that it weaned me away from any sort of hullabaloo, especially the turmoil and tumult that occur in Hell. Furthermore, I've recently been growing jaded. When I was young, I first heard that the demons in Hell whip the damned with iron rods—and I remember being terror-stricken by the thought of such cruelty! But now I hear on a daily basis: "Today we've boiled dozens and dozens of sinners in cauldrons or fried them in frying pans or hung them up by their tongues or their throats"—and it doesn't faze me in the least! Commonplace stuff!

And if while floating I happen to encounter famous Jewish comedians like Hérshl of Ostropólye or Sháyke Fáyfer or Móyshe Yog, I say: "How do you like what's happening in Hell?" And they nonchalantly reply: "Why should we care? That's what Hell's all about, isn't it? They've got it coming to them, the bastards! Serves them right for killing a flea on the Sabbath!" How do you like that for an answer?

But to get to the point:

First of all, I have to tell you that when I peered deeply into Hell, I was astounded! I didn't spot even a trace of what's written about it in *The Beginning of Wisdom* and other religious and moral tomes. Things were utterly different.

It all started with Paradise. Since the angels and seraphs were fruitful and multiplied day after day, even the endless number of heavens got overcrowded. So one fine morning they invaded Paradise and drove out all the saints (except for our Patriarchs and Matriarchs, whom they left in private quarters). And there they settled. They got hold of the Leviathan and the Wild Ox as well as the Cellared Wine (which are actually meant as food and drink for the righteous at the coming of the Messiah) and they started having a grand old time of it! The only souls they admitted into Paradise were those saints who were fit to assume the shapes of angels or seraphs. But since they couldn't really ostracize the other righteous souls, they allowed them to occupy several of the halls of Gehenna. So from a distance, the saints and sinners now seem alike—they're all in Hell! But actually it's the other way around. The wicked are rotting in Hell, while for the virtuous the Seven Halls of Gehenna have been transformed, so that they're no worse than Paradise and in some respects even better.

Let me briefly describe the seven halls as I saw them with my own eyes.

The first hall is bright and cheery. There are whole casks of Cellared Wine and chunks of the Leviathan and the Wild Ox and fat geese—all brought in from Paradise. And people eat and drink and live it up.

This hall is for the chosen few, the ardent Hasids and doers, outstanding for their fervor. They yell in turn: "Father, Father!," prostrate themselves seventy times a day, and sing with great haughtiness: "Thou hast chosen us of all peoples and Thou lovest us and Thou wanted us." And if they catch the slightest whiff of a sinner, they rant: "Pour out Thy wrath on the nations that do not know Thee," or "Then give fear." If they're feeling sad, they scurry into the other halls, where the true sinners are kept. There they feed wood into the flames under the limekilns, stick forks into the sinners frying in the pans, and shout that the fire in Gehenna isn't hot enough.

The second hall is almost as bright and cheery as the first but with less commotion. There's a holiday mood as if people were preparing for a wedding. These souls are pious, and there are a few anti-Hasidic ones who live in high style. They all firmly believe that "every cloud has a silver lining." They keep nodding their heads to the beat of their songs, humming, chanting, singing: "Thou art mighty in Thy Kingdom," and, while half rolling their eyes, they whisper, they whisper: "Thou art one and Thy Name is one."

The third hall is filled with twilight. The doors are half-open, both to the right and to the left. These people feel that they have to swear on a stack of Bibles if they're to be believed! They are sort of androgynous (spare me!): neither saints nor sinners. True Hasids regard them as the worst heretics, while the heretics regard them as pious idlers. In his right hand, such a person holds the commandments governing the life of an Orthodox Jew; and in his left hand, he holds the Russian legal code. They scour the Torah for some loophole to make pork kosher, they vituperate against the rabbis and the religious shalts and shalt-nots—but in secret they strive for a rabbinical ordination. For morning prayers they sit, half mournful and half cheerful, crooning: "Open the gates of

Heaven and Thy good treasure." And for evening prayers they croon: "How lonesome was Jerusalem." Some Angels of Destruction hover around this hall, but they don't touch anyone as yet.

The fourth hall is dark and cramped—a true Gehenna, though without cauldrons. However, there are Angels of Destruction with rods and other torture instruments. The people here are all illiterate in regard to the Jewish religion—they look down and don't feel the earth under their feet. Though making lots of mistakes, as illiterates are wont to do, they shout with great sorrow: "The heavens are for God and the earth is for man."

The last three halls—five, six, and seven—are combined into one. This is Hell as depicted in *The Beginning of Wisdom*. It's got cauldrons and limekilns, people are boiled, broiled, and flogged. These are sinners of substance—atheists, apostates for spite, the Ten Lost Tribes, plus Jews who spent many years beyond the Mountains of Darkness, and all sorts of other Jews who suffer from excessive chutzpah. The turmoil is immeasurable. And despite the harsh tortures, the quarreling and quibbling are intense. First place is occupied by the people who believe that "without food for the body there's no food for thought." And these believers are, in turn, divided into two sects: those who insist that what is done cannot be undone and those who insist that what is undone cannot be done. These two sects wrangle interminably with one another, and each twists its own melody for "Our masters have taught us" [the opening phrase of many Talmudic passages]. And with deep faith and utter ecstasy they all sing the tongue-twisting, jaw-breaking poem that Eliezer Hakalir wrote for Purim. It's mind-numbing!

Off to the side are the people who believe that "possession is nine points of the law." They're not particularly noisy. In fact, like the Lamed-Vovniks, the thirty-six hidden saints who justify the existence of the world, their prominent men stay out of the limelight. They sit off in corners and quietly study the Talmudic issues of "where is it?" and "with what may we light the Sabbath lamp?"

There are many other groups in this hall: the Reel-'em-Off Club, the Chaos-and-Confusion Brotherhood, the fraternal organization of Vanity of Vanities, and so on.

As you can see, my friend Shlemiel, the real atheists never get despondent. What agitated hearts they have—for Heaven's sake!

Your Friend,
Mótke Khabád (R.I.P.)

S. ANSKY (1863–1920)

Ashmedai

The final Yiddish text, Brif fun yener Velt, *is to be found in S. Ansky,*
Gezamelte Shriften, *vol. 8 (Warsaw: Farlag An-Sky, 1928): 5–80.*
For a discussion of Ansky's blending of folk material and satire, see my
introduction (pages xi through xix) and also my comments on "The
Ghost Writer" (pages 284 through 305). The verse form employed in Ash-
medai *(unrhymed trochaic tetrameter) was taken over during the nine-*
teenth century in Yiddish translations of the national Finnish epic
Kalevala *(by way of Russian and/or German versions). A number of Yid-*
dish writers then exploited this meter for humorous ends. American readers
should be familiar with its serious use: Henry Wadsworth Longfellow, in-
spired by the German translation of Kalevala, *used those four-foot trochees*
in Hiawatha.

1
Ashmedai and His Tower

Far from Poland, very far,
Far from Lithuania,
Way beyond the Mountains of Darkness,
By the road that leads to Hell,
Where the Sambatyon River
Seethes and surges, tosses rocks
(Though it rests on every Sabbath),
There a huge, high tower has stood
Since the ancient days of Nimrod. . . .
Please protect us, God, our Father,
From the master of that tower! . . .
There's no trace of any door
In that tower or any window.
On the roof just two tall chimneys

Loom there like a pair of sentries,
Bellowing and belching out
Two long streams of blazing flames,
Strands of fire like lightning bolts.
This vast tower is surrounded
By deep fear and trembling. . . .
In this place of sin the despot
Reigns with all his evil hordes!
Please protect us, Loyal Father,
From their might and mastery! . . .
    In a hall that's circular
Like a cauldron, sits the ruler,
Sits the monarch with his minions
Sits the king of all the fiends,
All the demons, all the devils,
Sits old Ashmedai himself. . . .
Terrifying, horrifying
Are his face and his physique!
Two short chicken legs support
A tremendous neckless body
Made up of a big fat belly
Plus a hundred ells of tail.
On the paunch a pumpkin head
With no trace of beard or earlocks
But with two enormous horns—
Long and sharp and sinuous.
No Hasidic shtreyml for him—
Just a crown of spiteful serpents.
And his eyes are like two flames,
Cold and dead and greenish fire,
Blazing, blaring—genuine sulfur.
And his mouth: a black abyss
With two keen and lengthy fangs
Like the tusks of a wild boar,
And his flaring nostrils spew
Billowing smoke and flying sparks.
His long hands, they have no fingers,
Only big, black, savage claws,
Pointed, piercing demon nails.
And his black and massive wings are
Woven out of actual darkness.

Ashmedai is coated over
Not with hair but with thin rods,
Yes, the iron rods of Hell. . . .
  The old Prince of Evil sits
At the center of the hall,
Lolling, lounging on a couch of
Human bones, right near a table
Made of old ablution boards,
On which corpses once were washed.
To his right the Golden Calf,
Which the ancient Israelites
Worshiped in the sandy desert.
To his left the coiling Serpent,
Cunning, cagey, cursed creature,
Who persuaded Grandma Eve
To betray the law of God
And to taste the apple from
The forbidden Tree of Knowledge.
In the back the bats and brutes
Fraternize with lizards, spiders—
Those accursed spiders, those
Loathsome creatures, fire bearers,
Who helped burn the Temple down.
  And on Ashmedai's big table
Stands the vast and loathsome furnace,
Where our great-grandfather Abraham
And the ancient holy prophets—
Hananiah, Mishael, Ezra—
Once withstood the worst temptations.
And the vast and loathsome kiln,
Brimming over with pitch and sulfur,
Simmering with pitch and sulfur.
The old Prince of Evil drinks,
Drinks from Nimrod's ample goblet
Drinks the burning beverage,
Blabbers, prattles, says: "To death!"
To the Serpent and the Calf,
And he drains the pitch and sulfur.
  There he sits, old Ashmedai,
From the morning to the evening,
In his mammoth cauldron tower,

Where the deathly greenish light
Radiates from his evil eyes,
Eyes that glisten in the dark,
Like the glowworms, sulfurous,
In the fields at summer's end.
And the deathly greenish light
Lends a terrifying look
To the brutes and to the beasts
That are in the tower now.
　　When the sun sets in the west
And the twilight gathers here,
Ashmedai gets to his feet
And he takes hold of the ember
That our foe, that criminal,
Evil Titus, once employed
To set fire to the Temple
And to burn it to the ground.
Ashmedai now huffs and puffs,
And the blackened ember starts
Flickering and flaring up,
Blazing with the same red fire
As beneath the mammoth cauldrons,
In the deepest, darkest Hell,
Where the Enlightened Jews are boiling. . . .
And the cauldron tower's walls
And the brutes, yes, and the beasts,
Even Ashmedai himself—
All burn in the blood-red blaze.
All the iron rods turn purple
On the flesh of Ashmedai.
Red as tinder is the Calf,
Red as tinder are the Serpent
And the lizards and the spiders.
　　Now it's time for evening prayers
(Maariv) and old Ashmedai
Spreads his wings so vast and black,
Makes the world so dark and dusky. . . .
And at midnight, when the roosters
Crow, and all the hordes come flying—
Devils, demons, imps and fiends,
Evil spirits, nasty sprites,

Wags and wantons, ghosts and goblins,
Incubi and succubi—
With their statements of accounts
For their ruler, Ashmedai. . . .

God Almighty, Loyal God,
Please have pity and protect us,
Us, Your blind and feeble children,
From the nets of sin and evil!

2
Ashmedai and the Archangel Michael
(Excuse my mentioning them together.)

All at once, a quiet tap
Was heard at the eastern wall.
Then a still small voice spoke up
(Like our beadle reverently
Tapping at a rich man's door,
Calling him to prayers on fast days).
And the blood-red lighting was
Sliced through by a lucid ray,
Like a ray from Paradise.
    And old Ashmedai—he frowned,
Furrowing his copper brow,
Glanced with naked sparks, inhaled
The aroma—and he knew
Who was tapping at his door.
He burst into happy laughter
And yelled in a voice of thunder,
"Welcome, welcome. It's been ages!
"Friend, come right into my tower!"
    An old angel now came flying
(Goodness only knows from where!)
Into the vast and sinful palace.
And the angel, in a prayer shawl
Woven out of rays so pure,
Was as tall as a lone cedar,
Had enormous sky blue wings
And a robe of pure white silk.
His shawl had an ornamental

Collar of the finest gold,
And his eyes were like two stars
Gleaming, glittering with mercy,
Piercing through the seven heavens.
Ah, no ordinary angel,
But the eldest one in Paradise,
And his name in our language
Is—I do believe it's Michael.
    When he flew into the tower,
He first floated all around—
For an instant he was wrapped
In a clear and airy cloud
To prevent the sinfulness
From befouling his holy robe.
    Then he stood not very far
From his old host and he murmured
With a certain naïveté:
    "Simple creatures—human beings—
"Think that you and I are foes,
"Wild and bloody enemies,
"Just because we fight each other.
"They don't understand—the fools!—
"That we're only messengers,
"Simple servants, loyal employees,
"And we only do the bidding
"Of the Good Lord, our Creator.
"Now I've come to visit you
"As a guest and as a comrade
"For a little chat about
"Worldly matters, heavenly levels,
"Paradise, yes, and Gehenna."
"True, so true, Archangel Michael!"
Ashmedai exclaimed, and then:
"I'm so glad to see you here!
"Have a seat, friend, don't be shy,
"Have a drink, please—pitch and sulfur!"
    "Why, I don't mind if I do!!"
Michael answered with a smirk.
"Let me be quite frank with you.
"I'm fed up with Cellared Wine,
"Which our saints all drink in Heaven.

"It's got no bouquet, no flavor. . . .
"So then let me wet my whistle.
"I would gladly have a swig
"Of some simmering pitch and sulfur!"
    And the ancient Prince of Evil
Filled a beaker at the stove
And respectfully handed it
To his visitor, the archangel.

    Michael took the beaker and
Wrapped his head in clouds and then
Softly spoke the blessing and
Sent it from the tower, from
This realm of iniquity.
Then he drank and drained his drink,
And his eyes rolled up so high,
And he snapped his fingers and
Said with endless ecstasy:

    "Wow, that really hits the spot!
"What delicious pitch, what sulfur!
"Ah, the flavor, the bouquet!
"It sets all my limbs on fire!
"Ashmedai, please tell me: Where
"Do you get this beverage?"

"Ha, ha, ha!" the host guffawed.
"Ha! A beverage? A bouquet?
"Where I get it? Hell? You're wrong!
"I get this concoction from
"Sodom and Gomorrha! Those
"Are the only sources of
"Pure and genuine pitch and sulfur. . . .
"How about a refill, Michael?"

    Time wore on for quite a spell.
These opponents, our Archangel
And our Ashmedai (forgive
Me for mentioning them in one breath!)—
Gulped refreshing pitch and sulfur.
Then they launched into their chat.

    The dark master asked his visitor
From the other world: "So tell me:
"What's the latest news at home,
"In your cheery Paradise?"

Michael held his tongue a while,
Sighed, then said so mournfully:
"Me oh my, there's no good news!
"Paradise is not so cheery. . . ."
      "What's the matter, what's been happening?
"In the good old days we heard
"Only miracles about Heaven:
"Paradise is bright and cheery,
"Paradise is beautiful.
"All the saints are in their prayer shawls,
"In their ornamental collars
"There they sit and read the Torah
"And delight in the shekhina,
"In God's glory and effulgence. . . ."
      "That was in the good old days,"
Michael ruefully responded.
"But those days are done forever.
"Paradise with all its beauty,
"All its rest, is gone, is lost!
"Modern times and generations,
"Modern deeds both good and bad,
"Modern Jews and modern Hasids.
"It's so hard to talk about it,
"Hard to tell about our troubles,
"Hard to lay bare all our wounds. . . ."
      For a moment, Michael paused
In a deep, deep melancholy,
Moaning, groaning on and on.
Then he finally spoke again:
      "Every day they bring me Jews,
"Hasids by the wagonload,
"Rabbis, rebbes, yes, and saints—
"Haggard, gaunt, emaciated,
"Sick with jaundice and consumption.
"Suffering from hemorrhoids,
"Sporting long, long beards and earlocks,
"Wearing floor-length gabardines.
"Duly filled with all the virtues,
"Showing just one teensy flaw:
"All of these illustrious Hasids,
"All these pure and righteous saints,

"All these judges, all these rabbis
"Haven't got a hair or spark
"Of a true-blue Jewish soul. . . .
"Please don't think they're infidels—
"God forbid! They're such fine Jews,
"Read the Torah, the Cabala,
"Pray with earnest ecstasy,
"Say 'Amen' with all their ardor,
"Dunk and soak in ritual baths,
"Follow all six hundred thirteen
"Shalts and shalt-nots, dos and don'ts.
"But what good's the Torah, worship,
"If their only purpose is
"To have a fine life on earth
"And a bit of afterlife? . . .
"I remember all the saints
"That we used to get in Heaven:
"Simple Jews—but true-blue Jews,
"Hearts so pure and hearts so big!
"Yes, they used to bring me souls,
"Souls from Spain or Germany,
"Souls so pure they shone like diamonds
"Purged by fire. Those Hasids knew the
"Taste of holy self-sacrifice
"For the weak and for the straying,
"For the truth and the community
"And for all their Jewish brethren.
"But these modern saints and Hasids
"Never have a spark of love
"For their fellow men—they never
"Care about their Jewish brethren,
"Never heave a heartfelt sigh
"For the sorrows of all Jews,
"Never have the slightest smidgen
"Of self-sacrifice at all
"When today's saints get together
"Up in Paradise, in Heaven,
"They are unendurable!
"Each thinks he's a VIP,
"Each one thinks he's higher, wiser,
"Holier, and far more pious

"Than our Moses or our Aaron,
"Than our David or our Solomon.
"They all put on airs and hate
"All their places, all their crowns,
"All they wait for is respect,
"They complain to God nonstop—
"Petty gossip, petty judgments,
"Petty gripes and grievances. . . ."
     Here the angel's voice trailed off
And he shed a pair of hot
Tears upon his silken robe.
     Our old Ashmedai just sat there,
Lost in thought, in deep distress,
Pondering the angel's words.
Finally he sighed and said:
     "Modern times in Paradise—
"Times are hard and times are bad!
"But don't think that business is
"Any better in Gehenna. . . .
"Hell is anything but calm,
"We've got our new troubles too.
"Long ago Gehenna was
"Packed with sinners like today.
"But can we compare those sinners
"With these modern rogues and rascals?
"With these renegades and rebels?
"Michael, you say there are few
"Genuine Jews in Paradise.
"You think Hell is any better?
"No, we've got the very same plague!
"Ah, where have the eons gone
"When they used to bring those Jews
"To me—fine Jews, decent Jews
"With such paltry peccadilloes:
"A stray thought . . . a word omitted
"From the prayers on Holy Days
"Or from a liturgical hymn. . . .
"Someone may have failed to follow
"The full formula when washing,
"Or he told a little white lie
"Or he killed a flea on the Sabbath. . . .

"Unimportant kosher sins! . . .
"It was such great pleasure doing
"Business with such perpetrators:
"They adored the punishments,
"Saw them as God's lofty love,
"Quietly slipped into cauldrons,
"Quietly baked in the ovens,
"Quietly lay on the benches
"And while being ripped by rods,
"Never wept and never hollered,
"Just recited psalms so sweetly.
   "Things are different today.
"Now they bring me shaven Jews,
"Deadly sinners, heretics—
"You would never ever think
"That these criminals are Jews.
"Oh, the nerve, the gall, the chutzpah!
"And they shout and shriek and scream
"And they brawl with all my demons.
"No one wants to suffer torture,
"No one wants to cook in cauldrons,
"No one wants to bake or broil!
"Nor be ripped by iron rods!
" 'Rods,' they counter, brash and brazen,
" 'Are the greatest shame for us!'
"And they won't endure a thrashing!!!
"Once we tried to whip them soundly—
"What a turmoil, what a tumult,
"What a brouhaha and hubbub
"In Gehenna, in the cauldrons.
"And then—all the sass and chutzpah:
"They fought off the senior demon
"And they almost smashed his horns!
"Awful! Dreadful! Fearful! Michael!
"What is to become of Hell
"If this state of things continues?! . . ."
   And these two old potentates
(One from Heaven, one from Hell)
Sat in deep and silent sorrow,
Mulling, musing, sighing, moaning,
Longing for the good old days
That were gone forevermore.

3
The Angel of Death and the Dumah
(The Guardian Angel of the Dead)

All at once a clap of thunder
Boomed and burst inside the garret,
Warning Ashmedai that midnight
Was approaching very fast.
Michael straightaway stood up,
Said goodbye to his old friend,
Folded his huge wings together,
Stretched out in the thinnest rays,
And, a second later, vanished. . . .
    Ashmedai, the Prince of Evil,
Got up from his lounging, lolling
And he yelled so loud and wild:
"Fiends and demons, imps and devils!
"All you ghouls and all you ghosts,
"All you spawn of sinfulness,
"Silent spirits, evil spirits,
"From the sea and from the land,
"From high mountains and deep valleys,
"From the fields and from the forests,
"From the graveyards and the ruins,
"And from vast and bottomless swamps,
"Succubi from towns and hamlets,
"Goblins from behind the stoves,
"Wags and wantons from the attics,
"Foul accusers, nasty sprites,
"From Poland, from Lithuania,
"From Berlin and from Odessa,
"And from Vilna and from Warsaw,
"And from little Jewish shtetls,
"All you hosts and hordes, fly here!—
"Smoke and dust and hurricanes
"Should sweep all your paths and roads!
"Dogs and wolves and werewolves, too,
"Should outbark your voices all,
"Roosters should outcrow them all!
"Fly here, fly here for the reckoning
"With your ruler Ashmedai!
"Fly, come flying! Midnight's here!"

In the twinkling of an eye
The black tower was surrounded
By a pandemonium.
In a powerful and angry
Roaring, whistling hurricane,
In cacophony and chaos,
Hosts of demons, hordes of devils
Swarmed and flocked and clustered here:
Big and little, fat and skinny,
Hurtling, flying, jumping, hopping,
Running, rolling, rollicking,
Prancing, dancing savage rounds,
Making grisly grimaces.
Squealing, barking, howling, crowing,
Singing dirty little ditties,
Talking filth so shamelessly,
A hundred thousand savage voices,
A hundred thousand frenzied gestures
In a storm of gleeful laughter.
    On one side, against the wall,
Keeping clear of all the legions—
There two earnest angels hovered:
The Angel of Death and the Dumah
(Guardian Angel of the Dead).
Both indeed looked very different
From the common run of angels:
Dreadful is the Prince of Death!
His entire powerful body's
Virtually cast in iron,
All his limbs are keen and cutting,
With a point upon his skull,
And his skinny nose is sharp,
And both cheeks are honed like knives,
And his shoulders, knuckles, ankles—
Thin and piercing, just like spears.
On his back a pair of wings,
Jet black as if forged of steel,
Small and sharp and curling, twirling,
Like two Turkish scimitars.
His body has a thousand eyes
Glittering, glistening in the darkness

Like a kosher slaughtering knife.
Eyes, a thousand, pitiless,
And they stab and lunge and plunge,
And they curdle all your blood,
And they throttle all your thoughts,
And they turn your breath to ice,
And they rob your senses blind,
And they holler, mute and wordless:
"All your hopes are lost, forlorn,
"Everything that lives must die."
A thousand eyes—a thousand deaths!
In the whetted talons of
His right hand the angel holds a
Sharp and flawless slaughtering knife.
On its tip a hefty drop—
No, not gall, but deadly poison.
And in his left hand the angel
Holds a sacred tome entitled
Crossing the Jabbok (the book of
Prayers recited by a dying
Person or by his survivors).
His irascible companion
Who is known as the Dumah
(Guardian Angel of the Dead)
Has a different appearance.
He is lank and awfully gaunt
And his body is drawn out
Like a cantor's cantillation,
Like a slinky, nasty snake.
He's got no face, just a beak,
Long and sharp, an eagle's beak.
In the middle of his forehead,
His reproving eye keeps shining
Like a big, black, bulging olive.
Two keen swords instead of arms,
Swords with which the Guardian Angel
Autopsies the silent corpses,
Who have lost all memory,
Who, so frightened of the Angel,
Have forgotten first and last names,
And who have no answer when the

Angel asks: "What is thy name?"
     These two horrifying angels
Have been friends for endless eons,
And when they do get together
They are very happy creatures.
     Here in Ashmedai's large court
These two angels stood apart,
Talking shop with icy smirks,
Chatting about doctors, nurses,
Prattlers, corpses, Gypsies, and
Burial societies,
Winding sheets and cemeteries.
     "Tell me frankly, Prince of Death,"
Said the Dumah. "For a long time,
"I've been meaning, friend, to ask you:
"With what instrument do you
"Kill a living human being?
"In your hand you've got a big knife
"With a drop of deadly poison.
"Do you poison? Do you slaughter?
"Or, as written in the Talmud,
"Do you simply pull the soul
"Through the kidneys or the mouth?—
"Like a hair from a glass of milk
"If the victim is a saint,
"Like a rope that's made of pitch
"If the victim is a sinner?
"Please do tell me, Prince of Death.
"I would really love to know."
     "No, I don't pull out a soul
"Through the kidneys or the mouth,"
Said the Prince of Death so coldly.
"I don't slaughter with my knife,
"I don't kill with lethal poison.
"I just hold the knife and drop as
"Signs that I'm the Prince of Death."
     Now the Guardian of the Dead
Was surprised:
"Then how do you
"Turn the living into corpses?"
     And the Prince of Death replied:

"With the gazing of my eyes,
"Little creatures—human beings—
"Cannot stand the icy glare
"Of a thousand cold sharp eyes.
"People feel a deadly horror
"And they simply die of terror
"At the sight of all my eyes.
"It may happen very seldom—
"Two or three times in a century—
"That a person peers straight into
"My eyes without fear or trembling,
"Calmly, deeply, with a smile.
"Those are people! That is bravery!
"Oh, would you believe it really?
"It makes me feel so despondent,
"I lose all my strength and courage,
"I cast down all thousand eyes
"And (you'll laugh) I fly away,
"Very much intimidated,
"Full of awe and full of shame."
    The Dumah was quite astonished:
"Do those people stay alive?"
    "No, they're killed by fellow humans—
"Killed on crosses or on gallows
"Or by bullets or by swords
"Or by other pains and punishments. . . .
"And it happens not so rarely,
"That they're killed by their own students.
"Human beings—merciful creatures!"
And the Prince of Death guffawed!
    "Frankly," said the Guardian
Of the Dead, "I envy you:
"Your profession is so noble.
"Beautiful, and so sublime,
"And it's got a deep, sound basis.
"You are always on the border
"Separating life from death.
"And the mystery of mysteries—
"It is open to your eyes.
"You see living human beings
"And you hold their fresh, warm souls,

"That have not yet lost their senses
"Or their human characteristics.
"Whereas all I see is corpses,
"Icy carcasses in shrouds,
"Icy graves and icy headstones. . . ."
    "Do not envy me, my friend,"
The Angel of Death declared.
"Icy corpses in their graves
"Are, I tell you, far more fetching
"Than a living human being
"Who's about to meet his Maker.
"You should see them trembling,
"Weeping, whining, begging, pleading,
"Clinging to their remedies,
"To their magic, to their charity,
"Grabbing on and holding fast
"To that sickly bit of life
"With alarm and zeal and fervor!
"If a person doesn't want to
"Die, if life is dear to him,
"Don't you think that he will do
"Anything and everything
"To preserve and lengthen it?
"Do you think that the expression
"'Human life' is sacrosanct
"Among humans everywhere?
"If you think so, you're so wrong:
"You will never find a thing
"Or a creature that considers
"Itself any cheaper than
"The life of a human being!
"I burst into nasty laughter
"When I hear the mourners shrieking
"By a bier or by a grave,
"Blaming everything on *me*.
"Morons, cretins, liars all!
"Are those human beings blind?
"Don't they see—those swindlers—that
"All I've got's a slaughtering knife
"With a single drop of poison,
"While they've got enormous cannon,
"Sabers, gibbets, pointed lances.

"Executions—Jews have four kinds:
"Death by fire, death by stoning,
"Death by sword, and death by strangling.
"Then there are the 'noble' tortures,
"Those that never pull the soul
"From the mouth or from the kidneys.
"Whom do people think they're fooling—
"Oh, those savages, those frauds—
"When they utter their laments,
"When they shout their pious words,
"About peace and unity
"About love and about mercy? . . ."
  Thus he spoke, the Prince of Death,
With cold hatred but no anger.
And the nasty guardian
Pointed his long beak at him,
Listened very fervently.
For a while they both kept still.
  "Well, what do you say to that?"
Asked the Prince of Death.
                         His friend
Answered: "Nothing to report.
"There's a hush in all the graveyards,
"All the graves are quiet too:
"Naturally in all the old ones
"Where the silent corpses lie—
"Such fine corpses, half decayed.
"But the fresher corpses—they
"Cause me agony and sorrow,
"Make me hit the roof and ceiling!"
  "Why is that?" the Prince of Death asked.
  "Well, just think about it, look.
"When I come into a grave,
"To a corpse in mint condition,
"Normally I find him there
"Fast asleep and very quiet,
"Tired from the funeral
"And the trip to the cemetery.
"It's not easy to revive him.
"First I have to yell and holler,
"Then I smack him with the chain,
"Till I finally wake him up.

"'What's your name?' I ask my new guest.
"I'm not talking about those corpses
"Who can't answer this simple question,
"Who have lost their memory,
"Can't recall what they are called.
"For such creatures, for such corpses
"With no name and with no memory,
"I just pass a summary judgment:
"Slice them up into two chunks,
"Send them off to Limbo. But
"If they've any memory left,
"If they stammer a response,
"They are simply simpletons.
"If they have some memory.
"When I ask them, 'What's your name?,'
"This is how they answer me:
"'Khaim, Borekh, Yankev, Henekh,
"'Tsirl, Khane, Beyle, Dvoshe.'
"Sometimes it gets even better:
"'Khaim-Borekh-Yankev-Henekh,
"'Tsirl-Khane-Beyle-Dvoshe.'
"And I furiously yell
"Out my question once again:
"And those creatures then reply:
"'Rich men, poor men, householders,
"'Merchants, tradesmen, artisans.'
"And these kinds of answers kill me,
"Make me hit the roof and ceiling!
"And so then I ask a third time,
"Booming like a clap of thunder:
"'WHAT'S YOUR NAME? WHAT IS YOUR NAME?
"'Tell me, damn it, what name did you
"'Leave behind you in the world!
"'Show the remnant, show the impact
"'That your deeds made in the memory
"'Of the many generations!'
"When I ask that simple question,
"Ninety percent hold their tongues,
"They don't have the foggiest notion."
      At these words the Guardian Angel
Of the Dead got very angry,

Banged his beak into the floor,
Wildly cast his eyes about,
Then went on with his lament:
    "That's below, inside the graves!
"What about upon the graves?
"All the headstones flaunt the highest
"Virtues, sing the highest praises—
"It's enough to numb the senses.
"Not to mention all the merits
"Carved into the marble slabs,
"For posterity to cherish.
"You would think the cemeteries
"Are chock-full of VIPs:
"Saints and sages, yes, and scholars,
"Generous philanthropists,
"Men with manners meek and mild,
"Valorous and modest women. . . .
"All these praises, all these falsehoods
"All about these silent corpses
"Truly got upon my nerves.
"So I figured I'd correct
"Lies on headstones and on tombstones.
"On a rich man's stone I wrote:
"'Thief!' And on a rabbi's stone
"In a shtetl I wrote: 'Moron!'
"On a grand and glorious stone
"For an intercessor's wife,
"Gilded letters said: 'A saint.'
"So I changed it to: 'A slut!'
"On the stately, sumptuous tombstone
"Of a famed Hasidic rebbe
"I wrote: 'Here lies buried a
"'Cretin and a hypocrite,
"'Who spent his entire life
"'Posing, posturing as a saint,
"'While he sucked the blood of paupers,
"'Charged a fortune for his blessing,
"'Fooled and fleeced his followers.
"'Cashed in on God's name and will by
"'Hawking charms and amulets. . . .'"

4
Hell: The Sin Trade

Boom! A clap of thunder crashed!
Myriads of savage roosters
Started cockadoodle-dooing!
Midnight was upon them now,
And the whirling hurricane
Of the hosts and hordes of demons
Spiraled upward toward the clouds
Like a column, like a drill,
Like a cantor's cantillation,
Leaning toward the left-hand chimney
Of the high and mighty tower
Of the ruler Ashmedai.
Now a second boom of roaring
Thunder, and the hurricane
With its droves and drives of devils,
Flew into the cauldron palace,
Whacked and walloped on the floor—
Silence! Not a peep or breath.
All the spirits stood like soldiers,
Wordless and expressionless,
Motionless and terrified,
Stood before the grim and gruesome
Face of the grand Ashmedai,
And the despot of the spirits
Gaped and gawked at his huge army,
Sat a while as if asleep,
Mulling, musing, meditating.
And then he began to speak:
    "Children, sons of evil, from
"All four corners of the world!
"Render, please, a clear account
"Of the vile and vicious deeds,
"Of the horrible temptations,
"Of the wicked cogitations,
"Of the dreadful infamies
"That you've sown and strewn and scattered
"Among people on this planet—
"Of the tricks and pranks and antics,

"Of the fakes and frauds and follies,
"Of the nets you spread to catch
"Pure and pious Jewish souls!
"All of you must tell the truth!
"But to keep from hindering you
"In your sordid, squalid job
"And to free you faster, too,
"I decree that all of you—
"Imps and devils, rogues and demons
"And the haggard, lustful tempters
"Of the little Jewish shtetls—
"Are to go to Hell and there
"Render your wretched reports
"To my greatest helpers: Síni,
"Sansíni, and Semanglóf.
"Write on parchment, using pig's blood—
"As is proper for a demon!
"Only one of you should stay
"In my tower here with me:
"The most famous and outstanding
"Evil spirit in Odessa.
"I would like him to regale me
"With the latest news and doings
"From my capital—Odessa!
"Tell me how the sinners there are
"Climbing, leaping, running, tumbling
"Into the net of my power."
　　In the twinkling of an eye,
From the tower's swamp that once
Engulfed Korah and his gang,
Came a blazing ball of fire.
Then the flames enclosed the demons,
And together they plunged down,
Through the marsh and through the mire,
To the very lowest Hell.
Just one individual
Now remained inside the tower:
An aristocrat—the greatest
Of Odessa's evil spirits.
Oh, the lowest Hell of all!
First I have to tell you what

Sort of place this region is.
  Not so very long ago,
In the days before the evil
Heresy began to rule
Our brethren, sons of Israel,
Hell was in a different place:
In the deep, enormous cellar,
Which is called *Shaúl Takhtíya,*
Underneath the massive tower
Of the Prince of Sin and Evil.
Way back in those pious times,
Hell was small and rather simple,
With two prehistoric brick kilns
And a dozen ancient cauldrons.
And the personnel consisted
Of just thirteen grizzled demons,
Sick and lame and feeble geezers,
Who spent all their time reclining
On the kilns or by the cauldrons,
Warming up their senile bones,
Moaning, groaning, and complaining
All about their bitter labor.
Hell was heated by old, rotten
Boards that all these deformed demons
Stole each twilight from the huge
Fence surrounding Paradise. . . .
In those days Gehenna was
Very calm and very silent.
Pious little sinners lay
Moralizing in the cauldrons
In front of the limping sentries.
And the demon gang would listen
And would think about repentance,
And, when nobody was looking,
They'd recite a morning prayer,
Say "Amen" and Kaddish too—
Sometimes even spit into
The large kiln and douse the fire.
And quite often a rich sinner
Swapped a couple of snorts of snuff
In exchange for his escape.

One snort for the demons and
One snort for the angels who
Guard the gates of Paradise.
And the wealthy miscreant
Quietly resettled in
The abode of all the saints.
And so things went on that way
Till the time of Moses Mendelssohn.
Oh, you Moyshe—Moyshe Mendelssohn.
Damn! Where can I find the curses
To curse you for all your sinning,
For the evil you inflicted
On the Jews with your Haskalah—
Odious Enlightenment?!
Since the heretic, the sinner,
Who made others err and sin,
Spread corruption among Jews,
Heresy and skepticism,
Speculation, cogitation,
Poisoning a million minds—
Since he built his synagogue
In Berlin, the modern Sodom
(City of reformist Jews),
Hell was being inundated
With new culprits, modern criminals. . . .
Within just a year or two
Hell became too small, congested,
And its cauldrons overcrowded.
Wood grew scarce—and the lame demons
Lost their little bit of power.
      When old Ashmedai found out, he
Promptly built a new Gehenna,
A colossal, cavernous Hell
All decked out with countless cauldrons
Heated not with wood but coal.
And he added new devices:
Telegraphs and telephones
And electric lighting too.
Then he posted a whole host of
Demon guards, young, strong, and healthy,
Sentries who know what to answer

With their tongues and with their talons.
        So much for the good old days!
Now no wealthy sinner can
Bribe his way out of Gehenna!
It's so big and beautiful,
Everyone is so well mannered!
Demons all say, "Sir" or "Madam,"
"Please" and "Thank you" and "You're welcome,"
To the biggest of the sinners
As they broil them in the ovens
Or they boil them in the cauldrons.
Everything is well arranged—
The last word in wisdom, logic.
But the torments and the tortures
Are so infinitely worse
Than they were in the old Hell. . . .
Ashmedai is smug and haughty
With his gorgeous modern building.
        When the old Hell was left empty,
Ashmedai converted it
Into a well-stocked bazaar,
Into a repository
Of all kinds of sins and wrongs,
And he staffed this shop with the
Finest famous spirits: Síni,
Sansíni, and Semanglóf.
All the walls are lined with goods
As in all the best boutiques:
Packs and packages of sins;
And at three long tables sits the
Trinity of earnest merchants,
Perching glasses on their noses
Clutching quills in sharpened claws,
And they write in big black ledgers
Filled with columns: "Credit," "Debit."
        When the multitude of demons
Flies into this lowest Hell,
Into the huge ball of fire—
Oh, the pandemonium,
Like three stock markets together!
First of all, the fiends and wretches

Hand in their reports (yes, duly
Penned in pig's blood and on parchment)
To His Highness, Prince Semanglóf.
Then the haggling begins.
Síni's table is surrounded
By a tiny group of demons,
The best-looking evil spirits,
Big and corpulent householders,
And with vanity and brashness,
As befits grand merchants, they
Deal and dole and do their business.
Some of them pay ready cash—
New and shiny coins, that is:
Rubbed out scraps of holy tomes,
Beards and earlocks that were shorn,
Spit that was spat during prayers,
Or defects in slaughtering knives.
Or bankruptcy IOUs. . . .
Others of these businessmen
Borrow their supply of goods:
Síni lends them merchandise,
He is glad to give them credit.
Evil spirits, householders
Love sins that are solid sins,
Fat and strong and hearty sins!
Even if they're not in fashion,
Even if they're quite expensive,
They must have a solid substance,
So that we can see and feel
That these articles are good.
      At Sansíni's table there are
Demons who are very poor,
Haggard goblins, evil spirits,
Paupers, beggars, drifters, vagrants,
And they weep and plead for loans,
Several dozen sins or so,
Even old ones, stale and musty.
And they swear by tails and horns
That they'll pay him later on.
Interest is agreed upon,
Promissory notes are signed,

And collateral is left.
And Sansíni frowns and glowers,
Curses all his customers.
Still he feels so sorry for them
And he gives each one a package
Of some rancid, rotten sins.
　　But the real, the healthy commerce
Thrives at Table Number Three,
Where Prince Semanglóf is seated.
Here you'll find a legion of the
Modern evil spirits and
Wags and fiends with "principles."
　　"Let me have a pack of sins,"
Squeals a teensy-weensy goblin,
"Fresh and hot, delectable—
"Yes, the latest trend and fashion."
　　"Please give me a package, too,
"Of the red sins bound and strong,
"Soaked and sodden in principles!"
Said a scraggy evil spirit.
　　"Give me something decadent,"
Said a lanky devil foreman.
"Give me sins filled with repentance,
"Filled with hallowed ecstasy,
"Sins of ice and fiery flames,
"Heating, cooling, burning, freezing.
"Sins emitting greenish fragrance,
"With a bright and pungent flavor.
"Sins that have the countenance
"Of a sweet and lengthy yawn
"Of an eagle in the desert. . . .
"Now I've got fine customers
"For such kinds of merchandise!"
　　Suddenly a raucous turmoil
Boomed and bellowed from Gehenna
What could possibly be wrong?
They had grabbed a little sprite
Who had quietly shoplifted
Several packages of goods,
Tasty and newfangled sins,
From Prince Semanglóf's own table.

And the thief had stolen off
To a corner and devoured
All his spoils with zest and zeal.
Now the captured robber started
Squealing, whining, and he wagged his
Little tail. He begged and swore
That he'd never steal again.
But they paid his tears no heed.
Grizzled demons, grizzled devils
And the three shopkeepers, too,
Síni, Sansíni, Semanglóf—
They conferred a little while,
Then they handed down a sentence,
Which was promptly carried out:
First of all, the nosher got a
Thousand strokes, and not with rods, but
With a tassel from a prayer shawl
(For the devils such a tassel
Is far worse than any rod,
Any whip, or any thorn).
Then they made him get a whiff of
Potent Sabbath incense too.
Plus he had to hear the blaring
And the blasting of a ram's horn.
Next he had to spend a thousand
Years in "jail": behind the stove of
A Hasidic synagogue.
    Business then went on as usual. . . .

    While the trade in sins kept seething
In the dark depths of Gehenna,
A discussion took place in
The black tower: Ashmedai
And the Satan of Odessa.
    This abominable spirit
Is a demon like all demons,
But he's fat, he's got a paunch.
And he's got a lovely pair of
Elegant and sharpened horns
And a long and curling tail,
Plus a pair of short pig's legs

With uncloven hooves to boot.
And his face looks like the face
Of a big and savage goat—
Except that a billy goat
Sports a little Jewish goatee,
While the Satan of Odessa
Is clean-shaven—and he wears the
Finest clothes: a top hat and a
Dickey with a white cravat
And a splendid black tuxedo;
A green poisonous toadstool serves
As the demon's boutonniere.

    Ashmedai kept still a while,
Sizing up his guest's attire,
Like a Hasid ardently
Scrutinizing and inspecting
All the tassels of his prayer shawl.
Then he said so mournfully
With a dollop of despair:
    "Oh, my boy, your dinner jacket
"Is no mix of wool and linen
"(Which a good Jew never wears).
"Tell me: How can you, the evil
"Spirit of Odessa, sport a
"Garment that is strictly kosher?"

    "Oh, my Lord, I must remind you,"
He replied with firm conviction,
"That a mix of wool and linen
"Is no longer fashionable. . . ."
    "That's a horse of a different
"Color," Ashmedai exclaimed.
"One must follow all commandments
"Set by fashion—fashion is not
"Custom, it is holy dogma,
"Sacred law for evil spirits. . . ."
    "Well, what else have you been up to?"
And the ancient king of demons
Leaned back comfortably on his couch,
All prepared to revel, wallow
In the tales of sins and wrongs.
    So the guest began to speak:

"Oh, grand and almighty monarch,
"Oh, omnipotent king of evil,
"All Odessa and surroundings
"Bow to you in utter meekness—"
    "Faster, faster, to the point!
"Cut your fancy rhetoric!"
    "Lord, the matter is so clear!
"In Odessa all the Jews
"Go around in shortened jackets,
"And no belts—Heaven forfend!—
"And no yarmulkes, no shtreymls,
"And no trace of any earlocks,
"And they sit with heads uncovered
"And they eat with hands unwashed,
"And they flout the laws of Sabbath—
"Carry handkerchiefs in the street!"
    "How exalted! How superb!
"How sublime!" roared Ashmedai.
"Just keep going! What else? Tell me!"
    "What else? It gets better! Listen.
"Ever since I started in
"On the burghers of Odessa,
"Indescribable things have happened.
"There are several thousand Jews
"Who now smoke during the Sabbath,
"And their kitchens aren't kosher,
"And they eat pork on Yom Kippur—
"And they openly deny God,
"And they're too ashamed to say
"That they're Jewish!"
                    "Shush, Accuser!"
Ashmedai boomed wrathfully.
"Shush, Accuser! Shush, Accuser!
"Don't you understand, Destroyer,
"That you're playing with fire now?
"You're relating stories that
"Smell like incense in my nostrils,
"Shriek like ram's horns in my ears.
"I dispatched you so you'd spread
"Petty Jewish peccadilloes.
"But instead you've turned the Jews of

"My Odessa into goys!
"You delight in telling me
"That the Jews who follow you
"Are a bunch of atheists
"And regard the designation
"'Jew' as an embarrassment,
"And you call such things fine sins—
"Though they're better left undone!
"One more step and then your Jews
"Will be rebels, turncoats, traitors,
"And they will be Jews no more
"Do you read me?—*Jews no more!*
"And no more in my control!
"What will happen if all Jews
"Lose their faith in God above
"And forget just who they are?
"What will happen if all Jews
"Become Christians and get baptized?
"I'll lose all control, all power,
"Might as well lock up the door
"Leading to Gehenna and
"Might as well disperse all devils,
"Demons, and all evil spirits!
"You forget that I've got power
"To spread out my devilish nets
"Only over Jews—no Gentiles!
"Goys have their abominations,
"And they have their own Gehenna,
"Their own wags and their own fiends,
"Sprites and spirits, ghosts and goblins.
"No, Accuser! You're playing with fire!
"Just fly back to your Odessa
"And proclaim on my behalf
"To all devils and all demons
"That from now on they should tempt
"Jews with Jewish sins alone,
"And that they should never touch—
"God forbid!—that Jewish spark,
"That quintessence of a Jew
"Hidden like the Holy Name
"In the Holiest of Holies,

"Like a Torah in the Ark,
"Like seeds in a pomegranate—
"Hidden in each Jewish heart.
"I command, I, Ashmedai!
"Fly, Accuser, don't delay,
"And proclaim my strict decree!"
    The Accuser of Odessa,
Mortified and terrified,
Bowed down deep to Ashmedai,
Sprang away, and disappeared. . . .

5
The Dreadful Denunciation

    "Cockadoodle! Cockadoodle!"
Crowed a multitude of roosters.
This was now their second crowing.
It announced that pious Jews were
Hurrying to synagogue
For the penitential prayers,
That the night would vanish soon,
Evil now would lose its power,
Its formidable control.
    From the deepest depth of Hell,
Through the swamp of Korah's grave,
Came the burning cluster of
All the armies of the devils,
Soaring through the old black tower,
Flying through the right-hand chimney.
And the spirits and the sprites,
Like the arrows from a bow,
Scattered now in all directions.
Over all the seven seas,
Over mountains, over valleys,
Over fields and over forests,
Over towns and over townlets.
    And old Ashmedai remained
All alone in his black tower.
For a while he sat there calmly,
Humming, humming something like
A liturgic melody.

Then his nails picked up a big
Flickering and flaming ember,
And he was about to snuff it—
When he heard a donnybrook.
Ashmedai saw that the Serpent
And the Golden Calf (both purple)
Were hissing and bellowing,
Shrieking in a savage rage,
Glaring at a corner there,
Shooting nasty, fiery looks.

    Ashmedai was quite surprised
And he peered into the corner.
There he saw a teensy demon
Hiding like a bad, black kitten.
"Reptile! Reptile! Show respect!"
Ashmedai yelled furiously.
"How dare you loiter in my tower?!
"This is what you'll get from me:
"One hundred fifty thousand lashes
"With the fringes of a prayer shawl!
"And three hundred fifty thousand
"Blares and blasts from a ram's horn."

    "Don't be angry, Lord and Master!"
Cried the frightened little demon,
Bowing deep to Ashmedai,
And he curled and twirled his tail,
As a devil's wont to do.
"Hear me out, your slave and vassal.
"I've remained here to reveal
"A great secret of all secrets—
"Which no demon must discover!"

    "You've got secrets to reveal?
"Evidently you've forgotten
"That I am Prince Ashmedai,
"And all secrets in the world
"Are exposed to my green eyes!"

    "I have not forgotten that,
"Lord of Evil," said the demon
Earnestly and quietly.
"Yes, all secrets are exposed
"To the glare of your green eyes—
"All except for female secrets.

"For example, Lord and Master,
"Do you know the whereabouts
"Of your missus, Lady Lilith?"
    "Lilith, Lilith!" Ashmedai was
Flabbergasted, and he asked:
"Where is Lilith now? Speak up!
"Just what are you driving at?
"Don't keep me on tenterhooks.
"Talk and tell me, loud and clear!"
    "Last night, after evening prayers,"
Said the teensy-weensy demon,
"I was in a little shtetl,
"Hunting down a Jewish scholar.
"I had stuff for him to study—
"Finally I persuaded him
"To go to the secular teacher
"(Such a famous heretic!)
"And converse with him in secret,
"All about the Torah and
"All about the modern books,
"About science and Enlightenment.
"And I never let my victim,
"My young scholar from my sight.
"And that night, as he was walking
"Silently from the teacher's home,
"Fascinated, lost in thought,
"I escorted him joyfully
"To the entrance of the synagogue.
"There I stopped—about to hurry
"To a swamp or to a ruin,
"Give my weary bones a rest.
"But then suddenly I saw a
"Feeble fire flickering,
"On a cheap and tiny candle
"In the window of the women's
"Balcony in the synagogue.
"Since I'm such a nosy fiend,
"I just had to check it out:
"Probably a pious lady—
"I assumed—an elderly crone,
"Botching up a Yiddish prayer.
"So I climbed up to the window,

"Had a look—and what a shock!
"On a bench right near a pulpit,
"Sat a matron in a bonnet
"And a pious marriage wig,
"Tearfully and gracefully
"Saying fervent Yiddish prayers.
"And who should the matron be?
"No one else but Lady Lilith!"
 "Lilith?! In a marriage wig?!
"Lilith?! In a synagogue?!
"Lilith sobbing, saying prayers?!
"Demon! Devil! Tell the truth!
"Just admit that you've been lying!
"Just admit that you've been slurring,
"Sland'ring my wife, Madam Lilith!!
"Tell the truth! Just tell the truth!
"Otherwise I'll rip you up
"In a million, billion shreds!"
Ashmedai kept railing, ranting
So ferociously that the columns
Of the big, black tower shuddered.
And the Calf was so unnerved
That it bellowed bitterly,
And the Serpent—it uncurled
Like a cantor's cantillation.
And the dark and tiny demon
Was so terrified that he
Lay inert, just like a corpse,
Waiting for the cataclysm. . . .
 But old Ashmedai recovered
All his senses and his sanity
And he shrieked and shrilled and shouted:
 "Demons, devils, and destroyers,
"Sprites and spooks and ghouls and goblins,
"All the children of all evil,
"Quiet spirits, nasty spirits,
"From the land and from the ocean,
"From high mountains and deep valleys,
"From the fields and from the forests,
"From the ruins and cemeteries
"From the deep and mammoth swamps,

"Fiends from towns and villages,
"Poltergeists behind the stoves,
"Ghosts that haunt the lofts and attics,
"Evil spirits, villains from
"Lithuania and Poland,
"From Berlin and from Odessa,
"And from Vilna and from Warsaw,
"And from little Jewish shtetls,
"Find my Lilith—on the double!
"Bring her to my tower here,
"Straight to me, just as she is,
"In the clothes she's wearing now! . . ."
        In the twinkling of an eye,
An enormous horde of demons,
Rushing, raging, rioting,
Instantly showed up with Lilith,
As she was, in her attire,
In her bonnet and her wig,
With one prayer book in her right hand,
And another prayer book,
Thick and huge, in her left hand. . . .
And the multitude of demons
Stood there, stunned and flabbergasted,
Gaping, gawking silently
At the newly pious Lilith.
Next the deeply saddened demons
Started leaving, one by one,
Mortified or terrified.
And they flew in all directions,
Saying: "Woe!" and "*Vey iz mir!*
"What's the world a-coming to?!
"Lilith—now a penitent!
"Oh, the shame, oh, the disgrace!
"Now we'll never look an angel
"In the face again! Oh, goodness!
"And old Ashmedai—poor thing!
"Oh, what sorrow! Oh, what heartbreak!"
        Only Ashmedai and Lilith
And the dark and little witness
Stayed on in the old black tower.

6
Lilith Appears Before Ashmedai

Lilith! . . . Meager is my language,
Poor in words and poor in colors—
It cannot describe her face!
Never has the world set eyes
On so ravishing a woman!
Rahav, the licentious girl,
Was a raving beauty, but
Lilith is a thousand times
Lovelier, and Lilith is
Lovelier than Sampson's Delilah,
Than the Queen of Sheba, or
Vashti, or young Esther, or
Tamar, even Shulamit.
Her eyes are a pair of diamonds,
Burning, glistening, glittering,
Summoning you and speaking to you,
Flattering you with compassion,
With a blend of grief and love.
And her gaze is velvety,
Slightly darkened by a tear or
Slightly shaded by a thought.
And her little nose is sculpted,
And her cheeks are like two roses,
And her lips are red and slender,
And her smile is so enchanting,
And her lips—they call your lips,
Draw you close from far away.
And her hair, oh, Lilith's hair
(Not her wig) is soft and silken,
Long and black and opulent. . . .
For an instant, deathly silence
Reigned throughout the old black tower
Ashmedai glared hard at Lilith
With two green and icy flames.
Tried to speak, to howl, to holler—
But he couldn't. Storms of thoughts
Blasted, bellowed through his brain,
Wild and dark and dreadful thoughts,

Drenched in violent cruelty—
Yet his heart was warm and weeping,
Glowing with uncanny love. . . .
Lilith quietly stood before him,
Staring straight into his eyes,
Waiting silently for his words.
    "Speak! Tell me the entire truth!"
Ashmedai was choking, gagging.
    And now Lilith told her tale.

Lilith's Tale

    Ashmedai! Oh, Ashmedai!
Hold your wrath and hold your rage.
Hear me out without your anger.
I would like you to remember
How I came into your tower.
Late one windy, stormy night,
You abducted me from my home,
From my Jewish family,
Forced me to come here with you.
And without a proper wedding
You made me your concubine.
    Next you poured the venom of
Sin and vice into my heart
And you simply blinded me. . . .
I was just a child back then,
I was just a shtetl girl,
And I comprehended nothing,
Viewed the world through your eyes only,
Felt the world through all your senses.
    In those days I worshiped you
And I bowed to all your wisdom,
To your beauty and your strength.
I did everything you told me,
Never argued or talked back:
Bared my bosom and my neck,
Like a harlot, like a trollop.
And I never shaved my head,
Never wore a marriage wig,
And I never wore a veil,

And I never visited
The *mikva*, the ritual bath! . . .
     Often you would send me to
Dreams of saints and of ascetics,
And I went obediently,
Sowing lust and lechery
In their hearts. But Ashmedai:
Even though you have great power,
There is someone in a shtetl,
In a little Jewish shtetl—
Someone mightier by far than
You and all your hosts of demons. . . .
That man brought me to my senses,
That man opened up my eyes
And made me a penitent.

     ("Who is he? Whom do you mean?
     "Tell me!" Ashmedai broke in.
     Lilith answered him directly:)

That man is the Linen Rebbe!
Maybe you have not forgotten
That during the Days of Awe
All the evil spirits and
All the powerful accusers
Wept and wailed in unison,
All because the Linen Rebbe
Gave them all a thorough thrashing,
So they couldn't do a thing
To the rebbe or his prayers.
It is easier to defeat a
Hundred Hasids and ascetics,
Hosts of rabbis, hordes of rebbes,
Than to touch a single nail
Of the left foot of the Rebbe.
     And so you commanded me to
Go to him and tempt and lure him,
And I went obediently. . . .

     (Lilith heaved a deep, deep sigh
     And she wiped her lovely eyes

With a corner of her apron,
Then resumed her chronicle.)

In an old and tiny room, the
Linen Rebbe lives his life
In great want and poverty,
It was midnight when I reached him,
And the Rebbe was awake. . . .
He was still in his white clothing,
All of it made of coarse linen.
And he sat there quietly
In a corner of his room,
Gazing upward at the heavens,
Silently and pensively
Harping on some wordless chant
Full of grief and gloom and sorrow
And yet also a strange joy.
At the time I failed to grasp
What that crooning really was:
A liturgic melody,
Or a prayer, a praise of God,
A confession filled with tears? . . .
    Late at night, past midnight prayers
And past penitential prayers,
When the sighing Rebbe lay down
On two bare and narrow planks
And dozed off, I sneaked inside.
First I murmured: "Evil spirit!
"Come to me, appear before me!
"And show me the shortest path
"To the famous Rebbe's heart!"
    A split second passed. Then I
Saw a creature crawling from the
Sole of the Rebbe's left foot.
Never in my life had I
Sighted such an evil spirit!
It looked like a skinny match,
Like a skimpy little goblin,
A sick and sepulchral sprite,
Crooked arms and crooked legs,
Broken bones and broken horns,

With a jumbo shtreyml on them,
With an earlock at each ear,
And a prayer shawl on his body.
Barely had the evil spirit
Crept along in pain and suffering
Than he washed his hands and said
Morning prayers with groans and moans.
And he softly asked in terror:
    "Woman, what is it you want?"
    "I am Lilith, and your Lord
"Ashmedai, the Prince of Evil,
"Sent me to your Linen Rebbe,"
I said to the evil spirit.
"Show me how to reach his heart."
    "All the roadways to his heart,
"Lilith, are already blocked
"By his conscience, the good spirit.
"He once drove me, the assassin,
"From the Linen Rebbe's heart.
"Slowly then and gradually
"He kept pushing, shoving me
"Until I came to this place.
"And here, in the Rebbe's sole,
"I lie in great agony,
"Fasting Mondays, fasting Thursdays,
"And I'm tortured all the time.
"And the Rebbe ruthlessly
"Breaks my bones both day and night—
"Arms and legs and other members
"Are already shattered now! . . .
"No! I cannot show you, Lilith,
"Any roadway to his heart! . . ."
    "That's no answer!" I retorted
Haughtily to the cripple. "Show me
"A path to his heart right now!
"Otherwise Lord Ashmedai will
"Flog you to his heart's content."
    Hearing what I said, the sickly,
Fearful, frightened evil spirit
Answered me with tearful words:
    "Only one road has remained—

"Not a road, a trail's more like it.
"Yes, a dark and twisting trail
"Through the Rebbe's left earlock.
"Try it, creep through his left earlock."
        "Well, if that's the way to go,
"Then I'll go through his left earlock!"
        And I didn't waste a moment.
I began to boldly creep. . . .
All at once the Rebbe raised his
Scrawny hand up to his earlock,
And he started scratching hard.
Down I fell and up I stood
In the middle of the room,
Naked, wanton, and without a
Marriage wig, just like a Gentile. . . .
And the Linen Rebbe now
Woke up from his light, light dozing
And he opened up his eyes.
For a moment he lay calmly,
Looked at me with no surprise,
Just with anguish and compassion.
Sighing from the bottom of
His heart, he got out of bed.
        Slowly he began to speak:
"It is raining cats and dogs.
"Cold and dark—a dismal blizzard.
"Since you've come here late at night,
"Through the wind and through the rain,
"You must have something important
"That you wish to say to me.
"Maybe you've got a request—
"Or perhaps a hurtful heartache?
"Well, just talk to me, my daughter.
"Tell me about your great sorrow,
"Your great heartache, your request.
"If it's in my power, I'll help you
"With a prayer to the Creator,
"With a word or with advice.
"Ah, my daughter," he continued,
Gazing with compassion at
My bare bosom and bare back,

"I see you're all torn and tattered.
"Clearly you've lost everything
"On the road: your bodice and,
"Yes, your mantles and your veil.
"Well, my daughter, here's some linen.
"Go and quickly cover up. . . ."
        I disliked the Rebbe's frankness—
But what could I do? I covered
Up my hair, my back, my bosom
With the Rebbe's coarse white linen
And I sought an answer to
His unsettling inquiry
As to why I'd come to see him.
All at once I hit on it—
An unusual idea,
Which had often helped me lure and
Tempt the highest, greatest rebbes.
"Rebbe, I'm a barren wife!
"My request: Give me a son!"
I said with a lecherous look.
But the Rebbe kept his head
And he didn't catch my leer.
After musing for a time,
He began to speak again:
        "You're a barren wife, my daughter.
"I can understand your sorrow!
"But how can I be of help?
"With a prayer to the Creator?
"Well, just think about it now.
"What can I tell the Creator
"About you and your request?
"If He doesn't grant you children,
"He might have good reason to
"Punish you with barrenness.
"Can I shout at the Almighty:
"'Lord, Your judgment is not righteous!
"'Please retract it. Give her children!'?
"That would be outrageous chutzpah! . . .
"I can give you good advice, though;
"Try to talk to God yourself—
"Not with words, no, but with deeds.

"Why, the matter's very simple:
"If you don't want to be barren,
"If you wish to have some children,
"Then show that deep in your heart
"You've got all maternal instincts."
        "How can I show all these instincts?"
I asked him without a leer.
        "That's so easy," said the Rebbe.
"Are there so few orphans here?
"Sick and needy homeless children
"Wandering about forlorn?
"Try to be a mother to them.
"Wrap them up in love, compassion. . . .
"In a town not far from here,
"There are paupers, there are orphans,
"With no one to care for them,
"Wretched, feeble, in poor health,
"Come along with me. I'll show you
"How to help them, mother them.
"Well, my daughter?" And the Rebbe
Gazed at me with tender mercy
And with deep and silent sorrow.
Ashmedai! Throughout my life
I've seen countless, countless eyes,
Lovely eyes, intelligent eyes,
Deep and reverent eyes, and eyes
Shining with the fear of God,
With religious ecstasy,
Or with icy, pious wrath, or
Under gray, thick, nasty eyebrows.
But I've never seen such eyes
As the Linen Rebbe's eyes:
Clear and azure like the heavens,
Plain and holy babies' eyes,
Simple and naïve and pure,
As if they were asking something.
And the power of his peering
Cannot be described at all!
His plain gazes penetrate
To the heart and to the soul,
And they ask you and they order

With deep love and with great might:
"Tell the truth! Just tell the truth!"
I don't know how many seconds
(Was it hours? Was it years?)
That I stood there like a statue
With the Rebbe's eyes upon me.
But I felt the Linen Rebbe's
Might and power with all my senses.
And the black stone of your poison
Melted, crumbled in my heart.
 And I followed him, the Rebbe,
Went obediently with him
To wherever he would take me. . . .
To the destitute, the needy,
To the widows, to the orphans,
To asylums for the poor,
To the schools for penniless pupils.
I was simply everywhere,
Doing what he told me to
With good will and with delight,
Weeping sweet and ardent tears.
And the homeless, wandering orphans,
Pale and hungry, sick and feeble
Children—they all called me "Mama!"
And these children weren't wrong.
I became a mother for them,
And I washed them, combed their hair,
Gave them food and gave them drink,
Cared for them and healed their hurts,
Taught them how to say their prayers.
 I don't know how many weeks
I spent in that little town.
Every evening the Rebbe
Came to see how I was doing.
He would comfort me and tell me
Tales about the Baal-Shem-Tov
And Hasidic masters, too,
And about the *lamed-vovniks*
And the other hidden saints—
Wondrous stories, miracles.
 Gradually I understood

How the Rebbe lives his life:
Not from payments for his wisdom,
Not with servants, not with beadles,
Not with groups of rapturous Hasids,
Not with sumptuous banquets served
On the Sabbath afternoons,
Not by giving followers
Holy remnants of his food.
No! The Linen Rebbe lives
From the labor of his hands,
Tills and sows like any peasant
(If I may mention them in one breath!)
On a tiny plot of land,
And he lives on what he grows.
     All his Christian neighbors and
All the Gentiles in the area
Beg him tearfully to bless
Their fields and their labor, too.
And the Rebbe blesses them, and
When they need them they receive
Rain and dew or sunny weather—
Never hail and never torrents.
     Once the Rebbe told me a
Lengthy tale about renowned
Penitents, and as I listened,
I began to weep and wail.
Unabashed, with no preamble,
I admitted to the Rebbe
Who I was and what I was.
Now I realized he had learned
Everything long since from Heaven.
He knew I was really Lilith.
     After listening to my story,
He sat still for quite a while,
Musing, mulling, lost in thought, with
The divine manifestation
On his pale and pious face.
And then with a silent smile, the
Rebbe spoke the following words:
     "The spark of a Jewish soul
"Is, it seems, so powerful

"That it never perishes
"Even deep in Lilith's heart!"
    I began to beg and plead:
"Mercy, Rebbe. For my sin
"Give me a great penitence.
"I'll do anything you say!"
    But the Linen Rebbe answered:
"Look into your heart, my daughter.
"There you'll find your penitence
"Based on your own thoughts and views,
"And your measure of remorse."
    I found my own penitence—
Sweet and deep instead of heavy,
Based on my own thoughts and views,
And my measure of remorse:
Every evening after working
With the poor and homeless orphans,
I go to the synagogue
(To the women's part, of course!),
I recite the women's prayers,
Dear sweet Yiddish prayers for women.
And I stay there till the morning.
That is my full penitence,
And I always feel reborn.
And my poor and homeless orphans,
And the sweet and pious prayers,
And the Linen Rabbi's prayers,
And the gazes of his eyes—
All these things have greatly changed me.
I've forgotten all about
All of Lilith's looks and leers.
And deep in my heart the feelings
Of a mother and a Jew
Have awoken potently!
    Ashmedai! Oh, Ashmedai!
Here I've told you the whole truth.
Nor am I the least bit worried.
Send your thunder, send your lightning!
Send me all your worst afflictions!
But remember that you've lost
All your power over me!

I no longer am your Lilith,
Now I am a penitent!
I'm back in the Jewish fold!

7
The Dreadful Judgment

Ashmedai responded to
Lilith's story on the spot.
Not with thunder, not with lightning,
Not with wild and dreadful shrieks.
No! He sat there cold and mute,
Never stirring, never moving.
But in Ashmedai's green eyes
Sparks of fiery feelings swiftly
Alternated with each other:
Now compassion, now brutality,
Love and hate and awful anguish.
The black tower was so terribly
Silent—silent as the grave.
Lilith stood there still and calm,
Waiting now for Ashmedai.
And the Prince of Evil sat there,
Still and stony, on his throne.
The big blazing ember flooded
Everything and everyone
With the red flame of its wrath.
Then, after a lengthy hush,
Ashmedai spoke quietly:
"I'll hand down my verdict shortly.
"So prepare for my decree."
And he started muttering,
Mumbling like a sorcerer:
"Oh, gray spirits, ancient spirits,
"From the deep and mighty Nile,
"From the faraway land of Egypt,
"Spirits of the pharaohs all,
"Of the illustrious stargazers,
"And diviners and soothsayers:
"Bring me three Egyptian wizards
"Of the oldest and the highest.

"They will judge my Lilith. I,
"Ashmedai, command you now!"
    In the twinkling of an eye,
All three conjurors were already
Standing in the huge, black tower.
They were tall, fat, gray, and old,
Haughty, all puffed up, and cold,
And their robes were long and black,
And their hats were high and pointed,
And their sticks were big and thick.
And they stood there and they murmured
Words in the Egyptian tongue,
Magic spells and incantations—
    "You Egyptian sorcerers!"
Ashmedai explained to them:
"I have summoned you from Egypt
"To pass judgment on my Lilith
"By the law of wizardry.
"Not since earth and the Leviathan
"Started swimming in the ocean,
"Not since the Creator made
"Paradise as well as Hell,
"Good deeds, yes, and evil sins,
"And as long as Ashmedai
"Has existed, not a single
"Demon ever has betrayed me
"Brazenly—but she's begun!
"Huge as are the Mountains of Darkness,
"Huger still is Lilith's sin.
"Judge her quickly, without mercy!"
    And the three old sorcerers
Listened to Lord Ashmedai,
Listened to the dark accuser.
Next they listened to Lilith, too,
To her tale, her testimony
And they stood there as before,
Stern and strict and all puffed up,
Muttering and mumbling,
Banging their staffs on the floor,
And they worked their wizardry—
Frightening and terrifying.

Finally the youngest of
The three ancient sorcerers spoke.
    "I will now hand down my judgment
"In the name of law and justice:
    "Lilith certainly is sinful.
"Well, but her temptation came
"From a mighty rebbe, who is
"Mightier than all evil spirits.
"He could even wrestle with
"Og the giant king of Bashan,
"Not just with a feeble woman.
"So my verdict is not strict,
"And I call for clemency:
"Let the demons tear her up
"Into billions of bits.
"And those bits should then be burned and
"Roasted in a mammoth kiln,
"And the ashes that remain
"Should be smelled eternally
"By great sinners who become
"Pious penitents in old age
"After losing all their teeth,
"After losing all their lust.
"This will be a lenient sentence,
"In the name of law and justice."
    "Sorcerer, this is no sentence,"
Ashmedai responded coldly.
"Sorcerer, it's just a joke.
"Why, I frequently inflict
"Penalties like that on demons
"For some measly monkeyshines.
    "Second sorcerer: State your sentence!"
    And the second sorcerer muttered:
"Ashmedai, in my decree you
"Won't find leniency or justice:
"Let the punishment fit the crime!
"Using her maternal feelings—
"That was how the Linen Rebbe
"Turned her into a penitent.
"Ashmedai! Make sure that Lilith
"Gets maternal punishment!

"This will be the harshest sentence:
"Give her children! Give her children!
"Let her bring them painfully
"Into this dark world of ours.
"Let her raise them by herself
"In great agony and anguish,
"In the deepest mortal dread.
"And then when her children stand
"On their own two feet at last,
"You can start to punish her.
"Turn them into rogues and wretches,
"Turn them into thieves and robbers,
"Scatter them in jails and prisons.
"Or send them to distant countries,
"Where they will be killed by bullets
"Or else die of thirst and hunger.
"When she's old, the mother will be
"Poor and miserable and lonely,
"With a heart that's raw with wounds
"That will hurt eternally,
"That will burn eternally
"From the salt and from the fire
"Of her hot and bloody tears! . . .
"This will be the stringent sentence!
"Let the punishment fit the crime!"

    "Sorcerer, that's what I call a
"Verdict!" Ashmedai responded.
"But for Lilith it's too lenient.
"You are certainly a great wizard.
"But the deep, deep mysteries
"Of a mother and her heart
"Are concealed beyond your ken.
"In the greatest, harshest sorrows,
"Amid hot and bloody tears
"Of a miserable mother,
"There are lucid tears that shine
"With forgiveness and with love!
"And they comfort and they heal
"All her welts and wounds like balsam.
"No, for Lilith such a sentence
"Is no punishment for her wrongs."

For an instant there was silence
In the huge, black, ancient tower,
And old Ashmedai now waited
For the third great wizard of
Egypt to hand down his sentence.
    Suddenly the witness squealed—
Yes, the dark and tiny demon:
    "Ashmedai, I've got a fabulous
"Punishment for Lady Lilith.
"Please allow me to describe it."
        "Speak, but tersely—and no frills."
        "Lilith is a penitent,
"And Gehenna has no place
"For her in a marriage wig. So
"Let me give you this advice.
"Send her to a foreign city,
"Berne or Paris or Berlin.
"Let her study medicine.
"When she gets there, they will ask her
" 'What's your name? Who are you, tell us!
" 'What's your nation? Show your papers!'
"After that, in a huge hall
"Filled with tubes and Bunsen burners,
"She will mutter, do her magic.
"And then she will cut up corpses—
"Just as ordinary devils
"Do the drudgery in Gehenna.
"Next she'll slice up living people.
"And along with all those pleasures,
"I can swear to you, great monarch,
"She'll be miserable there,
"Punished by her poverty
"And by slander—punished worse
"Than a thousand times in Hell. . . ."
        Without words and without anger,
Ashmedai grabbed the demon's tail,
Hurled him up the chimney, and
Then addressed the third great wizard:
        "Eldest sorcerer, speak your verdict!"
        "Short and plain is my decree,"
Softly said the sorcerer.

"Just let Lilith remain Lilith
"As she is—a penitent. . . .
"That is all I can inflict
"As a penalty for her sin. . . ."
    Ashmedai was flabbergasted:
"I don't understand, great wizard,
"What your verdict's all about."
    And the old gray sorcerer
Held his tongue a while as if
Slumbering. Then again he muttered:
"Lilith is a penitent now
"In a bonnet and a wig,
"With her hefty books of prayers—
"Yiddish prayers for Jewish women.
"She's so proper and so chaste.
"But please, Ashmedai, just peer
"Deep into her heart. You'll find
"All the features, all the cravings,
"Of the earlier Lady Lilith.
"And the source of deadly poison
"That you once poured there yourself.
"Trust me. It's all in her heart,
"Covered up with pious spices.
"So let Lilith remain Lilith
"As she is, with all her prayers,
"With her sins deep in her heart,
"With the poison and the spices.
"Just don't worry. In her heart
"There will be a true Gehenna:
"Dreadful struggles all the time
"Between all kinds of emotions,
"Between penitence and lust,
"Between Lilith and the prayers.
"So, Lord Ashmedai, she'll be
"An outsider in both worlds:
"Among humans, among spirits,
"Virtuous people, vicious demons,
"Far from awful depths of Hell,
"Far from radiant Paradise.
"For the saints she'll still be Lilith,
"For the sinners—still a penitent,

"For the pious she'll be wicked,
"For the modern—a chaste lady. . . .
"Alien to either side,
"She will wander, languishing,
"And on both sides all she'll see
"Will be nasty glares and gazes.
"All she'll hear will be vile curses.
"You will surely never find
"Tortures, torments worse than these!"
    For the blinking of an eye
Ashmedai just sat there, mulling
All about that last opinion.
Then he gawked and gaped at Lilith
As if struggling and wrestling
With quite different emotions.
Then he blurted out: "So be it!
"Let us execute the sentence
"Issued by the old, great wizard!
"Lilith, you'll remain forever
"An outsider for all people,
"An outsider for all demons,
"For the pious and the sinful,
"Far from awful depths of Hell,
"Far from radiant Paradise,
"Hellish torment in your heart.
    "And now, devils, demons, spirits,
"Go remove her from my sight!"
    And so Lilith promptly vanished.
Likewise the three wizards of
Egypt also disappeared,
And inside the big, black tower,
Ashmedai remained alone,
Filled with grief and melancholy.

    Multitudes of roosters were
Cockadoodling a third time.
Jews were hurrying to synagogue
For the penitential prayers.
And the eastern sky was growing
Lighter, clearer all the while.
And the crews of demons, devils

Started hiding everywhere:
In the earth and in deep seas,
In the ruins and in the attics,
In the forests and the swamps. . . .
　　Ashmedai sighed deep and long
And he put the ember out.
Next he took a giant knife,
Held a black wing out and cut,
Tore a hole to mark his grief
For the penitent, for Lilith.
Then he sat down on the floor
For the seven days of mourning—
And his lips were muttering:
　　"Lilith, my devoted Lilith!
"Lilith, you've abandoned me! . . .
"I, the exalted Ashmedai,
"I, the ruler of the spirits,
"I have been defeated now—
"Not by angels, not by seraphs,
"Not by wise King Solomon.
"No! I've been defeated by
"Just a plain and pious Jew,
"By the saintly Linen Rebbe! . . ."

Afterword

　　This is how the story ends:
　　Now I wash my hands and now I
Shake off Hell's impurities,
Which have lingered on my nails.
And I grab the pouch containing
My prayer shawl and my prayer thongs,
And I dash to synagogue.
My Creator, let me send You
Ardent prayers and avid praise—
"Thou restoreth, Lord, my soul
"With Thy great compassion, Lord"—
Now, today, and then on shabbes
To thank you for my escape.
　　And I also must admit
That while writing I kept shaking

Like a leaf for fear that Hell
Would catch me in its dark nets!
Mighty, marvelous miracles:
I escaped both safe and sane
With my head and beard and earlocks
From the Prince of Evil's tower,
From the depths of dark Gehenna!
    Don't laugh, Jews: My forebears helped me!
I am certain that my granddad,
Rabbi Zalmen, and my uncle,
Rabbi Yankl, both worked "there"
To keep me out of harm's way. . . .
Furthermore I was assisted
By an amulet and a pair of
Talismans a rebbe gave me.
    Here a final word or two.
As you see, my fellow Jews:
Yes, the might of evil is great.
But far greater than its power
Is a perfect Jewish saint.
Now you've hard a tale about the
Linen Rebbe. God should have
All Jews live for truth and justice
And become such perfect saints
As the Linen Rebbe was.
The Almighty will then send us
His Messiah, His redeemer,
And in our very lifetime
Hell and all the demons, devils—
They will disappear.
                                    Amen!

DOVID-LEYB MEKLER (1891–?)

The Dybbuk

The original Yiddish text was published in: Dem Rebns Hoyf / Talne, *vol. 2 (New York: Jewish Book Publishing Company, 1931): 135–41.*

Rabbi Dúvidl of Talne was famous both for his great wisdom and for his great miracles.

Many of his miracles were simply based on wisdom, but his followers were as delighted with those expressions of wisdom as they were with the tales of his real miracles.

Rabbi Dúvidl was also renowned as a healer, and people with all sorts of illnesses would visit his court, hoping that he would cure them.

The remedies he offered were not only blessings but also herbs, compounds, and salves, as well as amulets, talismans, and the like.

The rabbi owned a medical book that had been handed down through several generations: It contained treatments and remedies for various illnesses.

As a result his court was constantly besieged by patients with all sorts of mental or physical complaints and deformities—men, women, and children.

And Hasids tell one another all kinds of stories about his miraculous cures. Why, he even resurrected the dead. . . .

Needless to say, the most interesting stories are about dybbuks.

And there are many such stories. But they can be divided into two categories. In one group, the treatments are based on wisdom, intelligent ideas, and exact understanding of the human soul; while in the other group, the treatments derive from the rebbe's great power as a Cabalist and miracle worker.

One story is about a man who convinced himself that his legs were made of glass. He refused to sit down, scared as he was that if he bent his legs, they would shatter. Glass doesn't bend, and a man with glass legs is a miserable creature.

So he always stood on his straight legs or else walked about as if on stilts, and when he lay down, he would twist and turn, making sure not to bend his knees so that the glass wouldn't shatter.

People kept telling him that he had normal legs just like anyone else, that he could sit and walk and even dance. But no matter how much they talked away at him, it did no good. He stuck to his guns—his legs were made of glass.

So people said that a dybbuk had entered him and they took him to Talne, so that Rabbi Dúvidl could expel the dybbuk.

And expel him he did. The man stopped imagining that his legs were glass, and they became flesh and blood and bones again.

How did the rebbe pull it off? This is the story that the Hasids tell:

When the man was brought before him, the rebbe, without further ado, told him to have a seat.

"I can't, rebbe," he said. "My knees won't bend, my legs are made of glass."

"But I order you to sit down!" the rebbe shouted. "I order you to sit down immediately!"

The man was terrified. When the rebbe orders you to do something, you must obey no matter what may happen—even if your glass legs shatter.

The man sat down, and as he did so, they heard a loud racket like the breaking of glass. The "glass" legs burst, shattered, but they were mobile again—like the legs of a normal person.

"Now you can stand up and walk and sit and move like everyone else," the rebbe told him. "The glass has been shattered."

And the man left, fully convinced that his glass legs had returned to what they should have been.

What had happened? Not much. The rebbe had told his assistant to wait in the next room and break some glass the instant the man sat down. The man would then think that the glass fettering his legs had burst.

The idea was based purely on wisdom, and the rebbe's followers always cited it as an example of his great wisdom.

A very different dybbuk tale concerning Rabbi Dúvidl is told as follows:

In a remote shtetl, a feud erupted over a cantor. Such feuds were not unusual in the little Jewish towns. They would often end peacefully and very often flare up into bitter wars that dragged on for years, making entire families miserable.

The whole shtetl was Hasidic, there was virtually no anti-Hasid there. But the Hasids were split; they were followers of different rebbes, and these various sects were battling with one another. They fought every day of the year and they fought over nothing.

Naturally the war reached its climax when a new cantor had to be hired for the synagogue.

Now the old cantor had his friends and foes. Still, when a man has held a position for a long time, you don't hassle him. But with age his voice had become weak and raspy. And so his old opponents reared their heads. "Enough," they argued. "We need a new cantor."

And the dissatisfaction with the old cantor grew by the day until they brought in new cantors and tried them out.

The feud grew more bitter, erupting into an all-out war.

But the faction that wanted a new cantor was larger and stronger, and the other faction realized that there would be no peace in the shtetl until they hired a younger cantor, who could lead the prayers.

After managing to conciliate the old cantor, they took on a new one. The shtetl was now finally at peace. The new cantor did a good job of leading the prayers, and the congregation was satisfied.

The only dissatisfied person was the old cantor, whose broken heart could not be mended. There was no question of his finding another position. That was something a man of his age and with his voice could hardly expect.

So he had to remain in the shtetl and find some other line of work. But a wound remained in his heart, a deep, open wound. His heart bled when, rejected by all the world, he saw another man reigning in his place. No one so much as glanced at him or felt his great sorrow.

The old cantor started weakening by the day. He grew senile, he was bent and twisted, a shadow of his former self. His life was ebbing slowly, he was dying a bit more every day—until one day they discovered his corpse.

Only now did some people realize that the old cantor had been the victim of persecution and that his life had been shortened because the synagogue had replaced him with a new cantor.

His fiercest opponents now felt bad.

Unhappiest of all was the new cantor, who had pangs of guilt about the old cantor's premature death.

The old cantor died shortly before Rosh ha-Shana (the New Year), a time when every Jew has a need to repent.

The new cantor was miserable. You could tell that he was suffering, that his heart was broken, that he felt guilty about something.

And then Rosh ha-Shana arrived. The new cantor was standing with his choir, ready to sing the added morning prayer for the Sabbath and for holidays.

It was the first day of Rosh ha-Shana. The beadle had already knocked on the Torah table, signaling the cantor to start.

The cantor, in his smock and with his prayer shawl around his head, stood by his pulpit, surrounded by his choir, which was ready to accompany him.

The synagogue was filled with a deathly hush, aside from a few moans and a soft weeping from the women's section.

The cantor began.

He cried out the opening words, and the congregants shuddered.

It wasn't his voice, it was the voice of the old cantor, who had died.

It was exactly the same voice.

The cantor himself was frightened. He, too, felt that it wasn't his voice. Still, he tried to sing on. Perhaps it was only his imagination. But no, it *was* the old cantor's voice. There could be no doubt.

The congregation panicked.

A dybbuk had entered the new cantor. The old cantor had returned to take his position at his pulpit, where he had stood for so many years and which he had come to love and cherish. . . .

In mortal terror, the new cantor threw down his prayer shawl and his smock and dashed home.

But even in his home, the old cantor's voice sang through him.

The old cantor's dybbuk refused to leave him.

And the dybbuk haunted him more and more obstinately. "I want to be cantor here again," the dybbuk asserted, and he sounded exactly like the old cantor. "I couldn't do it while I was alive, so I'll do it now that I'm dead, through the new cantor."

The townsfolk tried everything. They prayed at the old cantor's grave, they measured the graveyard, they applied all sorts of remedies. But nothing helped. The dybbuk refused to leave the new cantor.

Finally they decided to take the cantor to the Rebbe of Talne. Rabbi Dúvidl had performed so many exorcisms that he would certainly be able to drive out this dybbuk too.

The rebbe ordered them to bring the new cantor to his home.

"Sing me something," said the rebbe to the cantor.

The cantor began, but all that came out was the weak and raspy voice of the old, dead cantor.

"I want to hear some singing!" snapped the rebbe. "That isn't singing. Try it again!"

The cantor began anew, but out came the same weak and raspy sounds.

"Can't you sing?" the rebbe snapped angrily. "You want to pray at the pulpit with a voice like that? Go back to your rest. You're merely disturbing the Jews who are trying to worship God as they should."

For a while there was silence. But then they heard a soft weeping.

"I love my pulpit so much."

"It is not the dead who will praise God," said the rebbe in response to what the dybbuk had said.

And the dybbuk didn't say another word.

"You cannot sing and you cannot stand at the pulpit anymore," the rebbe concluded.

A short time later, the rebbe, calm and collected, again ordered the new cantor to sing:

"Now sing in your own voice. The old cantor has returned to his rest. He has nothing more to do at your pulpit."

The new cantor began to sing, and this time he sang in his own voice. The dybbuk had left him forever.

SHLOYME BERLINSKY (1900–1959)

Blowing the Shofar

From Yerushe *(Buenos Aires, 1956): 75–78.*
Virtually a docudrama, as is much Yiddish literature, this brief and violent anecdote may reveal skepticism about dybbuks. However, in its emphasis on blatant sexuality, it nevertheless acknowledges the religious and psychological reality of a possession.

When I was a boy, my father would always take me to a great Hasidic court for Rosh ha-Shana. This time the courtyard was deserted. The hundreds of Hasids who had come from all parts of the country were in the huge square-shaped synagogue located in a corner of the estate.

The emptiness of the courtyard was terrifying.

It was before the blowing of the shofar.

From time to time a single Hasid would dash behind the court, head straight for the green pump in front of the synagogue, wash his hands, and then dash back to the other worshipers. Hundreds of voices could be heard from the synagogue: "Out of distress I called the Lord." The screaming was so bizarre, it sounded like a whole town choking.

I stood in the courtyard, unable to tear myself away, even though I knew that I was supposed to be praying in the synagogue—casting off so many sins: false witness, the use of faulty weights and measures, evil urges, and so many other offenses. But only one sin truly bothered me: I had found a silver coin on the Sabbath and buried it in sand, planning to dig it up again once the Sabbath was over.

Now, I was unable to tear myself away from the courtyard. I stood outside one of the windows of the synagogue, where the rebbe was. The glass was frosted, obstructing any view from the outside, and, to my eyes, the panes looked like small clouds, hiding dreadful secrets.

At that window, a woman had brought her child to the rebbe for the blowing of the shofar. She held the child in her hands, even though he was a big boy, some ten years old. Still, he was so scrawny that he

367

seemed to have just enough skin to keep his little bones together. He was also as yellow as wax and lame, unable to walk. The mother held him, and the boy, upon seeing me, began to smile at me. I would never have expected a boy like that to smile, but smile he did—with such gray little eyes.

I was so overwhelmed by his smile that I was ready to give him my legs. Let him walk a little, let him run around, let him play. Oh, how I would have liked to play with him, play for all we were worth!

But then I was separated from the boy. A girl and her mother came tumultuously rushing into the rebbe's court. The mother had her arm around the daughter and kept talking to her: "Blímele, don't embarrass me in front of other people, put on your kerchief. When you hear the rebbe blow the shofar, you'll be cured. C'mon, Blímele, put on your kerchief."

But the girl, who was tall and healthy, with a round face and coal black hair, and with black, playful eyes under thick brows, absolutely refused to put on the kerchief. "Mama," she yelled through her clear teeth. "Mama, I'm still unmarried, I'm not even close to getting married—why do you want me to cover my head?" And she pulled off the kerchief.

"It's all because of the dybbuk," the mother wept. "The dybbuk won't let you cover your head—oy, vey iz mir!"

"Mama, the dybbuk was so handsome, I met him in the evening, he caressed me—do you see, Mama? He caressed me right here on my cheek. He wanted to touch my body, my hair, he wanted to caress me— but I ran away. Now I yearn for him all night long. Mama, I want to find the dybbuk! Oh, how good it must be with the dybbuk."

The mother put her hands over the daughter's mouth, blocking the torrent of words.

And now they reached the rebbe's window.

The instant the girl heard the chanting from the synagogue, she began yelling: "So many men in there, Mama, it's so cozy! I wanna go into the synagogue!" And she tore away from her mother's hands.

But now the rebbe's assistant, a man with red hair and dense freckles on his face, came over. Grabbing a bucket of water, he emptied it over the girl's head.

The girl did calm down. But her soaked clothes, a white dress and a white blouse, clung so snugly to her body, revealing every part of it so sharply, that she seemed to be standing naked in the rebbe's courtyard— and Satan seemed to have won.

I stood there, with a pounding heart, waiting for the rebbe to blow the shofar. Now the synagogue fell silent, and a shofar blared out: "Ta-ta-ta-ta-ta," cutting through the courtyard.

The girl shrieked: "I don't want to! I don't want to!" The mother threw her arms around her and wept: "Blímele, darling, let the dybbuk go away! Blímele!"

And the woman with the sick boy lifted him up and shouted at the frosted panes: "Holy Rebbe, this is my only child! Split the heavens!"

I was haunted for a long time by all those sounds and voices.

And whenever I hear a shofar now, its trembling bellow resonates with all the unfortunates who stand with their arms stretched out to the sky!

ANONYMOUS

The Gílgul

The original Yiddish text is to be found in In der Velt fun Khsidis, *vol. 1 (Warsaw, 1938).*

Every Jew believes that his soul has come down to this world in order to right some wrong that he has done in a previous life. For it is only here on earth that he can devote himself to performing good deeds. All he can do in the afterlife is either reap the fruits of his earthly good deeds or suffer the punishments for his evil deeds.

There are sins, however, that cannot be cleansed by the agonies of Hell, the sinner must atone for them himself. That is why he is sent back to our world, where he is reborn with free will, the capacity to choose between good and evil. And he is put through a crucial ordeal. If he is willing to atone for the sin that has led to his reincarnation, then good for him. But if not—God forbid!—then he keeps getting reborn in various creatures and animals, until he is fully purged and allowed to go back to his source and his place of rest.

It is well known that all Hasidic rebbes have focused a lot of energy on the redemption of wandering souls. The greatest rebbe of each period encounters them at every step of the way, and much of his effort is aimed at helping them when they are unable to help themselves.

In regard to gílguls, the followers of the Rebbe of Rízhin tell a miraculous tale that occurred during his lifetime, in the year 5591 (1831):

An epidemic—Heaven preserve us!—was raging throughout Russia, leaving a trail of devastation and not sparing a single household.

Needless to say, the epidemic also reached the town of Rízhin. However, the inhabitants were full of hope that no harm would come to them, that they would be protected by the rebbe's merits. But how astonished were they upon hearing that the rebbe had shut himself up in his private study, admitting no one. He had sternly warned his assistants and his attendants not to let in a single guest.

His Hasids concluded that their leader was engaged in a tremendous conflict with the Devil, which required stupendous exertion and brain power. That was why the rebbe demanded that no one should disturb and distract him during his struggle.

But the Devil, who did not care for the rebbe's holy work, still tried to confuse him, and so the rebbe turned to one of his adjutants, a highly respected friend named Nethaneel. This man, in his sixties and a passionate Hasid, had once known and frequently consulted the rebbe's father (who had been the Rebbe of Probitsh). Nethaneel was ready to make the greatest sacrifice for the Rebbe of Rízhin, he was willing to go through fire and water for him. The rebbe likewise dearly loved his friend, and they would often engage in lofty conversations with one another.

Fearing the epidemic—Heaven preserve us!—many rustic Jews near and far had abandoned everything and fled to Rízhin with their wives and children in order to be near the rebbe and thereby escape certain death. They all tried to approach him and obtain his blessing—only to learn that he had strictly forbidden anyone to enter his study until he himself opened the door.

The people gathered here were grief-stricken by the news. Had they been Hasids, they would have understood that this was no simple matter, that the rebbe was battling to save the whole nation of Israel—a battle requiring his utmost rest and concentration. But these were simple souls without the slightest grasp of Hasidism, and so they inferred that if the rebbe refused to see them, it meant that the world was about to go under—God forbid!—and that there was nothing anyone could do about it: The Gates of Mercy were closed, and there wasn't even a flicker of hope that anyone would elude a bitter death. The rebbe's court was filled with these refugees, who wept and wailed so loudly that Heaven broke asunder. They saw themselves as doomed and wondered who was condemned to die in the next few hours.

Our Nethaneel roamed among these desperate men, women, and children, his heart bursting with grief. He knew that the rebbe's seclusion was not a simple matter, that the rebbe was laboring for the good of all Jews, but as a great lover of his people he couldn't stand watching them lose their final rays of hope. By showing himself to the refugees, the rebbe could spark their courage and raise their hopes. Nethaneel therefore considered entering the study and making the rebbe aware of what was going on. Nethaneel knew quite well that the rebbe would be annoyed at him, and that his annoyance could be deadly. But the compassion he felt for the Jews, for their misery and despair, was so overwhelming that Nethaneel decided to make the sacrifice. Come what may, he would enter the study.

Since he was a close friend of the rebbe, the assistants didn't keep on eye on Nethaneel. After all, he would normally visit the rebbe at any time of day or night! Waiting for a moment when no one else was around, Nethaneel opened the door and halted at the threshold.

"Nethaneel! Is that you?"

Nethaneel had not expected to be received in this way. His teeth chattered, and, barely managing to control himself, he cried out in a strange voice: "Holy Rebbe! The people desperately want to see you, they have to see your holy face, it will drive the demon of destruction from their hearts. Bless them, Rebbe, bless them. I can't stand it—I'm so filled with pity for the Jews!"

The rebbe stood there a while, lost in thought, gazing at his loyal follower. Finally he exclaimed: "Very well, go and tell them that I'll come to the window in the front room and give them my blessing."

Nethaneel promptly went to announce the good news. The terrified crowd came alive, and the rebbe then actually appeared at the window. He cordially looked at the Jews and blessed them so the epidemic would have no power over them.

And indeed, the illness spared all of them but one, who died that same day: Nethaneel.

Hasids claim that Nethaneel was felled by the announcement of the rebbe, who, because he had been distracted by the surprise visitor, could save only the local people, while for a time the epidemic kept ravaging other places.

Nethaneel's death had a strong impact on all the rebbe's followers. They had loved him deeply and they knew he had risked his life out of love for the entire nation of Israel. They drank to the redemption of his soul and said nothing but good things about him.

Two years passed. The holy Rebbe of Rízhin no longer mentioned his devoted Hasid—it was as if he had never lived.

One day, while going to the mikva (the ritual bath), the rebbe ran into a boy with a canary that he had caught in the woods. He was planning to sell it. The rebbe told his assistant to buy the bird and put it in a gold cage to be hung in the rebbe's prayer room. And even though his assistant found it bizarre, he did as he was told.

Every day from then on, the rebbe would stand ecstatically at the cage before prayers, listening to the bird, whose mournful and beautiful song would pierce your very heart.

The Hasids close to the rebbe realized there was more here than met the eye: They fully believed that the soul of a great saint in need of salvation had migrated into this canary. But no one could figure out the whys and wherefores.

At last, however, the secret was revealed.

It was the second day of the month of Nissan. During the first twelve days Jews read twelve passages successively from the Book of Numbers, and on the second day they read about the tribe of Issachar and about Nethaneel, the son of Zuar (Num. 1:8). That day, the rebbe's worship before prayers was fearful. His ecstasy was supernatural, and the canary sang lamentably. Its song was so heartrending that the agitated crowd waited in suspense, feeling that extraordinary things were about to happen.

Suddenly the rebbe cried: "Well, today is something of a holy day, the holy day commemorating the Biblical passage about Nethaneel, the son of Zuar. It's his day and his celebration—so let's go and pray!"

The rebbe ordered the prayer leader to croon a holiday melody, and the Hasids prayed with great rapture.

When prayers were done, the rebbe instantly opened the door to his prayer room and launched into the "Thy Will" more exuberantly than anyone had ever heard him recite it. He recited it in the Holy Tongue, of course, and so this is the Yiddish translation:

"Let it be Thy will, my God, the God of my forebears, that Thy vast grace ease the healing of souls that flutter like the birds and twitter and praise and pray for Thy nation Israel. Lord of the Universe! Bring in these holy birds to the holy place about which it is said: 'No eyes but Thine have seen it, God. . . .'"

At this moment, the canary thrust out its legs and died. Only now did the Hasids understand that the canary had contained Nethaneel's soul, which had been redeemed during the reading of the Biblical passage about Nethaneel, the son of Zuar.

PERETZ HIRSCHBEIN (1880–1948)

The Pledge

The original Yiddish text, Tkies-Kaf, *is to be found in* Gezamelte Dramen, *vol. 1 (New York, 1916).*

Characters

HÉNEKH, a miller
PÉSIL, his wife
KHÁNELE, their daughter
KHÁSHE
DÓVID, her son
PÉYE
FIRST BEGGAR
SECOND BEGGAR

Prologue

A large room with doors and windows left and right. To the right, DÓVID *is lying in a bed. It is night. On the wall an oil lamp is guttering, the oil is almost gone.* KHÁSHE *sits at the bedside, gazing at the patient. She looks scared and agitated. She stands up as if trying to decide whether to leave* DÓVID, *then silently takes the lamp and exits.*

DÓVID. (*Moans, then suddenly exclaims in fright.*) Khanele! You mustn't do it! . . . Wait till I'm dead! Go ahead! Tell me I'm dying! . . . (*Silence.*)

KHASHE. (*Returns with the burning lamp, puts it in its place.*) Are you awake, my child? The world's a nasty place. It won't allow me to be happy. I'm the talk of the town. . . . Sleeping again? (*She listens.* DÓVID *wakes up in terror.*) What it is, my child?!

DÓVID. When I close my eyes. . . . When I try to doze off. . . .

KHASHE. (*Kisses him.*) Pour out thy wrath on me, oh Lord. . . . What do you see, darling?

374

DÓVID. (*Moans tearfully.*) Mama, go to the mill. Khanele is getting engaged to another man. She's crying, she doesn't want to. . . . They're forcing her.

KHASHE. You're dreaming, my child.

DÓVID. No one's asking me. . . . Khanele, no one's asking me. They're shouting: "mazel tov!" Henekh's home is all lit up. The Sabbath chandelier, candles in all the sconces. . . .

KHASHE. You'll recover, my child. Khanele will be yours. The two of you will marry, God willing. You'll recover.

DÓVID (*Babbling feverishly.*) Remember? You gave me your word. You'd be mine. You promised. In the forest, on the Sabbath. Nobody knew. . . . Remember—gave me your word. . . . Wait till I die. . . .

KHASHE. My child, you'll recover. The Good Lord won't do that to your mother.

DÓVID (*More lucid.*) Tell me, Mama, why has Khanele stayed away for such a long time? Who's preventing her from coming? Mama, send for Henekh the miller. Tell him I want to ask her myself. She's getting engaged today. . . . Why aren't you saying anything, Mama? You know everything, tell me. You know everything. . . .

KHASHE. I've asked the people in the synagogue to recite psalms for you. You'll heal very soon. Look how miserable your mother is—she's surrounded by misery.

DÓVID. The whole town is there. The house is filled with guests. They're taking Khanele away from me. . . .

KHASHE. I'd give my soul for my child. Who wants to make his mother suffer? (*A pause.*)

DÓVID. (*Trembles, struggles to sit up, nearly falls from his bed.*) Mama!

KHASHE. Who's hurting my child? . . . Who's frightening my child?

DÓVID. They won't let me out of bed. I'm locked in. She's about to get married.

KHASHE. Who's tearing my heart to bits? (*She peers into* DÓVID*'s face.*) My child, what do you see? Your eyes are terrified. Look, your mother's right next to you. I'll do anything for you? And if it's God's decree, I'll tear it to shreds! . . . My child! My child! Look at me, look at your mother! . . .

DÓVID. (*Babbles*) I've died. . . . Khanele is crying. She's trying to get to me. They won't let her. I'm dying. . . . Khanele, I won't let it happen. . . . Mama, why are you sobbing?

KHASHE. (*Wretched.*) My darling. . . . My darling. . . . What do they want from my child?

DÓVID. You know everything. Tell me, tell me. . . . I know everything too. Look, they're combing her hair. . . . They're putting the bridal veil on her face. . . . I won't forgive. . . . No. . . . Never. (*Silence.* KHÁSHE *notices something eerie in* DÓVID*'s face. She peers around to see if anyone else is here. She then hurries through the left-hand door, immediately hurries back, her face chalky white. She tiptoes behind the head of the bed, wringing her hands, leans over, and gazes into* DÓVID*'s face.*)

DÓVID. (*Very loudly.*) Mama, where are you?

KHASHE. I'm watching over you.

DÓVID. Mama, where are you?

KHASHE. I'm guarding your bed.

DÓVID. No. . . . No. . . . I-won't-for-give.

KHASHE. (*Tears at her body, tears her hair. Keeps looking at the door. Pinches her cheeks in her horrible pain.*) My child! My child! (*Grabs his hands, yells louder.*)

My child! My child! (*People with pale, earnest faces file in and gather around the bed.*)

KHASHE. (*Pulls at* DÓVID) My child! My child! (*One of the* VISITORS *clutches* KHASHE*'s arms. Another* VISITOR *signals her to keep quiet.*)

Scene One

At the home of HENEKH *the miller. A whitewashed cottage. Two windows at the right; at the left, a door leading to another room. It is evening. Candles are burning in the Sabbath chandelier.* HENEKH *sits at the table, lost in thought.* PESIL *stares at him as if waiting for an answer.* KHANELE *sits on a window bench, her face buried in one arm.* HENEKH *stands up, self-assured.*

HENEKH. That's the way it is. How much longer can we wait? It's not my fault.

PESIL. It's easy for you to talk. You've forgotten the past, the terrible things. Once we had Rokhl—she was about to marry too. . . .

HENEKH. Stop harping for a while! I'm a father—a father. And you're a mother—let's hope we live a long life. Parents can take pride and joy in their kids. God himself commands. . . .

KHANELE. (*Goes and hugs* PESIL.) I'm so scared, Mama. . . .

PESIL. He wanted to stay alone with her. Did he say anything to you?

HENEKH. I wouldn't have allowed it.

PESIL. How can anyone prevent it?

KHANELE. The moment he saw me, he started crying. Crying softly, without words.

HENEKH. Ancestral merit caries weight. My father has never abandoned me—may he rest in peace.

KHANELE. Dóvid's eyes were pleading so earnestly. He stared at me without saying a word. We both cried.

HENEKH. You should have spoken bluntly to him. You should have told him that your parents are crying, our family is suffering. Your parents want to experience some joy from their child.

PESIL. Your mom's grieved enough—that's what you should have told him. She buried her beautiful child in the ground, and she's got only one child left in this world. She wants her one and only star to shine.

KHANELE. How can I say those things to him? I'll never tell him, never. You yourself told me to love him. And I did love him—more than life itself. He was so handsome at the engagement party. . . . You said so yourself, Mama. (*Silently kisses her mother.*)

PÉYE. (*Enters.*) Good evening.

PESIL. Look who's here! Are you alone?

HENEKH. It's no big deal walking alone at night. . . .

PEYE. If you have to, you do it. . . . How are you, Khanele? Such a spoiled child. Your home is so radiant. I hope your luck is radiant too!

HENEKH. The house was whitewashed. Everything was ready.

PESIL. Oh. . . . You can't ask God why.

HENEKH. I've never asked God why.

PEYE. (*Caresses* KHANELE, *kisses her.*) Khanele, my dear, why are you so pale? Didn't you get enough sleep? (KHANELE *is embarrassed.*)

PESIL. No child of mine sleeps late. She wakes up with the first sunbeam.

PEYE. Is that true, Khanele? Would you like to be my daughter? (KHANELE *hides her face.*) I won't pull any punches. When things changed, I was angry for a while. I had a good look at her when she was a child. . . . And I kept exclaiming: "She's the one!" A mother knows the right match for her son. You can see where you've all ended up.

HENEKH. Do I have any say? When God wants to punish, He finds the right place. I have to hold my tongue. I'm a simple man, a miller. But I do know one thing. I can see that the Good Lord sometimes sends His wind from another side. . . . So do I have any say? . . .

PESIL. A mother's heart is covered with wounds. What could I do?

PEYE. Now everything's clear. Everything's set to go.

PESIL. Nothing's known as yet. I can put someone in a dangerous situation.

KHANELE. He could die, God forbid. I don't want him to die for my sake. (*They all give her surprised looks.*)

PEYE. You silly child. A person dies for his own sins—that's written. It's the truth. An only daughter—God alone forgives.

PESIL. I won't say another word. I'm a suffering mother. God forbid that my child should lose even one hair—what good is my life?

PEYE. Now listen to me. I've just seen the rabbi. I told him the whole truth, I did. Henekh's daughter got engaged to Gavríel's son, Dóvid. But Dóvid's been sick for almost a year now. He's been through Hell—it shouldn't happen to our worst enemies. I tell you—Khanele is young. Her parents want to get some happiness from her. A year—how much longer? "Rabbi," I told him, "you have to untie the knot. . . ."

HENEKH. God protect him—what did the rabbi say?

PEYE. He said that she herself should go to him, she herself should ask him to release her,

KHANELE. I don't want to—I'm scared.

PESIL. Will you do it, my child? (KHANELE *doesn't answer.*)

HENEKH. Your mother's asking you something!

PEYE. The whole town is grieving. They're all praying for God's forgiveness.

HENEKH. I'm a simple man. If the rabbi himself issues an order, I obey.

PEYE. I heard it from his own pure lips.

PESIL. (*Goes and hugs* KHANELE.) I'm sick with pain and fear. Now listen carefully. I'll tell you what to say.

PEYE. The right thing, the right thing.

KHANELE. Oh, Mama, I can't, I can't.

PESIL. When you see him, cry. Tell him you'll pray for him.

KHANELE. Oh, Mama, I can't. He loved me so much. . . . I visited him the other day, and you can't imagine how much he cried.

PEYE. A Jewish girl shouldn't say such things.

(KHANELE *wipes her tears.*)

HENEKH. You should be ashamed of yourself—you're mortifying your father.

PEYE. You're the talk of the town. Everyone's praying for you—praying that you won't be punished, God forbid.

HENEKH. (*Kisses* KHANELE, *speaks tenderly.*) Listen to me. When a father says something, he knows what he's talking about. I'll go with you. Dóvid will have to forgive you. I'll talk for you. All you have to say is: "Father and mother, I'll obey you."

KHANELE. (*Weeping.*) Do whatever you like with me.

PEYE. My father was a rebbe, a miracle worker, and if he were still alive, I wouldn't go to the rabbi.

HENEKH. No, we have to go to a rabbi. A rabbi carries an entire town on his back. Khanele, I want you to come with me today.

PEYE. Today we're celebrating, we're celebrating! I'm prepared, and my son is willing. . . .

PESIL. (*She brings clothes from the other room and lays them out on the table.*)

Everything is ready, everything is all set. I feel so bad. I thought I'd wrap my child in silk and satin and lead her to the wedding canopy. I feel awful. I was so happy when my darling Rokhl got engaged.

KHANELE. (*Hugs her mother.*) Oh, Mama, if only you knew how scared I am! . . . If only you could hear how fast my heart is pounding. How can I say those words? . . . He's seen all these clothes. I told him about my wedding gown.

PEYE. Wedding clothes are lying on your table, and you're filling your home with grief! God help us all!

HENEKH. She's my child, my flesh and blood, I've got the right.

PEYE. I'm a mother too.

KHANELE. If I go to him . . . I won't be able to speak. Mama, maybe he'll recover, and I'll love him again, just as you loved him, Mama.

PESIL. I did love him, my child. He was the apple of my eye. But you're my whole life. If anything happens to you, I won't survive. Come with me, my child, we'll both go to see him. We'll ask him to forgive us, we'll cry. . . . He'll look at us and he'll see how miserable I am. Let him release you from your pledge. . . . Will you go? Will you?

HENEKH. It's fine with me. She'll go.

PEYE. Everyone's agreed. . . . Light more candles. Make the house radiant. Everyone's agreed. You two go, and I'll wait for you here, I'll wait till you return in a cheerful state of mind.

KHANELE. (*Buries her face in her mother's shoulder, weeps.*) Oh, Mama, Mama. I'm terrified.

Scene Two

In HENEKH'*s home. The room is half-dark. Pine splinters are burning in the fireplace. For a while there's no one around. All we hear is the crackling of the glowing pine splinters. Outside the window the wind blasts and howls from time to time. The wedding clothes are on the table.*

HENEKH. (*Enters from outdoors. Agitated. He feeds a few more pine splinters into the flames. The room grows brighter. The wind gets stronger.* HENEKH *goes over to the window and peers into the dark night. Talks to himself.*) I shouldn't have done it. I shouldn't have done it. The wind will carry the mill beyond the mountains. (*The wind wails outside.* HENEKH *hurries outdoors.* PESIL *and* KHANELE *come in.* KHANELE *has been transformed by terror.*)

PESIL. It's a curse! For whose misdeeds? For whose sins?

KHANELE. Hide my wedding clothes. I'm too scared to look at them.

PESIL. (*Carries the wedding clothes to the next room.*) My blood, my heart. God in Heaven—what happened? What happened? . . . (*Comes back.*)

KHANELE. I feel cold, Mama.

PESIL. (*Kisses* KHANELE, *wraps her in a shawl.*) I'm going to pray and pray, I'm going to pour out all my torment and suffering to God in Heaven. (KHANELE *sit wordlessly at the table, her terrified eyes wandering about.* PESIL *peers out the window.*) The storm came down on me too. What a horrible night. Alone in the mill. How will he manage all by himself? The storm will be pitiless toward the mill. Let's go and see how Papa is doing. (KHANELE *doesn't answer.*) My child, God will forgive us.

KHANELE. Listen, the wind is whistling. Can you hear it crying? *Dóvid*'s the one who's crying.

PESIL. My child, we'll all go over tomorrow. We'll mourn together there.

KHANELE. The wind is talking. On the way, I heard it calling my name—"Khanele." Just listen.

PESIL. God will punish only your mother, only your mother. . . .

HENEKH. (*Hurries in.*) You two are here? Don't just stand there, help me. We're in a terrible predicament! The storm will shatter the mill to smithereens.

PESIL. (*Bursts into tears.*) It's all over, Henekh, it's all over.

HENEKH. My hair feels like needles in my head. Come outside with me. (*Hurries out.*)

PESIL. Go to your father, my child. Winds, storms—punish me alone! Punish me alone! . . .

KHANELE. I won't go outdoors. Mama, don't leave me alone!

PESIL. He doesn't know as yet. He doesn't know. How can we tell him such awful news?

KHANELE. If I don't go, he'll drag me out, he'll drag me by my hair! . . . He'll yell: "Come with me!" . . .

PESIL. (*Peers through window.*) Slowly . . . slowly. . . . When God takes pity, He keeps His word. Praised be God! Dóvid will stay there without any strength. He will pass away. God help us!. . . . (*She peers hard through the window.*)

KHANELE. Tell me, Mama: Why did they drive me out of his home? I wanted to see him, I wanted to pray. . . . Tell me, Mama, you know everything. . . .

PESIL. He held it back. He binds the wings with chains. Praised be God! Praised be God!

KHANELE. I wanted to scream: "Dóvid, I'm yours." But they drove me out of his home. Tell me: Why were there candles burning on the floor? . . . Mama, tell me.

PESIL. (*Moves away from the window. It's obvious she's heard nothing that* KHANELE *has said.*) Why are you trembling so hard? Are you cold? God took pity. Pour everything out on me, on your mother! . . .

HENEKH. (*Enters, pale, terrified, panting, as if after a huge battle.*) Tell me what happened. Where do we stand?

PESIL. Sit down. You've lost your strength.

HENEKH. That was no wind. No, that was no wind. It crushed my fingers in the wheel. It shook the walls. No, it didn't shake—it howled like a wolf. . . . It spoke. I've plugged up all the holes in the walls, and it shook from all sides. . . . It was the first time. I tried to turn the wings aside—but it didn't help. The wind just blasted in from another corner. . . .

PESIL. (*Peers into* HENEKH*'s face, wipes the sweat from his forehead.*) The sweat on your forehead is cold.

HENEKH. Where were you two? And what happened?

PESIL. When did Peye leave?

HENEKH. The wind began to blast. So she went into town. It blasted her, and so she left. . . . (*He is lost in thought. The women stare at him.*) My heart is telling me something—did you have a good look at her? Are you sure it was Peye? . . . Was it Peye? Ha, why won't you say something? (*A deathly hush.*)

Khanele, why are you sitting like that? . . . Speak up, talk to me. . . . My heart's bursting—I'm so scared. Talk to me!

PESIL. Don't ask, don't ask. Let's pray. Get your father's psalter—recite, recite a psalm. Henekh, we're not alone.

KHANELE. (*Looks out the window.*) It's dark out, fearfully dark. (*Suddenly, as if recalling something.*) Tell me what happened. I don't recognize her at all!

PESIL. Things are bad, Henekh, bad. A terrible sin was committed . . . a terrible sin.

KHANELE. He didn't forgive us. He died and he didn't forgive us. . . .

HENEKH. And he'll demand his due! He'll demand his due! That's bad. He's slipped into the mill, opposite my windows. . . . He wanted to carry off my mill. He began with the mill. . . . We have to go to the rabbi! We all have to go to town—all of us! (*He nervously puts on his kaftan.* PESIL *goes over to him, gapes at him in terror.*)

KHANELE. Papa! Your hair. . . . Your beard. . . . They've turned white. . . .

Scene Three

Dusk. Outdoors. To the right, HENEKH*'s thatched-roof cottage. In front of it, an earthen bench. A well. In the background, a windmill on a hilltop. Not far from the mill, a sandy path.* HENEKH *sits on the earth bench.* KHANELE *is kneeling next to him.*)

HENEKH. We could drive a wagon into the forest and gather the snapped branches. The wind has caused enough damage. It all points to the storm.

KHANELE. Mama's been gone for such a long time. It'll be night soon.

HENEKH. Your mother has a very hard life.

KHANELE. Every night, before going to bed, you should bind the wings with solid fetters.

HENEKH. Yes, if it would help. (*Silence.*)

KHANELE. How could you be alone in the mill?

HENEKH. Your father doesn't want to go begging. (*Looks at the sky.*) A rainbow in Heaven . . . and a storm on earth.

KHANELE. Why didn't Peye come to the funeral? Why didn't she come? (HENEKH *is silent. His head droops.* KHANELE *looks at him. A beggar emerges on the road, carrying a large knapsack and clutching a bag and a long stick. He trudges over to the cottage.* HENEKH *and* KHANELE *don't notice him.*)

FIRST BEGGAR. (*Very close.*) Good evening, my friend! (HENEKH *and* KHANELE *are startled. She sits down away from her father and the beggar.*)

HENEKH. (*Coming to.*) Good evening! Where are you coming from?

FIRST BEGGAR. Good evening to you! The night's caught up with me. I need to rest a little. (*He removes the knapsack from his shoulders.*)

HENEKH. Have you come a long way?

FIRST BEGGAR. Not so much today. I spent last night just five or six miles from here.

HENEKH. Just five or six miles?

FIRST BEGGAR. (*Sits down.*) Oh, my legs won't obey me. In my good years I was a fast walker—horses couldn't keep up with me.

HENEKH. (*Sighs.*) That's the way it is. . . . And you can grow old in a single night.

FIRST BEGGAR. (*Eyes* KHANELE.) Is that your daughter?

HENEKH. My only child.

FIRST BEGGAR. Hmmm. (*Silence.*)

HENEKH. And there's no news from there—I mean the places you're coming from?

FIRST BEGGAR. You mean fires or what . . .?

HENEKH. That's what I mean. . . . There's no news? . . . There must have been a huge wind?

FIRST BEGGAR. Aha! That's what you mean? Yes, there was a powerful wind. It tore off roofs, it carried away the straw from barns—who knows where!?

HENEKH. (*Points to the mill.*) That's my livelihood. It could have been reduced to a pile of ashes. But God helped us.

KHANELE. My father stopped it all by himself.

FIRST BEGGAR. Can you give me a little water to wash my hands? I haven't said my afternoon prayers yet.

HENEKH. Khanele, go and get a jug of water. (KHANELE *hurries into the cottage.*)

FIRST BEGGAR. It wouldn't hurt to find her a husband and get a little happiness for yourself. (HENEKH *eyes him suspiciously.*) On the road, all four directions are east—God peers from all sides at the lonesome traveler.

HENEKH. Ah, how true that is! How true! People sometimes sin in word, in deed. . . . I'm a simple man, a very simple man. My eyes were opened only once. (*Points to his gray hair and gray beard.*) Do you see? It happened all in one night. . . .

KHANELE. (*Brings out water.*) I can draw fresh water if you like.

FIRST BEGGAR. That's fine, that's fine, my lovely girl.

HENEKH. You understand, friend. When a storm blasts, there's nothing you can do. It turns west into east and east into west.

FIRST BEGGAR. Ah, afternoon prayers, afternoon prayers. . . . (*He washes his hands.*)

KHANELE. (*To her father.*) Are you going to ask our guest to spend the night?

HENEKH. You're welcome to spend the night, sir, if you like.

FIRST BEGGAR. Thank you, that's very fine of you.

PESIL. (*Arrives along the path with a small bag on her shoulders. When she notices the stranger, she looks both astonished and delighted. She puts down the bag.*) God has answered my prayers!

KHANELE. (*Kisses her mother.*) You're so cheerful, Mama darling, so cheerful! . . . (HENEKH *eyes his wife in surprise.*)

PESIL. I found the sign next to my windows. God says it's time! . . . Who sent you to me, my friend?

FIRST BEGGAR. The night commanded me. When I was young and I couldn't find a Jewish house to put me up, I would rest in the field outside the village or under some tree in the forest. But nowadays, my age dictates.

PESIL. God sent you to me! My house is yours! My bread and salt are prepared for you! I'm going to send for all the wanderers in the neighboring villages and invite them to my home. I'll get up at sunrise and pray for their health.

FIRST BEGGAR. Yes, hospitality. Hospitality makes the lonely happy. . . .

HENEKH. Who put those godly words upon your tongue?

FIRST BEGGAR. I'm no longer tired, no longer tired.

HENEKH. I'm feeling better and better, I want to find out about the miracle. Your face looks like it's been reborn.

PESIL. This is what the rebbe told me: He said I should put up any and all wanderers for the night. I should fill them with my bread and salt. I should pour out my bitter heart to each guest, tell him about my misery. And every guest should pray for our home and our family! Khanele, my darling, my life! The whole world should pray for you. . . . (KHANELE *clings to her mother, peers into her eyes, astonished.*)

HENEKH. My child, use your common sense. Your heart might burst. Every creature can endure too much grief. But too much happiness, my child, is beyond our strength.

FIRST BEGGAR. Tell me what happened.

PESIL. Every day I will pour out my sufferings, and merciful people will pray for me in Heaven. My heart was turned to stone. I looked around my home without saying a word. I stayed up all day and stayed up all night around my child. I looked east, west, north, south. Where would my rescue come from? . . . Today I had the first sign. My tears were shed in front of God's throne.

FIRST BEGGAR. What's wrong?

HENEKH. For God's sake! What happened?

PESIL. A curse lay on my home—for my sins, for all my sins. The curse lurked under my window until you arrived. I was cursed. I lived with my soulmate, my husband, for ten years and God didn't want to raise my spirits with a single child. But in our eleventh year my prayers were answered, and I gave birth to a daughter. God in His mercy was gracious again, and He gave me a second daughter. All at once, my cup was full. My happiness overflowed. On Fridays I always lit candles at the Holy Ark and I peered fearfully in the silence and in the night, peered at my radiant fortune. I illuminated God's house of worship, and he blessed my home. . . .

HENEKH. It's true. . . . As true as his existence.

PESIL. My daughters grew like sheaves in the field. I was afraid to pronounce their names, it might draw bad luck. Rokhl, the older one, shone like the sun. Our home was always filled with her singing. When she was a child, she was already running to synagogue to light her own little candle. That was all the Good Lord wanted. . . . I arranged her engagement to a God-fearing man. But when it was time to sew her wedding clothes—my joy turned to sorrow. And my entire life remained sorrowful. My comfort, my soul. After the engagement her fiancé became terribly ill. It dragged on for a whole year. He was all skin and bones and he wasted away. . . . We wept and begged him to release us from our pledge—he didn't respond.

FIRST BEGGAR. And what happened then?

HENEKH. We broke the pledge.

FIRST BEGGAR. And now?

PESIL. Now. . . . Now. . . . They just had the funeral. And he'll be coming to demand his due.

FIRST BEGGAR. It's a gloomy matter. You'd need a huge amount of God's mercy.

PESIL. No, the prayers of many people would be accepted. That's what he said with his pure lips. I should seek out wanderers in need of hospitality. My home should become a nest for them. I'll wash their feet and drink the water. . . . (*She takes the beggar's pack.*) Please come into my home! (KHANELE *helps her.*)

FIRST BEGGAR. (*Musing.*) A lot of mercy, a lot of mercy. . . . (*Goes inside.*)

HENEKH. (*Wobbles on his legs.*) I'm ready. . . .

Scene Four

Inside HENEKH's *cottage. Daytime.*

FIRST BEGGAR. (*Stands in the middle of the cottage with his knapsack and his bag. Ready to leave.*) All blessings upon your heads.

KHANELE. When you meet other poor people, send them to us.

PESIL. (*Stuffing something inside his bag.*) Take this for the road, until you reach a village.

FIRST BEGGAR. Goodbye and good luck to you!

PESIL. Wait, wait, I've got something else for you. (*Hurries into the next room.*)

FIRST BEGGAR. This is Abraham's home. The doors are open for guests on all four sides.

PESIL. (*Brings a wrapped object, puts it in his bag.*) This is for your children.

FIRST BEGGAR. Abraham's home. . . . How can the Lord of the Universe raise His hand against such a home?

PESIL. Send guests to us from the four corners of the world. My door is open to everyone. My husband and I and our daughter will serve everyone.

FIRST BEGGAR. Holy, holy! Such deeds will not be ignored. No, no, they never will. . . . Goodbye, goodbye. (*Exits.* PESIL *and* KHANELE *gaze at him through the window.*)

PESIL. Now, my child, we'll attend to our own affairs.

KHANELE. I'm going to watch him until I can't see him anymore. (PESIL *gives* KHANELE *a worried look.* KHANELE. *leaves the window.*) He's gone. We're alone again. Mama, why do you look so worried?

PESIL. Let's attend to our own affairs. We're going to listen to your Papa when he comes back from town. . . . Well, my child.

KHANELE. I can't, Mama.

PESIL. The wax is soft and pure.

KHANELE. Perhaps no beggars will come here tonight?

PESIL. (*Puts wax and cotton wick on the table.*) I'll keep you with me. You'll stay very close to me. I'll watch over you all through the night. (*Cuts up the wick.*)

KHANELE. We'll all stay awake.

PESIL. (*Rolling the candles.*) I measured Rokhl's coffin nine times and the entire graveyard once. . . . Here, my child, take a wick and say: "May the soul of my sister Rokhl watch over me and prevent any harm from happening to me or my fiancé."

KHANELE. Oh, Mama, don't say such things. They make me feel so gloomy.

PESIL. Here you are. The candle's almost done. Roll it and say: "May the soul of my sister Rokhl pray to God for me and my fiancé.

KHANELE. Oh, Mama, don't say that. . . . My heart's pounding. I want to roll the pure wax candles, and, Mama, this is what I'll say: "My sister, my dear sister. The world is so beautiful and life is so good—I want to have life and I won't get married. . . ."

PESIL. Roll the candles, my child, roll the candles. The curse has been removed from our home. Your sister will come to the wedding. They'll remove the holiday curtain from the Holy Ark and put it on poles. Your canopy will be set up next to the Great Synagogue. Here's another piece of wick, it's already covered with wax. Roll, roll, and say:

"My sister, your grave was measured nine times. Our mother measured your remains nine times. Pray to God for your younger sister, beg God to remove the sin from our home." My child, say: "Our mother sinned. She broke her word. Our mother must be punished, but not her daughter's young remains. . . ."

KHANELE. Oh, Mama. I feel so anxious. I'll light candles at the Holy Ark. And this is what I'll say to the candles: "My mother measured my sister's remains nine times with your wicks. Burn, burn, candles. Let the flames rise to the heavens. Let them awaken all the angels in the heavens. Ask for mercy for Khanele, she doesn't want to get married."

PESIL. God help your mother! What are you saying?

KHANELE. I'll build a little nest in a secluded part of the green forest. I'll remain alone on the earth like the stars in the sky. And if a suitor comes to me, I'll say: "You be like a bird that has flown to a faraway land for the winter. I'll be like a bird locked up in a cage while her beloved flutters around it, banging his wings against the bars."

(PESIL *buries her face in her arm. Her entire body trembles with her weeping.* KHANELE *throws her arms around her.*) Mama, don't cry, I'll go to my wedding. I'll embroider radiant stars on blue silk. One for Rokhl and one for me. Tell me, Mama, who will be my bridegroom now?

PESIL. He will be a learned man, and the shekhina [God's radiance] will shine on his head.

KHANELE. And what should I say to him the first time I see him?

PESIL. Say: "I am a Jewish girl and I have a pure heart. . . . You will study the Torah, and I will sit in a corner, praying."

KHANELE. I'll say to him: "I already had a fiancé, and now his bones are rotting. . . ."

PESIL. My child! My child!

KHANELE. Don't cry, Mama. I'll do anything you tell me. I'll obey. And when my bridegroom and I stand under the canopy, he won't know that Dóvid is standing next to us, staring at us with his dead eyes. And he'll whisper softly into our ears: "Khanele once had a fiancé, his name was Dóvid. . . . She gave him her word. . . ."

PESIL. My child, I'll die of grief. . . .

KHANELE. Oh, Mama, I'll go to the wedding. And when I put on my wedding gown, I'll say: "I had a sister, and they made silk garments for her and they were about to lead her to the canopy. But her luck ran out, and she was buried in a white shroud. . . ."

PESIL. Who's speaking from your young heart?!

KHANELE. Your only child wants to live. My heart wants to live. And when I'm under the canopy, I'll be standing next to the Angel of Death with his sharp sword. . . . He will take me home from the wedding. . . .

PESIL. (*Hugs her tighter.*) Hush, hush. . . . The pain is shattering my heart. . . . (*Silence. They remain sitting, clasping one another. Voices are heard from outside the window.*)

KHANELE. (*Suddenly.*) I'm scared, Mama, I'm scared! . . . (*Bursts into tears like a child. Keeps clutching* PESIL.)

Scene Five

Inside the cottage. Late at night. A candle is burning in the chandelier. A mound of wax candles is on the table. PESIL *enters from the left-hand room. She is uneasy. She peers and peers through the window, and looks all around the room, as if noticing something macabre.* SECOND BEGGAR *emerges from the other room.*

PESIL. Don't leave my child by herself!

SECOND BEGGAR. Don't worry. It's all right. The mezuzahs are pure. I checked them. It won't hurt to have more people from town.

PESIL. What are you talking about?

SECOND BEGGAR. God is with you! I tell you: God will cure her. After all, she was fresh and healthy today!

PESIL. What do you mean?

SECOND BEGGAR. No harm will come to her. God doesn't punish such families. We'll wait till dawn. Morning always brings deliverance! (*He goes into the next room.* PESIL *peers through the window again.* HENEKH *comes in, pale.*)

PESIL. Well? What is it? Tell me! Now!

HENEKH. There's no cheer around us. . . .

PESIL. Did you see it with your own eyes?

HENEKH. I saw it with my own eyes. . . . The mill stood with its wings facing east. Go to the window, take a look. Maybe I didn't see straight. (*They both peer intently out the window.*)

PESIL. The wings are facing the cottage!

HENEKH. West! The wings toward the windows! It's bad, it's bad— I'm going crazy. Didn't I beg his forgiveness at his grave? Why am I being harassed.

PESIL. Hénekh, you're sinning!

HENEKH. A life for a life—I don't want to pay!

PESIL. I think the mill is screeching . . . as if someone were turning the wings.

HENEKH. (*From a distance he peers cautiously through the window.*) The wings are turning. . . . Look with your radiant eyes. Look, they're demanding a soul from my home—they're demanding. . . .

PESIL. I'd rather have my eyes gouged out!

SECOND BEGGAR. (*Enters from the next room, uneasy.*) You're both sinning with your lips. Something. . . . I'm not sure what. Her face has changed. Is she sleeping? . . . (PESIL *hurries into the next room.* HENEKH *is lost in thought. He holds his head in both hands.*)

PESIL (*calling from next room.*) Henekh! Come quickly! She's dying! (HENEKH *hesitates.*) Henekh! Henekh! (HENEKH *gestures hopelessly. Goes to next room.*) It's over. . . . (SECOND BEGGAR *touches the mezuzah, whispers.*)

HENEKH. (*Runs in, hugs* BEGGAR) I'm a fly, a sinful fly. I'll obey!

SECOND BEGGAR. C'mon, let's change her room. We'll bring her and her bed in here—we'll outwit the Angel of Death!

PESIL. Henekh! Henekh! (HENEKH *and* BEGGAR *go to next room. After a while they return, lugging in* KHANELE *with her bed.* PESIL *follows them, wringing her hands.*) That should drive the evil from her body! (*They place the bed in the middle of the room.* KHANELE *lies motionless, her eyes closed, her face bright.*)

HENEKH. Put her by the eastern wall!

SECOND BEGGAR. By the eastern wall, the eastern wall. That's where all the prayers fly up. . . .

PESIL. Next to the window. . . . No, no! In the middle of the room. . . . (*They stand around the bed.*)

KHANELE. (*Motionless, but in a clear voice.*) They're all standing around me.

PESIL. Dear Father in Heaven! . . .

HENEKH. (*Loud, as if crazy.*) Henekh! Today your house will collapse upon you!

PESIL. Shush, shush!

SECOND BEGGAR. Silence. Not a word!

KHANELE. Bring me my white clothes. The white clothes with the little stars—my wedding garments. . . . Bring me the veil. . . .

HENEKH. If someone calls, you can't refuse. (PESIL *signals him to hold his tongue.*)

KHANELE. Mama. . . . You're scared of your own child. I've always spoken like this. . . . Bring me my wedding clothes.

PESIL. Keep God's name in your mind, God's name!

KHANELE. My wedding clothes. Why are you silent? He's standing by my bed, he won't let me be. He won't forgive me. I have to marry him. He's wandering from world to world. He won't find any peace until he stands under the canopy with me. . . . Don't you see him here? . . . (*Silence. They all peer around.*)

PESIL. (*Whispering.*) Stones and bones have their peace. That's the kind of peace you should find. Leave my child. I'll pray for your peace every day!

KHANELE. Bring me my wedding clothes!

SECOND BEGGAR. (*Whispering.*) You have to obey. . . . You must obey. . . . (HENEKH *brings in her wedding clothes.*)

KHANELE. (*As they dress her in her wedding gown.*) I didn't keep my pledge. . . . I broke my word. . . . It's my fault he left this world. . . . He's being driven to carry me away. . . . He won't go without me. . . .

SECOND BEGGAR. (*Whispering.*) That's God's will, God's will. . . . You have to honor her wish. . . .

HENEKH. I will obey. . . .

PESIL. I hope my eyes go blind! . . .

KHANELE. The white wedding veil. . . .

HENEKH. I'm prepared for anything! (*He brings her the wedding veil. They put it on her face.* PESIL *gapes at him in terror.*)

KHANELE. Light the Sabbath chandelier. . . . A candle in all the sconces. . . . (HENEKH *lights the candles on the table and inserts them into the sconces. He shudders.*) Light the candles and stand around me. . . . With candles around me. . . .

SECOND BEGGAR. (*Trembles.*) Do it. . . . (HENEKH *hurries into the next room. They gaze after him.*)

KHANELE. Light candles around me. . . . Everyone with candles! (PESIL, *terrified, lights candles on the table and stands at the head of the bed.*)

HENEKH. (*Returns in his prayer shawl and his white linen robe. Yells.*) A candle for your father! . . . For me! (*He lights a candle.*) I am prepared. I will go with my child! . . . (*His legs buckle and he collapses next to the bed. . . .*)

CURTAIN

The Tale of the "Baal-Shem" and the "Dybbuk"

From: A. Litvin 1862–1943; Yidishe Neshómes (Jewish Souls), (New York: Star Hebrew Book Co., 1917), inconsistent pagination. Sónye the Wise Woman or Stocking Maker was one of Litvin's informants about folk material.

This is no fairy tale, it really happened.

In our shtetl, there was a bright young man named Móyshele. He was as smart as a whip, and also a good-for-nothing. Then all at once he disappeared, and no one knew what had become of him. About five or six years later, my dad had to take a business trip to a small shtetl somewhere in Volhynia. Upon reaching the inn, he found it packed to the rafters. The street was mobbed with people trying to shove their way inside. But it was no use—they couldn't squeeze in.

My dad asked: "What's going on?

Someone replied: "A baal-shem is in there. He's got amulets that can get women pregnant and they can also cure all diseases."

At that instant, the door to the inn opened, a man came dashing out in a fur hat and a white satin kaftan with a waistband. My dad took one look at him and cried out: "Móyshele, damn it! What the hell are you doing here? Are *you* the baal-shem?"

"Quiet!" said the "baal-shem." "Come along, I want to show you something!"

My dad climbed into the "baal-shem"'s wagon, and they rode off to the home of a rich villager. The "baal-shem" was supposed to drive out a dybbuk from the man's daughter. The girl, who hadn't slept for several nights, kept screaming that there was a demon in her featherbed.

When they arrived, the "baal-shem" asked to be taken to the girl's bedroom. He then ordered everyone out so he could meditate in seclusion. The eavesdroppers heard him yelling and chanting shreds of the Cabala. Suddenly he fell silent. The door opened. The "baal-shem" called out to the villager and told him to bring a ginger cat and a bucket of tar. After a long search, they finally found a ginger cat and delivered her, together with the tar, to the "baal-shem." He again shut himself up in the bedroom, but this time with my dad. The "baal-shem" took the cat, smeared her up with tar, cut the featherbed open on one side, and stuck the cat in. Next he opened the door and told his host to lug the bed and the featherbed over to the woods and to take the sick girl there.

"Now," he said, "you'll see me drive the demon out of the featherbed." And he began communing and twisting his face and spitting and whispering over a glass of water, into which he had slipped some citrine salt. He then added some soda powder—which the Jews here knew nothing about. The water began to seethe and bubble. The onlookers were terrified by this "dreadful miracle." The "baal-shem" then grabbed his stick and started beating the featherbed. A yowling emerged from inside, and while the witnesses were shrieking: "God help us!," some kind of black creature, covered with feathers and caterwauling at the top of its lungs, sprang out and hightailed it to the forest.

When the girl saw that the demon had fled, she calmed down. Now that she was able to sleep at night, she recovered her health.

The "baal-shem" received a nice bit of change for his work and he amply rewarded my dad. When the two of them were back at the inn, my dad had to admit that no genuine "baal-shem" could have ever come up with a brainier idea for driving out a "demon." And they both roared with laughter.

The Last Dybbuk

Collected by A. Litvin, Yidishe Neshómes *(Jewish Souls) (New York: Star Hebrew Book Co., 1917), inconsistent pagination. Litvin's dates are 1862–1943.*

Never, never had Láshkovits, a tiny village near Czortków, experienced what it experienced that Yom Kippur.

At the synagogue they were just finishing *musaf*, the extension of the morning prayer, recited on the Sabbath and on Holy Days. However, the worshipers had long since dispersed and only the pious elderly men were left in the synagogue. In one corner, the Rebbe of Láshkovits, wearing a prayer shawl and a white linen robe, was standing by the Holy Ark. He was the last scion in the dynasty of his grandfather, Rebbe Meyer of Przemysl. Now he was praying to God in profound ecstasy, calling for help, citing the merits accumulated by his holy ancestor, Urye-Leyb of Láshkovits.

For some time now, the marketplace behind the synagogue had been filled with a murmuring that sounded like ocean waves. Hundreds of people, young and old, had been arriving from Czortków and Buczacz, Oteny and Prosheve, and even from as far away as Tarnopol. They were here to watch the tremendous combat, the contest between the holy rebbe—the great-grandson of Rebbe Meyer of Przemysl—and the heretic, the "Shapírnik" (follower of the enlightened Rabbi Shapiro), Mékhel Válakh from Czortków, who had challenged the rebbe to a duel.

"Today the entire world will see which is stronger: the power of the tsaddiks and the sacred faith or the power of Satan—Heaven preserve us!" Those were the thoughts and words of the pious women, the old men, the followers of the holy dynasty founded by Urye-Leyb of Láshkovits.

"Today the entire world will see which power is stronger: the power of darkness and superstition or the power of light and enlightenment."

Those were the thoughts of the followers of the Haskala (the Jewish Enlightenment), the admirers of the heroic Shapírnik, Mékhele Válakh, who had dared to challenge the Rebbe of Láshkovits to this marvelous "duel."

However, the adherents on both sides were like drops in the ocean compared with the huge throng of rubberneckers. These people had come to see the great wonder, to watch the rebbe perform an exorcism in the square, out in the open, in front of the entire world, between *musaf* and *ne'ila* (the last prayer recited on Yom Kippur), in full view of policemen and constables. The rebbe was supposed to drive a dybbuk out of a young woman and into the mouth of the heretic, the Shapírnik, Mékhel Válakh. The cantor had already completed the *musaf* service, performing the ritual of taking three steps back. Not a soul was left in the synagogue, aside from Rebbe Urye and a few VIPs, who didn't want to leave him. A fearful but ecstatic lamenting came from his alcove and was echoed in the moaning and groaning of several old ladies who had remained in the women's balcony.

Out in the square, the thousand-headed mass was waiting eagerly, impatiently, and growing bigger and bigger. Not even the babies had been left at home. There were also peasants—old and young, male and female—from the shtetl or from the surrounding villages. At the center of the crowd stood, bold and brazen, Mékhel Válakh: a little man with a short, grayish-red beard and a constant smirk, which was more sardonic than ever. His small, gray eyes were burning with the passion of a hero who is ready to fling himself into a fierce battle with the enemy, a hero who is convinced of his victory, who knows for sure that his victory is the triumph of Light and Truth over falsehood and darkness.

Mékhel Válakh was a simple man, a shopkeeper. Until a few years ago he had been a Hasid and he had made fun of Rabbi Shapiro and his Shapírniks. But then suddenly—no one quite understood it—he started visiting the rabbi, borrowing his secular books, and leafing through the Hebrew journal *Hamagid*. Eventually he became one of the rabbi's most devoted followers and he would have done anything for the rabbi and for the Haskala.

One day Mékhel read in *Hamagid* that the saintly Rebbe of Láshkovits was sending printed letters all over the world, announcing that he could heal any illness, that his speciality was driving out dybbuks: He claimed he had already driven out hundreds and hundreds of those evil spirits and cured hundreds and hundreds of girls and women. Mékhel, who was very intrigued, began paying close attention and asking around: What was going on in Láshkovits? He happened to have relatives there;

and while they didn't really believe in the rebbe, they didn't dare protest openly. One thing was clear: The rebbe was busier than a one-armed paper hanger, and Láshkovits was crawling with dybbuks—a regular epidemic. Possessed Jews, old and young, particularly girls and women, came here from all sorts of towns and townlets. The air was heavy with dybbuks. No matter where you went, people would be talking about dybbuks and about the rebbe's great wonders.

At this point Mékhel decided to take matters into his own hands. He went to Rabbi Shapiro and revealed his plan: He would challenge the Láshkovits Rebbe to a "duel," make the supreme sacrifice for the Haskala. He would prove to the world that the rebbe was a fraud and a swindler.

Rabbi Shapiro tried to dissuade Mékhel from going through with it: Truth is not fought with anger and uproar, its ways are silent and modest. The Hasidic rebbe's lies wouldn't last long anyway, the darkness was bound to flee the quiet radiance of the light.

But Mékhel wouldn't listen. He took up the fight on his own, and his rabbi made no attempt to stop him.

Mékhel asked his relatives to convey his challenge to the Rebbe of Láshkovits: He, Mékhel, the Shapírnik, the adherent of the Haskala, laughed at dybbuks! It was all a swindle, a device for keeping simple people in the dark and fleecing them. If the rebbe stubbornly insisted that the tales about dybbuks were truth and not tricks, then he should prove it in public, before the eyes of the world. If the rebbe could drive out a dybbuk from one person, then he could certainly drive it into someone else. He, Mékhel, was willing to take in the dybbuk. If the rebbe could truly both drive out and drive in a dybbuk, then let him name the time and the place.

Mékhel's relatives transmitted his proposition to the rebbe. Meanwhile the story set tongues wagging in Láshkovits, Czortków, and all the surrounding towns and townlets. It was said that the Rebbe of Czortków encouraged Mékhel on the sly. Perhaps he did so because the Rebbe of Láshkovits had grown important: He was running his own court with pomp and circumstance and beadles, and taking payments for giving advice; he might thus become a competitor for the Rebbe of Czortków. Or perhaps the Czortków court was too aristocratic for such clumsy miracles as exorcisms and therefore looked askance at the Rebbe of Láshkovits. Nobody knew for sure. One thing was definite though: They told him not to get embroiled in a dispute with the heretics, for Satan was very powerful, and an accusation could make him victorious and disgrace the true believers.

But by now it was too late for the Rebbe of Láshkovits to back out. He had to pick up the gauntlet. He therefore treated the contest as a solemn and fearful encounter in order to intimidate his enemy. The rebbe also asked a lawyer whether he, the rebbe, would have to stand trial if the evil man were killed by the dybbuk. The lawyer replied that criminal law provided no penalty for verbal homicide. Next the rebbe tried to get Mékhel's relatives to talk him out of his insolence, warn him about the dire consequences. But Mékhel stuck to his guns. He was scared of nothing and ready for anything.

The rebbe then deliberately scheduled the duel for Yom Kippur, right before *ne'ila,* when every Jew is in dread of the Day of Judgment, the sealing of his fate for the new year. But once again, Mékhel was not intimidated. His friends in Czortków feared for his life and asked the local government to protect him: These authorities were also interested in the strange duel and sent policemen to the square in Láshkovits.

The dybbuk was likewise in the square. The victim was an old woman who kept moaning: "Dear me!," with her face twisting, her arms flailing, her head wobbling. She glared venomously at Mékhel. With teeth grinding and arms outspread, she lunged at him, trying to sink her teeth and her nails into his flesh. But Mékhel dug in his heels and even shook his fist at her: "Hands off, you dirty swindler!"

Finally, the rebbe, wearing his prayer shawl and his white robe, emerged from the synagogue; his eyes were gaping. Pacing slowly and solemnly while shooting nasty glances at Mékhel, he went to the middle of the square. The crowd starting milling, every single person shuddered. The suspense kept mounting by the instant. The onlookers made way for the rebbe in silent awe. No one dared to utter a sound, to draw a breath. The entire human billow was virtually frozen.

The rebbe halted, and with his forbidding eyes he peered about for his mortal enemy; upon sighting Mékhel, the rebbe raised his thick, dark eyebrows, which were like storm clouds. He then turned toward his foe with an ominous yet lyrical Hasidic intonation: "Just recently we said on behalf of the Good Lord: 'Repent, repent thy evil ways'—Give them up, give up your sinful habits. 'Let the evildoer turn from his path and the sinner from his evil thoughts. . . .' Today is a day of repentance, a day of begging for forgiveness. I therefore warn you, Mékhel, you sinner, you heretic: 'Repent for one day, for one hour before thy death. . . .' The Good Lord is a gracious and compassionate God, and I will forgive you as well. . . ."

But Mékhel's mouth twisted, and he let out an even more sarcastic guffawing. He confronted the rebbe in an arrogant and defiant pose and, dwelling on every word while casting triumphant glances at the surrounding audience, he announced: "Do your worst! I didn't come here to listen to your moralizing! I just want to show the world what a swindler you are! I'll open my mouth. So drive the dybbuk into me. Or else. . . ."

A dull murmur swept through the crowd. The frozen human billow shuddered again. "Heretic! Sinner! Apostate!" Those words were uttered here and there. But a resounding "Shush!" from the rest of the crowd restored the silence.

For an instant, the rebbe shuddered. He lowered his head, then raised it again, and furiously held out his right hand to the woman with the dybbuk. Gesturing wildly, she strained and twisted and tossed about as she charged toward Mékhel.

"Quiet, you sinful dybbuk!" the rebbe screamed. "Do you hear what I'm saying to you? I decree that you leave this woman through the little finger of her left hand and that you enter an evildoer just like yourself. . . ."

The human billow started murmuring once more, but then it froze again of its own accord. All eyes, in dread, focused on Mékhel.

But Mékhel was unconcerned about the thousand gazes drilling into him. His eyes twisted even more scornfully, and he stuck out his tongue at the possessed woman: "Well?! Well?!"

A minute wore by, two, three. Mékhel, the rebbe, and the possessed woman were still in the same posture, glaring venomously at one another.

Several more minutes crept by, then a quarter hour. . . .

The crowd grew impatient and started peering at the rebbe. The rebbe turned pale. His eyes glazed over, his arms dropped hopelessly.

Mékhel shifted, stood straight, tucked in his coattails, turned his backside toward the rebbe, and yelled: "Kiiiiiss myyyyy aaaaaass!" And skedaddled.

The exhausted crowd slowly dispersed, and the Jews stole into the synagogue for *ne'ila*. But it didn't feel like Yom Kippur, it felt more as if the Temple in Jerusalem had been destroyed. The rebbe didn't utter another word. He went to his alcove and burst out crying. After prayers, he shut himself up in his house, never came out, never spoke to anyone. For the next two years he never showed up in public, he lived in isolation, abandoned by the world. At the end of those two years he died, and with him the dynasty of Meyer of Przemysl was snuffed out for good. And as of that Yom Kippur there were no more dybbuks in Galicia. Mékhel Válakh had driven them out forever. . . .

Mékhel Válakh died in the 1890s, some twenty years ago, but in eastern Galicia and in Bukovina his name is still uttered with great respect, as the name of a martyr for the Haskala. Mékhel Válakh's son lives in Czérnowitz, at number 22 Russian Street, and if you ask him, he can tell you the entire story about the last dybbuk with every detail. I heard the story from Velvl Gold, who likewise lives in Czérnowitz. He's about sixty years old now, but at the time of the story he was a twelve-year-old boy in Yanovi, a village not far from Láshkovits. "I was already a heretic back then," he says. He came to Láshkovits that day with a group of some thirty youngsters in order to see the dybbuk. He remembers the episode as if, he says, it had just taken place a moment ago.

SARAH HAMER-JACKLYN (1905–1975)

Forgiveness

From Shtamen un Tsvaygn *(New York, 1954), 20–43.*

In a quasidocudrama apparently drawn from her own family, Sarah Hamer-Jacklyn explores the curselike power of a pledge that was not entered into by its unaware victims. Still, like Khónen and Leah, Tshípele and her husband have to pay the consequences. Whatever the religious laws may demand, the perhaps unjust situation reveals a profound anxiety about Jewish helplessness and vulnerability in a hostile world. The author neither attacks nor defends; aside from enjoying the act of literary creation, she, a virtually amateur ethnologist, wants to recall a world that was annihilated a decade before the publication of this story, but that still maintains its hold on the Jewish imagination.

The other large home of our big clan was headed by Aunt Shífre and Uncle Yóyel, the kosher slaughterer. He was nicknamed "the Krushnitser" because his parents had once lived in Krushnitse. We children—all thirteen of us—used to fight over a piece of rye bread in Aunt Khavve's overcrowded house. And we battled just as greedily for the colored candy that Aunt Shífre would hand out to us the instant we appeared at her threshold. Actually, we children used to go there for sweets and not for solid food.

But more than to the candy, the caramels, the chocolates, we were drawn to Genéndl, the maid. She would tell us fearful stories about dragons, about highwaymen in forests, about ghosts that arose from their graves after midnight, drifting like shadows among the living. No one could see them, but they could see everybody and they would slap sinners. . . .

I can clearly remember a certain incident: I got up in the dead of night and made my way through the darkness to the hidden box containing the freshly baked flatbread. Mama had warned us not to touch the bread because she was expecting guests on the Sabbath. All at once, just as I was fiddling with the bread box, my cheek reverberated with a good hard slap! I looked around but saw no one. Everybody was fast asleep. I was petrified, I couldn't move. My mouth was wide open but no sound emerged. I barely made it back to my bed. At daybreak I promptly ran over to Genéndl and told her about my terrifying night. After thinking briefly, she said: "You were slapped by a ghost who caught you stealing."

Throughout the shtetl the Krushnitse slaughterer's house was renowned for its comfort and its charity. Paupers would come from far and wide. Hungry people would go away with full stomachs. Brides would leave their dowries with him, and journeymen and tavernkeepers their savings.

Uncle Yóyel owned his brick house with its balcony facing the street, its four rooms, its spacious parlor, and its large kitchen. The huge brick oven was usually set with large iron pots emitting steam and delicious aromas. The women were constantly making jam, plucking chickens, cutting noodles—the kitchen was a factory!

Right next to the home there was a kind of long stable, which served as the slaughterhouse. Four times a week Uncle Yóyel would kill chickens there, and once a week he would visit the huge meatworks outside the shtetl and slaughter cattle there.

Aunt Shífre and Uncle Yóyel had five children—four boys and a girl. Three of his sons were yeshiva students, while the youngest, ten-year-old Yankl, had a private Talmud tutor. Tshípele, the daughter, was the eldest child, a tall, bright, good-looking girl with a solid figure and a clear, white skin. Her pale face was slightly flushed, her shiny eyes were large and blue, and her hair was thick and black.

Tshípele had a beautiful voice and she was famous for her expert needlework and embroidery. Using gold and silver threads, she would make curtains for the Holy Ark and mantles for the Torah scrolls. And when she burst into song, it was as enchanting as the warbling of a bird.

Matchmakers brought Tshípele countless offers, and her parents finally selected a bridegroom from a distant shtetl. A prodigy from a long line of rebbes, he was nicknamed Shlóyme of the Judges.

Tshípele didn't get to see her fiancé until the wedding. When she glanced at him under the canopy, a faint blush spread over her face, and, embarrassed, she bowed her head.

Shlóyme was tall and slender with a noble face and deep, brown eyes. His fine, black, silken hair crept out from under his fur-edged hat. His long earlocks were as shiny as his satin gabardine.

Uncle Yóyel took in the newlyweds for the stipulated period of five years, giving them their own, newly furnished room, where Shlóyme sat poring over the sacred texts. They had also agreed that Uncle Yóyel would teach him the craft of slaughtering.

When the young couple had their first baby, my Aunt Shífre became a grandmother, and our grandmother, Khaya, became a great-grandmother. The circumcision was as festive as a wedding, and we children didn't attend school for an entire week, having fun instead.

When Shlóyme became a father, he very earnestly studied the laws of kosher slaughtering and began thinking about practical matters such as establishing his own household. At an early point he and his wife talked about finding a shtetl that needed a kosher slaughterer.

Unfortunately, Borekh was a sickly child. His young mother and his grandmother had to constantly exorcise the evil eye, smear his little body with different salves, feed him all kinds of potions containing boiled herbs procured by midwives. Every evening, they licked Borekh's eyes and spit three times—a remedy against the evil eye.

If the mother and the grandmother grew tired, Genéndl, the maid, would watch over the infant. She sat there, rocking his cradle for nights on end. And if Borekh kept crying anyway, she would pick him up and walk back and forth, until the worn-out baby finally drifted off. It was Genéndl who discovered Borekh's first little tooth, and she simply danced for joy.

When the baby was nearly one, he again fell very ill. So they gave him another name, Khayim, Hebrew for "life"—to fool the Angel of Death. Next they took him to the greatest rebbes, they performed the ritual of measuring the cemetery, they summoned physicians. But the baby died right on his first birthday.

The young mother was grief-stricken. If Tshípele hadn't been expecting her second child, she would have been unable to endure her profound anguish. She kept crying and fainting, so that her family was afraid to leave her alone.

Genéndl, still unmarried and no spring chicken, was short and chubby, but had an agile walk. With a lion's strength she watched over Tshípele day and night, protecting her as if she were her sister.

A week after Borekh-Khayim's death Tshípele gave birth to a girl. They named the baby Rátse-Temerl after her great-grandmother, who had lived to a ripe old age.

Unlike her brother, who had just passed away, Rátse was a lovely and healthy baby, who would greedily clutch her mother's breast and suck so intensely that her lip smacking could be heard in all the rooms.

The girl fared nicely, bringing joy and filling the house with her infantile babble and laughter. Before you even knew it, Rátse was sitting on a chair, and at the age of ten months, she started walking. She was always clutching a piece of bread in her soft little hands, gnawing on it with her few little teeth. A red ribbon was tied around one wrist—to shield her against the evil eye.

When Rátse was eleven months old, she was given a little brother. The mother wept for joy, thanking and praising the Good Lord for granting her a son. But then when Rátse was almost one, she suddenly developed a high fever and became very sick. They called the finest doctors, who, however, immediately said that the child was doomed, she would not recover. And right on her first birthday, Rátse closed her bright blue eyes forever.

The slaughterer's comfortable home was shaken. The whole enormous clan, with the grandfather in the lead, saw a heavenly sign in the calamity: Like the firstborn, the girl had passed away at the age of one. There must have been a dark curse hanging over the slaughterer's house. Aunt Shífre decided to consult the Rebbe of Radoshits. She had been his follower for a long time, and whenever she was deeply troubled and couldn't find a way out, she would instantly travel to the rebbe and return with her mind at peace.

Once again Aunt Shífre set out with deep faith. But her heart was very heavy. Upon her arrival, she paid the rebbe's assistant a large fee as usual. Gazing up at the sky, she uttered a quiet prayer: "Almighty Creator of all the heavens, only Thou and the holy rebbe can help me!"

No sooner did Aunt Shífre step into the rebbe's study than she burst into tears. In a grieving voice, she told the rebbe about her daughter and the children that didn't survive: When they turned one, their lives were snuffed out like candle flames.

The rabbi was resting his head on his hands. Under his thick, white eyebrows, his lids kept drawing up and down. He placed his red kerchief on the open volume and stroked his white beard for a long time. From his yellow parchmentlike face a pair of sorrowful eyes gazed into the distance. All at once, without turning his head, he softly asked: "Wife of the Krushnitse slaughterer! Is there anyone anywhere who hates you? Have you, God forbid, sinned against anyone? Caused anyone grief?"

"Holy Rebbe, we are nothing more than sinful human beings." Aunt Shífre wiped her eyes. "My home, praise the Lord, is a place of learning and charity. We also fulfill the commandment to help poor brides get married. . . ."

"Have you ever canceled a match? Or shamed an orphan?"

"Holy Rebbe, we keep an orphan, Genéndl, in our home and we treat her like a member of the family."

The rebbe banged the table and snapped: "I won't hear anymore! Go home and rack your brains! Try to remember! And come back tomorrow at dawn."

Aunt Shífre left in a confused state of mind. What was she supposed to remember? And why did the rebbe want her to come back the next morning? He was perfectly aware that she lived far away, in Novoradomsk. It was a long trip. How could she return to the rebbe's court by dawn? She looked up at the sky, where a red sun was already half-set in the west. Soon night would fall, and she was all alone in a strange town. What should she do? . . .

As she stood there with her worries, a Jewish beggar appeared next to her, holding out his hand. She gave him a small coin. The man peered at the coin in great surprise and asked: "You're from another town?"

"Yes."

"Are you looking for an inn?"

Astonished, Aunt Shífre nodded. It was the only solution: She would spend the night at the inn, racking her brains. Perhaps she would remember something after all. . . .

Following the beggar, she mulled and mulled: Perhaps she really had sinned against someone?

"This is Sháye Nísele's inn," said the beggar.

Turning to where he was pointing, Shífre saw a white house with lots of windows and a huge open door. She handed the beggar another coin, thanked him for his trouble, and entered the inn.

Sháye Nísele asked her if she wanted to eat. It now struck her that she hadn't had even a morsel of bread all day. She ordered a snack, washed her hands, recited a blessing, and ate a little.

Night came. The innkeeper's wife showed her to a tiny room. The wooden bed had a large comforter and a mound of pillows. There was also a small table with a porcelain basin and a pitcher of water.

Shífre said her prayers, put out the kerosene lamp, and went to bed. She closed her eyes but stayed awake. She kept trying to remember whether she had indeed harmed another person. . . . Long-forgotten shapes, close and distant friends and relatives floated in the gloomy night. Shífre summoned the dead from their graves and the living from the farthest corners. Long-buried events unraveled once more like threads from a collar.

It was way past midnight. The shtetl was sound asleep. But Shífre still lay there half-awake, her eyes shut. Then she vehemently opened them and with fresh strength she tried to revive the past.

All at once something flashed through her drowsing brain. She hastily sat up and pulled off the comforter as if to dash away. But, sitting bare-legged on the edge of the bed, she cried in terror:

"Oh me! Granny Rátse—may she rest in peace! God Almighty!" She wrung her hands. "How could we have ever forgotten?!"

And Granny Rátse flickered in the darkness—Granny Rátse, the great-grandmother whose namesake had just died. Yes, yes! Shífre remember exactly! When Shífre's daughter Tshípele had been nine, Granny Rátse had already been in her late eighties. . . . Shífre could see her clearly now: Granny Rátse, a widow for many years, had been living with her daughter. She was very pious. She prayed three times a day, like a man, her body swaying to and fro during the Eighteen Benedictions. On weekdays she wore a linen cloth on her head, but on the Sabbath and on Holy Days she wore a bonnet. She was short and skinny, with a swift walk, and she loved dressing up. She enjoyed putting in her two cents, giving people advice, and she liked going to parties and funerals.

Having sewn her own winding sheet, she would often try it on. She frequently traveled to Zavyertshe to visit the graves of her parents and her brothers and sisters. If she wore her Sabbath bonnet and her taffeta coat on a weekday, everyone knew she was heading to Zavyertshe.

Rátse was almost ninety, she often forgot what she was talking about, and she readily lost her way. Her children refused to let her go out alone, which greatly angered her.

The last time Rátse got all dressed up in her Sabbath best and they refused to let her travel to Zavyertshe, she banged her fist on the table and yelled: "Mind your own business! I'm visiting my family in the graveyard. They're waiting for me! . . ."

There was nothing anybody could do. She went. Their only comfort was that whenever she traveled to Zavyertshe, she would stay with a relative, Dvoyre-Gitl.

Upon returning home, Granny Rátse informed the clan that she had arranged a match for Tshípele. Shmúel-Hérsh, the husband-to-be, she said, was twelve, only three years older than the bride. He was a yeshiva student, getting his meals at various homes, and was renowned as a prodigy. Rátse had met him at her relative's home, where he ate a meal each week. Dvoyre-Gitl told Rátse that the poor boy was a full orphan. Since Rátse really liked him, she had officially arranged the match, calling upon Dvoyre-Gitl as the witness. And so: mazel tov!

My grandmother and my aunt pounced on the great-grandmother: "How could you?! It's unheard of! You didn't ask anyone! How can you do such a thing?! Why, the girl's barely nine years old! . . ."

Uncle Yóyel's household was up in arms. Getting everyone to quiet down, he turned to Rátse: "Granny darling, tell me! Did you give your word? Did you sign an engagement contract? Did you break a plate?" (He was referring to the Jewish custom of breaking plates after the signing of a betrothal document.)

Unfortunately, Rátse was totally confused by all the fussing and yelling. She looked around the large space, and the deep creases in her parchment face dug even deeper when Uncle Yóyel asked her such knotty questions. So many people were bearing down on Rátse, trying to annihilate her. They hovered at a foggy distance, but their voices were so close! What did they want from her? Such a nice boy—that Shmúel-Hérsh. . . . A golden boy. An orphan—poor thing! . . . Oh, how good! She played with him as she had played with her Yánkele long ago. . . .

"I rode a merry-go-round with him," she murmured. "He fell off his horse. The poor thing was awfully bruised." She pushed up her glasses, wiped her eyes, and then continued her rambling. "Later on, both of us were up there." She pointed at the sky. "Everything will turn out for the best. Give me a glass of Holy Land wine, please, and a slice of sponge cake! . . ."

They all remained seated, gaping at Rátse. Uncle Yóyel gesticulated and said: "The poor thing is senile. She doesn't know what she's saying or doing."

Right after that, Granny Rátse became gravely ill, lapsing into a kind of stupor. She never regained her lucidity. And one week later, she died.

Soon everyone had forgotten about the "match." It was only since the rebbe had told her to rack her brains that Aunt Shífre had dug up the memory. And she now grasped how serious the matter was.

Toward dawn Aunt Shífre got out of bed, recited the morning prayers—"I am thankful to Thee, Eternal King. . . ."—and poured water over each hand three times. Then she stepped into the taproom of the inn, where a lot of Jewish men had already gathered—merchants, Hasids—as well as several women, who had come to see the rebbe. Shífre barely forced down a few spoonfuls of milky grits, but she couldn't eat the roll or drink the chicory. She then hurried off to the rebbe's court.

The moment she entered his study, she started weeping and wailing. She told him everything she had recalled the previous night.

The rebbe heard her out, shook his head, frowned, and then suddenly he snapped: "Wife of the Krushnitse slaughterer! You should travel to Zavyertshe immediately. Seek out the shamed orphan Shmúel-Hérsh. If his clothes are ragged, order new clothes for him. If, God forbid, he is a pauper in great need, give him money. Take him to the Rabbi of Novoradomsk and have him sign a document of forgiveness! And be sure not to let him go away until the baby turns one!"

"I don't understand, rebbe," Aunt Shífre said in great fear. "How can we find him now? He was just a little boy in another town! . . ."

"Don't query me, woman. Do as you're told, and the Good Lord will help!"

Aunt Shífre asked no further question. Terrified, she went over to the covered wagon that was to carry her home. Upon sitting down inside, she suddenly felt a great bliss and a profound faith in God.

The horses tramped through deep mud. The shaky wagon lumbered past harvested fields. Peasant huts with thatched roofs surged by. Shífre's face was lashed by an autumn wind.

Eventually she nodded off. All at once, Granny Rátse sat down next to her. She was in her winding sheet and her black taffeta coat.

"Granny darling," a terrified Shífre asked: "How'd you get here? Aren't you dead?"

"Only the sinful body dies," said Rátse. "The soul lives forever, it sees everything and knows everything. I can't rest in the grave. You should follow the rebbe's advice right away. I want to rest in peace! . . ."

Shífre woke up, opened her eyes wide, but saw no one. She cried out: "Grandma! Granny!!! . . ."

And she realized it was all a dream.

In Novoradomsk the entire clan assembled in the slaughterer's home. Aunt Shífre described everything that had taken place with the rebbe and what he had told her to do. They decided that Aunt Shífre and Grandma Khavve would leave for Zavyertshe tomorrow and find Tshípele's former fiancé, Shmúel-Hérsh.

The two women arrived at twilight. They had long known that their relative's husband was already in the next world, the World of Truth, but they now learned that she, too, was no longer among the living. However, she had left a daughter named Brayndl, a barren woman, who was almost seventy. Despite her age, Brayndl was familiar with everything that occurred in the shtetl. Mainly she knew which wife was expecting, what month she was in, and when she was about to give birth. The instant the mother-to-be started having pangs, Brayndl was the first to run for the midwife, and she actually became the midwife's right hand. And the moment the children saw the light of day, Brayndl would dash about, telling everyone whether it was a boy or a girl. She also knew about everything that happened near and far in the ramified clan, and it turned out that she very clearly remembered the engagement, which had been hushed up.

My aunt and my grandmother learned that Shmúel-Hérsh had often come here and complained. Brayndl's mother, who had lain in bed paralyzed, would tell him something with her twisted mouth; but no one understood. Suddenly he stopped coming, and they discovered that he had married someone else, a poor, frail girl. Upon becoming pregnant, his wife had fallen ill and she had died before giving birth. Shmúel-Hérsh had thereupon vanished and had never been heard from again.

The visitors wiped their eyes. Aunt Shífre wrung her hands and cried out in despair: "God help us! God help us! . . . Where can we look for him?"

"If we don't find him, God forbid," the grandmother added, "we'll be done for."

Brayndl reflected. The creases deepened in her pale, wrinkled face, her small, gray, watery eyes half closed. She lapsed into silence. The two visitors didn't want to interrupt her pondering: She might recall something that could lead them to their goal. The Good Lord would help, and they would find Shmúel-Hérsh.

Then Brayndl whispered: "Yes, yes, I remember. . . . He used to teach children. . . . After his wife's death he disappeared. Years later he showed up again in Zavyertshe, his clothes were shabby and neglected. But now he seems to have vanished once more. Someone said that he's living in a poorhouse outside the town. . . ."

That same evening Aunt Shífre hired a wagon, and the three women headed for the poorhouse.

They arrived before nightfall. The stench coming from the poorhouse was nauseating.

It was dark inside. A tiny candle shed a faint glow on the mounds of straw and rags, which moved calmly when the visitors entered. Heads, hands, arms emerged, soft murmurs drifted from one mound to the next, reminding the women that these were no garbage heaps, these were living people.

"Friends!" Aunt Shífre exclaimed. "Can anyone tell me where I can find Shmúel-Hérsh?"

Several voices replied at once, and fingers pointed at a heavy mass lying on a pile of straw.

Grandmother had brought along a twisted Sabbath candle, which she now lit, and the three women went over to that pile.

Brayndl said: "Shmúel-Hérsh, stand up. Your future mother-in-law has come to ask your forgiveness!"

The man remained inert, like a corpse.

So Aunt Shífre said: "Shmúel-Hérsh, we must tell you that the Rebbe of Radoshits has ordered you to forgive my Tshípele. None of her babies have survived—God help us! Each child passes away the moment it turns one. We beg you to forgive us for the terrible sin that was committed against you. . . . We'll give you money and new clothes. . . ."

And she burst out crying, unable to proceed.

Now the gravelike mound stirred. Shmúel-Hérsh hastily sat up. In the weak glow of the tiny candle flame a big head loomed up with disheveled hair, a crumpled beard, and bushy eyebrows forming a single line across the forehead. Two fiery black eyes pierced Aunt Shífre's face while the man kept obstinately silent.

"Shmúel-Hérsh!" my grandmother turned to him with a broken voice. "We'll take you out of the poorhouse and we'll give you anything you want. Please respond to our request. We've come a long way. We are two weak, sinful women. How can you watch a mother's grief and hold your tongue?! . . . Please tell me, Shmúel-Hérsh, do you remember Grandma Rátse?"

"I remember her."

"And do you remember your engagement to Tshípele?"

"I've never forgotten."

"You'll come with us to Novoradomsk immediately." Grandmother wouldn't be put off. "We'll take you out of the poorhouse. You'll stay in my home. We'll take care of you, we'll treat you like a member of the family, you'll lack for nothing—Heaven forbid! But you'll have to go to the rabbi and sign a document stating that you forgive our Tshípele for breaking the engagement."

Shmúel-Hérsh calmly stood up. They now saw a tall, broad-shouldered man in tattered clothes, with naked hairy skin showing through a frayed and dirty shirt, his feet stuck in baste shoes and wrapped in rags. Picking up a bundle, he replied: "I'll go with you."

"Leave that here," said Shífre. "You'll be getting new things now."

Shmúel-Hérsh dropped his bundle. All at once, shadowy figures leaped up from the mounds of straw, bellowing and fighting over the bundle of rags. And when the three women and Shmúel-Hérsh were already in the wagon, they could still hear what sounded like the roaring of enraged beasts.

After midnight, just as Grandfather had woken up, finished praying, and was about to study, the stranger entered the house.

"This is Shmúel-Hérsh, Tshípele's ex-fiancé," said Grandmother. "We found the unfortunate man at the poorhouse in Zavyertshe."

"Why waste words!?" said Grandfather Yóykhenen to Grandmother, and to the visitor he held out his wrinkled hand with its trembling fingers: "Welcome! May the Good Lord help us avoid any grief from this day forward!" Then, turning to Grandmother, he said: "Khavve, give our guest something to eat."

Meanwhile a radiant Aunt Shífre entered her home, which was still full of hushed and distressing sorrow. Tshípele lay in bed with almost no will to live. Her husband, Shlóyme, had spent sleepless nights poring over the Talmud.

Shífre announced the good news: They had found Tshípele's ex-fiancé, he was at her parents' home—and instantly the house came alive. Genéndl, the maid, lit the kerosene lamp, added some wood to the dying fire in the oven, and put up a kettle of water for tea.

Tshípele sat up in bed. This was the first time since her baby's death that she had shown interest in anything: She wanted to know all the details.

Aunt Shífre gave her a blow-by-blow description of everything that had happened from the moment they'd left town to the moment they'd returned with Shmúel-Hérsh.

The very next morning Grandfather took the visitor to the bath-house. They dressed him from head to toe. And when my aunt looked at him now, she gaped, unable to trust her own eyes: How he had changed! Flabbergasted, she told her daughter: "You wouldn't believe it's the same person! I tell you, Tshípele, he looks like a king—Heaven preserve us! The shekhina—God's radiance—is resting on him!"

"I'd love to see him!" said Tshípele.

"You'll see him on Friday night, dear—praise the Lord! I've invited him to our Sabbath dinner." And she confided her plan: "I'm going to have him get engaged to Genéndl. We'll be doing two good deeds— killing two birds with one stone. We'll be serving the old maid, the poor orphan girl, and, with God's help, we'll be making up for the wrong that was inflicted on Shmúel-Hérsh. . . ."

Feeling a silent shiver, Genéndl was especially cautious in preparing for the Sabbath and the guest of honor. She polished the silver candle-sticks, scoured the pots, and scrubbed the floor until the boards were white. Ahead of time, on Thursday night, she made the various kinds of meat kosher (by rubbing them with salt and draining all the blood) and she added more fat and sugar to the carrot stew than usual. She washed her hair with kerosene, and on Friday evening she put on her Sabbath calico frock and her new yellow shoes, which my aunt had brought her and which squeaked at every step. The high heels made Genéndl's short, chubby figure look a wee bit taller. She had also tied a red ribbon to her braids. Upon seeing her maid all gussied up, Tshípele smiled for the first time in a long time.

When Uncle Yóyel and his son-in-law came from praying that Friday evening and brought along the stranger, a holiday mood wafted through the house. Uncle Yóyel showed the guest his place at the table, and Tshípele came in from her room, wearing her Sabbath gown of green silk decorated with lace. It was the first time she'd appeared in it since her child's death.

"This is my daughter Tshípele," said my aunt.

Shmúel-Hérsh turned. Suddenly his fiery eyes opened wide. He was astonished by the beauty of his ex-fiancée. Confused, he stammered: "Good Shabbes, Tshípele. . . ."

A matte rosiness washed over her face. Gaping at the stranger, she softly responded: "Good Shabbes, Shmúel-Hérsh."

From then on, Shmúel-Hérsh spent every Sabbath dinner at Uncle Yóyel's home. He was treated practically as a member of the family. It turned out that he was learned and that he zealously studied the holy texts. Grandfather spent hours with him, hunched over the Talmud, and they were often engrossed in an intense argument.

The months flew by, and whenever the family reminded Shmúel-Hérsh that it was time for him to go to the rabbi and sign the forgiveness document, he would invariably answer: "Where's the fire? The baby's first birthday is a long way off."

One day Grandmother fell ill, and Tshípele came by to see how she was feeling. The instant Shmúel-Hérsh heard the young woman's voice, he stationed himself at the door to Grandmother's room and, virtually frozen, he stared at Tshípele. His black, fiery eyes bored into her face as if through a misty fog.

Tshípele gazed at him, kept silent for a while, then suddenly, almost terrified, she blurted out: "So long, Grandma!" And she swiftly left the house.

If anyone tried to discuss his marrying Genéndl, Shmúel-Hérsh turned a deaf ear. Genéndl stared at him with amorous eyes. She kept curling her hair, polishing her shoes to a high gloss, and very carefully preparing the finest dishes and bringing him the largest portions. But Shmúel-Hérsh didn't notice a thing.

The child, Avróm Méndele, was growing and thriving. At nine months he was already crawling around, and the house resounded with his infantile chatter and laughter. My aunt and my grandmother kept urging Shmúel-Hérsh to visit the rabbi and sign the forgiveness document, but he would always put them off with some lame excuse.

When the child turned ten months, Tshípele went and told her mother that she was pregnant again. Grandma and Grandpa whispered together, then entered Shmúel-Hérsh's room, where he was studying a holy text. They demanded that he accompany them to the rabbi without further delay.

Shmúel-Hérsh heard them out and after a long silence he announced: "Tshípele is my soulmate. I will never sign the forgiveness document—Tshípele is my *basherte!* . . ."

Aunt Shífre burst into tears and desperately asked: "What are you saying, Shmúel-Hérsh!? It's outrageous! Why, Tshípele is a married woman, she's a shattered and trembling mother! . . . Feel some pity, don't shame us! How is that possible!?"

"She can get a divorce!" Shmúel-Hérsh dug in his heels. "Ours is a match made in Heaven!"

Grandfather, who heard everything in silence, suddenly exclaimed: "Shmúel-Hérsh, the woman is with child, and your words are sins against her and against God Blessed Be He!"

Shmúel-Hérsh writhed. His head drooped. He shriveled up in the chair, stony and silent.

And Grandfather continued: "You're like a member of the family. For the shame and suffering we've caused you we beg you to forgive us. Why is poor Tshípele to blame in any way? Why are her innocent children to blame? . . . Shmúel-Hérsh! We'll treat you like a son and, God willing, marry you to Genéndl, a decent girl. We'll give you a nice dowry. You can use it to open a grocery shop, you'll be your own boss, you'll have your own home, and with God's help you'll make a good living. But please don't shame us!"

Grandfather uttered those last few words in a broken voice, choking back his tears.

And Shmúel-Hérsh murmured: "Yóykhenen, let me be. . . . I have to mull it over. . . . There's something I don't understand. . . . If we make it through the night, I'll give you my answer tomorrow, though I'm not swearing to anything now."

Grandfather told Aunt Shífre to say nothing to anyone, and she went home, completely crushed.

That night Shmúel-Hérsh did not sleep. He softly paced about from room to room, occasionally halting, squeezing his temples with both hands, lost in thought, rubbing his forehead with his fingers, then softly resumed pacing.

Grandfather didn't interfere, he let him pace and ruminate, and he didn't ask him anything.

Shmúel-Hérsh saw Yóykhenen close the sacred tome, recite his bedtime prayer, undress, and silently lie down to sleep. But no sleep came to

Shmúel-Hérsh. He sat by the window and peered into the black night, smoking his pipe. He stayed there for a long time, absorbed in his thoughts. A rooster's crowing aroused him from his reflections. He looked up at the sky, he saw the dawn turn blue. His entire body was icy. He stood up calmly, stole over to Grandfather's bed, and murmured: "Yóykhenen, are you asleep? . . ."

"No, I'm awake."

"Yóykhenen, I'll do what you want. We can go to the rabbi today. I'll sign the forgiveness document and I'll do whatever you tell me to."